also by Vickie McKeehan

The Evil Secrets Trilogy
JUST EVIL Book One
DEEPER EVIL Book Two
ENDING EVIL Book Three

The Pelican Pointe Series
PROMISE COVE
HIDDEN MOON BAY
DANCING TIDES
LIGHTHOUSE REEF
STARLIGHT DUNES
LAST CHANCE HARBOR
SEA GLASS COTTAGE
LAVENDER BEACH
SANDCASTLES UNDER THE CHRISTMAS MOON
BENEATH WINTER SAND

The Skye Cree Novels
THE BONES OF OTHERS
THE BONES WILL TELL
THE BOX OF BONES
HIS GARDEN OF BONES
TRUTH IN THE BONES

The Indigo Brothers Trilogy
INDIGO FIRE
INDIGO HEAT
INDIGO JUSTICE
THE INDIGO BROTHERS TRILOGY BOXED SET

Exclusively at Amazon in print and Kindle format

Just Evil

The Evil Secrets Trilogy
Book One

Vickie McKeehan

beachdevils
PRESS

Just Evil
The Evil Secrets Trilogy

Published by Beachdevils Press
ISBN: 978-1-4659-4329-3 - eBook
ISBN: 978-0-6156-3949-9 - Paperback
Printed in the USA

beachdevils
PRESS

Cover art design by Vanessa Mendozzi Design
www.vanessamendozzidesign.com

Visit the author at:
www.vickiemckeehan.com
www.facebook.com/VickieMcKeehan

For Gene and Keith,
who read and read until their eyes hurt and
offered up suggestions and critiques.
Thank you. Without you guys there
would be no books.

"Evil is unspectacular and always human,
and shares our bed and eats at our own table."
W. H. Auden, Poet
1907 – 1973

Just Evil

The Evil Secrets Trilogy
Book One

CHAPTER 1

So much for warm, sunny Southern California in the spring, he decided as he shivered under the jacket he wore and took another sip of hot coffee to warm his bones.

Sitting by the front window, he did his best not to stare at the reason he'd gotten up at the crack of dawn and driven in a steady downpour to check out the daughter. He took his eyes off the blonde long enough to gaze outside and watch rain pelt the glass. The wind picked up and sent loose debris flying in a gust.

It started to rain again—hard. It was just his luck he'd timed his trip to L.A. at the same time an El Niño storm arrived and dumped enough water on the area to make everything west of the 101 look like beachfront property. In a way the weather made him homesick for the land of his birth. But then, this was nothing compared to a bad-tempered Irish gale.

Sunny California my ass, he thought. Where were the bikini-clad women, the hot bodies sunbathing at the beach? Glancing out the window again, he decided that until the rain let up and the sun came out there was no chance in hell of seeing any bikini-clad bodies lying half-naked in the sun. No sun, no bikinis.

Doesn't matter, he decided; he was stuck here, rain or shine, until he was done. He took another long look at the blonde, and couldn't help but wonder how she'd ended up in such a backwater, out-of-the-way dump like San Madrid. How had Alana's daughter gone from Beverly

Hills to living in this Podunk little fishing village nestled up against the Pacific Ocean? If there were more than four thousand people living here, he'd give up drinking for a week. And why was she working in the bookstore-slash-coffee shop known as the Book & Bean where he was now sitting?

The shop sat in the middle of the block, off an old cobblestone main street, across from a town square complete with a picturesque free-flowing fountain.

Antique streetlights with old-fashioned street signs gave him the impression he'd wandered onto the back lot of a studio rather than a genuine town. If it hadn't been pouring rain, he might have wandered into a few of the shops along Main Street or walked down to the waterfront to check out the row of sailboats he'd seen from the Coast Highway. But sightseeing wasn't why he was here.

He watched Kit Griffin move with graceful efficiency behind the polished but worn oak wood counter waiting on customers streaming in out of the rain. He sipped his coffee and settled in, enjoying the ambiance of the place.

The Book & Bean, with its scuffed hardwood floors and retro furnishings, seemed to be a gathering place for everyone in town even in this miserable weather. Since he'd parked himself near the front door, harried soccer moms and dads rushed in and out with children in tow as a contingent of older folks tried to squeeze in around several small oak tables or stand to the side, waiting for one of the comfy, overstuffed chairs to open up. The place felt homey on a rainy day. Even the artwork hanging on the walls had him feeling melancholy. When he finally decided to retire, give up this lifestyle, he might enjoy living…

He scrubbed a hand over his face and tried to shake off his wistful mood. Jesus, what was happening to him anyway? Enjoy this backwater dump? Not in this lifetime. He needed to get a grip. This tendency to reminiscence had to stop. Jesus, the place was starting to get to him. No, he thought, not the place, the damned miserable weather was making him crazy. He needed to see the sun.

He took another long look at Kit Griffin—and relaxed. He'd purposefully saved her for last. And now after getting a good look at her up close and personal, he decided the two-hour drive in the pouring rain had been well worth every second he'd spent sitting behind the wheel of his rented Chevy.

He continued to stare at the pretty young thing with smooth, golden skin and soulful green eyes the color of fine Irish heather. Tall, maybe five eight or nine; it was hard to tell exactly as he watched her move behind the counter. Her silvery-blonde mane neatly tied back into a ponytail kept it from falling around her face as she diligently worked the counter, filling orders for the customers standing in line.

He couldn't say she favored her mother. No—Alana Stevens, the former actress, had lived in the fast lane too long to make a good comparison. And at this stage of the game there'd been too many trips under the knife to get the skin tightened. Yet, Alana's face showed the damage one would expect for a woman her age in spite of the Botox factory and every brand of wonder cream that promised to keep her skin looking supple. No amount of expensive cream could wipe away the damage that too many drugs and too much booze had wrought on her body. Nothing could bring back how she'd looked in her prime. And up to now, Alana had pretty much lived a life of excess, done whatever she pleased and with whom, but tonight he would remind her that all good things must come to an end.

That brightened his mood. As he sipped his coffee, he put down the newspaper he'd pretended to read and went over his plans again in his head. Biting into the tasty apple tart the pretty blonde had recommended as the house specialty, he tasted heaven. He momentarily forgot about his prey. The cinnamon-nutmeg combination had him smiling into the goddamned rain outside. Sitting back he relished the moment because he knew the drive back to L.A. in this stuff would be hell.

Taking another bite of his pastry, enjoying the view of the blonde from his seat by the window, he began to anticipate the night ahead.

⚭ ⚭ ⚭ ⚭ ⚭

Kit wiped down the counter for the umpteenth time that morning before she poured a fourth cup of coffee for Mr. Planter, who had to be ninety if he was a day. Nodding politely at his comment about the foul weather as if he'd been the first person to walk in off the street that morning and want to discuss it, she glanced out the window to check the nasty weather in question—and smiled.

At least the storm wasn't keeping her regulars away. Squeezed around one of the six little oak tables, they drank espressos or lattes, ate the homemade pastries she'd baked the night before, or simply lounged in several of the oversized chairs, reading the best sellers they'd purchased in the bookstore—her bookstore.

In spite of the dreary weather, Kit took pride in that.

And it was about damn time.

She knew even a glimmer from the past could send her into an abyss—if she let it. She didn't intend to let it. Whenever memories of childhood tried to jam their way inside her head, she simply pushed the bad to that corner of her brain where the vault kept the awful past locked away.

After all, she hadn't sampled normal until twelve, when her aunt Gloria had finally moved out West and provided an alternate place to go at times when life with Alana became unbearable, which too frequently had. But that was living life with a viper, one that could strike without warning, and was certain to leave a scar.

There was no point in dwelling on what was.

She forced a smile for her customers and worked her way through the tables and chairs, picking up empty coffee cups and trash along the way. With a determined push to her shoulders, she stepped behind the counter to make fresh coffee for the late morning rush still streaming through the doors.

$$\text{🪢 🪢 🪢 🪢 🪢}$$

In his Westlake Village office, Jake Boston sat at his desk putting the finishing touches on a multi-million dollar deal he'd been working on for the better part of a year—in Tokyo. It hadn't really taken a year to close the deal. Nor had it been necessary to fly six thousand miles to get it done. But being away from L.A. had given him distance and time to think about what was missing in his life.

A year ago, he'd been tempted to dip his toes into water he had no business getting near. He'd gotten close. She would have let him take her to bed.

It had been twelve long months since he'd seen her. He'd been back two weeks and had yet to pick up the phone. He'd never lacked confidence in anything before, but the idea of confronting her had him feeling—edgy.

He got up from his desk to pace. He'd had a year to think about Kit, sort things out. But he'd had to leave. Get out of L.A. Get away from the stain left by Claire. He'd gone to Japan without so much as a farewell adios. And that he knew had hurt Kit.

Gloria had given him hell about that for the better part of a year. Now that he was back, he could just imagine how Kit would react when he picked up the phone. It was only a matter of time before he had to face her, face the fact that he'd left her without a word. How was he supposed to tell her how much he'd missed her in the year since he'd been gone? She wouldn't buy it. And who could blame her? He'd have to do something about that. Buying the old Crandall House might be a start. But it would take more than renovating an old relic of a house to get her to believe he'd finally put his ghosts to rest, put the past behind him and was ready to take the next step—with her.

He thought back to that night a year ago when he'd taken her to dinner, how talkative she'd been—just like at fourteen. Back then she'd worked summer vacations in the file room at her uncle's law firm, just a kid, a very talkative kid. Three summers in a row he remembered now, from fourteen to sixteen. He'd been just starting out then, developing the software application that Gloria's husband Morty had encouraged him to create for his law firm. His company, Billing-Pro Software, had come from that. He'd used Morty's firm as his first beta site, coming and going on a daily basis as he tweaked the software and the lines of code, working the bugs out and testing the application before mass marketing it to bigger clients, larger law firms.

Kit had been a gangly teen who couldn't keep her mouth shut for five minutes without rambling on about movies or music or virtually anything that happened to pop into her teenage head. She'd had a major crush on him back then that had both flattered and embarrassed him.

That had been another lifetime ago: before Claire, before his marriage.

God, what he wouldn't give to go back and replay that part of his life, correct his mistakes. Unfortunately, he'd learned the hard way that you were stuck with the consequences of your fuckups.

He ran a hand across his face. Jesus, could he get any more maudlin for chrissakes? It had to be the miserable weather. He stared out the window at the rain and the traffic on Westlake Boulevard. He had a house in San Madrid under renovation. The woman he wanted was there. When was he going to face her? He was tired of waiting. He checked his watch.

Screw this, he thought as he headed out the door. Now was as good a time as any.

Jake was still going over the plan, how to play this whole thing out, when he pulled his Mercedes to a stop in front of the Book & Bean. Groveling might not be his first choice, but it was definitely on the agenda. He hadn't been worried on the drive up, but now his chest tightened as he shoved the gearshift into Park and cut the engine. For several minutes he sat there staring out the windshield, listening to fat drops of rain fall on the glass.

What was he doing here anyway? She'd probably take one look at him and tell him to go to hell. She had every right to feel that way. He hadn't exactly been nice to her. When he first met her she'd been far too young, but so...sweet-natured...so...eager to please. Through the years the timing for both of them always seemed to be off. But no more, he thought, as he sucked in courage, opened the car door, and stepped out into the pouring rain.

Tucking his keys in his jacket pocket, he pushed open the door to the bookstore. Once inside he glanced at the rows and rows of neatly organized books, at the people milling around the aisles. The aroma of coffee had him drifting toward the coffee shop where a busy crowd lingered, some with their noses stuck in a book.

And then he saw her.

She stood behind the counter working the espresso machine, her back to the entrance. He'd recognize that silvery blond hair anywhere. Dressed in jeans and a white cropped T-shirt, she moved with graceful efficiency doing two things at once. When she turned around to wait on another customer, Jake's attention moved from her body to her face. The heat of the machine gave her skin a healthy, golden hue, as well as making wisps of hair curl around her face. He watched her full mouth move as she tried to dissuade the flirtatious attempt of an infatuated teenage boy trying to act much older by ordering a double espresso. Jake couldn't blame the kid his efforts. A year of being away from her, of missing her, had him fighting for control to keep from embarrassing himself in front of a room full of strangers.

Seeing her again energized him. The nerves slipped away.

While he stood a couple of customers behind the teen, he worked on his opening line. He'd say something clever and funny, something about old times. He'd be smooth, confident, self-assured.

But when he watched her take the money from the customer ahead of him and count out change—he realized the nerves were back—enough to have him second guessing this whole scene.

When she turned back, he was face-to-face with her. She looked up, met his eyes, and blinked. Shock registered on her face. She started to say something. He knew because her mouth moved but nothing came out. In the next instant, he saw annoyance simmer in those jade eyes. How had he forgotten her eyes, the darkest shade of green he'd ever seen?

And they were boring holes through him.

"You snake-in-the-grass son of a bitch."

So much for sweet-natured, he thought, as he opened his mouth to speak, but the only word that slid out from the software genius was a weak, "Hey."

Before he had time to say anything more, she snarled, "You come crawling through my door after a year? Why are you here?"

He quickly regrouped. "Getting coffee." He hadn't choked like that since he'd struck out with bases loaded in the bottom of the ninth back in high school. The man standing behind him asked, "Hey buddy, do you intend to order any time soon? Some of us have things to do."

Out of desperation, Jake simply grunted, "Uh, I'll take a regular." *Damn, this was not going well.*

In a clipped, angry voice, she fumed, "I'm sure you want that to-go since to-go is what you do best."

"For here?"

She turned back to the tray to lift a ceramic cup. She fumbled with the pickup and it slipped out of her hands, dropped to the floor and shattered. He heard her mutter something. Then, she closed her eyes, took a deep breath, exhaled slowly, and filled another cup before setting it down on the counter with a slosh. "Surely the black-hearted cheapskate bastard would like a pastry to go with that."

"Ouch. What do you recommend?"

"That you stay on your side of L.A. and I'll stay on mine." But he ignored her and calmly started scanning the array of pastries in the glass case. She huffed out a breath when she thought he was taking too long, and grumbled, "Oh for God's sakes, order the apple tart, everyone knows it's the house specialty."

Jake gritted his teeth and got the apple tart. After paying, he took his purchase over to a vacant table by the window, sat down next to a guy reading his paper—and waited.

☙☙☙☙☙

Thank God she was busy was all she could think as she filled orders and tried to ignore him sitting at a table by the front window. The distance gave her time to get her balance back. But every few minutes, out of the corner of her eye, Kit looked his way, and wondered why he couldn't have choked to death on sushi over the past year. Or why he couldn't have lost every strand of hair on his stupid head. Life just wasn't fair.

He's just an idiot man—she decided—with a crop of black hair and expressive blue eyes. Thinking about his eyes pushed her back to her awkward teen years and her first dip into the one-sided pool of teenage love. But now she wasn't a shy girl admiring the man's tanned, lean, six-two frame but rather a full-grown woman who'd never been able to ignore the way this particular man filled out a pair of jeans.

Okay, she needed her head examined, but it would have to wait. She needed to find out why he was here in San

Madrid. He hadn't driven in traffic for two hours in the pouring rain on a Saturday morning to see her. That much she knew. After leaving her high and dry without so much as a phone call, she deserved an explanation.

After the line died down, she picked up a carafe off the burner and headed out to make the rounds. She took her time pouring refills here and there until after several eternal minutes, she reached his table.

The crowded shop tempered her language when she glared at his face. "You, Jake Boston, are a first-class asshole."

He set down his fork in mid-bite. "Just give me five minutes."

"Unless you were in a coma for a year and couldn't pick up a damned phone, it'll take longer than five minutes. I want you out of here."

"You'd throw out a customer?"

"Think of it as reserving the right to refuse service."

"Aw, come on, Kit. This apple tart is delicious by the way. Tastes better than the one my grandmother used to make."

Flattery from the arrogant jerk, now that was new. "You didn't drive two hours in the rain for pastry or coffee, Jake. There's a Starbucks across the street from your office."

"I owe you an apology. Why don't you sit down, get off your feet for a few minutes. I'm prepared to grovel."

Grovel? Jake Boston? That'll be the day, she thought, as she glanced at the counter. For the first time all morning there was no line; not a single customer waited there. Reluctantly, she sat down, waved her hand. "Okay, but make it quick."

"I had to leave, Kit. Get away. Put some distance between me and L.A. and what happened to Claire."

She sighed. So it was still about the wife. "That's it? That's your explanation for taking off without so much as a goodbye. That's weak, Jake. Japan? Could you have run any farther? Not a phone call, no e-mail. Not even a one-line text. The last time—that night we went to dinner, we almost…" She huffed out a breath. "I thought we were at the very least friends."

He put his hand on top of hers. "We are. Always. But…you knew what a hard time I was having with—everything. I had to leave, Kit, get my head on straight. At the time, I had too many problems. It wasn't fair to you."

"I see." She jerked her hand from the weight of his, drummed her fingers on the table. "You left and took off to the other side of the world…for me. Didn't call, didn't write, for me. Friends don't do that, Jake. I deserved better, I deserve…"

"You deserve better than a damned murder suspect. But I've put it behind me. I'm back. And ready to do better."

"Right. Until you decide that you need to put some distance between us again? I don't think so."

"Look, I'm back…to stay. You'll just have to handle it."

"Yeah. Right. For a smart guy you're really dumb, you know that? We both know that you coming back doesn't have a thing to do with me."

To hell it didn't. "I'm renovating the Crandall House."

Her heart dropped. "The Crandall House—the house on the cliffs? My Crandall house? You're moving here to San Madrid? Why?" With another wife probably, she thought, despising the woman already. No wonder he'd moved on. Her jaw visibly tightened.

"The house was a good investment. I can always fix the place up then put it on the market." He tried to sound convincing.

When the bell over the door signaled a customer, she stood up, picked up the pot of coffee and said, "I hope everything works out for you, Jake." Have a crappy life without me, she wanted to scream into the rain, but it just wasn't in her. She'd spent too many years caring about him to turn mean now. Oh, she wanted him to suffer for leaving, but she couldn't get her mouth to spout off all the nasty things she'd wished on him over the past year. And what good would it do? She forced her lips into a curve. "Just so you know, I'm over you. I've had the disease, gone through the cure, taken my shots. You can go infect someone else."

With that, she whirled around, and stormed to the counter to wait on her customer.

The man at the next table dropped his newspaper long enough to look over. Jake met his expression, saw the commiserating look and said weakly, "That could have gone better."

The stranger's lips twitched before ducking back behind his paper.

Jake sat there another hour watching the place gradually empty as the customers either left or went in to browse through the bookstore.

Since it wouldn't get any easier, he approached her as she wiped down tables. He patiently waited until she glanced up. "If you have some time later maybe you could ride out to the house, take a look, and tell me what you think. I could really use a woman's take."

Surprise crossed her face. "My take…you mean…you want my opinion on how to remodel it?"

"Yeah. I could really use another pair of eyes. Maybe there's something I've missed. I've never renovated an older home before."

He glanced around. "And you did such a great job when you took over the bookstore from Gloria, adding the coffee shop, remodeling this place. I could use all the advice I can get."

When he saw interest flick in her eyes, he quickly added, "Come on, it wouldn't take that long. What time do you close up?"

"Four o'clock."

"Then I'll be back at four." He looked out the window, saw the rain still coming down in sheets, and muttered, "Maybe, when the rain lets up, we can go sailing." And with that, he headed out the door.

Kit stood there, nailed to the same spot for several minutes before she said out loud to an empty shop, "Well for goodness' sake, what was that all about?"

☙☙☙☙☙

He sat across Main Street in the Chevy, listening to the pouring rain beat on the roof for what seemed like an eternity until the man finally came out of the Book & Bean.

There was obviously a connection between Alana's daughter and the man who had shown up out of the blue. He needed to know if this Jake posed a threat to his plans.

He re-read the notes he had on Kit Griffin. There was no mention of a man in her life. But if the man ended up being a complication, he'd have to eliminate him just as he would anyone else who got in his way.

CHAPTER 2

Jake was prompt. At four o'clock, just as Kit finished cleaning the last of the equipment, he walked back into the store carrying two umbrellas. As he watched her restock the condiment bar, he tried to gauge whether or not her anger might have subsided. When she turned to glare at him, he decided it was less than a fifty-fifty shot.

"I wasn't sure you'd actually show," she announced.

"Why's that?"

"You had several hours to kill. With the weather like it is, I thought you'd get tired of waiting and head back to L.A."

"Not a chance. It's still coming down out there though."

"This is some storm, but hey, a little rain never hurt."

"I bet that's what Noah said."

A joke. He'd cracked a joke. Unbelievable, she thought, and wondered if the storm had blown her into a parallel universe.

"Thinking of building an ark, Jake?" When she'd retrieved her purse from under the counter, turned off the lights, and grabbed her jacket off the peg, she reached for one of the umbrellas he was holding. Doing her damnedest to rankle him, she oozed sarcasm when she added sweetly, "Or do you suppose your row boat can handle this heavy rain?"

"Very funny. I remember a time when you were a whole lot nicer to me."

"Yeah. And look where that got me."

The trip through town, past the waterfront, and up the cliffs to the old Victorian Queen Anne known locally as the Crandall House took less than five minutes. But once they turned off the Coast Highway onto a spotty, gravel driveway they sat inside the car, waiting for the rain to let up. They kept the conversation light, sticking with safe subjects like building permits and contractors. He didn't mention Gloria had been the one who tipped him off about the house and how much Kit had talked about fixing it up.

"Have you ever been inside?" he asked.

She'd driven by the place a hundred times. But she saw no reason to open up and let him know, so she simply shook her head. "It's a great old house though. Did you know it was built in 1888 as a hotel, a stop on the Coast Stage Line? The place should be a historical landmark, don't you think?"

"You know the history then."

"A little. I like old things. I'm surprised you'd pick a house that needs so much work and as far north as San Madrid. Renovation's not only costly and time consuming, but living here will be quite a commute."

He ignored the comment. "But it's worth the effort, don't you think? They haven't been able to do much work to the outside because of the rain this week. But the inside…" Laughing when he saw the look on her face, he finished, "Is definitely under construction. You'll see what I mean when we get inside."

But Kit wasn't listening. Her gaze had fallen on the wraparound porch that ran the length of the house, its charming two-foot rock wall railing, and the ornate columns that looked like draped ivy. Her eyes drifted up to the curved second floor balcony and its rounded exterior. She'd often wondered if that wall meant there was a circular room, like a castle behind it. She'd always thought the place looked more like a castle than a house. Even with all the work it needed, she zeroed in on the idea of owning such a unique house with so much history.

"You ready? We might as well make a run for it; this rain isn't letting up." He flashed a wicked grin her way before throwing open the car door and flipping up the umbrella.

When he got around to open her door, he took her arm, and then just stood there looking down at her as the rain pelted the umbrella.

At first she thought he'd changed his mind about going inside, but when he turned her around to stand in front of him, he pointed over her shoulder and said, "Take a look at that view."

The house sat on the highest cliff above the little coastal town with the ocean in front and a forest of trees to the back. Looking out over the top of the car, she smelled the rain and the fishy scent from the ocean, but she had to admit she'd never seen anything quite like the view from this spot.

From where they were standing on the cliff, they faced the sea, looking through the mist and the spray to the gray horizon. From this height, the clouds were rolling in, drifting toward the car hugging the ground in an eerie fog that slowly began to eat up the ground and envelope them.

"How many times do you get a chance to see the elements come together like that?"

She drew in a ragged breath just thinking about him living here with someone else. It was a good thing she'd gotten past Jake Boston.

To keep from getting drenched, he began to move them quickly from the car, across the yard, around mud puddles, past equipment and materials covered by huge black tarps. They ran up five, slippery, saggy steps to the long, wraparound porch.

Jake opened one of the double front doors and let her go inside first before leaving the umbrella on the porch. She stepped into a wide entryway with a concrete floor, sheetrock walls, and not much else.

"At least you won't get wet. We finished the new roof before the rain hit. But the place needs some work, huh?"

That was an understatement. The place looked like the Addams Family wouldn't live there. And she saw now what he meant by his "under construction" comment. Everywhere she looked there were sawhorses, tools, fresh lumber, and materials stacked against the walls waiting to be used as either new cabinets, new walls, or new flooring.

As she caught the fragrant odor of wood mingled with the smell of rain, she imagined the possibilities of the old house. A cozy fire in the stone fireplace, pictures on the mantel, a real family sitting around the dining room table.

Whoa. Where had that come from? Down girl. This is not your house. One glance at Jake told her he was waiting for her to say something. She went with upbeat. "Who wouldn't want to live here just to wake up to that view outside every morning?"

"So you like it?"

"It has potential, Jake."

He blew out a breath before moving her along, pointing out what work they were doing in each room. But when she spotted the bridal staircase, she ran her hand along the mahogany railing, her heart dropping a little further with each step she took. Who was he planning to share this huge house with?

She made certain her voice never gave anything away as she started upstairs, chatty all the way to the top. "They don't make staircases like this anymore. If you don't mind I'd like to take a look at the view from that round balcony, though. It's got to be the master bedroom."

He watched her walk up the steps ahead of him, focusing on the way she moved, the sleek shape of her body. He couldn't remember a woman looking so damned beautiful wandering around the rooms of a cold shell of a house on a chilly, rainy afternoon and chatting the place up. It took all his will power to keep his hands to himself and not turn her around right then and there to kiss her boneless.

When they got to the landing, he took her hand in his and steered her to the left, down the corridor, to the spacious circular master bedroom. She oohed and ahhed over the floor-to-ceiling windows and the rounded fireplace in the corner. Then she stepped outside onto the wet balcony, taking in the view again.

When she finally walked back inside she spun around and asked, "Is there something you haven't told me? You planning to remarry, start a family? This house is huge."

But when he just smiled at her, she decided to check out the rest of the room.

She opened the door to a small bathroom then to an even tinier closet. The room started to whirl. A dizzying sickness engulfed her. The closet became a blur as she backed away from the tiny space. Panic squeezed her chest then moved up to lock tight in her throat. She swayed.

Jake saw her start backing away, slowly, inching further away from the closet until she stopped in the middle of the room.

She'd gone gray as death.

Jake caught her right before she hit the floor.

When she came to, he was holding her against his chest. She blinked, looked up at him and saw they were sitting on the bottom step of the bridal staircase. Sitting there with his arms locked tight around her, she felt the strength in his arms, the beat of his heart through his jacket, and began trying to get up.

He noticed her shivering and wrapped his arms tighter, securing her in place.

She desperately wanted to throw her arms around him and enjoy the moment. But no, she wouldn't make a fool of herself ever again, not with this man. Been there, done that. She wasn't going down that road again even in her sorry state. And would that ever change? she wondered. Something—he must have triggered something from the past to set her off like that.

"You want to tell me what happened?"

She lied. "I…I'm not sure."

"You went white as paste and then just dropped. One minute you're fine, checking the place out, looking in closets, and then wham. You want to tell me anything?"

She swallowed hard. "Like what?"

"Are you ill?"

"No. I'm cold." And she wanted as far away from him as possible.

"Then let's get the hell out of here and get you warmed up."

She pushed off his chest or tried to, started to get to her feet. But he held her there locked in his arms. With her squirming against him, his lower half started to respond. If he didn't let her go, he feared a response she wouldn't be too pleased about at the moment.

"Let me up."

"Now you're upset."

"I want you to let me up. We're not—I'm not—doing this again."

He released her. She struggled to get her balance before standing up. When she finally got to her feet, she pushed her hair back and insisted, "Take me back to the Book & Bean. Please. My car's there."

"I thought we might get something to eat."

"No." *Protect yourself; be firm this time. Don't give in.*

"Why?"

"I want out of your damned house, okay? I want to get back to my car. Is that too much to ask? You wanted me to look at your house. I've looked. Now I want to..." She'd almost said get out of there, to get outside where she could breathe. Instead though, she stomped her foot, turned on her heels, and headed straight for the front door. When he didn't follow, she huffed out a breath. "Fine, I'll walk back, but I'm taking the damned umbrella."

He let her get to the door to pick up the umbrella from the porch before getting to his feet. The entire time conceding the fact, he might have to alter his plan somewhat.

She was gonna need a helluva lot more convincing.

☙ ☙ ☙ ☙ ☙

All the way back to L.A. the wipers on the rental did a noisy double-time. He couldn't see a bloody thing out of the windshield. Even with the defroster jacked up to high, the windows kept fogging up. And he was chilled to the bone. Since leaving San Madrid behind, he'd even turned the heater up trying to get warm.

It was May, for chrissakes, in Southern California. He'd been told L.A. was warm in May. They'd obviously lied.

But they hadn't lied about the damned traffic. After sitting for several hours in bumper-to-bumper exhaust, he finally pulled to a stop across the street from a house in Beverly Hills.

He stared at the fifteen-room mansion. Alana's house. He sucked in a breath to let his nerves recover. The trip down the 101 had been brutal. He needed to settle down, focus.

What was wrong with him anyway? Where was the calm, cool detached man who did this for a living? He took a few more minutes to right himself, his mind, his thoughts. When he caught his reflection in the rearview mirror, he laughed at himself.

Here he was sitting in the dark in a parked car in the pouring rain, about to begin his mission, if you could call it that, feeling colder than he could ever remember feeling in Prague during the winter.

Bollocks to Southern California, anyway. He'd get his business done and get out.

So what if the lousy rain reminded him of another time, another place? God, he felt burned-out. But that was normal at this stage of the game wasn't it? Didn't most people tire of doing the same old thing year after bloody year? At his age, he should be sitting on a sandy beach in

Aruba using the nearest available hot body to warm his bed.

Sunny Southern California, my ass, he thought as he reached over and turned the heater up to high.

When the warm air from the heater made the windows fog over even more, he cursed under his breath and wondered if the nasty weather would keep Alana from going out tonight. Would she leave the house in this weather or decide to stay in? It didn't matter much to him.

Either way, it was her last night to live.

☧ ☧ ☧ ☧ ☧

A couple of minutes later, as if on cue, he watched as the garage door slowly worked its way up and Alana backed out her Lexus. Once out of the garage, she kept the engine idling in the driveway while the garage door shimmied closed. After she'd pulled away, he waited until she was a reasonable distance before shifting the Chevy into Drive. He followed her through the maze-like streets of Bel Air.

As soon as he was sure she'd stay put carousing at her favorite bar for a few hours, he'd head back to the house and wait for her to return. Because he knew she'd almost certainly take a side trip and spend part of the evening with her partner in crime, dear old Jessica, it would give him time to set up in the house.

After all, he had Alana's routine down almost as well as his own. He knew all about her nasty little secrets. Good thing she was a predictable sort, a creature of habit. But hell, who was he kidding? The vault full of lies and deceit he'd cracked open would be difficult for anyone to accept as the truth. That's why tonight it would be Alana up first. There was an order to this process, and he intended to follow the plan, a plan he'd been working on for two fucking years. It would take both his patience and his professional timing to pull it off. So what if he toyed with them a bit before each kill? He had to make a statement, didn't he? Because by God, before they died they'd know why and what it meant to him.

This time when he got to Alana's, he parked the car several streets over. He picked up the black bag that held his tools of the trade, slapped on a pair of thin leather gloves and made his way back through the darkened neighborhood in the pouring rain. When he got to the back door, he pushed a key into the lock and stepped inside, stopping to punch in the code at the control panel. He shut the door and went into the laundry room just off the kitchen to grab a towel to wipe up the watery footsteps he had dripped onto the sandstone floor.

He mechanically checked his watch. He'd plan on a minimum of two hours before she returned. He set the timer on his Tag Heuer. After mopping up the floor and disposing of the towel, he snapped off the leather gloves he'd worn and stuffed them in his bag only to dig further down and pull out a dry pair, which he promptly stretched onto each hand. Fastidious to a fault, he had been taught by the best, which made many of his habits outdated and probably unnecessary. But technology had changed a great deal over the years and in his line of work, one could never be too careful.

Suddenly hungry, he strolled into the kitchen to fix himself something to eat. As he dug into the refrigerator, he pulled out the makings for a hearty ham and cheese sandwich. He found the bread, a nice focaccia, and drooled. He did appreciate good food. The thought of a gourmet meal made Kit Griffin's delectable desserts pop into his head.

Would it be her turn before long? A pity, he thought. No matter what he'd seen today, if she was anything like her mother, she too was living on borrowed time.

As he assembled his supper, he considered the night ahead of him and what he needed to do. For the next couple of hours he'd hide out in the tiny back bedroom he'd found off the alcove, almost an afterthought of a bedroom. Because it was the room farthest from Alana's, it would suit his purpose perfectly.

When he thought about the possibility of Alana bringing Jessica back with her for the night, he knew he could easily kill two birds with one stone, so to speak. The thrill of killing them both at the same time had his body pinging. But then he quickly tamped down the urge. While the local police weren't exactly known for their sharpness, killing both women now would not serve his purpose. No matter how tempted he was to take care of them both at the same time, it simply wouldn't work to his advantage.

He reminded himself of the plan.

No, he'd wait until Alana was alone, even if it meant waiting all night, even if it meant waiting till morning. He could be patient when necessary.

Getting comfortable in the little guest bedroom, he threw his bag on the bed and dug out the movie he'd brought for the occasion. Turning on the television before pushing the button on the DVD player, he popped in the movie, *Psychos At Dusk*, made in 1968. The film certainly couldn't be considered one of Alana's best performances, but then, what was? She'd never bothered to hone her craft.

Settling back on the bed, he took a bite of his sandwich and enjoyed the movie, which he knew had a mood-lifting macabre death scene. He smiled to himself wondering how Alana would play her own death scene. For real.

It was after one in the morning when he heard Alana return home and get ready for bed. It was time to go to work. Technically, it was now Sunday morning, Mother's Day, no less. He could only hope the police would see the significance of it all.

Even though he'd been at this for years, he still couldn't fight that bit of adrenalin rush that came just before a kill. And he reminded himself this was a bit different; unlike his other jobs, he wasn't getting paid for this one.

He drew out the butcher knife he'd taken from the kitchen. It wasn't his usual weapon of choice, but then Alana deserved something a bit out of the ordinary. As he ran his gloved hand up and down the blade of the knife, it dawned on him how easy access had been up to this point. That, he knew, would change. After tonight it would be a little more difficult to get to the others. He shrugged, realizing he'd just have to make the best of it. But then he smiled at his dark reflection in the dresser mirror; he'd planned for that as well.

As he walked quietly down the Berber-carpeted hallway toward Alana's bedroom door, he thought about how it would play out. He was as good if not better than Alana and Jessica at setting a scene. And with this scene, he intended to have Alana Stevens play her part to perfection. Her best and final death scene would have as much drama and flair as he could eke out of her. Suddenly, he wished he'd thought to bring a camcorder.

He clutched the knife in his hand and opened Alana's bedroom door, stepping into the darkness.

CHAPTER 3

Thunder grumbled with a roar and shook the small bungalow like a mini earthquake. Intermittent flashes of lightning and the howling wind had Kit restless and edgy. As if the storm refused to give ground, it battered the house until she pulled the covers over her head, curling into a fetal position. She couldn't sleep. Something didn't feel right.

She didn't think it was the weather, either. She'd had the strangest sense of—something all day. It had started at the shop that morning, and then, out of the blue, he'd walked into the Book & Bean.

"Jake's to blame for this," she said out loud to Pepper, her rescued black-and-white border collie curled up beside her on the bed. At the intrusion to his sleep, the dog lifted his head long enough to stare at her.

"Don't look at me like that, okay?" she told the dog. But since Jake had dropped her off at the store around six o'clock to pick up her car, a gnawing, inexplicable fear chewed at her insides. Something bad was about to happen. She couldn't shake the ominous feeling and now she couldn't seem to settle down.

Maybe it was the panic attack at the house, she thought. And seeing Jake again must have triggered it. But she couldn't ignore the sense of danger she'd felt when she'd gotten into her Jeep. Not danger exactly, she corrected, maybe it was more like defeat that stemmed from watching him drive off down Main Street and head back to

L.A. and out of her life...yet again. Why did he keep doing that to her? And why did she keep letting him? And who was he planning on sharing Crandall House with anyway?

The questions buzzed through her head like angry bees as she stretched out her long legs and tried to find a more comfortable position. As she lay there she willed herself to sleep and simply wasn't convinced it was the panic attack making her so...tense and jumpy.

After a while, she decided she'd gone to bed way too early. But she'd been exhausted. As she blew her bangs off her forehead she thought about all the caffeine she'd consumed. Although maybe the problem stemmed from that television program she'd watched hours earlier about serial killers. That could be what had her jumping at every little sound outside. Or it might have been those six steamy chapters of the romance novel she'd read that had her juices flowing. That had to be why she couldn't get to sleep.

After all, a healthy, single twenty-four year old woman living in a little town like San Madrid who had just turned down dinner on a Saturday night with the man of her dreams had to be crazy as a loon. "No," she protested. "Jake Boston is not the man of my dreams. He's just a man from my...youth."

Hot now, she kicked off the covers and wondered what it was about living alone during a thunderstorm that made a relatively normal woman become such an insomniac.

Normal? Oh God, had she actually thought that? Well, that showed progress, didn't it? How long had she actually considered herself normal anyway? *Since moving to San Madrid*, she thought. Moving here four years ago hadn't just been a good financial decision for her but a personal one as well. She'd obviously needed to get the hell out of L.A. and make a change in her life long before she'd actually taken the step.

Normal. Wow. After three long years in therapy, wouldn't Dr. Strasburg be proud to hear her use that word to describe herself. Maybe she'd call him out of the blue and give him a progress report. "That's stupid," she said out loud. "The man has better things to do than walk down memory lane with a former mental patient."

Chilled now, she grabbed for the covers and pulled them back around her. Obviously her restlessness and odd feeling was no more than the rainy, sunless week of bad weather getting to her. She didn't know how people went for weeks, sometimes months, without seeing the sun like they did in the Pacific Northwest. She shook her head at the idea of living anywhere else besides San Madrid and told herself this was just an unusually long lingering storm that couldn't last forever.

As she shifted in the bed again, she reached past the slumbering dog, envious of Pepper's ability to drop off to sleep, and picked up the remote to the television. She clicked it on, then switched remotes and turned on the VCR. The VCR already held a familiar tape, one she hadn't yet converted to DVD. An old black-and-white image of her father appeared on the small screen.

Here was her go-to comfort zone. It wasn't the first time she'd relied on him or, rather, the image of John Griffin to lull her to sleep.

It had been years since she'd discovered some of her father's work on videotapes, videotapes that held images of him from his roles in movies or his guest-starring roles in the old '70s television westerns. When she couldn't sleep, like tonight, her father's appearance on screen, even briefly, captured an image that reminded her of what might have been. As a character in his western attire, sometimes playing the villain, sometimes playing the sappy hero, he stared back at her from the television screen and eerily came back to life for a few precious moments in time.

She knew how pathetic that sounded, but watching him in his various roles even for the brief few minutes he appeared on screen, were all she had of a man she hadn't seen in years. But in spite of his absence in her life, her father's presence on screen somehow always comforted her, and eventually she fell asleep.

☙☙☙☙☙

He was pretty sure no one would find her body until Monday morning when the maid showed up. But there was always an outside chance that Jessica Boyd might decide to pay her old pal a visit before that. "Well, she can't be with Alana now," he sneered into the damned rain as he drove back to his hotel. "At least not yet."

He'd cut that damned umbilical cord to ribbons, hadn't he?

He smiled at that and wondered if dear old Jessica's death would be as sweet. He tried to picture how the infamous "family" lawyer would spend Mother's Day with her self-centered brood.

He snorted as he considered Jessica and Sumner Boyd's family; their worthless three sons, Connor, Cade, and Collin, all lawyers. He knew firsthand the private image didn't jive with the public persona they'd skillfully crafted over the years. He shifted easily from the focus on Alana to checking off his list of the others and how they'd made their fortune, every dirty little dime.

When he was finished here, the family law firm, Boyd Boyd Geller & Gatz, the largest and most successful law firm on the West coast, would have to hope for a miracle in order to survive his onslaught, because he was about to crack open the family vault...then sit back and watch what slithered out into the light.

If things went the way he planned, all of them were about to pay the ultimate price for their success, one by bloody one.

CHAPTER 4

When the alarm sounded at her usual five o'clock, Kit crawled out of bed, nudging Pepper off her legs, and dragged her body into a hot shower. She'd spent her day off, a quiet and uneventful rainy Sunday, doing what she usually did when she was in a mood: she baked.

She'd made dozens of individual chocolate pecan tarts and a couple dozen batches of brownies, and if that weren't enough, a chocolate cheesecake.

As she stepped out of the shower, she realized she might have overdone the chocolate thing. But she'd been in a mood for chocolate. It was the weather, she decided, as she threw on a pair of well-worn jeans and an ancient red T-shirt emblazoned with the words "Born to Bake" on the front.

She bound her hair back with a bright red scrunchie and left the bedroom to head downstairs, the dog at her heels.

On the way to the kitchen, she contemplated whether or not the rain was really the root of her mood. She hadn't slept well after waiting until almost six o'clock the night before to call Alana to wish her an obligatory happy Mother's Day. When she hadn't answered the phone, Kit had left a brief message on her mother's answering machine.

Kit was so overjoyed that she hadn't actually had to speak to her, she could have danced. And didn't that just sum up nicely her entire relationship with Alana?

Afterwards, she'd had no problem picking up the phone and talking for almost an hour to Gloria about everything from recipes to life in general.

It wasn't her fault she had more in common with her aunt than she'd ever had with Alana, the woman who'd given her life. As Kit saw it, Alana was the one with the problem and always had been.

Kit's first taste of normal and belonging hadn't come along until Gloria and Morty had moved from Maine to L.A., opening up a whole new world every time they had praised her or showed her affection. Both had given her a taste of self-worth for the first time in her life. And whenever she was around them, she had noticed how they took pleasure in the small things of everyday living. Like cooking.

Like so many rooms in that Beverly Hills mausoleum that passed for a house, Alana's kitchen had been off limits. No exceptions. No daughter of hers would spend time in the kitchen doing something as lowly as cooking. To Alana, the only people who cooked were, well, cooks. Kit winced, remembering the ugly screaming-match between the two sisters the day Alana had walked into Gloria's kitchen and found Kit making a hearty Bolognese from scratch. Kit had been fourteen.

But time spent with Gloria meant she got to do normal stuff.

With her aunt's encouragement, the reserved, shy girl had made the most of it. With the freedom to cook and bake at Gloria's, Kit found she not only liked it but that she was good at it. Gloria had pushed her to experiment with recipes and try her hand at spicing up some of the age-old favorites and creating her own dishes, such as the chocolate pecan tart, a velvety saucy chocolate version of her own making, a dish so rich her customers hounded her to make it. And every time she did, it sold out before noon.

"Well, come and get them, folks. I baked enough for the whole town," she said to herself as she walked into the kitchen, mechanically turning the oven to preheat. She poured herself a cup of coffee from the fresh steaming pot, already brewed thanks to the automatic timer she'd set the night before. After feeding Pepper, she started digging in the pantry, assembling the ingredients she needed to make fresh orange-cranberry muffins to offset all the chocolate goodies she'd made.

When she'd poured the last of the batter into the muffin pans, she realized she had an excess of fresh orange juice and rind leftover. She wondered if she had enough time to roll out dough for orange cinnamon rolls. One glance at the clock told her she needed to get moving. Maybe tomorrow, she thought, and started clean-up detail.

By the time she reached the store, carrying the first tray of baked goods, the sun was just creeping up, turning the horizon into brilliant shades of orange—the sun's first appearance in days.

After starting several different flavors of coffee including regular brew, she went to the front door and flipped the sign around to Open.

Thrilled with the prospect of a sunny day, she stood at the window with a smile on her face and watched as the little fishing village she called home slowly came to life.

☸ ☸ ☸ ☸ ☸

At about the same time Kit opened her store, a maid used her key to unlock the back door at 15222 Bel Green Drive and made her way into the kitchen to start breakfast. When she'd finished preparing the meal, she started a load of laundry, and then waited patiently until seven-thirty or so before going upstairs to check on why her employer hadn't come down for breakfast.

When she got to the master bedroom, she noticed the door stood slightly ajar, which was a rarity. Not wanting to spy on her employer, but curious as to why she'd left the door cracked, she peeked inside…and froze.

Blood was—everywhere. A scream hung in the back of her throat as she backed out of the room and ran down the hallway until she tripped on her own two feet. Picking herself up, she fled down the stairs two at a time and ran screaming out the front door to the nearest neighbor.

⎈⎈⎈⎈⎈

By eleven o'clock that morning, veteran homicide detective Max St. John and his younger counterpart Dan Holloway had identified their victim as Alana Stevens, a former actress and owner of a real estate company. Her nude body had been left on the floor of her bedroom, cut up like a piece of meat with at least twenty stab wounds—and the coroner was still in the process of counting. They'd also found the murder weapon, a nine-inch butcher knife from the kitchen, dropped in the bathroom sink with no apparent effort to conceal it.

As St. John and Holloway stood in the hallway directly outside the bedroom, waiting for the crime scene unit to finish up, Max said flatly, "Whoever did this was pissed."

"Overkill, pure hate, pure rage. No forced entry, Max. I'd say she knew her killer."

"Yeah, which means we start with family, friends, boyfriends, and acquaintances right up front. I didn't eyeball a single print on the knife, but you never know. You canvassed the neighbors, right? Did they hear or see anything?"

Dan shook his head and stifled a low chuckle. "You don't want to know."

"Now you've piqued my interest."

"Okay, but you asked for it. The neighbors are so damned scared they think Manson might've made parole or one of his followers did and came back after all these years, killed her like this to make a statement; another actress, butchered, murdered."

"Manson? You're kidding." St. John drifted back inside the bedroom, and Holloway was forced to follow.

"Nope. A couple of the neighbors still remember the Manson family slayings up in the hills not far from here." Eyeing the uncertainty on his partner's face, he went on to clarify. "A lot of the same neighbors still live here. They remember the Manson murders in '69. For years afterward they were scared, thought Charlie pulled some kind of bad mojo strings from his cell in San Quentin. Now they think he somehow made parole, started his killing spree all over again not far from the original murders."

Dan watched Max roll his eyes. "Hey, you asked. I'm just repeating what they said. Old people believe wild conspiracies. The way they see it—a former actress, a mother, killed on Mother's Day, their imaginations kick into overdrive." He flipped through his notes. "I did find out the victim has a kid. A daughter, an estranged daughter, so say the neighbors. And there's an odd message on the answering machine from her that came in Sunday night around six. Sounds kind of...weird. You might want to take a listen. Could be she staged the call to throw us off. According to the neighbors mother and daughter had issues. Since the murder occurred on Mother's Day, the daughter might be our starting point, and we spread out from there."

Looking at the bloody, lifeless body still on the carpet, Max agreed, "When you think about it, it makes sense: wealthy woman with a fat bank account, greedy relative like the daughter wants her dead for the insurance and the money, chops her up like meat on Mother's Day. Doesn't take a genius to imagine greed as a motive, but why kill her like that?"

"Obvious rage," Dan said, glancing again at his notes. "A murder with so many stab wounds, you figure it was either a crime of passion or pure hate. We'll know more details after the autopsy, of course."

And even as he said it, Holloway winced as he watched one of the crime scene technicians scrape at blood splatter from the wall then slip the evidence into a plastic baggie. After only three years in Homicide it still made Dan cringe a little. He remembered why he'd wanted to remain outside in the hallway. So when the M.E. spoke it caught him off guard. "Got something here, found something foreign in the mouth."

Holloway watched as the portly medical examiner pulled a shiny, metallic object from the mouth of the victim and dropped it into another evidence bag.

"Define foreign," St. John demanded.

The M.E. held up the bag. "Looks like it's about the size of a toy soldier, only it looks like," he squinted, before adding, "a gold something, maybe a cowboy. It doesn't belong in the mouth, that's for sure."

Holding up the bag himself, St. John remarked, "What the hell? What's that doing in the mouth?"

"More like stuffed down her throat. Hey, you guys are the detectives, you tell me."

"Can you give me a time of death?"

The M.E. shook his head. "Too early, but I'm guessing more than twenty four. My best guess is sometime after midnight Saturday night, maybe early Sunday morning."

St. John pressed, "When will you have more?"

"Don't get pushy, Max. Tomorrow morning tops."

Settling for that, Max and Dan returned to the hallway and stood at the top of the stairs, where both men paused long enough to formulate their next move. It was Dan who wanted clarification. "Okay, we check out the next of kin starting with the daughter. Did she benefit from her death and so forth? If so, how much does she gain? Find out if the victim had any enemies. If so, who hated her enough to slice her up like that?" He went through his notes once more. "There's a sister in Agoura Hills."

Just as they started down the staircase, harsh feminine shouting suddenly drew their attention to the open front doorway. An older woman with short black spiky hair, meticulously dressed in a raspberry colored suit, was trying to bully her way past the two patrolmen standing guard. The woman was yelling obscenities, making threats about someone losing their job if they didn't let her pass. She was also explaining to them in no uncertain terms that they didn't know who they were dealing with.

Tired of listening to the woman's shrill voice, St. John yelled, "Lady, this is a crime scene. Back out of here now or I'll arrest you for obstruction."

"Crime scene? I'm Jessica Boyd." She pulled out a business card, coolly palmed it into St. John's hand. "Boyd Boyd Geller & Gatz. No doubt you've heard of us. I'm Alana's attorney and best friend. What the hell is going on here? Where's Alana?"

They recognized the law firm and the woman, who was perhaps the most famous female lawyer on the West Coast and the wife of Sumner Boyd. Together the couple made up half of the founding partners. The legal eagle stepped into the entryway as if she owned the place.

Both men exchanged exasperated looks.

Not wanting to make a mortal enemy of the high-powered law firm but wanting to keep his dignity intact, St. John simply offered, "Perhaps you'd be good enough to ID the body for us." It wasn't one bit necessary, but the lawyer didn't know that.

"The body? What are you talking about?"

"Your friend's been murdered."

"Oh my God. How?"

With no intent to share specifics, St. John countered, "When's the last time you saw Ms. Stevens alive?"

Shaken by the news but not enough to lose her head, Jessica jockeyed from lawyer to concerned best friend with the innate skill of a chameleon. As she calmly searched inside her Louis Vuitton handbag for a tissue to dab at her dry eyes, without missing a beat, she softened her voice and replied, "Saturday night we went out for a girl's night out—in Beverly Hills, of course. We left around ten, headed to my house for some girl-talk."

The cops didn't have to know they'd ended up having a threesome with a gorgeous hunk they'd picked up at the bar. "She was fine when she left around midnight."

"Any idea who might have hated her enough to murder her?"

Without once considering that maybe a member of their Saturday night tryst had followed her back to Beverly Hills for a private rendezvous, Jessica's mind began to consider more important objectives. When her brain found one she couldn't bulldog down, her eyes lit with newfound concern. Deliberately she suggested, "That ungrateful daughter of hers tops my list. Then there's her Loony Tunes sister, Gloria Gandis. They both hated Alana. And Kit…well, Kit Griffin has a violent streak. I've seen it firsthand."

St. John's eyebrows went up. "And when was that?"

"When she moved out of the house, she went into a violent rage and attacked her mother, slapped Alana right across the mouth. I remember it like it was yesterday. If Alana hadn't already been kicking her daughter out, she would have called the police."

Holloway's heart raced as he formulated different scenarios. "And how long ago was that? How old is the daughter now?"

Jessica looked rather annoyed. What possible difference did it make how old Kit was? "She's twenty-five. I know because she's the same age as my youngest, Collin."

Both detectives wanted specifics, but it was Holloway who insisted, "So she moved out recently?"

Exasperated now, Jessica put some force behind her argument. "She was sixteen. The point is she's shown violent tendencies."

The lawyer pondered her next comment, before adding, "And Kit spent years under the care of a psychiatrist."

Holloway didn't make much out of a nine-year-old incident, and hell, half of L.A. was seeing a shrink, but he pressed on and asked, "Were there any other more recent violent episodes between mother and daughter that you witnessed personally?"

"Every time Alana tried with Kit there was always some issue from the past. All I know is that Kit hated her mother. Alana never knew why. Poor woman, it was such an embarrassment and a shame for her to have such a daughter like Kit. From the time she was born, Alana tried to give the girl everything, but she was impossible to deal with from the beginning. Some children are like that, you know. But I was there. I saw what a difficult time Alana had with her."

The whole time she talked, Jessica noticed the younger detective jotted down her every word. As the two detectives escorted her back outside to her car parked in the driveway, they listened as the accusations piled up against the daughter.

The claims, Holloway noted, were mostly from her teen years. But both men couldn't dismiss the seriousness of her charges. Jessica, the stubborn litigator in court, took the opportunity to use every bit of Alana's theatrical influence to make the detectives aware just how dangerous Kit Griffin had been in her youth when she handed them her final parting shot. "The woman not only has a violent streak, there's multiple personality disorder. And as Alana's attorney I know she had recently decided to change her will, leaving the little leech nothing, not a red cent. So yes, Kit Griffin would be my best guess."

There, she thought, that should give them a nice place to start. She watched as the two detectives exchanged looks, and knew for certain she'd left a mark.

If she played this right, she'd deflect any suspicion away from the family or the firm. The police would be so busy investigating the little bitch it would give her ample time to take care of any necessary loose ends.

As she climbed behind the wheel, she considered what she needed to do. She'd have her oldest son, Connor, handle Alana's probate; that way she wouldn't actually be the attorney of record. By the time she made the necessary changes it would cement motive. There would be a nice money trail, one significant enough to make any homicide detective with a brain sit up and take notice. Not all of Alana's money of course, that would be foolish, but enough so no one would question, least of all naïve little Kit.

Why had she felt such panic earlier when she'd learned Alana had been murdered? This would be so much easier than she'd originally thought.

As the two detectives watched her drive away, Holloway commented, "That woman is one piece of work. Did you notice her eyes were completely dry the entire time she wanted us to think she was crying?"

"Oh, I got that. Check out her alibi. Make sure it holds. She admits to being the last one to see the victim alive. Send someone out to that bar in Beverly Hills. And this daughter sounds like a nut case. Where's she live anyway?"

"San Madrid."

"Shit. Let's start with the sister in Agoura Hills and work our way out to the boonies."

⚭ ⚭ ⚭ ⚭ ⚭

As Jessica pulled away, a wide smile on her lips, she wasted no time hitting the speed dial on her cell phone, giving orders at a rapid pace to her oldest son, Connor. They'd organize a press conference for that afternoon. In a matter of days, she'd have the police so convinced of Kit Griffin's guilt it wouldn't surprise her one bit if the girl's ass wasn't sitting in a jail cell before Alana was firmly in the ground.

And who knew, Jessica thought, maybe the little mouse had finally found a spine. Maybe she'd finally exacted her revenge after so many years and actually killed Alana. Maybe she was guilty as hell. Either way, it didn't matter much to Jessica; as long as the police believed Kit capable of Alana's murder, it would keep them from digging anywhere near her, Sumner, or for that matter, her precious law firm.

⚭ ⚭ ⚭ ⚭ ⚭

Hours later, after St. John and Holloway left her house, a distraught Gloria Gandis dialed Jake Boston. She'd sensed Kit was in danger, that much was true, but she'd never thought the danger would come from the police. She hadn't seen that coming.

And that was unusual for her.

They'd thought she was crazy, even as a child, especially Alana, and then later, Jessica. Both women had ridiculed her very existence. But she couldn't help what she was. She'd had the gift all of her life. And she knew now something was very wrong. She felt the wrong. She'd been fighting the feeling since the horrible nightmare had resurfaced Saturday night.

Gloria did her best to calm down. But after listening to the two detectives for almost forty-five minutes, it was blatantly obvious their investigation was headed straight for Kit. They repeated things to her that Jessica had told them, terrible things that they'd taken completely out of context without knowing all the facts. She'd tried to correct the misunderstanding of what had happened between Alana and Kit years earlier. But nothing she'd said seemed to matter. They'd jumped to a ridiculous assumption. The police thought Kit had murdered Alana. She was their prime suspect. But they didn't know her. The idea was preposterous. Gloria had tried to convince them of that to no avail.

At the notion of Kit arrested, her stomach clenched with dread. She forced herself to calm down enough to speak intelligently into the phone. Jake would know what to do. He had to help Kit, he just had to. Thank goodness he was back.

When his secretary Ginger answered the phone, she informed Gloria that he was in his usual Monday afternoon staff meeting. Gloria pleaded with Ginger to go drag him out. While Ginger put her on hold, Gloria went over everything the two detectives had implied.

She needed to keep her head, but the minute she heard Jake's voice, she started sobbing and babbling uncontrollably.

Through the tears and the hysteria, Jake managed to get the gist of the situation. Kit was in trouble, the kind of trouble he knew something about. By the time he'd hung up the phone, he was halfway to the elevator with his jacket in his hand, apparently taking an unexpected trip to San Madrid with a promise to Gloria that he'd do his best to help Kit stay out of jail.

᭜ ᭜ ᭜ ᭜ ᭜

When two men dressed in suits walked up to the counter in the bookstore portion of the Book & Bean and asked for Kit Griffin, Baylee Scott, Kit's lifelong friend and her part-time employee for the past five months, immediately sensed cop. Instinctively protective of Kit, Baylee went into cautious mode. "Who wants to know?"

Holloway looked down at the pretty, petite brunette with her chin jutted out, fierce gesture on her face, and flashed his badge. "Homicide. I'm Dan Holloway and this is Max St. John."

Shock crossed Baylee's face, then confusion. "Homicide? What's this about? Are you sure it's Kit Griffin you want?"

At this point, his patience running out, St. John took over. This obviously wasn't Kit Griffin and it had been a long trip out here and an even longer damned day. "Is Kit here or not?"

The brunette cocked her head, started walking into the coffee house portion to the left of the front door, and offered, "Follow me."

Kit was behind the counter scrubbing the equipment when she looked up and saw Baylee with two men. "Hey Kit, these two guys are Homicide. They want to talk to you."

When Kit heard the words her mind went blank and a sudden chill went all the way through her bones straight to her heart. She drew in a deep breath before wiping her hands off, giving the detectives her full attention. "What's happened? Is it Aunt Glo? Has something happened to Glo?"

"Aunt Glo?" replied Holloway. "Would that be Gloria Gandis?"

Kit swallowed hard, nodded.

"No," St. John grunted. "I'm sorry to have to tell you this, Ms. Griffin, but we have bad news. It's about your mother. Alana Stevens has been murdered."

Once again, Kit heard the words but couldn't seem to get them to fully register in her brain. A fogbank moved in. Alana murdered? That was impossible, she couldn't be dead. They were mistaken. Alana was too...what...too...*mean*, to be...dead.

Baylee saw Kit go pale and stepped between the two men. Taking her arm, she forced Kit into the nearest chair. When Kit just sat there staring into space, Baylee's curiosity kicked in. She asked the two men, "How? When?"

Disappointed that the questions hadn't come from the daughter, St. John took out his notebook, more out of habit than necessity, and clarified, "The how, stabbed. The when, occurred sometime between Saturday night and early Sunday morning. Where were you then, Ms. Griffin?"

For the first time she looked directly at Holloway before turning her gaze to see St. John's piercing, accusing dark eyes. It finally sunk in. "What? What? You want to know where…" Noting they were serious, she blinked again before stammering, "I…I was…at home Saturday night and all day Sunday. I…I baked all day Sunday."

"Anyone with you? Can anyone verify that?"

"I…I…don't know…I…I'm not sure."

Baylee saw the doubt form in their eyes as they stared at Kit, stared at her as if they were waiting for her to confess her worst sins. Oh lord, thought Baylee, this is bad, really bad. Her first thought listening to the two men question Kit in more detail was that her friend desperately needed a lawyer and preferably not one named Boyd.

With each question, St. John got more agitated as the interrogation grew more intense. Frustration ruled as he desperately tried to get information out of the woman who refused to give them anything. After a half hour went by, Holloway suggested that the brunette leave them alone. But Baylee looked him in the eye, shook her head, and told him, "I'm not going anywhere." Baylee took up guard behind Kit's chair, with one hand on her shoulder for support, refusing to budge.

St. John ignored the brunette. "We've spoken to Jessica Boyd. She seems to think you had more reason to harm your mother than anyone else. Why is that?"

Kit looked up when the bell jingled over the door to see Jake walk in. At her wit's end, she'd never been so glad to see anyone in her life.

Without waiting for Kit to respond, Baylee took exception to the question. "Now wait a minute. I see where you're going with this. Kit wouldn't hurt a fly. But Alana, now there was a woman who made Joan Crawford look like Mother of the Year."

Jake walked up just in time to hear Baylee's revelation and understood the implications right along with the two detectives. Jake wasted no time. "That's it. Interview's over. Kit's not answering any more questions without her lawyer present."

St. John wheeled around to confront the man who'd interrupted their questioning just as things were getting interesting and came face to face with Jake Boston, a face from the past, a face he knew only too well. "Good to know you're back in town, Boston. Now I won't have to fly half a world away to arrest your sorry ass." St. John turned to his partner and reflected, "You remember the Claire Boston murder, don't you, Dan? That brutal murder over on Neptune where the woman was beaten to death in broad daylight. Do we have any other persons of interest in the Claire Boston homicide?"

Dan shook his head. "Nope, never did. Mr. Boston, here is it."

"Maybe you'd like to talk about your wife's murder, or do you need your lawyer present for that, too?"

"We can go through it again for the hundredth time. When Claire died I was either thirty-eight thousand feet in the air or at work. But that's a fact you chose to ignore." He took a step closer to St. John. In a low, menacing voice, Jake vowed, "You won't do to her what you did to me, so back off. Interview's over. If you want to grill Kit any more today, call Reese Brennan, make an appointment. She'll be there."

St. John's face grew red before turning back to Kit to tick off his points, one by one. "You have no alibi. No one can vouch that you were home Saturday night or Sunday morning during the time in question, which I might point out was Mother's Day. We have a problem here, Ms. Griffin. Jessica Boyd says your mother was about to change her will, leaving you nothing. And then she's conveniently murdered."

When Jake started to interrupt, Holloway held up a hand in warning. "Don't go anywhere Ms. Griffin. This isn't over. We'll be in touch." And with that both detectives turned to leave.

Once they were out the door, out of earshot, Jake turned to Baylee, almost not recognizing the woman with brown hair. "I know you were trying to help, but you couldn't have said anything that hurt Kit more. You handed them a motive."

"But I didn't mean…I'd never…"

Nerves frayed after more than an hour of intense questions, Kit snapped back, "Don't jump down Baylee's throat. They would have found out eventually, if they didn't know already." But if they'd known, why hadn't they mentioned it?

Jake's voice softened when he asked, "I had no idea Alana hurt you. Why'd you never say anything?" And why hadn't Gloria, whom he considered an old friend, never mentioned it?

"Talk about it, you mean?" She shuddered at that. "It was a long time ago."

Jake reached out for her hand. "Come on, I'll take you home." When Kit went to get her purse, Jake turned to Baylee. "I'm sorry. I didn't mean to jump…"

"No, you're right; I should've thought before I opened my mouth. I wasn't thinking. But Jake, they were trying to say that Kit…"

Jake squeezed her hand. "You were trying to help, trying to defend her. That's what happens when the interview gets out of hand, gets heated. They pound and pound. They count on people saying things they don't intend to say. Don't worry about it. I'll get her home."

⚭ ⚭ ⚭ ⚭ ⚭

Fifteen minutes later, Jake pulled into the driveway of a small, tri-level Spanish-style bungalow yards from the beach. The stucco house belonged to Gloria, but had been Kit's home for the past four years where, like the Book & Bean, she'd put her own personality into the place.

She'd painted the outside a warm gold, the trim a cool red. With no yard to speak of, she'd taken advantage of the tiny courtyard at ground level and set out Adirondack chairs to watch the waves. On the second level leading up to the front door, she'd set out colorful pots containing an assortment of blooming flowers and fragrant herbs. She'd fixed the little house up and made it a home, the first real home she'd ever had. After the last couple of hours, she couldn't think of a single place she'd rather be right now.

And then there was the man sitting next to her. He'd rushed to her defense. It had been wonderful to watch. She did her best to tamp down the feelings he always managed to bring out.

"Are you okay?" he asked quietly

She gave him a weak smile, and opened the car door. "I'm fine. Want to come in?"

"Sure."

The minute Kit opened the front door Pepper jumped two feet off the floor to greet her with a sloppy, wet tongue.

Jake followed her and the dog into a small but tastefully decorated rectangular living space with walls painted buttercup yellow and floors of polished hardwood. The space felt cozy, homey. Pepper ambled off to his bed in front of a rounded kiva fireplace in the corner. To complete the room, two red loveseats sat facing each other separated by a blanket box that doubled as the coffee table.

Jake looked around. She'd taken advantage of every square inch of space by turning the area underneath the staircase into her office. Here a mahogany desk held an assortment of books, a laptop computer, and a printer.

Framed artwork, a collection of beach scenes done in everything from acrylics to watercolors to charcoal, dominated the walls. The signature reminded him she could draw and paint. When she'd been a teen, she'd always taken the time to create her own funny little greeting cards to hand out. But the paintings here showed real talent.

An old upright piano in the far corner of the room caught his eye. He went over and started thumbing through several sheets of music messily propped up and remembered one musical recital in particular from the past. Alana had shown up and embarrassed Kit with a slew of insults in front of everyone. She'd been drunk.

Jake racked his brain. A lot of Kit's past clicked into place. Had Alana ever had a good word for her daughter? Skimming through the stack of music, he finally found what he was looking for. "I always liked this."

Kit walked over to the piano. "Let me guess." Without even glancing at the sheet music he held in his hand, she sat down and began playing *Cliffs of Doneen*. She smiled broadly and added, "You and my father."

But after a brief rendition she abruptly stopped and headed for the kitchen. "I need coffee. What about you? If St. John has his way, my arrest could be imminent. Perhaps I should plan on getting blitzed tonight."

Following her, he laughed. "Not a good idea. You want to talk about it?"

"No."

Just then the phone rang. One glance at caller ID told her the call was from someone at BBG&G. "Great. Just what I need. Jessica already told the police I did it. She isn't my favorite person to talk to right now." She let the answer machine take the call.

Seconds later, Connor Boyd's authoritative voice held court in the small house as his message filled the air. "Kit, we need to talk. I'm handling Alana's probate. It seems you're a very wealthy woman. You've inherited Alana's entire estate. Call me. I've got some papers you'll need to sign so we can move this forward."

Suddenly shaking, she lost control. "God, I can't handle this right now. They've made a mistake. Alana would not leave me a dime, let alone her entire estate."

And one more reason they'll think she killed her mother, Jake thought sourly, as he wrapped his arms around her while she cried her eyes out.

☙ ☙ ☙ ☙ ☙

From his vantage point on the beach, he considered Kit Griffin.

From the beginning, the plan had been for her to get the blame, at least initially. So far, everything was going according to plan, but for some reason, for the first time in years, maybe for the first time since he'd been doing this job, he didn't like the taste it left in his mouth.

What would they think when the others fell? Would they figure it out then, let the daughter off the hook? How long would it take the police to take off their blinders, maybe start thinking outside the box? What if that didn't happen?

He'd underestimated Jessica Boyd. And that he would correct.

CHAPTER 5

To get her mind off St. John, Jake took Kit to Pirelli's down at the waterfront for dinner. In spite of an overcast evening, they dined outside in the open air on steak and lobster and were on their third bottle of wine when Jake insisted, "How about we take a walk on the beach, walk off this meal, head down to the marina. I'll show you my boat."

"You really love that boat, don't you?"

"It isn't so much the boat. I like being out on the water." How could he explain that, after being the person of interest in a murder investigation for the better part of a year, he'd needed to make some life altering changes?

Waking up one day and finding his perfect life wasn't so perfect after all but rather an illusion had sent him into a tailspin. The humiliation of it all had him searching for an outlet where he could lock himself away from the pressures of his business and forget how he'd fucked up his life.

Sailing had been it for him.

But he revealed none of that as they left the restaurant and walked outside into a heavy lingering marine layer. They headed south, toward the marina. With only streaky bits of lowering sun, the breeze right off the water made the gray May evening feel chilly. He took one look at the slinky, form-fitting black dress Kit wore and asked, "Are you cold?"

She shook her head. "I enjoy being outside. When I was a kid I always hated being cooped up inside. I'm like my father that way. He was an outdoor kind of guy."

They'd just reached the outer fringes of the downtown shops when Kit abruptly stopped and asked in a wobbly voice laced with emotion, "Do you think you could find out for certain what happened to him? My father, I mean. Alana told me he died when I was fourteen on location in Spain filming a western. I always wondered if she told me the truth."

Kit saw the questions form on his face. "He and Alana hated each other. They divorced when I was a baby. There were long periods of time when I didn't see him."

Jake looked out over the water, furrowed his brow. "I could do a search online, start with the union, the Screen Actors Guild." When he saw her puzzled look, he explained, "He had to belong to the union in order to work. As an actor, they'd keep track of his residuals. Might be a good place to find out who's getting what. I take it that's not you."

Again, she shook her head.

The implication of it all hit him then. He suddenly resented being put in the position of pointing out to Kit the sad possibilities about this whole thing. "He could have arranged for his residuals to be part of his estate through his will and the residuals are going to the person named in the will. Isn't it possible he might have remarried or for that matter had other children? Do you have stepsisters or stepbrothers? I've never heard you mention any."

Looking at the puffy eyes from where she'd cried earlier, Jake realized talking about this couldn't be easy. Taking in those sad green eyes, he wanted to take away the hurt. "This must be difficult for you, but I don't know any other way to do this except to strip away the layers one at a time."

A tear slid down her cheek. "I don't care about his residuals. I got used to the fact that I wasn't exactly his primary interest a long time ago. He never mentioned that he remarried or had other kids, but then he was usually a half a world away. It's entirely possible he had other children. Even though, to tell you the truth, I hadn't considered that possibility until right now. Alana might have been right. I'm not exactly the brightest bulb on the tree."

They stopped momentarily, long enough for him to knuckle the tear off her cheek. "Get his social security number. I'll check a little deeper than just surface stuff, find out more details, maybe even contact the authorities in Spain for any information they might have about his death. If you know the name of the film he was working on when he died, maybe we could find out more, find out who some of the actors were, get in touch with them. They might remember something."

Kit looked at him as if seeing him for the first time. He was willing to take the time from his busy schedule to find something out about her father. Maybe this man was different from the self-absorbed guy she'd known for so many years. As they started walking again, she suddenly thought of something. "Why on earth is your boat docked here instead of Marina del Rey?"

He flashed a smile at her and lied through his teeth. "There was some problem with the boat permit at the time. I thought it would be better to move the *Sea Warrior* rather than fight with the marina. You know I stopped by the bookstore a couple of weeks ago when I got back. You'd already closed up for the day."

"Why didn't you just call me at home while you were here? We could have gotten together for dinner."

He raised a brow. "After the chilly reception I got Saturday, I can just about picture how well that phone call out of the blue would have gone."

"Ouch. Direct hit. But it seems I had an epiphany this afternoon in the form of two police detectives. They didn't exactly have my best interests at heart. It reminded me that in a spot like this, a person can't have too many friends. And we're two mature adults who both care a great deal about Gloria." It was the wine putting her in such a generous mood.

Deciding that friend was a huge step up, he said, "We've never had a problem being friends, Kit."

"You can't say I haven't tried to be more over the years."

"Yeah. The timing was always off."

"For you maybe. Not for me."

There it was. That reminder that he'd hurt her. He redirected his focus on getting her to open up since he had to admit, he'd never been curious about her childhood. "Talk to me, honey."

"What do you want to know?"

"All of it."

She sighed. He'd just keep bugging her till she did. "Alana and my father were always at war with each other. Their life—my life— after the divorce was a war zone. They had no interest in getting along for the sake of a child, that's for sure. I don't think I've ever seen two people more opposite in their approach to life in general or their attitude toward me.

"I see all these horrific custody cases in the news and my heart goes out to the kids because I've been through it, in the trenches, pulled apart by two people who wanted conflicting things for me." She shrugged her shoulders before going on, "I don't know when their animosity started, but it had to be before I came along.

"Look, growing up with divorced parents was no big deal. Half the kids I went to school with were in the same boat. Being a product of divorce was never the issue. These two people were so volatile, sometimes it seemed as though I was no more than a pawn, something to be fought over, fought about, and then when one side won, I was quickly cast aside as an afterthought.

"The year I turned five, he petitioned the court for full custody." Sadness crept into her voice. "Obviously he gave up the fight. Later he told me it was because Alana had Jessica on her side and he knew he couldn't win, but as I grew older I suspected there was some other reason."

"Like what?"

She grew quiet, willed the tears away.

As soon as they neared the edge of the water, Jake watched as she slipped off her shoes and walked along the sand in bare feet.

A light wind hit her cheeks as she glanced upward to watch a noisy flock of seagulls that flew overhead and landed just on the other side of the rocks jutting out into the ocean. The clouds so thick and full earlier had parted and left huge holes in the sky so that the stars glittered. She spotted the full moon and sat down in her good dress.

"How about if we sit here for a while?" Looking up at Jake, she patted the sand, knowing he was reluctant to sit down in his good clothes. "It's not that damp."

He sensed she somehow thought he was hesitant to sit down and muss up his clothes, so he followed her lead.

But he couldn't believe she'd just plop down on beach sand in that sexy black dress. Claire would have been downright offended if he'd suggested such a thing. But then he smiled, propped his hands on his knees.

Kit was nothing like Claire.

She took in several deep breaths of ocean air, dug her bare feet into the cold, damp sand and gazed out into the water, listening to the sound of the waves.

Jake sensed the break was significant, that she'd stopped talking for some reason to avoid the fact that her father hadn't fought harder for custody. Instead of prodding her, he kept quiet and said nothing, waiting for her to regain her composure.

When she began talking her voice was so hushed he had trouble hearing her over the sound of the surf.

"I remember almost every one of his visits. There weren't that many really when you add them up over fourteen years."

It wasn't lost on Jake that she'd gone in a completely different direction. He wasn't going to find out tonight why her father hadn't fought harder for custody. Hell, maybe she didn't even know why.

"He'd often drop by unannounced to take me to the Santa Monica Pier for a ride on the carousel or the Ferris wheel, or for long walks on the beach. Alana would be furious that he hadn't called first. I think he did it to piss her off. But he always had a good excuse or story at the ready. The man excelled at telling a story. He always made whatever story he came up with sound so real, so believable. But I was a child and kids tend to believe every word their parents tell them; that is, until they don't. I know I fell for his stories and his excuses on more than one occasion."

She thought back to the father-daughter Valentine's Day banquet at school when she'd been eight. She'd dressed up in her red dress and waited for him in the foyer for two hours to show up before realizing he wasn't coming. She'd cried her heart out for two days. His telephone call several days later and the excuse he'd used stuck in her head. Some work thing had come up, or movie thing or television thing that always seemed more important than his daughter.

She needed to make Jake understand though. "The thing is, he would spend time with me doing stuff I'd never do with Alana. He taught me how to ride a horse. He'd take me hiking at Malibu Lagoon, or camping at Lake Arrowhead, or skiing up at Big Bear. When I turned eight, he bought me a surfboard and taught me how to ride a wave. And when I wanted to play volleyball and softball, he supported my efforts. While Alana grumbled and refused to sign the permission slip, he'd do it behind her back, which would, of course, piss her off to no end."

"Lots of girls play sports. My sisters played tennis, ran track."

She laughed. "Alana thought sports were for boys. When I made the varsity volleyball team in high school, it embarrassed her so much she bitched about it the entire time." Even now she remembered the arguments, the accusations.

"Once I got to college she had no say in the matter. I made the varsity volleyball team as a freshman, got to play all four years. For once I could play without the thought that she might show up during the game and embarrass me. Dad never got to see me play though."

Even in the growing twilight, Jake could see the pitiful look on her face, the sad eyes. He'd thought he had his feelings pegged, but his heart turned over—and she didn't have a clue.

"Then there was my love of art. I've always loved to draw and paint. As a child it was my only outlet…at times…when…" She caught herself. "Dad encouraged me. You see, I didn't do very well in school. It seems I always had to play catch up for one reason or another. The usual subjects like math and English didn't interest me much, but I knew I had a talent for drawing and painting. Unfortunately, that wasn't good enough for Alana. She didn't think I was talented enough to make a living at it so it wasn't worth my time.

"Mainly what Alana wanted was a carbon copy of Alana, girly through and through. It didn't matter that my interests weren't in those things. No daughter of Alana's was going to be a tomboy. What she didn't count on was the fact that when she wanted me to do something, anything at all, I usually did the opposite, especially as I got older, and deliberately headed in the other direction from what she wanted.

"When she couldn't mold me into what she so obviously wanted…" She took a deep breath and just blurted it out, "She tried beating it into me at an early age. But I was headstrong. I battled her at every turn even when I was small. I paid for that stubbornness, but as I got older, either she drew the battle lines in the sand, or I did. It was a tossup. I fought her so often it became a way of life until I moved out."

"Aw, honey." He reached out and put his arm around her. Hearing it now, Jake was sure his earlier instinct had been right; that St. John would see that as motive. But tonight he refused to go down that path. Even though his heart went out to her, he wanted specifics, and was determined to get the answers. "Kit, how many broken bones did you have as a kid?"

At first the question startled her, but then she looked away. "My right arm was broken at three, left leg at four, my left arm at five. Those were her rage years. I mostly just tried to stay out of the woman's way. But when I was little, she was a force to be reckoned with and sometimes it was difficult to avoid her. She was so much…bigger."

Jake swore. "How could she hurt you like that, something so beautiful?"

"I'm pretty sure Alana didn't think of me as beautiful, most of the time she was just pissed about something and I got in the way."

If he'd known she'd had such a lousy childhood, maybe he'd have…what? What could he have done about it back then? It was Jake's turn to fall silent.

As if Kit sensed his mood, she purposely pushed the memories away. *Enough of this. Why did it always seem like she embarrassed herself with him?*

She took in several gulps of ocean air, welcoming the slight breeze that fanned her face. All the wine she'd had over dinner made her flush. She took another deep breath and filled her lungs with the moist ocean air before going on, "By the time Gloria and Morty moved out to L.A., dad's letters with postmarks from places like Africa or Spain came less frequently and then one day stopped coming altogether. When I was fourteen, Alana told me he died in Europe and that was that. John Griffin disappeared from my life. I never saw him again."

Jake squeezed her hand and kissed the top of her head. "Kit, I'm sorry I made you go through all that again."

She shrugged. "I guess I better get used to it. I'm afraid it's like you told Baylee, with the abuse, the police will jump to the conclusion that I had a motive. Even though it doesn't make sense that I'd wait so many years later and do...*that*. I swear I didn't kill her."

"No one who knows you could possibly think that, Kit." But he was pretty sure Max St. John wouldn't let up until he got all the gritty details. He pictured the man's face, the tough-talking, no-nonsense detective.

Jake inwardly winced. He knew St. John would run with past abuse as the motive. And what about the media, what would happen when they got wind of it?

Jake watched as she picked at several broken pieces of purple and black fan shells. In one swift motion, she tucked her dress around her so she could bring her knees up to her chest. She wrapped her arms around her legs and with her fingers, started playing with her feet, then her toes, brushing the sand away. She rocked back and forth, watching the waves. "You've never once said what you thought of Alana."

"Vain, materialistic, a piranha in business. Right after I started the company, I needed venture capital, needed investors to keep it going. I was young. Banks weren't exactly lining up to make loans to a fledgling software business. Gloria and Morty pointed me in Alana's direction, thought she might be interested in providing some capital. Alana offered me the entire amount. Taking her money would have solved my cash flow problems, but she wanted controlling interest."

He paused, thinking back to the encounter. He didn't mention that Alana had also tried to get him into bed. He'd been twenty-four. The memory had him even now feeling nauseated, especially at learning what Kit had gone through. He turned to look out at the water. "That isn't unusual for a venture capitalist to expect controlling interest if they invest heavily, but it was the way she conducted the meeting that bothered me. When I declined the offer, she threatened me, said she'd personally see to it that no one in Southern California did business with me. I eventually got most of the money I needed from Morty in the form of a loan. I would have shut the doors before I let that woman take control of my company."

When Kit heard that, she stopped playing with her toes. Her lips curved in a wide smile. Suddenly, she changed her sitting position to a kneeling one and set about patting wet sand between her hands, shaping and molding the wet stuff into sand creatures. Soon the sand took on various shapes of animals, creating a menagerie of sorts.

When he recognized the shape of a crab, he said, "You're very creative."

"You create an expensive software program worth millions and you think I'm creative with sand? You're a riot. Why don't you try it though? Working with your hands can be very cathartic."

In the light from the moon, he looked over and saw the sparkle in her jade green eyes as they went from dark to light depending on her movement. When she caught him staring, he got busy rolling the wet sand into a ball then forming it into clusters of shapes.

They sat there, two adults, grimy up to their knees in their good clothes, playing in wet sand.

After several artistically ingenious minutes with the sand, Kit proudly displayed her collection. "My animals look better than yours."

"That's how much you know; I'm not making animals."

"Good, because whatever you're making, you aren't doing a very good job."

"Such a critic, you obviously have no appreciation for abstract art."

"Oh, I appreciate the abstract, but that doesn't look like any art I've ever seen. Besides, my elephant is going to flatten your abstract art." With a devilish look in her eye, her elephant-shaped sand creature swooped down to obliterate his artwork.

He fired back, "That's war." Going on the offense, he hovered for a moment over her sand creatures before blasting them with handfuls of sandy artwork.

Both on their feet, the battle raged on as they threw handfuls of sand back and forth at each other, dodging each other's aim and trying to avoid defeat.

At one point, attempting to evade Jake's constant bombardment, Kit ventured out a little too far into the surf, got carried away by the current, and ended up floating, albeit momentarily, out to sea.

Gallantly, Jake tried to fish her out, but with the constant tide, the current strong, she easily pulled him down into the water with her. Together they struggled to regain their footing. Like two ten-year olds, they played and splashed around in the water, as if it were an everyday occurrence.

Once out of the water, back on sandy shore, they sat down trying to catch their breath. But it didn't take long sitting in wet clothes before it grew colder. Jake took one look at Kit and declared, "You've ruined that dress. Come on, let's walk over to the boat and dry off."

They headed toward the marina. As they trudged through sand, she chose her words carefully. "I know you lived on the boat after Claire…because you couldn't go back to the house. What's it like living on a boat?"

"You learn to make use of every inch of space, learn to downsize. Have you ever sailed?"

She looked out over the water again. "Once. Dad took me out to Catalina Island for the day when I was a child, so long ago it seems like a dream." She thought for a moment. "Come to think of it, maybe it never actually happened. Maybe I just dreamed he took me to Catalina."

Jake noticed the sadness in her voice. "We'll definitely put sailing on the agenda then. Get you out of port and on the open sea first chance we get."

She smiled and Jake's heart double-clutched in a feeling so foreign his knees wanted to buckle.

Hand-in-hand they walked across the wooden bridge to the pier until they came to a row of boats, where he stopped in front of one with the name *Sea Warrior* emblazoned on the side.

He helped her onto the starboard side of the sleek fifty-foot French-built sloop. An immediate sway and give was the first indication she'd left land. In spite of all the wine she'd had with dinner, she managed to steady herself.

☙☙☙☙☙

Still wet from the beach, Jake guided her below deck, rubbing her chilled arms as he went. "Let's get you out of the cold." He gave her a quick tour, pointing out things like the galley and the engine room on the way to a large bedroom, or stateroom, where he dug into a bin for towels.

As she accepted a large beach towel and began to dry her hair, she looked around the master stateroom, saw the queen-sized bed, and suddenly wondered how many women he'd had in this floating love nest. She knew she had no right to think that way, but all the resentment over the past bubbled to the surface, leaving her feeling ridiculous standing in his bedroom.

Would she ever learn? Hadn't she figuratively been right here, in this same spot, the year before? Not on the boat of course, she silently corrected, as she did her best to get into the spirit of the tour.

By the time they ended up back in the salon, however, Kit's ridiculous feeling had turned into a slow boil directed at her stupidity. She watched rather impatiently as he played with a panel, and went over all the things it controlled, a stereo system, a DVD player, a television. With a cell phone, a laptop computer, and Internet access, he pointed out he had all the comforts of home, or as she decided, enough toys on board to keep any grown man content as he sailed off into the sunset.

Kit took a seat on an L-shaped sofa, feeling suddenly exhausted. But her eyes drifted to the wall lined with photographs. Scanning the pictures, she noted none were of Claire, but rather photos of friends and family.

There were pictures of a much younger Jake skiing with his friends Dylan and Reese, several others that showed a group of people wearing UC Berkeley shirts, obviously taken during college tailgating at one of the football games. Good times, Kit thought, times of his life she'd had no part of. The slow boil of anger simmered to belated resignation. She had to face facts. There was a huge chunk of his life she'd had no part in and never would.

Jake noticed her staring at the pictures on the wall and then saw the sad look in her eyes. "You look tired."

She closed her eyes, leaned her head back on the sofa. But, as if she'd memorized the photos, she said quietly, "You have such a terrific, supportive family, Jake. I always envied that."

"They were great through all of it, the accusations, the embarrassment, the media blitz. It was hard on them. But their support never wavered. Dylan and Reese hung in there, just like Baylee and Quinn will for you."

"But at least you had family."

"Gloria's your family. And I know Baylee and Quinn are like family to you."

She opened her eyes. Green speared blue. "Why are you here, Jake? If it's because Gloria called you…"

"It isn't."

"Then why?"

He leaned over, tucked a strand of wet hair behind her ear. "I want to help you get through this. You don't have to go through it alone"

But that had her sitting up straighter. "And just like that, I'm supposed to forget you left for Japan like you did? Another night, just like this one, we were taking that first step, or the next step, something different. Then you panicked. You must think I'm incredibly stupid and naïve to believe you now. Naïve Kit, she'll believe anything you tell her. How can I trust you to be here tomorrow or the day after?"

He stroked her hair before pulling her to him. The minute his lips touched hers, he felt her body go loose, melt against him. He let himself enjoy the taste, the tingle. He took the kiss deeper. And then suddenly she broke off. "You son-of-a-bitch. You're doing it again. Will you be here in the morning, Jake, or will you find some place to run, some reason to slither out of town because you've had second thoughts? You always seemed to have second thoughts where I'm concerned."

Jake got to his feet. "You're exhausted and saying things you haven't thought through. I've told you I'm back to stay. How many times do you want me to say it?" He ran his hands through his hair. "And you're the one who keeps using the word *friends*." His sigh filled the small space. "Look, I'll go jump in the shower, get out of these wet clothes, and take you home."

When she didn't say anything, Jake stormed off down the hallway.

Soon she heard water running, and she sunk back into the sofa. Feeling drained; the fight went out of her. The wine from dinner kicked in and she went from buzz to exhaustion in a heartbeat. In her damp dress she was chilly, so she tucked her bare feet under her legs and looked around for a blanket. Spotting an afghan draped on the back of the sofa, she wrapped herself up like a cocoon and curled up in a ball. Before settling in, she released the barrette holding the twisted knot of hair at the back of her head. It felt good to free her hair from the clasp. For some reason her head hurt. But soon drowsiness overtook her and she fell asleep.

The ten-minute shower helped Jake get rid of the wine buzz. Wide awake now and refreshed, he quickly toweled off and threw on a pair of jeans and a T-shirt. Slipping on his topsiders sans socks, he grabbed his wallet and car keys, and headed back toward the salon. As he rounded the living area, he stopped in his tracks when he saw her sleeping on the part of the couch that made up the L.

She'd fallen asleep curled up in a ball, lying half on her side and half on her stomach, facing toward him with a fist placed just so under her chin.

He bent down to her level, rocked on his heels to get a better look. Inches away from her face, he studied her full mouth, the cute nose, the gold colored skin. She'd loosened her hair and strands of it fell across her face. On instinct, he nudged a few locks away, letting his hand rest on her hair.

Even curled up in a ball, snuggled under his mother's knitted afghan, she was all legs. Suddenly, a jolt of lust hit him. How could he let her spend the night thinking the way she did? Gently, he rubbed at her arm before shaking her back and forth. But after drinking so much wine earlier, she didn't so much as stir.

Wasn't he looking at the very reason he'd made some changes recently? The timing had always been off, and he intended to change that.

But now she was the one in trouble. He tried all the reasonable lines before reality took over.

Oh hell, he thought, as he reached down, picked her up, and carried her to his bed.

CHAPTER 6

In the dark, he hid inside the backseat of the Benz—waiting—patiently waiting for the prey to come to him was all part of the process. But the spider-waiting-for-the-fly-game was always incredibly boring. And by jeezus, she was taking her sweet time.

He tried not to think about what she was doing—inside that house. He wondered if her husband knew about her little sex nest, all the trysts she'd had inside. Funny, he thought, everyone thinks she's such a pillar of the community, such a workhorse; if they only knew. Underlings do most of the legal work, except of course for the work she doesn't want anyone to find out about.

Prophetically, poetically, philosophically: for he thought of himself as all those things, prophet, poet and philosopher, he wondered if anyone ever really knew another person. Oh, they think they do, would swear that they knew another's heart. But does one person ever really know the evil that lurks inside another?

He laughed about how often they'd be wrong.

Finally he heard heels clicking on pavement, heard the beep of a keyless remote opening the locks. She was so distracted she never realized her security had already been breached. The car door flew open. He waited for her to start the car before popping up from the back seat.

"Nice of you to finally join me."

When she started to scream, he calmly clamped a hand over her mouth. The other went around her throat. In a whispered brogue, he told her, "Shut up. Just shut the fuck up. Do you understand?"

When she nodded, he removed his hand.

"Don't rape me," she breathed out raggedly.

So that was it. Well, he'd set her straight on that score. "Look lady, with all the people you've screwed over the years and I mean that both physically and metaphorically, the last fucking thing I'd want is to exchange bodily fluids with you, not even with a fucking condom, not even if you were twenty years younger. Right now, I hate having to get this close to you. Unfortunately, it's necessary. Now drive. Were you headed home after your little rendezvous? You'll head to The Enclave now."

When she didn't answer, he went on, "Jess, Jess. Your little press conference this afternoon was quite a performance. 'Lana would have applauded your efforts; that is, if she could. But did you really think your charade would go undetected forever? Now, take the Coast Highway. And let me tell you a story. Once I'm done, you'll never see me again." He saw her relax somewhat.

"How...how did you get inside my car?"

He smiled, held up a little black scanner. "I love technology."

"What do you want? Don't hurt me."

"I want you to listen to a story and see if a hotshot lawyer like yourself can argue your way out of this one." He put his hand in his pocket, touched the 9-millimeter Glock pistol, and wondered if the police would be able to solve this puzzle. Would they take the easy way and blame it on the woman with the big green eyes? *Well, we'll see what we will see about that*, he thought, as Jessica's car headed up the ramp and toward Malibu.

☙ ☙ ☙ ☙ ☙

The Malibu Police patrol car flipped on its lights as it circled the black late model S420 Mercedes Benz, parked in the left turn lane near the 1600 block of Cross Creek Road. Before he got out of his car, Officer Mark Wilson noted the time as 1:55 a.m. and ran the California plates. Parked in a random fashion next to the median, the vehicle was a road hazard. Believing he had a well-to-do drunk driver who had merely passed out at the wheel in a very inconvenient location, Officer Wilson parked his cruiser behind the Benz, and grabbed his flashlight.

However, when the beam hit the driver's side window, the blast of blood splatter on the glass had him automatically trying to open the driver's door. Finding it locked, he tried the other three doors and found them locked as well. He backtracked to his cruiser and radioed dispatch for backup and requested a CSI unit, explaining that he had what looked like a suicide.

After several minutes another patrol cruiser pulled up. Backup had arrived in the form of Officer Bill Schroeder. Promptly Wilson explained the situation to Schroeder who went back to his police car, opened his trunk as if searching for something, and pulled out the auto thief's age-old tool: a pry bar. This time when the officers walked up to the passenger window, Schroeder slid the metal between the glass and the frame. The passenger door popped open.

A White female in her sixties sat behind the steering wheel, slumped back as far as the seat would allow in a recline position. Blood stained the leather seat and saturated the victim's clothing, coagulating inside the crevices. A 9-millimeter Glock 17 semi-automatic pistol lay on the passenger side floorboard. The Glock had caused a sizeable hole in the woman's left temple.

"Why commit suicide in the middle of an intersection?" Wilson asked Schroeder.

Just as perplexed, Schroeder pointed out, "Not only that, but there's not much recoil to a Glock, how'd the pistol get on the passenger side floorboard when the bullet wound is in the woman's left temple? That's on the opposite side."

Without disturbing any of the blood evidence, both officers combed the car for a suicide note. There wasn't one. They looked around the interior of the car with a flashlight until Wilson focused the light on a shiny gold object lying on the front seat of the passenger side. "What do we have here?"

"Looks like some kind of toy soldier." Without picking up the toy trinket, Schroeder focused his flashlight on the object. "No, it looks like a cowboy. See the horse? The cowboy is sitting on top of a horse. There's a sunset in the background."

Schroeder asked Wilson, "You run the plates?"

"Plates came back clean, no outstanding warrants. The Mercedes is registered to Jessica Geller Boyd."

� ♆ ♆ ♆ ♆

Max St. John had hoped he could wrap up the Stevens murder in a neat, tidy package. But Jessica Boyd's murder muddied the water. Considerably. Since three-thirty that morning, he'd known he had a problem. He had two murders and two victims who knew each other. And both murders fell into that high profile category. Throw in another gold cowboy trinket left at the scene and he had a complication. At least this time the thing hadn't been shoved down the victim's throat. Another reason, he thought, to suspect Kit Griffin.

"Maybe she wanted to silence her mother's lawyer," Max pointed out to Dan.

"Max, where are you going with this?"

"Dan, we have a mess on our hands. For now, we'll let people think the Boyd woman committed suicide. But we both know we've got two women, friends, pillars of the community—"

"And two identical toy cowboys left at the crime scenes."

"Which we'll keep to ourselves for now."

Driving along the Malibu shoreline, St. John pulled his police issue Crown Victoria up to a gatehouse where a security guard with a clipboard stepped out of his hut to stop his progress.

"Detectives Max St. John and Dan Holloway to see Sumner Boyd," St. John said as he held up his badge for inspection. After glancing at the shield, with a nod of his head, as if he'd been expecting them, the guard pushed a button inside the hut, opening the iron gates, allowing them to enter the grounds toward the massive compound known as The Enclave, a cluster of multi-million dollar homes snuggled up against the Malibu cliffs and the Pacific Ocean.

As they pulled away from the guard station, Holloway joked, "Not a bad gig if you can get it; sitting in a hut, stopping traffic. But all this security didn't help Jessica, now did it? If someone's got it in for you, a guy with a clipboard isn't going to stop a determined killer."

Over the wrought iron eight-foot-tall fence, St. John noted that the Enclave looked more like a bustling resort at the height of the busy season rather than a row of private residences. Behind the iron gates, three families lived within walking distance of each other and chose to use golf carts as a means to go back and forth. *Rich people, he thought, could afford such luxury.* The mansions shared the one common gatehouse, hence the security guard. After that, a private road took visitors along the water for almost two miles in either direction, winding by driveways belonging either to a Gatz, a Geller, or a Boyd.

Impressed at the Boyd mansion, Holloway looked at the lavish tri-level, contemporary- style, forty-thousand-square-foot main house and recalled he'd seen a tour of the place on the Home Channel one Sunday afternoon during football's off season. He remembered the program had boasted that the house had ten bedrooms, eight full bathrooms, a theater room, and a law library. He wondered if the rumors he'd heard about the place over the years were true.

The Boyds' had purchased the property in the late '60s after they'd won their first major court case in 1967, a David-versus-Goliath type lawsuit that had pitted a small-time rancher against a mega construction company. Just when it looked as if the fledgling law firm was going to lose, they'd pulled a bona fide miracle out of thin air, producing not only flawless documentation at the eleventh hour that proved liability but a surprise witness who had testified that the construction company dumped toxic waste on the rancher's land, killing his cattle.

The court had awarded a record fifteen-million-dollar judgment that had gone on to bankrupt McKetrick Construction. At the time, the case had been the first monumental court victory of its kind on the West Coast against a major environmental polluter.

The court victory had been so impressive that, even today, law professors used it as a model. That one case had put Boyd Boyd Geller & Gatz on the proverbial map to overnight success. To celebrate their victory, every year on Memorial Day Sumner and Jessica held a decadent festival known locally as The Boyd Bash.

For four days beginning on Friday and ending on Monday, they opened The Enclave to close friends and business associates, including some of Hollywood's biggest celebrities as well as guests from all over the world. Dan knew the local legend. Each year the parties got a little raunchier. He wondered as he looked the place over if this year they'd still carry on the tradition.

&&&&&

In spite of his seventy years and his snow white hair, Sumner Morgan Boyd was a good-looking man. Trim and fit at six feet tall, he made sure he ran three miles every day and hit the links at least three times a week, which explained the perfect golf tan. Life's setbacks were new to him. He simply wasn't used to failure or disappointment. In fact, he didn't permit it.

Those who knew him said he was tough. And he was. But it was important to Sumner that people believe he was a regular guy, a self-made man. Proud of the fact that he came from humble beginnings and made something of himself, he didn't want his sons forgetting that he had grown up in a blue collar neighborhood in Grand Rapids, Michigan, the oldest of six children.

Because of that he was proud that he had never taken a cent from Jessica's wealthy parents. He knew Jessica's father, old Jacob Geller, had disapproved of him the moment he'd set foot inside the man's front door. Jacob Geller had made no secret that he thought Sumner Boyd had been after his daughter's trust fund.

When Jessica had announced her plans to marry Sumner in their last year of law school, Jacob Geller had done the only thing that a wealthy, stubborn father could to get his way: he threatened to cut her out of the family fortune if she went ahead with the marriage. But instead of breaking off the relationship Jessica had dug in her heels. She decided she could do without a few of life's luxuries. After all, she was deeply in love—if not a bit naïve in her stubbornness.

Giving up family money couldn't be that difficult, or so she'd reasoned. She'd simply make her own. They'd start their own law firm and money would roll in. At the time her stance went a long way to alleviate any rumors that the poor-boy law student had married the wealthy debutante for her money. And in the beginning they'd been blissfully happy.

Unfortunately, the bliss hadn't lasted very long.

As Sumner stood looking out onto the majestic Malibu cliffs and the Pacific Ocean beyond, he reflected back to that time when they'd been looking professional failure in the face. But they'd overcome the odds. That one case had turned the corner for all of them. If they'd turned a blind eye to ethics every now and then through the years, it just showed they would do whatever it took to win. And as long as it was a Boyd, a Gatz, or a Geller doing the winning that was fine with him.

He watched his beloved sons Connor, Cade, and Collin take their place around the huge mahogany conference table.

From the moment his informant inside the police department had let him know Jessica was dead, Sumner had feared that someone had discovered their secret. But that was impossible. No one alive knew what they'd done, how they'd gotten their start. If someone had it in for his family it didn't have anything to do with that. And no matter what they had done, he would fight back with all he had to protect what was his.

He stood there in the library waiting for Jessica's sister Eva Geller Gatz and her sons Jacob and Adam to get settled around the table along with Frank Geller's four children. Sumner's eye twitched in annoyance as he remembered that Frank was honeymooning somewhere on the Riviera with his fifth wife.

Never could count on Frank anyway, Sumner thought miserably. Looking back on his forty-two year marriage to Jessica the woman he'd married in Las Vegas the day after they'd both graduated law school. He decided hands down, those early years had been the very best. But because he'd lost Jessica, he could indulge himself today, to look back and wonder what would have happened if things had gone the other way. He shook his head at that. It had all worked out for the best. And it had been a helluva ride.

When everyone had settled, Sumner took a deep breath. "I won't permit anyone to intimidate this family. We'll get whoever's responsible."

A slightly drunk Collin stood up. He was a preppy-looking younger version of his older brothers with dark hair and dark eyes like their mother, and announced, "You know suicide is bullshit."

"Yes. That's why I've prepared a cursory list of our enemies. After forty years of success, we've created a few."

"Is it possible someone found out?" a concerned Connor asked.

Sumner didn't want to rule anything out. There could be any number of reasons for his wife's murder—as well as Alana's. The nonsense about Kit being involved in Alana's murder was just that. He'd read the papers, knew the girl as well as he did his own sons.

When he realized they were waiting for an answer, he said, "That isn't possible. But I've put Auslo and Taft on it. They're good for grunt work such as this. But let me make this clear, from here on out, no one makes a move without consulting me, understand?"

His middle son Cade spoke up, "So we leave it up to Auslo and Taft? I don't like it."

A rather loud knock on the door broke the moment. "That will be the police. You let me do the talking. Understand?"

As heads bobbed in agreement, a butler in a black tux showed St. John and Holloway into the law library.

☙☙☙☙☙

The smell of expensive leather and polished mahogany hung in the air as Max took in the tight-knit consortium. They looked as if, for the first time in their lives, they'd suffered a major defeat. And they weren't used to losing. Looking around at their faces, he remembered all the triumphant press conferences he'd seen over the years with these same people, touting their courtroom wins, and decided they didn't look too victorious now.

After introductions all around, the family listened as Max delved into the coroner's preliminary findings, keeping most of the gory details to himself.

Max had done this many times before. It was never easy. But he never failed to search the faces of family members for a certain type of reaction, an emotion, an indication of how they took the news. Now was no exception.

Sumner Boyd had practical questions, so before wrapping up their visit, St. John briefly addressed the family's concerns about how long it would take before the autopsy was completed and how long the body would remain at the morgue. After answering a few more pertinent questions about what happened next in the investigation, both detectives were escorted from the room by the butler.

Once they were out of earshot, Dan turned to Max and said, "Well, they didn't buy the suicide angle. But that's the damnedest thing, Max. Did you notice the lack of tears, no crying, no hysterics, no emotion from any of them, just cool, collected faces? Am I jaded? What happened to telling the family about a death and having just one family member in the room show some grief, or shed a few tears over the deceased?"

"The whole scene reminded me when we told Gloria Gandis the news about her sister. She didn't shed a tear. And when we told Kit Griffin there were no tears there either."

"Might have been in shock." Dan's gut told him Max was heading down the wrong path as far as Kit Griffin was concerned. But he had no wish to butt heads with his partner.

"They may not cry, but they do drink. There wasn't a sober face in the crowd, and it's what, a little after seven in the morning? You don't find that odd?"

"Yeah. Do you think old Sumner Boyd would do something stupid on his own?"

"No. The family's got more money than God though. He'd hire it out if he had to. Wouldn't get his own hands dirty, now would he?"

"So what's the significance of those gold cowboys left behind? Any ideas?"

Max shook his head. "Not sure. But I know we find out where our number one suspect was when Jessica Boyd died."

Baffled at his partner's attitude tcward Kit Griffin, Dan turned to stare before deliberately causing his face to go blank. "You think Kit Griffin did this?"

Stubbornly, Max thought of Jake Boston and set his jaw. "Yeah, I do." And he so wanted it to be true.

CHAPTER 7

Kit's eyes opened slowly, squinted against the bright sunlight pouring in from the skylight above the bed, temporarily blinding her. Intense pain in the top of her head made it feel twice as heavy, twice as big. The bed gently rocked. This wasn't home. When she tried to sit up, the throbbing in her head increased. She tried to think, but it hurt to form a thought. Her fiber-dry mouth yearned for water. Her stomach flip-flopped.

All she could think about now was the wine she'd had last night at dinner. She wasn't much of a drinker, but last night, like the idiot she was, Jake had kept pouring and she'd kept picking up the glass.

Now when she rose to a sitting position her head spun and matched the roiling in her stomach. It was then she noticed she wore only her bra and panties. She looked around the master stateroom. Her sand-stained black dress from the night before was nowhere in sight. Still a little dizzy, she eased her legs over to the side of the bed. A glance at her watch told her it was a few minutes past eight.

She wondered if Baylee had opened up the shop. Right now, with her head doing a drum solo, she didn't much care. When she tried to move, tried to look around for her cell phone, her head and stomach had other ideas. Okay, so she hadn't been up at the crack of dawn to bake goodies this morning. So what? First time in four years, she thought, as she sunk back down a little. So, she'd be late. And she wouldn't have baked goods to offer. Big deal.

And oh, how her head hurt.

A soft knock on the door gave her reason to finish the weak crawl the rest of the way out of bed. She stood up on shaky knees. Grabbing the top sheet from the bed, she loosely held it around her body before answering in a weak voice, "Come in." The sudden reach for the sheet left her lightheaded. Her head hurt so badly she thought she might go cross-eyed.

Jake slid open the stateroom door and asked, "How you feeling?"

"I've had better mornings."

He walked further inside the room, dressed ready for work in tailored pants and a white shirt, tie-less. Why did he always look like he'd just come from an executive version of a hot body contest while she resembled a drunk on a three-day binge?

He reached his hand out to hers and turned her palm up, dropped three aspirins into it and waved a cold bottle of water in front of her. As if reading her mind, he said, "The aspirin is for the pounding in your head and the water's for your dry throat. I'd take several sips of water before trying to swallow the aspirin."

Grateful for the thought, she reached to take the water and lost her hold on the sheet. It dropped to the floor in a puddle at her feet. Her head was pounding so hard she let the sheet fall without contest as she stood in the man's bedroom in her black underwear.

Having seen the underwear in greater detail last night and for a good deal longer, in a playful mood, Jake's eyebrows went up as he told her, "I like this view way better than with the dress on."

Self-conscious, she tried to disregard the moment and in a hushed voice simply said, "Thanks for the water and aspirin." Per his instructions, she opened the bottle of water and took several gulps before downing the aspirin.

He laid two towels on the bed and some clothes. "Why don't you take a shower? You'll feel better. You can wear one of my shirts and a pair of my shorts."

With no intentions of arguing the point, she merely nodded, and muttered, "Good idea."

Twenty minutes later, she walked out of the stateroom carrying her dress, which she'd found hanging in the head, but was now wadded up in a ball under her arm. She sat carefully down in the salon with her wet hair braided down her back, dressed in Jake's clothes: a dark blue Cal Berkeley T-shirt, and a navy pair of baggy athletic shorts that Kit had pinned to fit.

At that moment, Jake grinned at her and she recognized it for what it was. That delicious smile of his had been at the root of her drinking one glass of wine after another trying to prove to him she was no longer a kid. As if he knew what she was thinking, he avoided the obvious, quietly asking, "Feel better? How's your head?"

She didn't answer, but instead looked down at her bare feet, and mumbled, "I can't find my shoes."

"They're around here somewhere. They can't go far on a boat. They'll turn up before we leave."

Barely audible, she asked, "Why are you so cheery?"

"Am I? I've been up longer. Would you like some breakfast?"

If she ate right now, she'd up-chuck for sure. "Coffee. Black."

He poured her a steaming cup and set it on the table in front of her, then slid in across from her.

The aroma of the brew gave her hope. She didn't trust one hand to hold the cup steady, so she used both to pick up the mug and hold it to her lips. She blew into the liquid until it cooled enough to drink, then took a long, slow sip. Never one to remain quiet for long, she asked in a low tone, "How long have you been up?"

"Long enough to pop a couple of aspirins. I had a hangover, too. Finishing off that third bottle of wine might have been a mistake."

Kit nodded slightly, beginning to enjoy the jolt of caffeine kicking in. "I like your boat."

"You didn't get dizzy or seasick last night, did you?"

"Oh no." She'd slept like the dead. "Not at all. Well, I got dizzy this morning when I got up, but it certainly wasn't from the boat, more like from an intense alcohol stupor. Poor Pepper's been home alone all night. He probably thinks he's been abandoned."

He rested his chin in his hand and enjoyed the view from across the table. Even dressed in baggy men's clothing she was all woman. A simple shower had her smelling like spring flowers. Listening to her voice, watching her mouth move as she talked, he knew what he'd like to do with that mouth. And the recent memory of getting her out of her dress would stay with him for some time.

Kit felt his intense stare and glanced up. Her eyes found his, locked. She steadied her gaze. Even with the throbbing in her head still evident, she picked up on the heat between them, a sexual energy she wasn't sure she'd ever felt until now. Below the pit of her stomach, a spark of lust ignited, settled in. Wetness pooled between her legs. And she was pretty sure it wasn't leftover from her shower.

If her head hadn't been pounding, she might have acted on the urge. She tried to tell herself it was the hot coffee making her feel so warm, not the sparks of lust from his gaze.

Why was he staring at her like that? Never dropping her eyes from his, she said in a soft voice, "I didn't mean to put you out of your bed last night."

"How do you know that isn't where I slept? I just got up first."

Her face flushed crimson. "Oh really? Then maybe next time I'll be awake and you won't have to take advantage of the situation."

"Next time…you'll be awake. Probably all night. And if I had wanted to take advantage of the situation, I pretty much could have. You were out for the night. Do you always snore so loudly? You should probably get that snoring checked. I'm hoping I don't have a complaint from the neighbors."

She chewed on the inside of her mouth. "I see. You're rather self-assured there will be a next time. Just so you know I don't make a habit of falling asleep in strange beds without my clothes on. Don't you think I deserve to know how I got out of my dress?" With green fire lapping in her eyes, she added, "And I don't snore."

"Getting you out of the dress was the easy part. Your dress was wet. You can't sleep in wet clothes. But the moral dilemma hit me when I got down to the black bra and thong. Leaving those on, now that was much more difficult. It took all the restraint I could muster, a great deal of willpower to take the high road when you were so out of it. I deserve a reward for being such a saint."

This playful side to him was new. And the tide had turned. There was heat here, enough to light a match. "Did you develop a sense of humor in Japan, Jake?"

He ignored her comment. Instead his thoughts drifted to the sort of activities they could spend the day doing if they both cancelled work. The idea hit him that maybe he could persuade her not to be in such a hurry to leave. "Let's blow off work, take the boat out. I'll take you to Catalina for the day."

"The workaholic playing hooky? Okay, what have you done with the real Jake?"

"When you own the company you can take the day off."

"Since when? This from the man who's known on three continents as Mr. Software, the one who's the first to get to work in the morning and the last to leave. I'll say it again, what have you done with the real Jake Boston?"

"Maybe I'm changing."

"What's the old saying, something about a leopard can't change his spots? I won't believe you can change until I see proof."

"You want proof, fine. Let Baylee handle the shop. Let's spend the day sailing. We go out now, come back late this afternoon. How's that?"

Kit had to admit, the invitation was tempting. Loving the outdoors like she did, she couldn't help but wonder what it would be like to sail. But then she thought of Baylee and then little Sarah. Her face fell. Baylee would have to deal with customers both in the bookstore and the coffee house, knew she'd be jumping all day and with Sarah she'd have her hands full.

"I can't," she finally admitted. "I only have Baylee part-time and she'll have Sarah with her today. It's too much to ask with the baby. Maybe we could do it another time, unless of course you're planning to take off again."

"How long do you plan on throwing that up to me?" Then he quickly changed tactics. "And what's this about Baylee and Sarah? When I left last year there was no baby."

"Baylee's not talking. See what can happen when you disappear for a year." She stood up, downed the last of her coffee, and headed into the galley to wash her cup out in the sink. "As soon as I find my shoes, I'll be ready to go. The aspirin's starting to kick in, my head feels better."

Jake followed her, watching as she rinsed out her cup. When she turned around, he moved to stand directly in front of her, blocking her way before placing a palm on either side of the counter, boxing her in. "I'm not running now, Kit. The question is what are you going to do about it?"

His nearness made her pulse quicken, her breath become erratic, but she didn't move, just looked into the depth of his lake-colored eyes. This is what she'd wanted...for...years. She didn't answer him. Instead she stood there staring up at him in wonderment. No longer one-sided, this mutual attraction took some getting used to.

He took her demeanor for something else, though, and drew back. "There's no reason to be afraid of me, Kit."

That brought her back to earth. "Afraid? Of you? No way. Nervous maybe. But I'm not scared. I've been waiting for you too long."

That was all he needed to hear. His hands went around her waist, bringing her into him. He intended the kiss to be tender, gentle. But then their lips met. Sizzle met burn. Opened-mouths devoured each other. This was exactly what she'd wanted for so long that now that it was happening she ached with such longing she didn't care about work or anything else. She could stay here in the moment wrapped in his arms for an hour, a day, a week.

Kit ran her fingers through his hair, took a good hold on his head. Their tongues played tag until a burst of need had his hands rubbing at her lower back, and then dropping further to her rear, molding her, fitting her body between his legs.

Kit felt the hardness and moved to wrap him into her. She couldn't get close enough. She wanted to eat at him, be devoured by him. The heat between them was enough to melt arctic ice. When they at last came up for air, Jake rested his head on her forehead just to get his balance back. Kit tried to recover by cracking a joke. "I waited a long time for that. And I just want to say, it was worth the wait. Can we do that again?"

"That's the plan."

As he bent his head to show her, his cell phone went off. He swore. Within minutes, he was embroiled in the middle of a conversation that sounded to Kit like a crisis situation with Dylan Burke, his VP of Research and Development.

At that moment, she heard a muffled ringing coming from her handbag. As she rounded the counter to reach her purse, she felt her swollen lips and reluctantly snapped open the bag. The ringing grew louder and brought back the heavy pounding in her head. When she retrieved the annoying phone, the number appearing in the digital readout belonged to Aunt Glo. Stepping back into the stateroom, she answered a bit breathlessly, "Hi Glo."

"Where are you, sweetie? I've been trying to call you all morning. It's all over the news."

"What is?" Kit tried to sound as if she hadn't spent the night in Jake's bed.

"Jessica Boyd's dead. It's on the news. She's dead, Kit, just like Alana."

ᐃ ᐃ ᐃ ᐃ ᐃ

Kit spotted his car, a sporty little black BMW convertible, parked haphazardly on the street in front of her house with the driver's side door open and music blaring from the car stereo.

But it wasn't until Jake pulled his Mercedes into her driveway that she actually caught sight of Collin Boyd sitting on the bottom step with a bottle of whiskey in his hand.

Jake pointed to Collin and said, "What the hell is he doing here?"

As soon as he cut the engine, Kit grabbed his arm and pleaded, "Don't leave me alone with Collin." Kit saw his questioning eyes and quickly added, "Please. He's an asshole in the best of times, but drinking makes him impossible to handle."

Jake looked past the fear in her eyes and sensed there was something more. He didn't want to believe what he was thinking. But he'd been gone a year. Anything could have happened during that time. He had only to think about Baylee and how a year had changed her life.

Not one to act without having the facts at hand, he wanted to know what he was walking into. "Am I stepping into the middle of something personal between the two of you?"

Kit gave him an incredulous look. "Personal? You mean like couple stuff?"

"Yeah, like couple stuff."

She stared at him in disbelief. "No. You should know me better than that. I've known him my whole life. We kind of grew up together, but we've never gone out. Think for a minute. He's just found out his mother's dead and it looks like he's already three sheets to the wind."

At that moment her cell phone rang and she looked to see who was calling. When the digital readout displayed the number of the bookstore, she pushed the button to answer. "This is Kit."

Baylee, breathless and scared on the other end, informed her, "That asshole Collin was here looking for you. He's drunk, Kit. The bastard's drunk. After what happened last time, I thought I should warn you. I'm pretty sure he's headed to your house. Don't let him in, Kit. Do you want me to call the police or come over?"

"Thanks for the warning and the offer, Baylee, but Collin's already here, sitting on the stoop. I have no intentions of letting him inside though. Jake and I will try to get rid of him, but if we can't, we'll call the police."

"You're still with Jake? Is that why you didn't open up?"

"I'll explain when I see you. And Baylee, thanks for getting the store open. Obviously, I'm going to be a little later than I thought."

Kit hung up the phone and turned her attention to Jake, who still had questions. "Okay, so he finds out his mother's dead and this is the first place he thinks to come. Why here? Why come to your house, Kit?"

Kit bit her lip, puffed air in her cheeks and blew it out. Frustration from childhood rose up like a brick wall, but this wasn't the time to hold back. "A long time ago, Alana and Jessica got it into their heads for some reason that they wanted the two of us to get together."

When the light didn't come on in Jake's eyes, she rolled hers and made it clear, "Marry, Jake, they wanted us to marry. Kit and Collin, Collin and Kit, that's all I ever heard from both of them ever since I was little. When Alana wanted me to do something, what did I tell you last night? I did the opposite of what she wanted me to do, that's what. I wanted no part of Collin Boyd or his family. But Collin kind of liked the idea, always has. Sometimes he's tough to dissuade."

"So there's never been anything between the two of you?"

Kit smiled. Was that a hint of jealousy sputtering in the depths of his blue eyes? "Collin's tried—several times."

The smile left her face and she turned somber. "As kids we did share a history together, a history based on mutual neglect. I told you I spent a lot of time hanging out at the Boyd compound when I was a kid. It was practically my second home before I turned twelve. But we were just kids then, Jake."

Satisfied, Jake moved to get out of the car.

In no hurry for a confrontation she'd had several times in the past, Kit took her time approaching Collin. She stopped long enough at the convertible to turn the key in the ignition, shutting off the engine and putting an end to the loud music.

Together Jake and Kit moved closer to the steps and to Collin, a man about as tall as Kit with brooding eyes that went with his black hair.

Dressed in a Hawaiian shirt, navy shorts, and flip flops, Collin looked as though he'd just stepped off a tropical island with enough booze in him to drown a sailor.

"Well, well, well." Disheveled, with day-old stubble on his face, Collin held up his bottle of Scotch as if toasting the air and took a big gulp, not bothering to replace the cap on the bottle.

"I find out at five o'clock this morning my dear sweet mother departed this earth and I come over here for a little comfort…just a little comfort, mind you, between two old friends. A friend that's recently lost her mother. What's it been, Kit-Kat, two days? And what do I find instead? I get to see Kit-Kat coming in from an all-night party with Mr. Software himself. And she's not even wearing her own clothes. I didn't know the two of you were an item."

He stared straight at Kit, accusingly. "I thought you were over this son of a bitch. Tells you how much I know. Been grieving Kit-Kat, over the loss of Mama? And you've found comfort in a most unlikely place." Anger welled up inside the man as he took another gulp from the bottle.

"Collin, you're drunk. And you're disturbing the peace, disturbing my neighbors. I'll call you a cab; you aren't fit to drive. You could hurt someone in your condition."

"Goddamn it, I don't need a cab. I can drive. I just drove here, didn't I?"

Kit started to press the call button on her cell phone anyway to make the call, but the gesture set Collin off.

He pointed at her and screamed, "Don't you dare call me a fucking cab, you understand?" Collin leaned over in the direction of the two of them and lowered his voice, "But I am drunk, that much is true. Goddamn right I'm drunk. I find out my mother's dead; I start drinking. What's wrong with that? At least I took my mother's death with some emotion. And we know my mother didn't have a suicidal bone in her body. How about you, Kit-Kat? What emotion did you show? The police think you did it, you know. You're a person of interest. That's what the papers said this morning. They think you killed the wicked witch. Isn't that what we used to call her, Kit-Kat? The wicked witch is dead."

He started laughing so hard at his own joke he almost stumbled down the steps. "Now they're both dead." He weaved over to one side before telling Kit, "I want to come in. I won't disturb the neighbors, if you let me come inside. Ask me to come inside your house, Kit-Kat."

But Kit shook her head. "No, Collin. I have to get to work. And there's still a restraining order against you."

With the bottle, he pointed to Jake accusingly. "Does he get to come in? He gets to come in and I don't, is that it?"

Jake spoke up, "We'll all stay outside until you leave."

"Like hell we will. I'm stayin' right here until Kit-Kat asks me to come in. You let this son of a bitch inside your house, inside your panties, but not me? Is that it? You spend the night with him but not me. I was never good enough for you, but this guy is? For chrissakes, Kit-Kat, he killed his goddamned wife."

Calmly, Kit said, "You're embarrassing yourself."

"Embarrassing myself? I'm not the one wearing someone else's clothes for chrissakes. I'm wearing my own clothes. You aren't." Proud that he'd pointed that out, aggression swam in the liquid pools of his eyes as he concluded, "I can pretty much guess what happened to your fucking clothes."

Collin swayed before heading further up the steep set of steps toward Kit's front door. He was having a hard time keeping his balance when he turned, as if used to having his orders obeyed, pointed a finger at Jake, and demanded, "I want you to leave." To Kit, he said, "And you, I want you to invite me inside the fucking house."

Matter-of-factly, Jake said, "We don't always get what we want." Rubbing his chin, he turned to Kit, half-joking, barely above a whisper and pointed out, "This might be a good time to mention that I haven't been in a fight since junior high."

"Don't shatter my illusion that you're my hero. You're bigger than he is; you're sober, and frankly if you can't take him in the state he's in, then I'm going to be sorely disappointed. But whatever, I'm not letting him inside my house even if I have to kick his ass myself."

Turning serious, she added, "Two years ago I made the mistake of letting him in because he said he just wanted to talk and he practically...well...he got very...physical. I got away from him, called the police, and got a restraining order."

In a loud agitated voice, Collin ordered, "Stop that whispering. I want to come inside the goddamn house. Is that too much to ask? Is this any way to treat an old friend you've known since birth?"

Jake looked at Collin, tried reason. "You're upset about your mother. No one's taking that away from you. But you can't show up here drunk and take your frustration out on Kit. She's already told you she wants you to leave."

The expression in his eyes turned violent. "Go fuck yourself, Boston. Or is my little Kit-Kat doing that?"

Jake took a step closer. "You don't talk about her like that."

"Don't mess with me…" Collin started down the steps toward Jake.

It all happened lightning fast.

The moment Collin reached the bottom step, he grabbed for Kit's arm. Jake reacted on instinct, spinning Collin around to face him. When Collin threw a punch to Jake's head, Jake dodged, pivoted, and threw a solid left jab that connected with Collin's nose.

Blood oozed down Collin's face as he staggered back. Regaining his balance, he realized his nose was broken. Stumbling, he made his way to his car in defeat. But before crawling behind the wheel, Collin turned back to both of them and yelled, "You'll regret this, you son-of-a-bitch. You both will. Nobody messes with a Boyd."

When he'd driven away, Kit grinned at Jake. "Wow, my hero. How's your hand?" With a twinkle of mischief sparkling in her eyes, she cracked, "Do you think he'll sue?"

Jake shook his left hand, flexed his fingers back and forth. "Probably."

Reaching out, she took the hand and inspected it. "You didn't break anything did you?"

"No, but maybe next time you'll take me up on the offer and go sailing. We could have been halfway to Catalina by now."

CHAPTER 8

"**H**ow long has Collin had this thing for Kit?"

Gloria's head snapped up. She was a ten-year younger version of Alana with short wispy platinum blond hair, stunning green eyes and a tall, svelte figure. She sat more erect on the sofa in Jake's office as she sipped a cup of herbal tea. "What do you mean? Collin knows better than to come around Kit after what happened last time."

"Really? I don't think he got the message." Jake paced back and forth in front of the bank of windows in his office, remembering the look of longing in Collin's eyes. It made him edgy, and a tad jealous.

"He showed up this morning drunk, maybe high, and left with a broken nose." He turned to stare at the woman on the sofa he'd thought of like a second mother. "I need more information, Gloria. Why am I getting this feeling you're holding back? If I'm going to help Kit, you need to be straight with me. I didn't feel comfortable asking her a bunch of probing questions up front what with the police giving her a hard time. So I didn't push it. But, now I'm asking you. Why did Kit consider The Enclave a second home when she was a kid?"

"She said that?"

A question for a question. Interesting. "It was because of the abuse, wasn't it?"

"You remember don't you, how Morty and I lived in Maine before we moved to L.A.?"

He took a deep breath for patience. What that had to do with anything at this point he wasn't sure, but as calmly as he could, he replied, "Yeah, Gloria, I remember."

"We didn't get to L.A. very often to see Kit back then because I lived three thousand miles away. Don't you see, I wasn't here when she needed me the most? It's true, as a child Kit spent a lot of time with the Boyds' whenever Alana and Jessica disappeared for weeks at a time to fly off to some exotic location. Those two women were forever traipsing off some place, taking a vacation to some resort or spa. Whenever they traveled, they'd leave Jessica's three sons and Kit in the care of Jessica's nanny, Maya. By the time Kit turned three, she'd stayed with Maya so often that Kit took to calling the nanny Mommy Maya. That used to just break my heart to hear her say that over the phone and she'd…she'd sound so sad." Her eyes filled with tears and with some trepidation she quietly added, "Not that Alana would have let me see her. She thought I was a bad influence, you see, kept telling me and anyone that would listen that I was crazy. She didn't want me around Kit."

Jake handed her a box of Kleenex, waited for her to pull herself together enough to continue.

Dabbing at her eyes, in a broken voice, she went on, "Kit's visits to the Boyds' were frequent, especially in the summertime, when she'd get dropped off for a stay that ranged anywhere from overnight to several weeks. When Kit got to be about six, I started pestering Alana to let her come and spend her summers with me. Alana used every excuse in the book not to let that child come visit me, though, even telling me at one point that Kit was just too much of a handful, and that the bed and breakfast I managed at the time might suffer because the guests wouldn't want to put up with all the noise a child makes. But I knew that Kit wouldn't have been a bother. I wanted so much to see her. But Alana wouldn't allow it. I think maybe she thought I might just keep her, not send her back. But whatever the reason, Alana wouldn't let Kit visit.

"After a while, I got the idea that maybe we'd move, relocate, I'd get a job out here, Morty could sell his law practice. I used to dream about picking up and moving to L.A. so I'd be closer to Kit. I started to...to bug Morty about it. But his practice was thriving back then and the idea of moving three thousand miles away just didn't work for him. Then at twelve, after...after Kit...turned twelve...Morty finally; he finally relented, he saw how serious I was about spending more time with Kit. By that time I'd bought the B & B I had managed.

"After Kit...after Kit turned twelve, we sold it, sold the law practice too, and relocated here to L.A." Gloria sniffed into the Kleenex Jake had given her. "We met you a couple of months later. You were right out of college then and Morty encouraged you to start your own company, develop your software. After that...Alana not only let Kit spend the summers with us, but I'd take care of Kit while Alana was off to Europe or wherever.

"Once Morty and I made the move to L.A., Kit was no longer forced to stay with the Boyds. Then later of course Kit started working at the law firm, in the file room, just for something to do, to have a little spending money." Gloria stopped talking and stared off into space. "It's true when Kit was small she spent too much time at the Boyds', it wasn't her home. Most of the time, she had to feel like an outsider there. But there was one saving grace—at least she wasn't with Alana."

That inference was clear enough. But Jake wanted to hear Gloria say it, so he pushed harder. "Exactly what issues did Kit have with her mother, Gloria?"

"Why would you ask that?"

Jake's instincts told him Gloria was volleying back and forth with him for some reason. It was rare for her not to be straight with him about anything.

What was she so nervous about? "It's obvious, isn't it? Her relationship with Alana is at the very core of why St.

John suspects her. He sees a daughter who doesn't get along with her mother, doesn't show enough emotion to suit him, and she's got a built-in motive. Why, Gloria? Tell me straight."

Gloria sat there with a pained look on her face, silent as the dead. She searched every fiber in the carpet as if looking for the secret to life. But she never looked at him.

Patience gone, he blew out a breath. "The cops are going to use the abuse as motive, Gloria."

"Oh…God, no."

"Gloria, Kit's in serious trouble. The police are pursuing her as their main suspect and unless we can convince them otherwise, she's in danger of being arrested. When the media finds out about the abuse, they'll come after her as well. I need you to be up front with me, tell me anything you can to help Kit out of this mess."

"But she didn't kill Alana."

"I know that and you know that, but Max St. John doesn't give a damn about what we know, only what we can prove."

Later, when Gloria finally left Jake's office and headed for her car, she was angry. And she rarely got this upset. Where Kit was concerned, however, she had a short fuse. As soon as she got to her car, she pulled her cell phone from her purse and dialed a number in Malibu.

When he answered his private line, his voice sounded gruff. "Sumner here."

"It's good to know you haven't changed your private number after all these years."

"Who is this?"

"Gloria Gandis."

"It's nice of you to call and express your condolences. How have you been, Gloria?"

"This isn't social, Sumner. I didn't call to express anything except outrage. Your son is at it again. He's been to see Kit."

"I don't believe that. Collin knows better. I warned him to stay away from Kit after the last time. No, Collin promised me he wouldn't do that."

"Sumner, I didn't call to argue the point. Believe it. Ask him how he broke his nose. I'm tired of this. It can't happen again. Do you understand? It seems every two years or so, Collin gets it in his head that Kit's going to change her mind. She won't. I don't doubt you tried, but he's got to be dense as a stump to do this again. I won't put up with it, either. You care about Collin and I care about Kit, it's as simple as that. If he ever crosses the line, I'll see to it they lock him up and throw away the key. That much I can assure you. You aren't the only one who knows people. Do you understand me? You get that son of yours to somehow understand that or put him under lock and key yourself. He's dangerous where Kit is concerned and you know it. I don't want to have this conversation again."

"I'll take care of it." As soon as he hung up, he dialed his youngest son's cell phone number. When Collin picked up the phone, he heard his father say simply, "I want you here in ten minutes."

Collin made it in eight. When he'd answered his phone, saw it was his father's number, he knew what to expect.

As he walked into his father's study, Collin braced himself for what he was sure would come. In a matter of seconds, he directed all of his fury at the woman responsible. As he stood there waiting for his reprimand, all he could think about was making Kit pay for the lecture he knew was coming.

As soon as Sumner looked up and saw the bandage across his son's nose, he swore. The veins in his neck popped to a bulge, his blood pressure rose, and his anger doubled. "Goddamn it, what the fuck were you thinking?

The last time you pulled this stunt you spent the night in a holding cell. Evidently, you have a short memory."

"All I wanted to do was talk. I swear that's all I wanted to do. I was upset about Mother. Every time I go near Kit, she overreacts. Typical female reaction if you ask me."

"No one's asking you, Collin. When do you intend to stop this obsession with the woman? She's made it clear she doesn't want you; why can't you leave it at that? I understand Kit is a beautiful, vibrant woman, but she isn't the only skirt in town. You could have any woman you wanted, so why not leave her alone if she doesn't show an interest?"

"We grew up together. It wasn't always like this. I can't help it if I...I guess I'm in love with her."

Sumner already knew that and hearing it didn't sit well. "Get the fuck over it. This feeling you have happens to be one-sided and one-sided never works. How many times do we have to have this conversation for you to understand that? You're too old for this and you aren't stupid, although apparently you aren't as smart as I had hoped you were. If you don't stop this, one day...one day...you'll cross a line and I won't be able to help you, no one will. You can't keep doing this. For God's sake, leave the woman alone. Do you understand me? You go near her again I'll break more than your nose myself. You got that?"

ॐ ॐ ॐ ॐ ॐ

Kit and Baylee had been so swamped they'd barely had time to do more than grunt at each other. So as soon as the line died down, Kit pushed Baylee from behind the counter, telling her, "Go sit down. Take a break. Sarah will be awake soon."

While Baylee settled in at one of the tables, Kit poured both of them a fresh cup of amaretto coffee and listened to Baylee talk about her morning. "When I opened up, I had a line out the door and people grumbling about having to wait. I hadn't even made the coffee yet. I sold out every pastry you had left over from yesterday by eight-thirty and then the customers got really bitchy."

"I'm sorry you had to open up." In spite of her harried morning, Kit's business acumen kicked in. "You sold the day-old pastry?"

"Every crumb. Apparently these people will eat anything." Baylee eyed the stack of papers on the counter that Kit had brought in with her. "What is all that?"

"Connor Boyd sent over papers he wants me to sign about Alana's estate. Can you believe that?" Kit missed the cautious glaze that settled in Baylee's eyes at the mention of the oldest Boyd son. "He wants to make sure Alana Stevens Realty continues to run smoothly through the transition. He spent ten minutes telling me that Alana's employees would continue to eat if I'd sign this, sign that. He wanted me to know I should be grateful I now own a business." She rolled her eyes before picking up her mug to enjoy the coffee she'd poured.

Despite the fact that Sarah was a mere five feet away napping in her Pack 'N Play, Baylee's voice rose as she threw her arms out wide. "What the hell does he think this is—a hobby? Damn those Boyds. They never gave you credit for anything"

She grabbed Kit's arm. "Don't sign anything. I don't trust them. Promise me you'll get someone to look at this stuff, maybe get your own lawyer. Just don't sign anything on Connor's say-so alone, check it out first. Besides, since when would Alana leave you her business?"

"That's what I wanted to know." Connor had sent over enough paperwork via special courier to choke a horse. Then followed up with the phone call to make sure she understood he was on a tight deadline and needed to get her signature on the papers for probate as soon as possible.

"I'm still reeling from the news of Alana's death and he wants me to sign papers. It's hard to believe she'd leave me anything."

When she'd been able to think, she'd considered Alana's apparent about face. That didn't sound like the same woman who'd always told her she'd never get a dime.

Alana had told her time and time again she simply wasn't bright enough to run a bookstore slash coffee shop, let alone Alana's precious real estate business. Knowing all that, Kit kept wondering why Alana would change her mind about something that meant so much to her.

And now, Connor expected her to step in and fill Alana's shoes, be prepared to take the reins of a real estate company she had no interest in running.

When Kit realized Baylee was saying something, she zoned back into the present, focusing on Baylee's hair. She still couldn't get used to Baylee with brown hair, and wondered why she'd colored it from the natural blond she'd had all her life to the dark chestnut color that now fell down to her shoulders. In fact, there was quite a bit about Baylee lately she didn't get. "I'm sorry. I'm a little spacey. What were you saying?"

"I'm worried about you, about what happened yesterday with the police." When the baby stirred, Baylee walked to the port-a-crib to put Sarah's pacifier back in her mouth.

Keeping her voice soft, Kit told her, "I'm worried about me, too. But in the meantime life goes on."

Kit watched as Baylee patted Sarah's little body, soothing her back to sleep. Kit couldn't help wondering when her friend had become so moody, so secretive, and worse, such a cynic. Kit feared Baylee was a few Sweet Tarts shy of turning totally bitter.

It wasn't the Baylee she'd known forever, when they'd confided their darkest secrets to each other. No, that Baylee had disappeared a year ago with a half-baked story about spending time in Europe looking for the mother she'd never known, which had been a lie, Kit thought now.

Baylee hadn't gotten pregnant in Europe. She'd been pregnant when she'd left L.A. and hadn't confided in anyone about it. No, Baylee had gone off to God knows where alone to go through childbirth without her friends. Kit still didn't know the whole story because Baylee refused to discuss it.

Even though Kit hadn't for one minute bought the story about her quest to find her mother, she hadn't been prepared when Baylee had arrived on her doorstep last Christmas Eve with an eight-day old baby tucked into an infant carrier. After getting over the initial shock that Baylee had a baby—and that had been the easy part—the hurt had settled in knowing that Baylee hadn't felt the need to confide in her friends about the pregnancy, that she'd gone through it alone, gone through childbirth alone.

Even after Baylee had been back for several months, Kit still couldn't get her to talk about the last year and what had happened to make her leave L.A. If it hadn't been for the fact that Baylee's father, William Scott, the renowned director, had fallen ill with a brain tumor, Kit doubted Baylee would have re-surfaced with Sarah until the child was ready for college. A theory that had her feeling uneasy for both mother and child. They were running or hiding from something or someone, Kit was sure of it. She just didn't know who or what. Yet.

After getting the baby back to sleep, Baylee sat back down. "How'd you get rid of Collin?"

"Jake broke his nose."

"What a guy! And you spent the night with him?"

"I passed out on his boat."

"This just keeps getting better and better. You don't usually drink enough to pass out. You were trying to impress him, weren't you?"

Kit chuckled; Baylee knew her too well. She explained the circumstances about last night right up to waking up on Jake's boat, minus the sexual vibes. She kept those to herself. Then she told Baylee about Collin. "But you already knew he was drunk when he stopped here."

"The bastard should be in jail."

"No argument there, but guys like that with enough money to buy a small third world country rarely spend time in jail. He didn't last time."

Baylee could relate only too well. Her sudden urge to protect was instinctive as her hand reached out to Kit's. "I thought about you last night, worried sick about this whole mess." She didn't say what was really on her mind. Baylee didn't think it was a good idea for Kit to get involved with anyone right now when what she should be concentrating on was getting out of the mess she was in.

The timing with Jake had sucked for years and now was no exception. Baylee wanted Kit to put herself first for once, instead of Jake Boston. She only wanted what was best for Kit. "You've got Quinn and me in your corner. Gloria's there too. You don't need Jake Boston to come along now and mess with your self-confidence all over again."

Kit blew out a breath. There was that bitter tone she heard Baylee use now toward men, one that she'd never had until recently. "But I'm not fifteen anymore, struggling with low self-esteem." Her brain zoned out and into thoughts of pure lust as she replayed that kiss on the boat. Absently picking up her coffee and tipping the hot liquid to her mouth, the stuff only made her hotter.

"About yesterday, about what I said. What do you want me to tell them when they ask about...about Alana? You know, about...your childhood."

Kit shook her head and held up a hand as if to stop her from going any further. "I don't want to talk about it. Just tell the truth; don't even think about lying. You've got Sarah to think about, so when they get around to asking, just tell them how it was, just like you did yesterday." After baring her soul to Jake last night, she wanted to get on with the business at hand. She gave Baylee a pleading look before quietly adding, "I just can't talk about it, okay? Please try to understand."

"I do, too well. I tried to put myself in your situation last night. If Dad...when he isn't here anymore, what issues will I be dealing with about my own childhood after he's gone? If you need to talk, I'm here, but if that isn't enough maybe you should go back to see Dr. Strasburg, talk to him about...how you feel...now that she's dead."

"I don't think I'm so far gone I need to do that."

"You're in serious trouble. If the police...you have to be prepared for..." For what, she thought, for an arrest? She wouldn't think like that, couldn't.

The bell above the door jingled and Quinn Tyler stepped inside the shop, dressed in jeans and an old faded Bruins T-shirt. Kit watched the exotic-looking woman and brand new hospital resident toss back her long black mane of hair before heading straight to the Pack 'N Play. Bending down to peer at the now wide awake baby, Quinn announced, "Hey, guys. Check this out. Sarah's got a tooth."

Baylee scooted over to look. "Is that the future pediatrician talking or wishful thinking on the part of her Auntie?"

To prove the teething diagnosis was true, Quinn picked up Sarah and poked a finger in her mouth, rubbing at a little white sprout. "Don't tell me you haven't noticed her teething, Mama?"

"As a matter of fact, she was a little fussy at four this morning and didn't want to go back down until six."

Kit turned to stare at Baylee in wonder. "And I thought I had a rough night. How do you do it?"

Baylee simply shrugged and said, "Since I'm staying at Dad's, Tanya's always willing to lend a hand in the middle of the night." Tanya was pushing seventy, but she was the closest thing to a mother Baylee had ever known. Over the past few months Tanya had proved once again she could handle an infant.

"By the way, when was anyone going to tell me about Alana? Yesterday I was on the downside of a thirty-hour shift when I look up at the TV; saw Jessica preening for the press. And this morning I turn on the tube only to find out Jessica committed suicide in the middle of an intersection. Geez, they're dropping like flies." Quinn stood alternately bouncing and nuzzling Sarah, then stopped long enough to look accusingly at Kit. "I called you four times last night, worried."

Before Kit could respond, Baylee chimed in, "The police were here yesterday, questioning Kit. They think she—" Baylee bit her lip, looked at Kit then Quinn. "They think she did it."

"Did what?" When Quinn finally figured it out, her jaw dropped. "You're joking. They couldn't."

Kit took another sip of her coffee. "Unfortunately, they're serious, I have no alibi. As of yesterday, according to Connor Boyd, I inherited the bulk of Alana's estate. I'm sure the police will use that and anything else they can…as motive."

At that moment, a customer walked in, and Baylee went to wait on the man.

"I don't know what to say, Kit. You told them you couldn't go back into that house, didn't you? How could they think that? And since when would Alana leave you her estate? When did that happen?"

"I have no idea, but I'm supposed to," Kit waved a hand toward the files on the counter, "go over this paperwork, sign where indicated, and get them back to Connor ASAP."

Just as Baylee had done, Quinn snuck out one of her hands from around the baby and took hold of Kit's arm. "Don't sign anything. I don't trust those vultures. Take all this stuff to a lawyer. Get a second opinion. Don't take their word for anything." When Sarah began to fuss and root around like she needed to nurse, Quinn relinquished the baby to Baylee, who'd finished up with the customer and sat back down at the table.

Quinn pulled up another chair, plopped down. "Did either of you catch that joke of a press conference yesterday afternoon? The Unholy Three standing by Jessica's side the entire time? Icing on the cake since it was Jessica's farewell performance."

Hearing Quinn mention The Unholy Three, the nickname they'd given the Boyd sons when they were kids, sent chills down Baylee's spine. She looked away and began nursing Sarah.

But Kit shook her head and sneered, "Quinn, I was a little busy getting the third degree from Homicide."

"Oh, right," Quinn said, sheepishly. "Sorry. But this was must-see TV. You should have seen the way Jessica held court with her three little lap dogs around her. They made such an ass out of themselves vying for mommy's attention. It was pathetic. That's nothing new of course, but it was sickening to watch Connor, Cade, and Collin twisting in the wind whenever Jessica opened her mouth to speak. And Cade was the worst."

"There was a time you didn't think so."

"Hey, the minute Cade hit me; I called the police, didn't I? They hauled his sorry ass to jail. Thank God for the restraining order."

"Like that did Kit any good," Baylee pointed out.

But Quinn gave her a quick, questioning look, "You should have seen the way Jessica went on and on about what a saint Alana was. She ticked off all her charity work, which I don't remember at all. The woman I knew didn't have a benevolent thought in her head about anyone, and she sure as hell wouldn't give a dime to a charity.

"Then Jessica couldn't keep her trap shut long enough for Connor to get a word in edgewise. He tried, he really did, but every time he opened his mouth to say something, Jessica interrupted him. That was the highlight of the whole thing really, watching those three grown men try to support mommy when mommy hogged the spotlight." The idea had her snorting with laughter. "And now she's gone and killed herself."

Quinn's outburst triggered a reminder of something Collin had said earlier that morning. Quietly Kit said, "I don't think she killed herself, Quinn."

"But that's what they said on the news. They said her car was locked from the inside. The police said…"

"Doesn't matter what they're saying. Can you honestly sit here and tell me the woman you knew was prone to suicide?"

She had a point, Quinn realized. "Well, if she didn't kill herself, then that means…oh my God, Kit…"

"First Alana, now Jessica."

"I guess they finally pissed off the wrong person."

Baylee had her own dark thoughts. She'd purposefully kept quiet, but now listening to Quinn talk about the Boyds had her desperate to run from the room. But while nursing Sarah that was a little hard to do at the moment. To keep from hearing anymore about the Boyds, Baylee changed the subject and blurted out, "You'll never guess who Kit spent the night with last night."

An eyebrow arched over one eye as Quinn noticed Kit send Baylee a disgusted look. "Okay, I've clearly fallen into The Twilight Zone. Alana's been murdered. They think Kit did it. Jessica's dead. And Kit's having sex. I must be dreaming. This is a parallel universe, right? Obviously the two of you have kept the best for last."

She stood up with renewed energy, looked around. "I need coffee." She held up a staying hand when Kit started to speak. "No wait, I can't handle all this yet. I need caffeine. And chocolate. Point me in the direction of anything chocolate."

"We sold out of chocolate yesterday. And since Kit didn't bake this morning we can only offer you a day-old muffin I saved for later. Sorry."

Kit looked sheepishly at Baylee, grinned. "Well, I did put back a pan of double fudge brownies yesterday. For emergencies," she added quickly.

"Now we're talking," Quinn said, rubbing her hands together.

"Where'd you hide them?"

"Mini-fridge behind the half and half, the orange storage container."

Amused, Kit got up and walked behind the counter, began to arrange brownies from the fridge onto a tray. She took her time just to string out Quinn's chocolate craving.

When they'd settled back around the table without saying a word, Quinn noticed the stupid grins on their faces. Hoping to get the conversation going, she hurriedly poured everyone refills of coffee. Staring at Kit, waiting for the dam to burst, got her nowhere.

Quinn noticed Baylee looked like she'd swallowed a canary whole and was about to explode with feathers. Not in the mood for a long drawn-out guessing game and never a patient person, Quinn was about to detonate with curiosity when she finally boomed, "Okay, spill, who's the lucky guy?"

When Baylee's grin turned into a snicker and Kit simply sat there gloating with information, an exasperated sound came out of Quinn's throat. Baylee finally threw out a hint, "Think back to the past; who has Kit been in love with since she was old enough to lust?"

When Baylee saw no recognition, obviously enjoying the moment, she couldn't resist another hint. "Think older man," she offered and wiggled her eyebrows up and down.

Quinn's eyes grew wide. "You mean...Jake Boston's back in town?" She exchanged a knuckle bump with Kit.

With her free hand, Baylee touched her nose. "Ding, ding, ding. We have a winner." With all the movement from her mother, Sarah stopped nursing long enough to look up at all three women and grin as if she were in on the joke, too.

"So you finally did the deed with Jake. How was Mr. Hottie?"

Without bothering to clear up the misconception, Kit watched Baylee enjoying herself as she threw in, "And Jake broke Collin's nose this morning when he showed up drunk."

Quinn's eyes glazed over with confusion. Still trying to wrap her mind around Kit being a murder suspect, Quinn struggled to digest everything she'd heard, rubbing at her forehead as if it hurt.

Kit took pity and explained everything including what happened with Collin. When a couple came in looking for tips on how to play poker, Kit left them long enough to help the customers. After ringing up the sale, Kit settled back down and dug into the batch of double fudge brownies with her friends.

As the chocolate and caffeine kicked in, Quinn began to think more clearly. "You say Collin comes by your house all liquored up, making an ass out of himself, and then Connor phones you confirming Alana's so-called generosity. Don't you think it's odd that Connor's on the clock, working, the very morning he finds out his mother's killed herself in the middle of an intersection?" Eyeing Kit's face, she added quickly, "Okay, maybe mommy doesn't kill herself, but she's dead and the guy's on the clock a couple of hours after he hears the news, dealing with Alana's will. That's weird."

"I hadn't thought of that," Kit said, thinking back to the conversation with Connor. "Collin wasn't hard at work mere hours after mommy's death. In fact, he looked as if he'd never gone to bed."

"Get a lawyer, or better still, ask Mr. Software for some advice. It'd be a good way to test him and see if he really is, you know, interested in something more than a quick roll in the hay."

Kit had already decided to do just that, but she couldn't let go of the subject of Alana's will. "Don't you think it's odd she left me anything?"

"Yeah, I do. But hey, maybe she suddenly grew a conscience." Quinn stuck her finger in a meaty brownie, pulling out a chunk of chocolate, and then stuck the whole thing in her mouth, letting out a laugh. "Okay. Not. Just testing to see if everyone's paying attention. But all kidding aside, maybe the woman said all those things to you just to be mean, get a reaction, and then leave you the whole enchilada."

"I don't buy it. She did everything she could to convince me I wasn't smart enough to answer the phones at her real estate office. Remember how she reacted when she found out Gloria and Morty gave me the gofer-slash-file clerk job at the law firm? The woman was mad as hell for weeks."

They all three nodded, remembering those bad years. Then out of the blue, Quinn changed the subject back to Jake. "You went out with this guy last night, right? Please tell me you got all gorgeous, wore that little black dress that leaves nothing to the imagination, and made the jerk sit up and take notice."

"I was so gorgeous he was rendered speechless."

"That's my girl, make him suffer. Make him suffer, then have mind-blowing sex, right? Good plan. I like that plan. It's time you had great sex."

Kit gave her an embarrassed stare. "Sex isn't on the agenda. It was just dinner...and wine...lots of wine. He doesn't even like me. Very much. Remember, he's never liked me." And then her brain recalled that mind-blowing kiss.

Baylee snickered. "Yeah, right. If he doesn't like you then why'd he take you to dinner? And break Collin's nose?" Like they'd done in their teens, Baylee mimicked Kit's words, and then all three women burst out laughing.

"Wait a minute, seems to me I remember the night you saw his wedding announcement in the paper, you went home, choked down a pint of Chunky Monkey, and cried your eyes out for a week. Is this guy really ready for a relationship or is he still hung up on his wife?"

"Geez Quinn, give me a break."

"Okay. But if this guy hurts you, he'll have to answer to me."

"And me," Baylee said, before adding in a low voice, "If he's the kind of man that won't take no for an answer, he's a user, a rotten bastard you don't want to be around anyway."

Kit and Quinn shot each other a knowing look. Was this the opening they'd waited for? Was their friend on the verge of sharing more? But when their look lasted a little too long, their answer came when they noticed Baylee take a step backward, figuratively, in retreat. It wasn't so much her body language as it was the mortification that crossed Baylee's face that had Kit deciding this wasn't the time to open up a festering wound and pry.

Instead of reaching over and shaking Baylee unconscious until she spilled her guts, Kit turned to Quinn and chided, "Let me get this straight, a minute ago you were all ready for me to jump the man's bones and now you're trying to protect me?"

"You're vulnerable. You're going through a rough time. I don't want to see you hurt."

"Just having sex," added Baylee, trying to keep the mood light. Already willing to put her momentary lapse of control behind her, she simply wanted to enjoy being around the two people she considered her sisters. She told herself she needed this time with them. She wondered if she too might have to take off again for parts unknown in the middle of the night. Putting that worry aside for now, Baylee considered when the three of them might be together like this again. It wasn't Quinn's brutal schedule at the hospital that might keep them apart, but whether or not Kit stayed out of jail.

Turning more serious, Baylee pointed out, "You've only dated a couple of times since you moved here, right? If you haven't had sex in a while, don't just jump in bed with Jake because you think you know him. It's been a year. People change. Guys change."

"Good advice. Just because you knew him way back when doesn't mean you know him now. Has it really been four years since you've done the deed? If so, I think that makes you almost virginal, a saint or something," Quinn pointed out.

"Hardly. But thanks for the vote of confidence."

When Quinn stood up to leave, she held up a curved pinky in the air on each hand, a gesture they'd practiced since they were eight, a symbol of their unity. Kit held out both of hers, linked one with Quinn's and waited for Baylee to put Sarah back in her crib to perform the ritual. Now forming a small circle, in unison, in sing-song fashion, the three repeated the words, "Together we let no one hurt us. We are most powerful when we are one. We draw strength from each other. One."

With that, they fist-bumped each other.

Kit sighed. "I don't know what I'd do without you guys."

"We don't intend to let you find out," Baylee reminded her with a hug.

Quinn grew serious. "I'd get someone to look at those files Connor sent you, the sooner the better."

"I could call Jake, see if he has time to sort through the stuff, but I don't want to leave Baylee by herself. She was swamped this morning."

"Don't worry about me. I'll be fine. You go ahead. It's important to get this taken care of quickly. I'd rather you go see a lawyer though," Baylee reasoned.

"Look guys, I've got to get going. I pull another long shift at the hospital tonight, so I may be a little scarce for a while. Doesn't mean I'm out of the loop or that either one of you can't reach me if you need me."

Sending a quick what-if-Kit-gets arrested look in Baylee's direction that confirmed they were both on the same page, she winked and added, "But if things heat up with Mr. Hottie, text me. I'm never too busy for those kinds of deets."

CHAPTER 9

Before leaving for Jake's office, Kit was wiping down the counter when the towel she was using knocked off something shiny near the cash register. The object went flying through the air and landed on the hardwood floor with a thud. Kit reached down to pick it up. The object was a little larger than a toy soldier, except that it wasn't a soldier. She felt the heavy weight as she held it in the palm of her hand. The piece was pure gold, minted in the shape of a cowboy sitting astride his horse in front of a rounded sunset in the background.

The artist in her appreciated the intricately woven design of the sunset interspersed with the painstaking detail of the cowboy. A lot of work had gone into minting this piece, she thought.

She didn't know why, but all of a sudden, her mind wandered to her father. In an instant, her imagination kicked into overdrive and the cowboy depicted on the gold trinket resembled him. She shook her head.

What was wrong with her? She blew out a quick breath and ran her hand through her hair. It was a toy, nothing more. Baylee had probably found the thing somewhere in the store. A child had dropped his toy as he'd shopped with his mother. She tried to remember if she'd seen kids in the store earlier in the day, and then remembered she'd been late getting there.

It didn't matter, she decided and shook off the weird feeling. Why finding such a thing would have her feeling so edgy she didn't know, other than the fact that since Saturday she'd had the strangest sense about everything.

And look how that had turned out.

When she heard the door jingle she looked up—and smiled. Absently she stuck the toy cowboy in the pocket of her jean skirt and walked over to Gloria, who entered the store with her little Chihuahua, Morty, so named because Gloria was convinced the dog was her late husband's reincarnated soul.

"You must indeed be psychic, Glo. I was just thinking about you earlier and you show up out of the blue. What are you doing here anyway?"

"I was worried. I wanted to see for myself you were okay. Jake told me about your encounter with Collin."

Kit leaned over, hugged her aunt, and kissed her cheek. Then in a stern voice, she went into lecture-mode. "Worried, huh? Enough to call Jake Boston to the rescue? Did you send him out here on Saturday, too?"

Gloria sat down at one of the tables with a bewildered look on her face that made it seem like she wasn't sure which fork to use to eat her salad. "I don't know what you're talking about. I called him after the police left my house yesterday. I panicked. Sue me. Aren't you even going to offer me a cup of tea?"

Kit walked behind the counter, grabbed a teabag, poured hot water into a cup, and brought it over to her aunt. She sat down across from Gloria eyeing her face for any indication she was evading the issue.

"Oh for goodness sake, I merely asked an old friend to look in on you, where's the harm in that? It's ridiculous that the police think you could have had anything to do with Alana's death. Since the man went through a similar situation when his wife was murdered, I thought he'd know what to do, how better to handle the situation. Lord, the police hounded that man for the better part of a year. Was it wrong of me to think that perhaps he could provide some insight we might overlook?" Gloria took a sip of her tea before setting Morty down on the hardwood floor to sniff at Pepper, who'd wandered in from the bookstore to look over the Chihuahua. Despite their difference in size, Pepper and Morty were longtime buddies and soon Morty had snuggled up at Pepper's side for a nap.

"So you didn't call him to come out here Saturday?"

"He was here Saturday? Whatever for?" She knew, but she had no intentions of tipping Jake's hand.

She gave Gloria the short version about Jake renovating the Crandall House. Her reaction seemed genuine to Kit.

"Why would he buy that huge old house?"

"That's what I wanted to know. Investment maybe? His boat's here, too."

"Really. He didn't say a word to me. But he's been acting a little weird since he took off for Japan."

"Weird how?"

"It's like he finally buckled under the pressure of that whole year. He couldn't stand the humiliation. He's a proud man, Kit. Being a murder suspect just broke his spirit."

He'd said he'd needed to get away. She hadn't realized how bad things were for him during that time right after Claire died. The man had always seemed so capable, so invincible. She thought back to last year and decided she should have done more, should have gotten in touch with him sooner than she had. Instead she'd kept her distance, thinking he needed some space, time to grieve for his dead wife.

"What are you thinking?"

"That I should have been there for him sooner when he needed a friend."

"It wasn't your fault."

Kit reached out and patted her aunt's hand. "Look Glo, I hate to bring this up, but I don't see any way around it. We have a funeral to plan. I know Alana bought a plot out at Whispering Oaks, but it looks like the details fall to you and me." Then as delicately as she could, she told her about Alana's will.

"You think I'm upset because she didn't leave anything to me. Well, I'm not. Put that right out of your mind. I don't need Alana's money, nor would I want it. But frankly, I'm surprised she didn't leave everything to Jessica."

"Me too. Would you like the house? I have no use for it. I can't even go back inside."

"Listen sweetie, put the house on the market, get the best price possible, and keep the money. Think of it as payment for the kind of childhood you had. Use one of those estate liquidators for the furnishings. They'll take care of everything. You might want to think about keeping the baby grand, though." Looking into Kit's eyes, she added wistfully, "Your father would like that, don't you think?"

Kit nodded; even though she didn't have room for the piano in her tiny house, the sentiment was there. Her father had given it to her for her eighth birthday. She smiled. "He paid for the piano lessons all those years. I'm pretty sure it was only to rankle Alana. Speaking of my father..."

Gloria shifted into an emotional void, bracing for the question. Talking about John Griffin always put her into rage mode.

"Glo, do you think he remarried, had other kids?"

Gloria hadn't been prepared for that. "Why would you ask such a thing?"

"Jake pointed out he might have remarried, and had other kids I don't know anything about."

Gloria took her time thinking. "No. No, I don't know about that. It's possible, isn't it that he remarried? He spent a lot of time overseas. Why wouldn't he? He could have had other children I suppose. Why are you dwelling on this, Kit? I know that the man should have taken you away from Alana when you were five...actually long before that. But he didn't; he left you with her time and again. Don't dwell on this. Move on. This is weighing on you and you need to put this behind you—you need to put him behind you, the sooner the better. Deal with Alana's death and move on with your life. It isn't fair, I know, but...you've got to come to terms with the past...with him for leaving you there especially after..."

"But I can't stop thinking about him, Glo. It's as if I'm going through all of it again in my head, all my childhood memories are coming back to me. Not just what happened at twelve, but...everything."

"I don't doubt that. But it won't do any good to dwell on it. You're thinking about all of this too much. Kit, the man was never around all that much. He stayed gone for months and months at a time, didn't he? Think about that before you spend any more time on these walks down memory lane."

Surprised at Gloria's coldness on the subject of her father, Kit groaned, "I don't understand how you can be so callous about this. This is important to me. John Griffin was more like a father to me than Alana Stevens ever was a mother. At times he was all I had. He at least acted like a father when he was with me, whereas Alana didn't even pretend to have maternal instincts. There were so many times over the years that he was there for me."

And times he wasn't, thought Gloria. She took a deep breath, gentled her voice. "You say he acted more like a father, but yet he left you time and time again with Alana. If he truly cared for you, truly loved you, how is it he didn't get you out of that situation? Perhaps the man was a better actor than we gave him credit for. You can't know what went on between them. Animosity runs deep in contentious divorces. Stop torturing yourself. He never truly appreciated you, Kit, and from what I remember about the man, you were his greatest achievement."

☙ ☙ ☙ ☙ ☙

Later, those words came back to Kit as she headed to Westlake Village. On the drive she tried to convince herself to put Alana and her father behind her for good.

But it had always been a struggle. Now with Alana gone, it might be possible, although inheriting her business would be a problem. Surely, a smart guy like Jake could help her find a way to turn Alana's business over to someone else. Not only did she know nothing about real estate, she'd spent years avoiding any type of corporate setting, including the one Jake had created for himself.

Maybe it was time she did something about that.

Sitting in traffic on the 101, she remembered the driven man he'd been at twenty-four, and knew even then she hadn't fit in to that business side of him.

She'd been around at startup, of course, but then so had Morty and Gloria. She might have been no more than a teenager, but she'd watched from the wings with proud fascination at Jake's transformation from gifted programmer to software developer to CEO.

She recalled all the times he'd talked and she'd listened. She hadn't understood half of what he'd said. She'd been young, that was true, and as Alana had often reminded her, she hadn't been particularly bright. But she'd listened to him, or tried to, as he'd outlined his dreams of taking his software company global.

She'd been smitten; it was embarrassing to think about it now, but she'd watched as he lived and breathed software applications, marketing campaigns, and spreadsheets. If it were a little hero worship in the fact that he'd taken a program he'd developed from scratch and turned it into a multi-million dollar company, she could admit that now.

She'd watched from the sidelines, always from the sidelines, as his world grew more successful each year and finally expanded to include Claire, the woman he'd married. Claire had fit into his world perfectly. She'd been sophisticated and classy, an asset to any up-and-coming businessman's agenda, the complete opposite of Kit both then and now.

Thinking about the conversation with Gloria earlier, Kit was reminded that no matter how much he'd been on top of the world before Claire's murder, Jake didn't walk on water.

In one night everything had come crashing down around him. She supposed she could have been a better friend during that time. But God how she'd hated the idea of approaching him when he'd been grieving for Claire.

As she exited onto Westlake Boulevard, she wondered if he was finally over Claire, the love of his life. She hoped so for both of them. Because that kiss this morning had been one lip-lock worth following up on. The man knew what to do with that mouth.

She pulled into the parking garage of a bank building, parked her Jeep on an upper floor, and took an elevator down to ground level. She walked through the bank lobby and took another elevator to the tenth floor.

When she stepped out into an elegant, tastefully decorated reception area, it was obvious to her that she'd entered an upscale corporate world the complete opposite of the Book & Bean. She suddenly lost her nerve and regretted coming. She hadn't dressed for a stuffy corporate setting, hadn't even considered there might be a dress code involved or how everyone else might be attired until this moment. Wearing a short jean skirt with a white top and sandals, she felt self-conscious and considerably underdressed.

That's when she remembered Jake wore suits to work.

It was at that moment she realized how good she had it working in her little world, in her little book shop in little backwater San Madrid where she never had to dress to please anyone but herself.

It wasn't too late to jump back on the elevator. Just as that thought slid into her head, an anorexic-looking petite redhead no older than twenty, who was stationed behind that elegant reception counter, popped her head from behind her computer and asked, "Can I help you?"

A little intimidated in this world, Kit had to think why she'd crossed the bridge to the other side in the first place.

She fumbled the words out. "Jake Boston; I'm here to see Jake."

The girl eyed her up and down as if passing judgment on a homeless person and wanted to know, "Do you have an appointment?"

Kit shook her head. "If he's busy...I can come back another time."

"Are you selling something?"

"Uh, why no, I'm not." Kit took the question as a tad on the rude side. What if she owned a law firm and wanted to purchase billing software? How did the anorexic young woman know she wasn't a customer? Of course, she realized she didn't look like she owned a law firm that needed software, but then in her world she wasn't in the habit of treating customers in such a rude fashion. Her customers usually came in right off the street. But then she realized she had wandered in right off the street. Worst of all, she was dressed like she had.

The thin redhead picked up the phone, telling her, "I'll let Ginger know you're here. She'd be the one to know if Mr. Boston has time on his busy schedule to see you."

Great. Yeah, you do that, thought Kit. Is this a power trip or what? Now she was just suddenly pissed that she'd fooled herself into thinking the timing might be right after all these years. They had nothing in common. She thought back to his arrogant demeanor years earlier.

This was the world he'd wanted to conquer, found so important, so driven to achieve success in, and he'd done just that. That fact hadn't changed. They really didn't have a single thing in common. Now she was seeing it for herself, the fact hitting her full force between both eyes. No longer uncomfortable about being here, she was glad she'd made the trip. *Face the truth, Griffin, the two of you have about as much in common as two opposing political foes.*

Just then, a woman in her mid-forties dressed in a light pink Donna Karan suit, with jet black hair streaked with gray and warm brown eyes, approached the reception area.

"Hi, I'm Ginger Starks, Jake's secretary. Can I help you with something?"

At Ginger's sudden appearance, Kit took two steps toward the elevator. "Well no, not really. I was here to see Jake. And no, he isn't expecting me. I was in the neighborhood and decided to drop in; however, I see now that was a bad idea." It wasn't just the lie; she was babbling, and worse, she knew it.

Ginger eyed the attractive blonde with interest, clutching an assortment of file folders to her chest. "Jake's on a conference call, but if you'll take a seat, I'll wave a note under his nose to let him know you're here. May I have your name please?"

"Kit, Kit Griffin." She inched closer to the elevator. "But I've changed my mind. I don't want to interrupt him."

After eight years working as Jake's secretary, Ginger knew every aspect and detail of the man's calendar and schedule by heart. It was her job to know. She was certain this woman wasn't on his schedule. But Jake rarely had visitors who were so pretty and so young. For some reason she thought that he'd be upset if she let this woman leave without letting him know that she'd been here.

Ginger flashed an easy smile. "I'll be right back. Would you like something to drink while you wait?"

"No thanks. I'm fine. Look I don't want to bother him. If he's busy, I'll just see…I'll see him some other time…I'll see him…later."

Ginger was still smiling at Kit and oozing warmth. "I'll just let him know you're out here. Please sit down. I'll just be a minute."

When Ginger reached her desk, she wrote Kit's name and the fact that she was in the lobby on a Post-it® note with a purple marker. She peeled off the yellow paper from the pad's dispenser and, without knocking, opened Jake's office door.

He was listening to a man's voice over the speakerphone, showing a mild interest in the conversation, when she waved her finger with the note to get his attention.

He looked slightly annoyed for about two seconds until he saw what it said. Without waiting to interrupt the caller, without saying a word to Ginger, he shot up from his chair and left the person on the other end of the phone talking to air.

Ginger smiled. Some days it just paid to have a hunch. Amused, she took a seat in one of the comfortable leather chairs in front of Jake's desk with her steno pad. In Jake's absence, she dutifully scribbled down whatever the caller rambled on about, all the while wondering about the blonde.

Jake was in the lobby in under two minutes flat. And when he saw Kit, it was as if he hadn't seen her in days rather than hours. When he'd dropped her off at her house after they'd dealt with Collin, she'd been wearing his clothes.

Looking at her long legs in the short slice of denim skirt, a rush of adrenaline caused his heart to skip a beat. She was holding some file folders clutched to her chest.

Keeping his voice level, he said, "What a surprise. I'm glad you stopped by." Glad didn't cover the way he felt. He wanted to throw her down on the lobby sofa and start nibbling down her body inch by inch.

But then he noticed how uncomfortable she acted, how tense she was. Had something happened?

At the sound of his voice, a funny thing happened. When Kit turned to face him, the image of the kiss they'd shared that morning popped into her brain, and she had to remind herself to breathe. The pissed-off feeling about their differences vanished, and she stood there trying to get her mouth to work. After several seconds of just staring, her brain finally kicked into drive and worked in sync with her mouth. She tried to sound casual and cool when a few words squeaked out. "Just thought I'd see how the CEO lived." Mortified, she realized she sounded fourteen again. But he seemed genuinely pleased to see her.

"Come on back to my office. I'll give you the grand tour after I get off the phone."

"But you aren't on the phone."

He shot her a wide grin. "Technically, I am. I'll show you my office first."

As he took her hand and led her down a hallway, it occurred to Kit that if they had sailed to Catalina they might have explored more than a day at sea: but each other's bodies as well.

And she would really love to find out what was under his starched shirts and pressed pants. Just picturing him sans clothes caused a spike in her lust factor. Maybe it was the hope of kissing him again or the prospect of something more. Whatever the reason, desire flooded her. The emotion was so strong she was annoyed with herself, annoyed at how seeing him sent her into cardiac overdrive.

Back in his office, Jake patted the empty leather chair beside Ginger and motioned for Kit to sit down. Ginger automatically handed her notes off to Jake. But before getting up to leave, she flashed Kit another warm smile. Less self-conscious, more comfortable now, Kit smiled back.

Reading Ginger's notes, Jake slid back into his chair and picked up the conversation as if he'd never left the room. After asking a few relevant questions of the caller about the man's current billing system, he then ran through a checklist of the software's features before ending the call.

"Sounds like you wear many hats. You get the usual commission on that sales call?"

"Only when it closes. I'm glad you came. Did I tell you that?"

Self-consciously, she put the file folders down on the floor next to her. "I'm ashamed to say I brought you my father's social security number and some files Connor Boyd sent me that I was concerned about. But after seeing you in action, I don't expect you to waste your time looking at them now. In fact, I can't possibly ask you to make time for my problems."

"Hey, if Connor Boyd sent you papers, I'd like to take a look."

"Okay, if you're sure. But promise me you won't spend more than ten minutes on the stuff."

This woman had an innate sweetness about her and she didn't get it from Alana. Alana could have played the wicked witch of the north every day of her life in the role of a lifetime. Kit was looking at him intently, waiting for an answer. Finally, he said, "Sure." His mouth curved into a sly smile. "Would you like the grand tour?"

"I'm not exactly dressed to meet your co-workers. Maybe…"

Before she could put up much more of a protest, he was in his element, telling her, "What are you talking about? You look great. Come on."

The tour took her through accounting, marketing, and testing, ending up in the engineering department, where Jake left her in the capable hands of Dylan Burke while he took an important call from Japan. Despite knowing Jake for as long as she had, she'd never actually met his friends.

With his dark blond hair pulled back into a stubby ponytail, Dylan looked more like a cross between surfer and rock star rather than a programmer in charge of research and development. His blue eyes were warm and friendly, and since he was dressed quite a bit less conservatively than Jake in worn jeans and a golf shirt, he put Kit more at ease.

After Kit showed interest in the surfing pictures hanging on the walls of his office, Dylan kicked back in his chair, put his feet on the desk, and Kit listened as he talked about curls and waves and the best spot he'd ever surfed, which was hands down Angourie Beach on the north coast of New South Wales.

As soon as Dylan found out she enjoyed surfing, he grinned and said, "Then I should probably tell you about Jake's first time up on a board. It wasn't pretty. We were twelve. The three of us—Jake, Reese and I—went to spend a month of summer vacation at his grandmother's house in Santa Cruz. We were novices just starting out. Even though the guy could out-lap either of us in a swimming pool, Jake kept falling off his board; never got the hang of it that day. So we kept going back every day for a week until he finally stayed up longer than twenty seconds."

When he laughed at the memory, Kit heard genuine affection in his voice as he talked about his friends. This was special, she realized, like what she had with Baylee and Quinn. "How long have you known Jake?"

"Came from the same neighborhood in the Bay, been buddies ever since grade school, where we were alphabetized, Boston, Brennan, and Burke in Mrs. Kurth's first grade class. Mrs. Kurth was really big on organizing and order. I'm pretty sure trying to handle the three of us in the same class for nine months probably drove that woman to drink. I can't much blame her, we were a handful back then."

"And you've all matured so well now, right?"

They were laughing when Jake came through the door.

On the way back to his office, Jake made a side trip into one of the empty conference rooms. As soon as he shut and locked the door, Kit saw the flicker in his eyes and knew why they'd made the stop.

Leaning his body against the door, he positioned her between his legs, pressing her body to his. He lowered his mouth to hers. A flash fire ignited. Kit kissed him back with such force, their teeth knocked together. She felt him harden like stone.

When a knock on the door interrupted them, Jake swore under his breath, closed his eyes and hit the back of his head lightly on the door. Curious, she asked, "Is it always like this?"

Without opening his eyes, he nodded. "Most times it's worse."

"Years ago, that software you created turned out to be a living, breathing monster, didn't it? It's like one of Alana's horror movies, the monster just keeps growing, getting bigger and more demanding."

He laughed and some of the tension drained away. As another knock sounded from outside the door, Kit pulled the weight of her body off his. Surveying his condition below the belt, realizing his disadvantage at the moment, she touched his face with her fingertips, kissed his cheek and offered, "I'll answer the door. I don't think they're going away anytime soon."

"I might need a minute." He moved away from the door while Kit switched places with him. Taking a deep breath before gradually turning the lock, she opened the door so that no more than a crack was revealed and saw Ginger.

"I'm looking for Jake."

"He went to get me a soda from the break room, said I should wait for him in here. He's been gone a few minutes, might have made a pit stop at the men's room on his way to get me the drink."

"When he gets back could you tell him Chuck is on the phone from New York? There's a problem with the Eastman contract and it needs to be taken care of tonight because it has to be in the client's hands by nine o'clock in the morning—that's nine o'clock New York time, but six o'clock here. Hence, the problem with the contract will need to be resolved tonight."

"Got it." Kit closed the door, looked playfully at Jake and winked. "Looks like you'll be conducting Crisis Management 101 for the next few hours now that all hell's broken loose because some guy named Chuck waited until the eleventh hour to do what he should have done several days ago. The contract isn't ready and now it seems he's hit the panic button because it's due at the client's in the early morning AM."

Jake grinned at her assessment of the situation. "You're pretty good at this."

"I'm pretty good at a lot of things."

"Will I ever get to find out?"

"Maybe."

"Do you want to wait here or come back to my office with me?"

She looked at her watch. "I should get going. Traffic will be brutal."

"Stay. I'll take you to dinner when I'm done with Crisis Management." He reached out, took her hand in his, brought it to his lips, kissed the palm. "Stay."

She looked into the depths of his blue eyes and realized she didn't want to go. What was it about him that she was so attracted to anyway? Since the first time she'd looked up and found him standing in the doorway of the file room in Morty's law firm staring at her so many years ago, she knew she loved him. She sighed and gathered up whatever strength she could muster and said softly, "I can't, Jake. I've been gone from the shop most of the day. I promised Baylee I'd get back in time for her to take Sarah home."

"What about—later?"

"Sure. Will you be finished up here by say, six-thirty or seven?"

"I guarantee it."

"Then come for dinner."

A lightheaded feeling hit him at the prospect of spending another evening with her. "I'll walk you out."

She shook off his offer. "Not necessary. Besides, you have a crisis to manage."

"But if I walk you out, I get to spend more time with you." It sounded like the most juvenile comment he'd made in twenty years.

As she opened the door to the conference room, her lips curved, "But wouldn't your time be better spent wrapping up that crisis so you'll be on time for...dinner?"

He drew in a deep, shaky breath. He wanted this woman. He'd known her when she was a kid, knew what she'd looked like at fourteen. Wasn't there something wrong about that? But God, she was like fresh air he needed to breathe. His raging hormones made him feel like a randy fifteen-year-old struggling with his libido.

When they got to the elevators and the door opened, tired of waiting, he took Kit by the arm and pulled her into the elevator with him. As soon as the doors closed, he drew her into his chest and gave her a mouthwatering kiss every bit as good as the one he'd given her in the privacy of the conference room.

She was pretty sure the only reason she remained upright was that he had hold of her. Her bones were like pools of mush that matched her brain. When the elevator dinged at ground level, he released her, and they both walked out into the lobby trying to act as if nothing had happened.

Kit put her fingers to her lips, found them swollen from that kiss—no she corrected, from two of his kisses that had been like heat-seeking missiles. Kit looked up at him once again, needing some reassurance they were on an equal playing field. "I do have one question."

"What's that?"

"That kiss just now and the one, the other one in the conference room, and the one on the boat this morning, am I to understand that after all this time you no longer think of me like a little sister?"

To keep from touching her again, he shoved his hands in his pockets and leaned in where only she could hear. "News flash Kit, not now nor have I ever thought of you as a little sister. If I had, it would have made things so much easier."

Before she could respond, he'd hit the elevator button, the doors had opened and he'd disappeared inside, leaving her standing there with her mouth open.

☙☙☙☙☙

Jake had just gotten back to his office to deal with Chuck and the Eastman contract when Dylan appeared in his office doorway. "Where in the world did you meet a woman like that when you've been in Japan for a year, won't leave the damned office long enough to go to happy hour, and the closest thing to a social function you ever attend, if you can call it that, is a software convention?"

In the midst of everything else he was feeling since he'd left Kit standing in the first floor lobby, the last thing Jake wanted to discuss was the woman in question. And the last man he wanted asking him anything was Dylan. So Jake ignored him.

But that just made Dylan more determined. Dylan scratched at his cheek. He knew how to get a rise out of the man. "She's a little young for you, don't you think?"

Jake was up out of his chair like a shot and in Dylan's face. "Goddamn it, Dylan, get out. I don't want to talk about Kit."

"Oh I can see that, but she is…" He meant to say something special, but at the last minute, still wanting to needle Jake, he said, "Not your usual type."

"And what type would that be? You mean like Claire, a materialistic viper of a woman who slept with anything in pants except maybe her own husband? And because I really didn't give a shit, I never got around to filing for a divorce. Just lucked out when the stupid bitch got herself murdered and the police tried to pin it on me. Is that my usual type, Dylan? If that's who you're talking about, it's time I changed my goddamned type. Now, shut the fuck up and get out of my office."

Dylan watched as Jake stuck his hands in his pockets and stared out the window onto the street and the traffic below. Realizing he'd opened up old wounds that needed stitches, he tried to make it right. "Jake, I could back up, start over again, but I'd just find a way to piss you off, especially if I wasted my breath and reminded you that Reese and I begged you not to marry Claire. The woman came on to me the first time I met her, for chrissakes. And what did you do when I told you about it? You laughed, said it was her outgoing nature. Bullshit. And never once during the entire time you knew her did she act as if she gave a crap about anything except your bank account. She was an opportunistic bitch, nothing more. You just don't like being reminded. And Claire's misfortune stemmed from the fact that she finally pissed off the wrong person and somebody took it personally.

"This Kit, she seems nice enough. Hell, there was a time Claire was too. But maybe this Kit might be another money-hungry woman with a great-looking body interested in nothing but your money. You need to…"

"No, you need to stop right there before you say anything else and make me rearrange your face. Kit doesn't need my money. Kit's Gloria's niece, for chrissakes. You remember Gloria and Morty Gandis. She's…" He stopped, what was she anyway? "She's in some trouble right now, similar to what I went through with Claire. St. John thinks she killed her mother. Gloria asked me to help. I'm helping as a family friend, nothing more."

Like hell, thought Dylan. He'd seen the way his friend had looked at the woman, had watched the way he acted around her. His reaction to criticism told Dylan all he needed to know. And it had nothing to do with being a friend of the family. Jake looked like he had it bad.

Because of that he'd just have to keep an eye on Kit Griffin, Gloria's niece or not. He refused to sit back and watch while another woman sunk her greedy nails into his best friend…again.

Kit was still trying to recover from his bone-shattering kiss when she stepped off the elevator into the parking garage. As she walked to her car, she considered their age difference somewhat minor when she realized what those years represented. That kiss came from a man far more experienced than she was in everything sexual. She had very little history in relationships: three to be precise. She had never even experienced the big O like Baylee and Quinn had.

The first time she'd just turned twenty and finally lost her virginity to Brad Traynor, a hunky but rather serious-minded geomorphology major that had packed up after eight short weeks and headed off to study the landforms of South American jungles.

The other two relationships had come right on the heels of Brad and were even shorter. From there, she'd moved to San Madrid, where most of the male population fell into three distinct categories. They were either kids, happily married, or well over fifty.

She even considered herself to be a rather naïve chump where sex was concerned. She liked it okay, but didn't understand what the fuss was all about. The guys she'd been with hadn't exactly been stellar in bed. But then she was no prize there either.

What was it about Jake anyway that always tied her up in knots?

She reminded herself that she wasn't a kid now but rather a grown woman. And the grown woman wanted him now more than she'd ever wanted him at fifteen. Maybe she could find a book on sex at the store that would fill in some of the gaps. Because a man like Jake, who kissed her blind like that, had to be better than first-time Brad.

Lost in lusty thoughts, and trying to search her brain for the inventory of books back at the store that dealt with sex, she looked around the darkened parking garage.

An eerie feeling crawled up her spine, making the hairs stand up on the back of her neck. Even though it was still daylight outside, that creepy feeling had her increasing her pace toward the car.

But the faster she walked, the more it felt like someone was following her. Fighting the urge to panic, she quickened her pace as her Jeep came into view. She was tempted to look behind her, but thought better of it.

Was someone here? She realized how silly that was. It was a place where hundreds of people parked their cars.

Even though she felt ridiculous, she readied the keyless remote a good fifty feet before actually getting to the car and then pushed the button on her key chain to release the door lock. Sliding quickly into the driver's seat, in one swift motion she locked the door, fumbled a bit in the dimly lit interior to insert her key into the ignition. She hurriedly started the engine, grabbed her seatbelt, and buckled it around her.

Taking a quick look around, she put the car into Reverse, and gunned the car out of its parking space. As she braked to put the vehicle into Drive, a shadow passed to the left and behind her. Something struck the backside of the car with a heavy thud. Looking into the rear view mirror, she made out the shadowy form of a man. Frantic, Kit floored the accelerator and the car lurched forward, narrowly missing a row of parked cars.

Glancing back in the mirror, Kit saw the man run between the cars and disappear into a darkened corner of the parking structure.

By the time she drove to street level, still shaking from the experience, she wondered what the hell had just happened.

CHAPTER 10

As soon as Kit walked back into the Book & Bean, she took one look at Baylee's brooding glare and knew something was up. So she wasn't surprised when Baylee announced, "We need to talk."

True, she'd been gone longer than expected, but she didn't think that was the reason Baylee looked so anxious. Slipping her purse under the counter, she tried to gauge that look on Baylee's face. When was the woman going to get over these mood swings?

Over the past several months, Kit and Quinn had discussed Baylee at length, repeatedly trying to get her to open up about the past year, even suggesting at one point she seek advice from a professional. Maybe, get her to go back in and see Dr. Strasburg.

As Kit braced herself for whatever Baylee had on her mind, she stuck her hand in her skirt pocket and felt the gold cowboy she'd found earlier. She pulled out the trinket. "I can see you're upset about something, but before we get into that, can you tell me where you found this?" She held out the miniature cowboy nestled in the palm of her hand.

Baylee picked up the cowboy and inspected it briefly before telling her, "I've never seen it before."

Kit frowned. "I found it this morning on the counter by the register. I thought maybe a child lost it in the store and you picked it up."

"Wasn't me." Wringing her hands, Baylee blurted out, "Look, I need to leave."

"Sure. Okay. I know I should have been back an hour ago but…"

Baylee was nervous. "No. No. Not that. I need to leave L.A." She'd thought about it while Kit was gone and decided it was the safest thing she could do.

Panic stuck like a wad of cotton in Kit's throat. "No. You. Don't."

Looking into Kit's eyes, Baylee decided on the spot to put a spin on the truth. "I do. I can't stay with Dad any longer. He's getting verbally abusive, Kit. He's started drinking again." That part was true. "I'm sure it's because of the illness, but you know how he is when he drinks. I don't want Sarah around that. Even if he is dying, he can't verbally abuse us like…" Before, was the word she wanted to use, but instead her voice trailed off as she considered the shaky past with her father. She wouldn't get into that today, not with everything going on in Kit's life right now. The time to talk would have been…no, she wouldn't go there either. Things were just getting too complicated to handle. And Collin had come into the shop this morning. It was just a matter of time before he got around to mentioning something. She had Sarah to protect.

Kit laid her hand over Baylee's. "Of course you don't. But you don't have to leave L.A., Baylee. You can move in with me." She'd spent a week with Kit at Christmas before moving back into her father's house. She could move back in now. Problem solved.

But Baylee shook her head. "Not this time. Remember how crowded we were for a week? You don't have the space. Don't look at me like that. If it were just me, I'd bunk at your place, but it isn't. Sarah's things take a lot of room. Besides, she's starting to teethe. And we spend five days a week together as it is. I can't ask you to take me in…again." The idea was humiliating.

"You didn't. I offered. Baylee, you can't just take off again, where would you go?"

"I've got a friend in Denver. Remember…"

"No. You aren't leaving. What are you running from, Baylee? Is it Sarah's father?"

Baylee went dead pale and rocked back on her heels as if she'd been slapped. "Don't ask. I can't drag you into my problems. I won't. You have enough to deal with without me adding to it. Just know that it's better for Sarah and me if we go away. Tanya will call me when…if…Dad gets any worse. I can come back."

Kit's temper snapped. "Well, of course he'll get worse, Baylee. The man's dying. He has a brain tumor. What is it with you lately? You and I have been like sisters. We've always confided in each other because we didn't have anyone else. Then Quinn came along and we made a nice little circle, the three of us closer than real sisters."

Kit started pacing back and forth, getting worked up. "Then after high school we venture out on our own, room together all through college, tell each other everything. But then a year ago, you lie to me." Eyeing Baylee's defensive expression, Kit shook her head. "No, there's no other way to describe what you did. You lied to me. Then seven months later you show back up with Sarah."

By now, Kit's fury raced along the fast track, heading for the finish line after all the months of holding back. "I try to give you some space, try to let you deal with whatever you're dealing with in your own way, in your own time. But now, you tell me you want to just take off again. Like hell you will. If you won't stay with me, then move in with Quinn. She'll be at the hospital most of the time anyway. She's got space. It'll work."

"No, it won't." Baylee had already thought of that for about five seconds. "When she's home Quinn needs to sleep. Sarah's a great baby, but she cries. I can't intrude on Quinn's downtime like that."

"Oh, for Pete's sake, Baylee, you're trying my patience; since when can't you intrude? You're my family. Why are you acting like this?"

Then as if she'd just thought of something, she snapped her fingers. "Wait a minute. I wonder if Gloria's guest cottage is still empty. A couple of months ago, her long time-tenant moved out, a travel writer from Europe who met this hunky carpenter and moved in with him. If it's still available, it'd be perfect for you and Sarah."

Baylee looked skeptical. "You really don't want me to leave."

Dialing Gloria's number, Kit muttered, "Idiot. Of course I don't want you to go. What's wrong with you? Why would I want you out of here?"

"I…because I've kept things to myself. I haven't been a very good friend lately."

As she waited for Gloria to pick up, Kit declared, "No kidding. Baylee, the last few months getting information out of you has been like trying to interrogate an undercover cop afraid of blowing his cover."

When Gloria picked up on her end, Kit got right to the point. Yes, the guest cottage was empty, and no, Gloria didn't mind if Baylee moved in as soon as possible. In fact, the arrangement would work for both of them.

When she hung up, Kit turned to Baylee, tapping her finger on her bottom lip. "You can move your things in tonight. I'll keep Sarah. I've been trying to get her to myself for months now anyway. And Baylee, don't you ever just up and leave again without being honest about where you're going and why. Don't you know there isn't anything you can't tell me that I wouldn't understand? Whatever it is, whoever's hurt you, we can deal with it together. Whenever you're ready to talk, I'll be right here."

When she saw tears pool in Baylee's eyes, Kit drew the shorter woman into a hug. "Now that that's settled, what do you need me to do?"

Baylee patted the water from her cheeks with her fingertips, began to plan what needed to be done. "We can switch out the car seat from my car to yours, load up the Pack 'N Play. She can sleep in that. I'll pack a couple extra bottles of breast milk, but remember to save one to give to her when you put her down for the evening. She goes down around seven, wakes up again around midnight. I'll be back long before then, of course. I'll pick her up around nine. Is that okay?"

"Perfect. I invited Jake to dinner."

"Ah. Then you'll need to take the baby monitor." She saw the puzzled look cross Kit's face and broke out in a huge grin. "In case you get distracted, you can still hear Sarah over…heavy breathing."

Kit rolled her eyes. "Well, things are…heating up."

"Nothing wrong with heat in the early stages. Look, I'll call Tanya, take the chicken way out and let her tell Dad I'm gone after I'm gone. That way I can avoid a blow up with him."

When Kit gave her a doubtful look, she added, "I can't deal with him, Kit. Even if he needs me to be around, I can't be there when he's drinking. Lord knows we were never close, but for the past couple of months I thought we'd turned a corner. And then…anyway, I was trying to give him the benefit of the doubt. But now, I don't want Sarah around him if he's going to drink like that."

"Well, good for you." In spite of her dinner invitation to Jake, Kit offered, "Can you get your stuff and Sarah's by yourself or do you need me to go with you?"

Checking her watch, Baylee decided. "I can get it. I don't have that much." And wasn't that pathetic, she thought. "Maybe I should stay and feed her when she wakes up. Yeah, that'll work. And Kit—thanks."

Later, Kit was dealing with diaper duty and contemplating closing up fifteen minutes early when the bell over the door jingled and a customer walked in.

Used to customers coming and going in and out of the store all day, Pepper usually gave them no more than a quick once-over before ignoring them completely while they went about their shopping.

But now as the man, not all that tall and with salt and pepper hair, approached Kit and the baby, Pepper took up a genuine guard-dog stance. Head ducked low, growling, Pepper watched the man advance. Kit couldn't believe what she was seeing. Her usually docile dog had gone on the attack.

She gave Pepper a look, snapped her fingers and commanded, "Sit. He's usually not like this," she told the man. As Kit stood up, she swung Sarah to her hip, and watched as Pepper reluctantly obeyed, sitting in place on his haunches, nervously eyeing the customer.

"May I help you with something?" Kit politely asked the man who continued to stand just inside the doorway, eyeing the dog as if he weren't sure the canine was friend or foe.

Looking around tentatively for several seconds, he answered with just a hint of a brogue. "I hope so. I was in here the other day getting coffee and noticed you have several paintings on the walls."

He nodded toward the coffee house. He'd come back not just to take another look at Kit Griffin but to satisfy a curiosity that had been nagging at him, one he couldn't shake. "I was wondering if they were for sale. There's one...I'm interested in the one where the woman with the long flowing blond hair appears to be floating on water. None of the art had a price."

A confused look crossed Kit's face momentarily before realization dawned. "Oh, the paintings..." Some were hers, some were Baylee's, but there was only one that fit his description and it belonged to Ella Canyon.

She tried to think whether or not in the four years since it had been hanging on the walls of the coffee shop if anyone had ever shown an interest. That had been her original intent to showcase local artwork on the walls of her store where customers might see the paintings and buy them. But here in San Madrid the idea fizzled. The town wasn't exactly a hotbed for art lovers.

"Imagine my surprise at finding such art in a backwater place like this, or the fact that anyone here would recognize such artistic expression."

Certain that she and her shop and the town had just been insulted, Kit tried to offer up a smile when she pointed out, "It's done in oil. One of Ella Canyon's works; she called it *Woman Rising*." She jostled Sarah as she walked over to stand beside him under the painting. All the while Pepper continued to stand guard.

The painting was of a semi-nude woman, draped only in a sheer white gown, standing in a greenish pool of water on an oversized canvas. "Notice the golden color of the woman's long hair, as if you could simply reach out and touch it, and the way the artist uses contrasting colors around the woman's form to create a reflective effect. I think that's what causes it to look like mist rising slowly out of the water. And as you can see, there's no busy background to detract from the subject of the painting, which is of course, the woman."

When she turned to get his reaction, the man had turned white as a sheet and looked to be on the verge of hyperventilating. Fearing he was about to faint, or worse, suffer a heart attack, Kit snapped out instructions, "Sit before you fall down."

It didn't take much effort to push him into one of the overstuffed chairs. "Do you want some water? Are you on medication? Is it time for you to take a pill or something?"

He didn't answer her, but continued to look as though he might be having some kind of attack. She took off clutching Sarah, ran to the counter, and grabbed the phone, dialing 911. While she waited for help to come on the line, she slid behind the counter to grab a bottle of water from the mini-fridge. She ran back past the register to where he was sitting and found him pointing at the canvas. "Where…did you get it?"

The minute the dispatcher came on the line Kit stared at the man, wanting to know, "Do you need an ambulance?"

The man shook his head.

Kit explained to the dispatcher that she'd thought a customer was in trouble but that now he seemed to be fine. When she hung up, she noticed the man continued to stare at the painting. Watching him, Kit grew more uncomfortable. Bizarre was the word running through her mind as she mentally measured the distance to the front door.

"Do you know the woman in the painting, Ms. Griffin?"

This particular painting had been hanging in the apartment she'd shared with Baylee and Quinn for several years before she'd moved here.

Quinn's mother had given the three girls the painting as a housewarming gift. But when Kit had moved out, Quinn had insisted she take it with her to hang in the shop. Eyeing the man's face, Kit decided he'd made a connection to this piece. He deserved to know its history. "The painting was a gift from the artist. Are you familiar with Ella's work?"

He shook his head. "Does the artist—does she look like the woman in the painting?"

"Why…no, it isn't a self-portrait."

"Was she ever in Ireland?"

"Ireland. Well, of course! That's where Ella met Quinn's father, Nick Tyler." When she saw absolutely no recognition at the name on the man's face she added, "Nick Tyler, the lead singer for Shatter, the Irish rock band. As I understand it, Ella lived there for several years. Quinn was born there. Ella used to be quite the artist." When she wasn't on drugs, Kit thought, seeing no reason to share that little tidbit or the fact that Ella no longer bothered with painting and hadn't for years.

When she noticed the man still hadn't taken his eyes off the canvas and simply sat as if in a trance, she went with instinct and asked, "By any chance, do you recognize the woman in the painting?"

"She looks—there was someone once. She looks—like my wife." As he made mental notes, his mind whirled with possibilities. The artist had lived in Ireland. Was it possible? "Do you know where in Ireland?"

"I have no idea, but Quinn could tell you."

"When did she live there? What was the timeframe?"

She racked her brain, throwing out the date. She knew for sure Ella had been there during the height of the band's popularity when she was Nick Tyler's girlfriend. But beyond that, Quinn's early years were sketchy at best, even Quinn didn't know details.

His brow tightened. If true, the timing was right. How could he tell her what having this painting meant to him?

He was staring at her and acting strange again, Kit thought when their eyes met. She saw the pain in his eyes. "This isn't just a connection to a painting, is it? You actually believe the subject of the painting might have been your wife."

"Aye."

Obviously, this man had loved her very much. His reaction to the painting was one of the most remarkable responses to a work of art she'd ever experienced firsthand.

Talk about art reaching out to a person, Kit thought, and not ten minutes earlier this man had come into her shop with a bit of an attitude, insulting her, and now sat in the chair as if he'd undergone some sort of epiphany, or at the very least a change in personality.

Tentatively she asked, "Would you like the painting?"

The man simply nodded. Another difference in his attitude, thought Kit. Just a few minutes ago he'd been making fun of her store, the town.

"Okay. I'll wrap it up for you." She put Sarah down inside the Pack 'N Play without a fuss then walked a few feet away to the closet and dragged out the step ladder. When she'd climbed up a couple of steps to reach the painting, she heard Pepper give a low growl and turned to see that the man had finally moved out of the chair and was standing over Sarah at the Pack 'N Play.

Kit panicked. "What are you doing?"

"I...I was just looking at the baby."

An uneasy feeling hit her. She thought of him now not as a customer, but a complete stranger who'd walked in off the street pretending to want a painting she'd had hanging on the wall for four years. And she'd been stupid enough to fall for his story. She knew nothing about this man, this odd-behaving man who for all she knew could be Baylee's long-held secret, Sarah's father, who was here in the store to distract her while he kidnapped Sarah and took her off to God knows where.

While Pepper continued to hold the man at bay with his low guttural snarling, she walked slowly down the ladder one step at a time, hitting the floor with heavy feet. She inched closer to the portable phone on the counter. "Well, well, she's…fine. She doesn't need you to be…that close."

The man looked up and saw the panic in the woman's eyes. He stepped back from the baby. Closing the distance between them to within a few feet of where she was standing, he stopped short when he realized it wasn't just panic he saw in her eyes, but genuine fear.

Wanting to correct her misconception, he told her, "I meant no harm…to the baby. I…"

Kit watched him rub at his forehead and close his eyes. Watching his increasingly odd behavior, the uneasiness quivering within her grew to major red flags. She heard herself telling him, "Maybe we should do this another time."

He nodded, opened the door to the coffee shop, and was gone.

When he was all the way out of the store, Kit ran to the door and turned the lock. Then ran to the front door of the bookstore, did the same thing there. She leaned her back against the door and tried to stop shaking.

It wasn't until she'd settled down and had gathered Sarah in her arms that she replayed the scene. As she stood there clutching the baby to her chest, she remembered he'd called her Ms. Griffin. She was pretty sure they hadn't taken the time to exchange names.

And that, she thought, made the whole incident even more unsettling and creepy.

CHAPTER 11

It was after seven when Kit heard a car pull into her driveway. It was all she could do not to run out of the house and act like that awkward teen she'd once been.

She had to take a couple of deep cleansing breaths to force herself to continue chopping veggies for the salad she was making.

As she dried her hands on a dish towel, she cast a please-help-me glance toward baby Sarah who sat in her swing gnawing on a fist. "You're my buffer tonight, Sarah. I won't let my hormones rule while you're here. And hey, I'm no longer that goofy girl I once was. You're going to prevent me from doing anything really stupid tonight. Aren't you, pretty girl?"

When the doorbell finally rang, Kit picked up her support system from the swing and made the baby gurgle at getting free of her confinement. As Kit wiped drool from Sarah's chin, she smoothed out the baby's yellow romper, taking her time getting to the door.

It wasn't easy, but Kit managed to let him cool his jets on the front stoop a couple of seconds longer than was absolutely necessary, giving her some much needed time to appear more composed than she actually felt. But she made the mistake of looking through the door's peephole. At the sight of him standing on her porch with a bottle of wine in his hand, her heart jumped. She clutched the baby tighter, leaned her forehead on the door, trying to ignore the flash of heat she felt in her lower belly.

How could she possibly feel this glad to see a man she'd left mere hours earlier? Lord, help her, but she wanted so badly to jump the man's bones. This feeling was worse than any she'd ever had at fifteen. After taking another set of cleansing breaths she got herself more under control, opened the door, and gave silent thanks to Sarah's presence.

Jake shot her that killer grin, held up the wine and hedged, "Please tell me fifteen minutes after doesn't mean I'm late. Traffic was terrible." Eyeing the baby in her arms, he asked jovially, "Are we babysitting?"

"No, you aren't late, and yes, we're babysitting. Baylee had something she needed to do tonight and as it turns out it was at the last minute. I wasn't really sure if you'd make it. The crisis must not have been that critical."

He had no intentions of telling her that he'd verbally kicked Chuck's ass for waiting to the last minute to make corrections to a contract that should have been finished two weeks ago. Then, to the surprise of everyone within shouting distance of his office, he'd delegated the rewording of the contract to Dylan and left him to deal with the Eastman contract. It had been a first, but he hadn't wanted to risk getting bogged down in the minute details and consequently be late for dinner.

He followed them from the tiled entryway through the long, open rectangular living room into the small but homey kitchen. He watched Kit put Sarah in the swing without a fuss and hand the baby a bright yellow plastic teething ring to play with before turning back to the counter to start work on a marinade. Noticing the wine he was holding, Kit asked, "Does that wine need to breathe or chill or something? Despite helping you polish off three bottles last night I'm not a wine connoisseur."

He chuckled as he shrugged out of his suit jacket, draped it over a kitchen chair. "A beer sounds good."

She dug into a drawer for the corkscrew before reaching into the fridge for a beer.

"And this is an Australian Shiraz 2004 that goes well with just about anything, and since I wasn't sure what was on the menu, I thought it was a safe bet."

In one motion, she twisted off the cap to the beer and handed him the bottle. "It's such a nice evening, why don't we throw some steaks on the grill, eat outside, and enjoy the view from the deck?"

She took down two wine glasses from the cabinet and carried them outside to the table already set for two. When she got back inside, she found him watching the baby as if Sarah were an alien with several heads.

When he caught her looking at him, he turned his attention to the view beyond the open French doors, enjoying the picture-perfect sight of shimmering water merging with a crystal blue spring sky.

For a few moments he stared out at the ocean until his eyes drifted back to where the baby sat prettily in the swing. Curious, he leaned down in front of the swing and asked Kit, "How old is Sarah?"

At the mention of her name, Sarah chortled and cooed and tried hard to throw the teething ring in Jake's direction. The thing landed at his feet. Jake reached down, picked it up off the floor, and handed it back.

As Kit poured the marinade over the steaks, she acknowledged proudly, "She'll be five months Sunday. And she got her first tooth this morning." Turning from the counter, she caught their exchange. "Oh look, she's trying to give you the toy. You obviously have a way with babies. Go ahead, reach out your hands. See if she'll come to you."

"Come to me?" He'd played with a niece or two at this age. The idea that she might actually want him to pick her up intrigued him so much he held both hands out to the baby.

In response, Sarah went to kicking out her little legs and cooing again. Willing to oblige, he reached out, scooped her up with his big hands, and brought her up to his shoulder like an old pro. Patting her gingerly on the back, he issued a couple of soothing words until Sarah gurgled and waved her little arms in the air.

Kit stood there amazed. She had no idea he'd actually pick her up. Well, who knew? Weren't most men scared to death to handle a baby? The man obviously had a way with children. Kit watched as Jake headed outside to the deck, bouncing the baby in his arms while carrying on an animated conversation, talking to her about the ocean, the sky, and the setting sun.

After about fifteen minutes of sightseeing though, he brought Sarah back inside just as she started to fuss. "I think she's getting tired. She's starting to—make noise."

Kit wiped her hands on a dish towel before turning to take the baby from him. "Well, aren't you just the best-kept secret since daycare?"

"I'm an uncle several times over. I have nieces. My oldest sister Sophia has two girls, six and five. Hannah has a little two-year-old girl and she's expecting another." As if that explained everything, he grinned.

Testing his good mood, Kit asked, "In that case, with all that experience under your belt, maybe you'd like to change her diaper, give her a bath, or get her ready for bed? Pick one."

The man visibly paled. "I've never changed a diaper in my life. I have, however, taken the garden hose and wet down a couple of sticky little girls before letting them set foot in the house. But something tells me that isn't what you had in mind."

She stalled in mid-step and turned to look at him. "Well, no. A garden hose?"

He grinned and grabbed his beer. "It seemed like the most practical way to get rid of several layers of caked on dirt since they were making mud pies all afternoon."

"Somehow I can't picture you caring for two little girls."

"Piece of cake as long as there are no diapers to change."

When Sarah began to cry for real, Kit reached into the depths of a gigantic diaper bag until she found a pair of lavender pajamas and a fresh diaper. For good measure, she searched again, finally pulled out a little red rubber duck she could use for Sarah's sponge bath. "Be right back," she yelled as she turned the corner and disappeared.

When he heard water running, he took his beer and stepped back outside to stand at the rail.

He stared at the waves, watched the people strolling on the beach and the sinking sun. Pepper ambled up to him, and he reached down to pet the dog and let this purely domestic scene envelope him like a warm, fuzzy glove.

He stood there listening to the waves and let the day's events just melt away. The encounter with Collin forgotten, as well as the problems with the Eastman contract and dealing with Chuck, peace settled over him and the day's tensions fled.

He began to relax. Instincts told him this was the something he'd been missing. Kit. It occurred to him that even with her difficult childhood, her innate sweetness would make her one hell of a mother someday.

Were kids and marital bliss really in his future? he wondered.

Thinking like that had a nasty tasting fear inching its way up his throat. He'd wanted kids once. And look how that had turned out. But Kit wasn't Claire, he reminded himself. The two women were polar opposites in every way.

That settled him down.

When he heard Kit come back into the kitchen, he went inside to get another beer and met her at the fridge. Kit grabbed the baby's bottle of milk, he a beer. Their eyes met and held.

Suddenly, Kit offered Sarah out to him and asked, "Will you hold her a minute while I heat up the bottle in the microwave?"

Once again, he held Sarah in his arms, breathing in her powder-and-lotion, her baby smell, while he watched Kit punch in the time on the microwave. While the bottle heated, she dug into the deep interior of the diaper bag and came up with the baby monitor.

When a tired Sarah began to wriggle in Jake's arms and fuss in earnest, Kit took the milk from the microwave, tested the temperature, and handed off the bottle to Jake, who promptly stuck it into Sarah's eager mouth.

While she nursed, making little sucking noises, Kit motioned for Jake to follow her into a minuscule bedroom right off the living area. "I have to hook this thing up and get it working before I put her down so we can hear her while we're outside."

When Kit had trouble getting the monitor hooked up, the geek in him couldn't stand watching her struggle with it and finally volunteered, "Let me do it."

Grateful for the offer, they switched duties. Kit took the baby and began to rock her gently in her arms. With each back-and-forth movement, the baby's eyelids fluttered with sleep and soon closed.

While Jake worked on the monitor, the room fell silent. Instead of feeling awkward, it settled into a comfortable atmosphere where the two of them were engrossed in nothing more than getting the baby down. Soon Jake had the monitor up and running and Sarah was fast asleep.

As they walked back to the kitchen, Jake admitted, "That was fairly painless."

"She's a good baby."

"I take it Baylee's on her own."

Kit nodded as she tossed the salad. "I wasn't kidding earlier. Baylee's clammed up. She disappeared about the same time you did last year and showed up Christmas Eve with Sarah. I don't even know who Sarah's father is."

"That doesn't sound like Baylee. No idea what happened?"

"Not a clue."

Changing the subject, he offered, "What can I do to help?"

She handed him the platter with the steaks and said, "You can get these started."

As he went outside to put the steaks on the grill, something kept rolling around in his mind. Baylee had to know Kit's past. And knowing that, some relief tore through him that at least she'd had someone to confide in, someone to turn to. But then just as quickly, that relief vanished when he decided that turning to another kid wouldn't have been much help in Kit's situation. What she'd needed was for her father to step in and get her out of there.

But he hadn't done that.

Kit joined him at the railing just in time to see the remnants of the sun drop into the water. "Ever thought of having one of your own? A baby, I mean."

In spite of his earlier thoughts, her direct question caught him off guard. Kit merely shrugged. "Hey, last night I bared my soul. Tonight's your turn. I've never asked you about Claire; never wanted to go there."

Much like she'd felt the night before, he didn't want to dwell on his past, didn't want to talk about it. But if they were headed toward a relationship, and he thought they were, it was better to get things out in the open.

He took a pull on his beer. Kit watched as he swallowed the liquid, gathering his thoughts. He finally set the bottle down on the table. "I knew from the start I'd made a huge mistake. When you marry someone based on a lie, there's no other direction to go but down when the truth comes out."

That was the last thing she expected him to say. A tug of sympathy formed in her heart. "Why'd you marry her then?"

With the tips of his fingers he rubbed both eyes before drawing out a sigh. "She told me she was pregnant. But two weeks after the wedding I walked into the bathroom, caught her taking a birth control pill out of her pill pack. She tried to make me believe that she'd miscarried, but I wasn't quite that stupid. She'd lied and got caught, simple as that. There were plenty of red flags before we were married that spoke volumes about what kind of person she was, but like an idiot, I ignored them all. I thought once we were married, she'd change."

He shook his head. "People don't suddenly change their behavior because you stick a ring on their finger. But knowing she'd lied about being pregnant, I was done. I knew she couldn't be trusted."

Suddenly Kit understood the infamous Claire had tricked the founder of a multimillion-dollar software company into marriage for his money. As she listened intently, she walked to the grill and turned the steaks, intrigued that the confident, arrogant man she'd known could have been fooled so easily into believing a lie like that.

But he must have loved her.

"We were married twenty months, just a little more than a year and a half. It was the worst time of my life. I was miserable. I spent more and more time away from the house and buried myself in work. It wasn't that hard to do, I had a pretty full plate at the time trying to keep sales up, keep the software current, and meet strategic marketing deadlines on three continents. I had to travel a lot back then, so I was gone most of the time. Our marriage became more like a roommate situation. We shared the same house, but lived in separate bedrooms If I suspected there were other men, the truth is, at that point, I just didn't care. I was too busy with work to pay much attention to what Claire was doing, how she lived. As long as she left me alone, I didn't care."

"Why didn't you get a divorce?"

"And admit to everyone they'd been right about her. A part of me was humiliated that I'd been so stupid. Then... That day—I'd been out of town for almost two weeks. I landed at LAX at seven-fifteen in the morning from Germany, went directly to the office, put in a sixteen hour work day, I didn't get home until well after midnight. When I walked upstairs the first thing I noticed was the blood on the carpet in the hallway. Then I walked into the room—I'll never forget that as long as I live. There was blood everywhere, on the bed, the walls, the floor. There'd obviously been some kind of a fight..." His voice trailed off.

How horribly sad, Kit thought. But she had to stop him from going any further. She didn't need those kinds of details. She reached out and took his hand in hers, pressed it to her face. "Jake, you don't have to do this. It isn't necessary. I get the picture."

He squeezed out a forced laugh. "The thing is I wasn't entirely sure about the men, the affairs; I mean, I had no confirmation of that until after she died. It was St. John who asked me real nice like to come down to the station for a little interrogation, a little one-on-one, and then he hit me over the head with that information right between the eyes. Of course, I wasn't all that surprised, but hearing a police detective tell you that your wife is screwing anything in pants is a pretty low point in your life. And just when you think things can't get any worse, you learn that the police plan to use her infidelity, her affairs, as your motive for killing her. Honest to God, that was perhaps the lowest point in my life. When I found out I was a murder suspect, I hit rock bottom. I'd embarrassed my parents, my sisters, my friends, my employees, myself.

"St. John just assumed I knew about the affairs—and cared enough to kill her or have her killed. I swear I didn't know about the affairs until after she died; I didn't know that every day while I was at work, she was sleeping with her aerobics instructor, or her tennis coach, or her personal trainer. And I paid for all of them. I paid for her lifestyle, the car she drove, the house; I picked up the tab for every goddamn thing she did because I just didn't care enough to get a divorce. How stupid is that?"

"Oh Jake, I had no idea."

"I'm convinced one of the men she was seeing killed her. I tried to get St. John to follow that logic, but he refused to go there. It didn't stop me though. I hired a private detective, and for almost seven months I hoped he'd turn up something, anything at all to show everyone I hadn't done it. But as it turns out it was a waste of time and money. He found no new leads and eventually, I had to let it go."

A stressful sound escaped his throat, as he admitted, "I've finally let it go, Kit."

"I'm glad, Jake. Life takes turns we're not always comfortable with and we can't change the past, can't go back. It is what it is. You were right to let your past go. I'm sorry you went through that kind of hell." She waited a beat before looking into his eyes. "I was pretty upset when I got an invitation to the wedding."

"An...an invitation to the wedding? Claire must have...ah, I see."

"Do you? Needless to say I passed. But when I read about it in the paper, I cried for days. I assumed the infamous Claire was the love of your life."

He stared at her, speechless. What was she telling him? But when he looked into the depths of those deep, green pools, he saw the answer in her eyes. He saw the honesty, the truth of what she was saying. The knowledge humbled him. He thought about all the pain and hurt she must have suffered as a child, considered what his rejection must have felt like back then.

And then it hit him. She hadn't been a teenager when he'd gotten married. "You had to be what, nineteen or twenty?"

"Twenty. When I came out of my funk I decided it was time I lost my virginity, time to quit waiting for—" With a toss of her head, she took a stab at lighthearted. "I picked a very serious-minded geomorphology student. It lasted two months before he bolted to South America."

She smiled as she stood up to check the steaks, but wasn't quick enough; Jake had her wrapped up in his arms, settled on his lap. He rested his forehead on hers. "Kit, I don't know what to say to that, other than I wish with all my heart that I had never met Claire, let alone married her.

I wish I could change the past for both of us, change what's happened to both of us over the years. All I know is that we can start fresh right here, right now, and go forward from here. If you want to, that is."

"Okay."

He didn't need more incentive than that. He turned her mouth up to his, gently parted her lips. She opened, slipped her arms around his neck. The kiss started tender, gentle, until he deepened it. Desire stirred within, filled her with longing.

This is exactly what she'd wanted. She was pretty sure she'd never felt this kind of aching need, and it felt so right. When Jake's hand moved to her breast, Kit broke the kiss, reluctantly pulling away, and said shakily, "I have to check the steaks…" Her voice trailed off with a sigh.

Jake dropped his head and for several seconds just held her in place on his lap. With a sharp sigh of his own, he let her go, but said, "Any man that prefers the jungle to spending time with a woman like you is nuts. He didn't deserve you, Kit."

She forked the steaks onto a plate. "And you do?" She saw the hurt look on his face. "Well, with me, it seems men are always running off somewhere."

"I'm done with running."

"You think so?"

It was time to level with her. "I was attracted to you—and mortified to know that attraction was to someone so young. A grown man shouldn't—isn't supposed to have thoughts about someone so young."

Amazed at the revelation, she turned to him. Holding the plates with the meat, she wanted to know, "That's why you were such a jerk." It wasn't a question.

"You were fifteen but you didn't look fifteen. You were tall for your age. One day I saw you in the file room and thought wow, maybe you were a young-looking eighteen. Eighteen wouldn't have been so bad; at least eighteen is legal. But when one of the lawyers mentioned that he thought you were just sixteen, I—"

"Ran the other way," she finished for him.

"Exactly. And then a week later, Morty mentioned that you had just turned sixteen. I wanted nothing more to do with you. I couldn't afford the office gossip. So I deliberately discouraged you anyway I could."

"Actually, I was fourteen. I thought...I thought it was because...of...what happened to me, the abuse. I thought you knew and you didn't want to have anything to do with someone like me. I thought Gloria might have said something."

He stood, went to her then, and set the plate on the table before taking her chin in his hand. "Aw honey. That wasn't it at all. I didn't even know. If I'd known, I'd have..." What, what would he have done about it? "Why didn't Gloria help you?"

She shrugged. "What could she do? She moved out here, kept an eye on me as best she could after I was twelve." She desperately needed to change the subject. "I'll get the salad. The meat's getting cold. We need to eat." Uncomfortable, she hurried off to the kitchen.

Over the meal, they laughed about some of her and Baylee's choices at making money during college. "Hey, don't knock it. We were eighteen and didn't have much of a skill-set back then. It was either that or work the drive-thru at McDonald's. We both loved art, both loved to draw and paint. It made sense to go that route. In addition to working at Morty's law firm in the summers, Baylee and I painted houses on the weekends."

"Blondes Paint, I remember."

"That was us. We had business cards printed up and everything. At first, we painted houses, inside and out, then we started painting murals. The murals were my idea. Who would have thought that painting murals on the walls of nurseries for pregnant moms could be so lucrative?" She laughed just thinking about how many Winnie the Poohs and Barneys she'd painted back then. "Granted, it was a little unorthodox, but the fact is it was a pretty good way for two college students to work their way through school."

He sat a little straighter at the table. "Alana didn't help you with college at all?"

"Not a penny. Baylee and I started saving every cent we could get our hands on. We weren't brilliant like Quinn who got an academic scholarship. If Baylee and I were going to college, we'd have to put in extra work to make the grade. And after one particular nasty argument too many with her stepfather while still in high school, Quinn moved out on her own. Of course, it didn't take long before she discovered she needed help paying the rent. When she approached us about moving in with her, we jumped at the idea. I couldn't wait to get out of Alana's house and Baylee couldn't wait to leave hers."

Prone to rattling on, she realized she'd drifted from the point of the conversation and got back on track. "Anyway, since the painting business was just a sideline, so to speak, and not much of a business, when I found out Gloria intended to close the bookstore here, I jumped in with both feet. I knew I didn't want a regular nine-to-five, structured, corporate kind of job."

At that, she shot him a solemn look, adding, "Sorry, but it's just not my idea of bliss, spending nine hours every day in a stuffy setting where other people tell you what to do, file this, e-mail that. Sitting at a desk for hours unable to get outside when you want to would drive me over the wall. It didn't take long to discover that every time I found myself stuck inside that file room for hours at Morty's."

"It isn't for everyone."

"No, it isn't. This afternoon at your office, the idea hit me that if I had to work in your environment for very long, I'd go mad." She puffed out her cheeks and blew air out. A habit, Jake had come to realize, she had when she was nervous or exasperated and didn't know what else to say or do.

"It is pretty stressful."

"It isn't that, Jake. It's confining. Take your receptionist for example; the woman can't even get up and walk around, can't leave her post, not even to go to the bathroom when the urge hits. I'd go crazy surrounded by four walls, chained to a desk all day. I feel sorry for her."

Hearing this confirmed, once again, her sweet nature. Her empathy for the receptionist Deidre was just another example of her even temper. And then something else occurred to him. "Kit, by any chance are you claustrophobic?"

Her face went white. Oh, God. She'd said too much. She stammered, "Well. I'm...not sure...I'm...maybe. I don't know. Why?"

"It sounds as if you don't like small, cramped spaces, don't like to be confined indoors, love doing things outside." He reached across the table and took both of her hands in his. "It's okay, honey. Lots of people are claustrophobic."

Flustered now, she realized she'd drifted from the topic yet again. She tried to pick the story up where she'd left off. "Well, once I got the idea in my head to add the coffee shop, it just wouldn't go away. I knew I didn't want to design websites or something equally boring; that's what some of the other art majors wanted, but not me. So, I bit the bullet, put a proposal together for a business loan, made a trip to convince the nice loan committee at the bank I was worthy of a loan."

Impressed, he asked, "How'd it go?"

"What I did was make a total ass out of myself asking those stuffed shirts for a loan. They turned me down flat. Well, why wouldn't they turn me down? I was a college senior, a woman at that, with no real business experience other than freelancing as an artist painting a bunch of storybook characters on walls and working another part-time job at a coffee house. I left the bank in tears, cried on Glo's shoulders, not knowing she'd interpret my pathetic existence as something she could fix. She offered to co-sign the loan for me, but that didn't sit well. I didn't want her to go out on a limb like that. What if I couldn't make a go of it and the bookstore went bust; it was already in trouble. What if I lost her money and she didn't have anything left for retirement? I just couldn't let her take a risk like that."

Jake didn't have the heart to tell her that he was pretty sure Morty Gandis had left Gloria in a position where she didn't have to worry about money.

"Still, the idea of getting the bookstore back on track appealed to me. So, I dug into my hard-earned savings and took the plunge. Quinn was dating a contractor at the time. He came up with a bid I could afford."

She paused and looked skyward, held up her wine glass in salute. "Thank you Steve Harper, wherever you are. I'm just glad Quinn kept him around long enough for him to finish the remodeling." Her laugh came from deep down in her throat. "With my investment in the coffee house, Gloria made me an equal partner. And once again I have Gloria to thank for being there when I needed her."

"What do you mean?"

"She's been coming to my rescue, been my saving grace for so many years, ever since, I…when I…well, for a long time."

She'd almost said something else. He was sure of it, but then he remembered what he'd found out that afternoon and the moment was lost. "By the way, I found out a little more about John Griffin's death."

Telling her was difficult. "I think maybe, your mother, uh, Alana that is, told you the truth on this one. John Griffin's date of death came up as November 2. The cause of death is listed as accidental. He fell from a horse doing his own stunts while on location in Santiago, Spain, suffered a head injury, and died about six hours later at the hospital."

"I never knew when he died. She never told me…November 2 would have been three weeks after my fourteenth birthday. He missed my birthday because of the shooting schedule." Tears filled her eyes, ran down her cheeks. "But he sent me a birthday present, an autographed poster of the last movie we saw together in July when we went to a premier showing of *Men in Black*. He was like that. He knew how much I enjoyed the movie."

Jake put his hand over hers.

"I should have been curious enough to find out for sure before now when he died. Instead I spent all these years hoping like a silly child that Alana had been trying to hurt me by telling me he was dead. I thought he'd come back, you see." She wiped at her eyes. "How stupid is that? I always thought he'd come back."

"It isn't stupid to hope for a different outcome, honey. But Kit, your father had a son. He's been receiving his residuals since his death. His name's Ben Griffin. He lives in Galway, Ireland."

The stunned look on her face and the tears running down her cheeks made Jake feel like the biggest heel. Why did he have to be the one to tell her this?

When she just sat there, as if in shock, he pulled her onto his lap, wrapped her up in his arms, and rocked her. "I'm sorry. I guess I could have thought of a better way to tell you."

"No, it's okay. He had a son. Where has he been all this time? Ireland, you say, he lives in Galway. Imagine…a brother, six thousand miles away. That's the second time today someone's mentioned Ireland to me. How'd you find out all that?"

"You crack the right database you'd be surprised what you can learn if you know where to look."

"I should contact him, this Ben Griffin, get in touch. If I didn't know about him, he probably doesn't know about me. He'd be family, Jake, my only family besides Glo, of course."

It was like her to want to do that, thought Jake, as he rested his head on her forehead before telling her more.

"I also read over a couple of those documents Boyd sent you. I brought the rest home with me. But I have a few questions, Kit, about the ones I read. According to the will, you inherit close to twenty million dollars, correct?" When she nodded, he went on, "That's including Alana's real estate business. But the business itself is worth that much, maybe more, and that's a conservative estimate."

"What are you saying?"

"It doesn't add up, Kit. There's the house in Beverly Hills, which is probably worth about seven or eight mil, a small lot she owned in Malibu but never built anything on, which is probably worth another three mil because it's in Malibu, and miscellaneous checking and savings accounts. According to the bank statements Connor sent, there isn't a lot of cash on hand in the accounts, not even the business account. That's odd to me. I mean, twenty million sounds like a lot, impressive; it's enough to get your attention, but when you add it all up, there ought to be a lot more there than twenty million."

"Jake, Alana spent money like it grew on trees. She probably ran through all of it."

"Maybe. But what if that's what Boyd wants you to think. Think about it, there's no question you've got a house you can sell, a business you can sell, property you can sell. In other words, you inherit stuff, assets, but hardly any cash. Do you see where I'm going with this?"

She thought for a moment. "If the business is worth more, then why did Connor tell me I'd inherited twenty million? What you're saying is I get Alana's stuff that I can liquidate, but there are no millions of dollars in cash sitting around in her bank accounts?"

"Exactly. I think we should check her bank accounts, find out when the cash went south. I'd bet it was recent. Like I said, the assets listed in the will far exceed the twenty million dollar amount Boyd told you. So where are the rest of the assets, the cash she had on hand?"

"Maybe Connor was upset about Jessica's death; maybe it's an honest mistake. Quinn pointed out that he was on the clock this morning right after his mother was found dead."

"Could be an honest mistake, but a lawyer should know the value of his client's business. It would have been appraised at some point. The fact that he doesn't know isn't a good thing. He was either upset, just made a mistake, or the error was intentional and meant to conceal the withdrawals to the accounts."

"What should I do?"

"Don't sign anything. I'll look over the rest of the documents tonight and if anything else surfaces, I'll let Reese take a look at them. Those Boyds are damn clever lawyers."

The doorbell rang. She suddenly realized how late it had gotten and crawled off his lap. "I think that must be Baylee coming to retrieve her daughter."

Jake followed her to the front door. When Kit started to open it without checking who was on the other side, he grabbed her arm just before she turned the lock. "I'm sure you're right, but humor me and make sure."

She stared at him, saw genuine concern in his eyes. By now the ringing doorbell had turned to frantic knocking. She looked out through the peephole and smiled. "All I see is one anxious mama."

When Kit unlocked the door and Baylee stepped inside, Jake still couldn't get over the dark hair. And then he noticed how edgy she acted. The relaxed, lighthearted Baylee of old was gone, replaced by a wariness he'd never seen before. Now, pooled in her huge aqua-colored eyes, he saw an almost distant look, much like he'd seen recently in Kit's.

Remembering what Kit had told him earlier, he wondered whom Baylee thought she was fooling with the different colored hair. To him, she still looked like Baylee.

Kit led her into the kitchen with an arm draped over the petite woman's shoulders, "Did you get all moved in?"

"Oh, Kit, the house is lovely, just perfect for us. It's like a little doll house. I'm so grateful to be there. How was Sarah?"

"A sweetheart. Would you like a glass of wine or tea or something?"

With her mind on her daughter's next feeding, Baylee slipped into a kitchen chair and sighed just thinking about how long it had been since she'd enjoyed a glass of wine. The temptation was there, but instead of taking it, she said simply, "Iced tea will do."

⚛ ⚛ ⚛ ⚛ ⚛

While Kit poured the tea into a tall glass, she told Baylee, "Jake and I were just finishing up dinner. Have you eaten? I have leftovers."

"Thanks, but I picked up a couple of fish tacos at the drive-thru."

"Jake was telling me that I have a brother in Ireland. His name's Ben Griffin. I can't wait to get in touch with him."

Instantly suspicious, Baylee turned accusing eyes on Jake. "A brother? Where's he been all this time? Are you sure about this? You know you're getting her hopes up, don't you? She's wanted family for as long as I can remember. And what if this so-called brother turns out to be a real jerk, what then? Or what if this brother wants no part of her? He could, you know, he could hurt her."

Protective, thought Jake, and angry, very angry. Right before his eyes, Baylee turned into a mother bear ready to defend her cub at the drop of a hat.

"Okay, but what if he doesn't know about her? And what if he wants to know his sister, Baylee? Doesn't Kit have the right to know a half-brother? I realize there's a possibility he might not feel the same about her; that's why I'm going to contact him and give him the option of getting in touch with Kit." He saw the flash of concern on her face and thought he knew what it was about. "I won't give him the opportunity to reject her face to face."

Those aqua blue eyes went suddenly cold as steel, piercing Jake like daggers. "Fine. But I'll tell you this: if she gets hurt in any way, I'm holding you responsible."

"Down Mom," Kit said, as her hand fell on Baylee's shoulder. "There's no point in jumping down Jake's throat. I wanted him to do this. He was trying to find out anything he could about...my father and he discovered this. I'm grateful for his help."

Baylee let out a loud pent-up breath, immediately remorseful. "Oh. You want to know if he's really...gone. Oh Kit, did you find out if he's...really...dead?"

Jake grimaced. "He died just as Alana told her."

Baylee's eyes went moist. "I...I'm sorry, Kit. I know you wanted it to be...not true. But that doesn't change how I feel about this so-called brother. You know nothing about him."

Confused by Baylee's behavior, Kit quietly told her, "He's my brother, Baylee. That's all I need to know."

Baylee downed a gulp of tea and stood up. "It's getting late. I'll start loading up Sarah's things and save Sarah for last."

"We can help you load the car, Baylee." But she was talking to Baylee's back. With a sigh, Kit started packing up Sarah's diaper bag.

Noting the tension emanating off Baylee as she left the room, Jake quietly asked, "Is she okay?"

Kit took a deep breath. "No. Not for a while now. She's gone through a lot over the last few months. I can't put my finger on exactly what's wrong. All I know is something isn't right."

He stood up. "I'll start loading the car."

"Could you switch the car seat from the Jeep back to hers? That would be a big help. I'll go talk to her."

Jake had just finished getting the car seat adjusted in the back seat of Baylee's Range Rover when she stepped around the car. "Look, let's just get this over with. I'm not apologizing for what I said in there. I don't think it's a good idea for her to try to find some stranger and to make him part of her life. Even a brother—a brother, I might add, that hasn't made one move to try and find her all these years." She put her hands in the back pockets of her jeans, rocked on her heels. "I don't want her hurt."

"She's been hurt enough, don't you think?" He stared straight into the woman's eyes.

"Yeah, she has."

"What about Collin Boyd? Has he ever hurt her?"

Baylee eyed Jake as if deciding just how much to confide in him and then remembered he'd been the one to confront Collin earlier that day. "He's tried. Like the rest of his family, he refuses to take no for an answer. He isn't just an arrogant jerk with money, but one who has never been held accountable for any of his mistakes. None of them have. The Boyds think they can do anything and get away with it. It's in the genes. Collin's had a thing for Kit for as long as I can remember. But she's never given him the time of day, probably because it's what Alana and Jessica wanted. Kit never fell into that trap."

She briefly looked away before turning back again to look up at Jake. "They've never dated, never gone out. I think that's what pisses him off the most. Every so often, like this morning, Collin pushes the envelope." She took a deep breath and took hold of Jake's arm. "He scares me where Kit's concerned. Watch out for her, won't you?"

"Absolutely."

Ten minutes later, standing on the porch, they watched as Baylee's SUV backed out of Kit's driveway and headed down the street.

"Thanks for dinner."

"Thanks for helping me with Collin. I'm not sure I said that. It just seems like there's so much coming at me all at once, I can't think straight. I'm a little nervous about Alana's funeral. With everything going on, I'm feeling a little overwhelmed."

"I know, but don't try to do everything yourself," he suggested as he rubbed her back. It was then and there he decided that as much as he wanted her, it wouldn't be tonight.

She'd just discovered she had a sibling she'd never met. She was dealing with the fact that in the past forty-eight hours both Alana and Jessica had been murdered. On top of that, she'd just admitted that all of this was coming at her too fast. He wasn't about to screw this up now by rushing her.

"I need to take that next step in finding Ben Griffin. If I come by your office in the morning do you think we could find out more info about him?"

"Sure, why not? But Kit, I meant what I said to Baylee. I'll be the one to make contact with him. There's no point in you getting your hopes up and then having them dashed if he doesn't want to meet. You come by in the morning and we'll see what we can find."

With that, he reached around her waist and dragged her into him. Her wet mouth tasted sweet and a little spicy.

Like the other times he'd kissed her, this was no hurried kiss, but rather a slow seductive mating of tongues. "Why don't you come back inside, Jake?"

"I want you, in bed."

"I know." It surprised her when he shook his head.

He patted her on the rear and pushed her toward the front door. "You've got too much going on." He pointed to her head. "Too much to think about tonight. When I take you to bed the first time, I want your complete attention." He grinned at her and swatted her bottom again. "Now go back inside. Lock the door. Get some sleep."

It was on the tip of her tongue to tell him it was him she needed now. But he knew her too well. If he stayed she'd talk it to death, then start dwelling on the past, dredging up what might have been, along with all kinds of painful memories. Reluctantly, she went inside.

When he heard the lock click, Jake headed to his car, and eventually, to a cold shower.

CHAPTER 12

Over the next few days, Kit couldn't escape painful stabs at her psyche as she dealt with the details of planning Alana's funeral. It didn't help that St. John encouraged the coroner to drag his feet in releasing the body. Keeping it an extra couple of days caused the arrangements to get pushed back, drawing out the whole process unnecessarily, creating several anxious days and sleepless nights for Kit.

For the most part she kept the service low-key as Gloria hovered, determined not to let her take on any chore that might dredge up anything hurtful. But in spite of Gloria's watchful eye there were still stress-related facets that had to be handled.

When the funeral home called about Alana's dress for burial, Gloria found a suitable outfit. When the issue of pallbearers came up, Gloria recruited men from Alana's army of real estate agents, with only a few refusing her request outright.

Kit handled the flowers and music. She filled the chapel with pink roses and orchids, two of Alana's favorites, and worried that somehow Alana would find fault with her efforts. But when it came to the music Kit went with sentiment. She chose uplifting and inspirational songs, and at the last minute for no good reason added the traditional Irish song, *The King of Love My Shepherd Is*, telling Gloria, "It makes me feel as though I'm putting my own touches on our goodbye, my own way."

But on the day of the funeral, it came and went in a series of surreal, clipped images. Snapshots of condolences, concern, and sympathy amid a parade of mourners as they walked past Alana's closed casket. Friends Kit hadn't seen in years blended with others who'd driven down from San Madrid to pay their respects.

And through it all Kit knew Holloway and St. John were there, lurking just beyond the fringe, watching her every move, her every action.

Thanks to Jake, Gloria, and Quinn, she somehow got through it. Even though Baylee had helped with the flowers and music, she had been noticeably absent from the memorial service. Kit couldn't help but worry about Baylee as she crawled into the waiting limousine afterward. But at that point all Kit wanted was to get as far away from Whispering Oaks as she could get, and preferably, as fast as the limo could take her.

From his position on the hill overlooking the cemetery, he watched as the mourners gathered around the gravesite and a flower-draped casket. As the minister recited his prepared sermon, he spanned the crowd, taking note of those in attendance.

He didn't miss the searing glares Collin sent Kit every now and then, or the leering stares Cade paid to Quinn. But when he spotted the two detectives watching their prime suspect walk to a waiting limo, he smiled.

Soon, they'd be even more confused by it all.

As he watched the car slowly make its way through the cemetery and out the front gates, he planned the demise of yet another.

Collin was furious. After watching Kit wrapped around Boston at Alana's funeral, his rage took on a harder edge.

As he sat around the pool with his brothers, he wasn't the least interested in his father's agenda anymore. He didn't give a rat's ass about the future of the firm, or his father's warning, or the fact that everyone seemed worried that Auslo and Taft hadn't yet found what they were looking for.

Nothing much mattered to Collin other than making Kit pay for rejecting him yet again.

"If she hadn't been such a cold fish, we might have had a couple of kids by now. Why can't she see she belongs with me? She never did appreciate what was right in front of her. It's been like that since we were kids, all the times she interfered with our plans, busted in on our games, always tagging along where she wasn't wanted." She'd made him fall in love with her all those years ago and then shunned him. And now, she'd taken up with Jake Boston.

She had to pay.

As the brothers threw back Johnnie Walker Blue, Connor and Cade let him rant. It wasn't the first time, but it was getting old. And it was starting to sound a little creepy and incoherent. Or at least that was Connor's take.

Cade, on the other hand, wanted to fan some of Collin's hot wrath to flame. "Yeah, like the time we killed that old cat, just to get it out of its misery. Kit ratted us out to Maya, who got us grounded when she told Dad what we did."

"I know she's behind what happened to Mother. I just can't prove it. I want her to hurt like I'm hurting."

Cade might've been on his way to getting drunk, but hearing that had him pointing out, "Kit was always a timid thing." Staring out over the water, he gave it more thought, and remembered a shy, skinny girl with eyes too big for her face. Kit was the opposite of Quinn. No spunk. No one could say Quinn was afraid of her own shadow. And wasn't that too bad, he thought. "I can understand you thinking she might have killed Alana. God knows that bitch was the antichrist, but what's Mother's murder got to do with Kit? Why would Kit want to kill Mother?"

"He isn't making sense. He's boning for her, that's all," Connor said. "And she won't give him the time of day. That's the problem, little brother; you've got the hots for her just like you did when you were both twelve. And look at your nose, some impression that's going to make at your own mother's funeral tomorrow, you with a bandage across your honker. What are you going to tell the reporters when they ask what happened there?"

It didn't help when Cade added, "And if Dad hears you talking about Kit the way you are, he's going to personally ship you off to Siberia. He wants you over this Kit thing."

The razzing he was used to, but damned if Collin would admit the truth. After all, hadn't his mother reminded him every time Kit rebuffed him what the girl was? "Mother always said Kit came from Hollywood trash."

Cade wanted to know, "Since when did you ever listen to Mother? You're acting weird, bro. What's this about anyway?"

"She's fucking that software prick." Hadn't he followed her to Boston's office, saw it for himself? He'd wanted to confront her about it right then in the parking garage, but she'd taken off. Why was she always acting afraid of him?

Cade thought a moment before turning to Conner. "Software prick?"

Conner replied, "Boston? She and Jake Boston? Well, now that's interesting. The police never arrested that son of a bitch for killing his wife. They let him get away with it."

"Had her killed more likely," added Collin. "And she'd screw anything in pants."

The memory had Connor smiling into his whiskey. "Now that was a nice piece of ass."

Cade and Collin exchanged looks before Cade asked, "And you would know that how?"

Connor lifted his glass. "Been there. Done that." Just thinking about her—he rotated his shoulders. "How about we order a couple of hookers for tonight?"

Cade wiggled his eyebrows up and down. "Now we're talking. I could use a distraction. I'm tense."

Not even the idea of hookers had Collin feeling any better. In fact, he desperately wanted to use his fists on her. He'd done it before. Sitting here humiliated, he knew he would have to make her pay, big time. His mother would want that. But that's what Auslo and Taft were for. As he saw it, the minions now worked for him and his brothers. And it was their job to do what they were told.

Kit had deceived him by fucking Boston. She'd rejected him for the last time. He would meet with Auslo and Taft and up the ante. No matter what his father said, it was time to get results. Kit Griffin had always been his. He'd loved her since they'd been kids.

She'd shacked up with Boston. And now, he'd make her pay.

⍝ ⍝ ⍝ ⍝ ⍝

Sailing offered escape. And after Alana's funeral no one needed escape more than Kit. Standing on the deck of the *Sea Warrior* with the wind in her face, she watched Jake navigate out of the harbor and head for the open sea.

He'd hovered over her during the funeral, never leaving her side for a moment. It was finally over. And now, just getting outside, getting on the water, she felt like a weight had been lifted.

Jake kept an eye on Kit's willowy body as it moved fluidly to the rail in a pair of low-rise Capri jeans and a short white tank top that showed off her bellybutton.

She was barefoot, with her loose hair billowing in the breeze, her chin to the wind. He watched her take pleasure in the moment. He'd been worried about her during the funeral, especially when she'd caught sight of St. John and Holloway.

She'd turned a pale shade of white and hadn't lost the pallor until he'd gotten her onboard the boat. For a while at the sight of the two detectives she'd turned to jelly, but then she'd pushed back her shoulders and sucked it up. She'd gotten through it.

"Hi," she said as she joined him at the helm, putting her arm around his waist.

"Having fun?"

"The best. This was a great idea. It's just what I needed after this morning."

"Want to take a crack at the helm?"

"Is there any chance I might run us aground?"

A laugh escaped before he assured her, "I think you're safe. Come here."

Edging up to him, the boat rolled and pitched, but he steadied her in front of him before putting her hands on the rudder, letting her guide the boat while he turned to work the sails. He cranked the winch, and the mainsail unfurled into the wind. She heard the wind snap into the canvas, could feel it power the boat through the water. After cutting the motor, he continued to trim the sails, and showed Kit how to work the jib. A slight spray slapped her face. "This is the best. Is it always like this?"

"It's different every time, but for me the basic rush is always the same."

With his hand over hers at the helm, Kit wasn't shy about wanting to know everything she could about the *Sea Warrior*. She asked a dozen questions in rapid succession. How fast does the boat go with the motor versus the sails? How much fuel does she carry? Does it take longer to sail from north to south or east to west?

Jake appreciated her curiosity. He really did. But after a while answering her questions, watching that mouth move, she was driving him crazy. It didn't take much thinking on his part to know what he'd like to happen between them, was even picturing in his head what he'd like to do to her beneath him in bed. He wanted Kit in bed, under him, naked, moaning, and preferably not asking him twenty questions about sailing.

The boat lurched and she leaned into his chest. He took full advantage of the sway, the unsteady ride, keeping her body pressed up against his to balance them both.

When Pepper began to bark at a flock of seagulls, they turned to look and saw the gulls following a large dolphin pod with babies.

Jake took the helm to navigate alongside the mammals while Kit hung off the rail as close to them as she could get with her camera. She marveled at the way he maneuvered the boat without scaring them off. At one point, he got them so close to the pod she could see the schools of fish swimming after the dolphins and in turn watched as the sea gulls took turns bomb diving for lunch.

As the pod took a southward turn, Jake maneuvered the boat farther out to sea. He made a few entries in the captain's log while Kit checked the pictures she'd taken with her digital camera. After scanning the disk, she showed off some of the shots. "Look at this one, look how clear that water is. You can plainly see it's a couple of dolphins. And look at this one; you can see the baby swimming next to the mama."

Jake got a kick out of her enthusiasm. Like everything she did, she got the biggest thrill from the little things, like taking pictures of baby dolphins.

A while later, she spread her arms out on the bow, turned to Jake, and said, "This is like heaven. How about we lean out over the water, you know, into the wind like the scene in *Titanic*? Have you ever done that?" Just as she started to step up on the bow to make the scene a reality, he grabbed her arm. "You're crazy. You can't do that."

She giggled, moved into him, and whispered, "Gotcha."

He laughed, but when their eyes met, instinct had him bending his head to touch her lips. The kiss began soft, playful, but just as his tongue played tag with hers in earnest, the kiss turned fiery. When a passing speedboat blew its horn, they broke apart.

"You aren't still pouting about not being able to find out any more about Ben Griffin, are you?"

"Not exactly." But it did rankle. "He must have moved recently, that's all. Just shows how difficult it can be to track someone down." Especially, if they didn't want to be found, he thought briefly. "I'm not giving up."

Giving him a stern look, she warned, "Don't pout about it. It's wonderful you found anything at all. I'm impressed with your hacker skills. We'll both look…tomorrow. I knew it might not be easy."

But it should be, he thought, as he began to lower the staysail. Turning to Kit, he showed her how to work the jib on her own, stopping the boat's forward progress. As they hung off the starboard railing arm-in-arm, Kit turned to Jake and said, "It's so peaceful here. I feel like you've brought me to another world." She snuggled into his chest.

And the urge to take her right there hit him all the way to his toes. He had to remind himself she needed comfort today, nothing more than relaxation after the tension-filled funeral. Granted, he should have his head examined for thinking that they could spend the day sailing, just the two of them in such close proximity to one another, confined on a boat where he'd be forced to watch her every move, listen to her every word, visualize taking her to bed. And there was a very comfortable, very convenient bed below deck, just waiting for them to enjoy each other.

Oh, perfect, he thought, that's a reminder he didn't need at the moment. The reality of it had him gently setting her back from him, getting her the hell away from his body. He needed a distraction. A cold dip in the ocean might just do the trick. "How about a swim?"

Even though the sun was shining bright and warm, Kit looked at him as if he were crazy. "A swim? Without a wetsuit? You're kidding, right? That water's got to be freezing."

Jake raised an eyebrow in both invitation and challenge. "No colder than sixty-five degrees, I'd imagine. Probably ten degrees colder another ten feet down. But if you swim around you shouldn't notice the cold too much." He took a few steps toward her, grinning like the devil.

Noticing the glint in his eye, she backed up. "What are you doing?"

"How about I toss you in and you test the water? See how cold it is. If you don't want those clothes you're wearing getting wet, I'd start stripping down to that red bikini you've got on underneath." He wiggled his eyebrows up and down.

She backed up even farther. "Now who's crazy?"

But when he started toward her, she ran to stern and in one smooth motion, shed her T-shirt and jeans, skidded to the railing, and took the plunge off the aft deck into the cold Pacific Ocean.

Jake was still getting out of his clothes when she surfaced, shaking off water from her hair, rubbing her hands on her face as she bobbed up and down. "Could you be any slower? What's taking you so long anyway? I could swim to China and back before you even get wet."

Just as she got out the challenge, he stripped down to his trunks and dived in, landing with a splash five feet from her head. She lit out after him at a fast clip, making a weak attempt to dunk his head under the water. But Jake swam just out of her reach until they were both darting in and out of the water much like the dolphins had earlier. When Kit broke stride, she yelled, "You were right about the water. As long as you move around it's not so cold."

Wasn't cold? It was downright freezing. Feeling a little sheepish about prompting her to swim in that bikini, Jake confessed, "I've got wetsuits on board."

"Now's a fine time to tell me," she said as she dived again while he followed after her. Despite the cold water, his blood was pumping and did nothing to ward off the sexual tension he felt. They surfaced again.

As they bobbed on the water, there was no ignoring Kit in that bikini. Or the fact that she was cold. Through the fabric he tweaked her erect perky nipples. Why was he torturing himself like this? But he wanted a taste, just a taste of her to get him through the long day.

He toyed with her lip with his teeth, nipping and urging her to open, until he felt her quiver. A yearning glaze settled in her eyes. He deepened the kiss, plunging headlong until he lost all thought of anything but her.

The frigid water did nothing to cool his need; he reluctantly released her. She shimmied toward the boat and he followed. Squeezing the water from her nose, she shook her hair back and said, "That's it for me. What about food? I'm starving. Nothing like a swim to build up the appetite."

Yeah, Jake thought, and nothing like working up a different kind. He'd just have to suffer.

But he wasn't happy about it.

When Kit reached the boat she climbed the ladder onto the deck where she'd left her clothes. With Jake right behind her, he pulled out several dry towels from a storage locker then pointed to the outdoor shower, turned on the water. "Get some of that salt off your skin."

She gave him a quick look before turning to stand under the running spray to wash off. Jake stepped into the spray directly behind her still wearing his swim trunks.

She felt him behind her, felt the heat of his body, the sexual tension hanging in the air between them, sensed what was going to happen before he actually touched her. When he did, when he reached for her, she turned and all but melted into his wet chest like ice in August.

He wrapped his arms around her. Their bodies touched. They went from slow slide to a fast hot, molten furnace. The air sizzled. By the time he deepened the kiss, her bones had turned liquid from head to toe.

One of them moaned.

He shut off the water and leaned his frame against the tile behind him for support. Kit kept her arms wrapped around him, rubbing her hand along hard-toned flesh. She put her lips to his, opened her mouth. His mouth devoured. One hand snuck around the back, unhooked the clasp, and began an exploration of her breast, settling on a ripe nipple, tweaking the peak between thumb and forefinger while the other hand probed beneath the bikini bottom, fingers reaching damp heat. "God, I've spent a year missing you."

Just then, a loud static crackle from the boat's radio broke the moment. A frantic SOS call filled the air. "Mayday, mayday, this is *Wind Dreamer* we're taking on water, going down; we need help. Somebody help, over."

They bolted apart. Dripping wet, he ran to the controls, while Kit grabbed for her clothes. "It's a distress call." Once he reached the helm, he adjusted some instrumentation on the control panel, and then picked up the radio. "Roger, *Wind Dreamer*, we copy. This is *Sea Warrior*. Give me your position, over."

Dead air, then static before finally they heard the voice rattle off GPS coordinates. "Roger that, *Wind Dreamer* we have your position and understand the situation. Will radio your position to the Coast Guard. We're en route to your location, ETA approximately ten minutes. Can you hold on ten minutes? Over."

Breaking up now, the voice sounded panicked. "...will try...we're going down fast...don't know how much longer...radio...will work...over."

Jake started the motor and didn't bother raising the sails, turning the boat 180 degrees southward and to the east. He placed the call to the Coast Guard, passing along the GPS coordinates for the *Wind Dreamer*, hoping the Coast Guard would get there ahead of them.

Kit handed him his shirt, and he handed Kit the binoculars, telling her, "Look for any movement in the water, a capsized boat, a raft, anything floating. Keep an eye out for debris of any kind."

Five minutes out, scanning the horizon with the binoculars, Kit spotted a dot in the distance, a speck in the sky closing in on the *Sea Warrior* from a northwesterly direction. She pointed to it, realized it was a helicopter; and Jake told her, "Let's hope that's the Coast Guard."

But in spite of her constant scan of the horizon, Kit still didn't see a boat in distress or anything moving up and down on the water. Soon Kit watched as the helicopter overtook the *Sea Warrior*, bypassing them, heading in a southeasterly direction. Jake followed the chopper's path, grateful the Coast Guard had shown up first.

Finally, in between the swells, bobbing in the water, Kit spotted something that looked like a boat turned sideways, and shouted, "There. Over there. There's a small boat." As Jake veered that way, she told him, "I don't see anyone on board, or anyone in the water, though."

As they got closer, Jake could see the sloop was old and listed noticeably. Even though he didn't see anyone in the water, he knew they could have drifted with the tides.

They watched as the helicopter circled the capsized boat. As the *Sea Warrior* drew within a hundred feet, the sound of an explosion pierced the air, knocking Jake and Kit backward to the deck. A huge ball of fire sent flames skyward. Black smoke engulfed them. As they picked themselves up off the deck, debris began to rain down on both of them.

� � � � �

Hours later, after filing his report at the Coast Guard station, Jake went in search of Kit. As he wandered the hallway looking for her, he remembered the words Petty Officer Mac Brown had told him, "If you'd been fifty feet closer to that old boat, you and that pretty lady of yours might have been blown to bits. That sloop was a derelict, unregistered. It certainly wasn't the *Wind Dreamer*. But you did the right thing, you responded to what you thought was a legitimate distress call."

So they'd reacted to a bogus signal from a boat that didn't exist.

It didn't make any sense. And if they'd been seconds faster, arrived sooner, they'd be toast right about now. Could the whole thing have been staged for their benefit?

He couldn't prove it, but he was sure of it. Had the intent been to scare them? Or something far worse, and for what purpose?

He found Kit curled up sound asleep on a bench in the hallway. He bent down, rocked on his heels in front of her to watch her sleep. Awake, the woman was a dynamo, talking, energetic. Asleep, she made such a peaceful, serene picture; he hated waking her. He couldn't help but chuckle to himself; this was the quietest she'd been all day. If he woke her...

His ringing cell phone did it for him. At the sound, she stirred, waking from a sleepy daze. When she realized Jake was there with her, she sat upright all at once and put her arms around his shoulders, felt the tension in him. He touched his fingers to her cheek and simply smiled at her. The ringing phone persisted and he answered it in his usual brusque manner, saying merely, "Boston."

"Someone hacked our system," Dylan informed him on the other end.

Jake asked the obligatory questions. Did we lose any data? Was their client information compromised? Was it virus related? If so, where did it attack first?

When he hung up, he'd resigned himself to a long night ahead and wrapped his arms around Kit, telling her, "Baby, as much as I'd like to finish what we started this afternoon, it looks like I've got another crisis at work. I'll take you home. You look wiped."

CHAPTER 13

*E*ven at two in the morning, high in the Hollywood Hills, the blistering heat that had gripped the city of angels for most of the summer refused to let go. The thick night air, just as hot and humid as it had been before the sun went down, hung heavier now that the car was approaching ranch country, that forgotten part of L.A. where barns once outnumbered studios.

Even with the windows rolled up on the sleek Mercedes, the earthy smells of manure managed to drift inward and penetrate the air conditioning cranked to max.

As the vehicle climbed higher, zipping along through the canyons, hugging the curves of the winding blacktop, rock music blared from the radio with Mick hoping you'd guess his name. The music had their blood pumping. But it was the mix of amphetamines and cocaine running through their systems that gave them that extra kick they needed to do the job, a job they'd planned since last spring.

As the Benz picked up speed, roared past the weathered sign marking the turnoff—barely more than a wide spot in the road—the driver missed the turn and threw out a string of profanity. For the next few seconds, the sound of grinding gears popping into Reverse replaced the chirp of crickets that hummed along the roadside as the vehicle backed up, squealing the tires in protest.

When the driver tried to squeeze through the opening, make the narrow turn, the front bumper clipped the rural *mailbox, leaving the metal canister hanging sideways in a twisted heap. But the driver never bothered to hit the brake. Instead, with the accelerator gunned to the floor, the car lurched forward, shooting along the long, unlit driveway like a missile, kicking up gravel, sending sharp pings into the car's underbelly.*

By the time the vehicle screeched to a stop mere feet from the side of an isolated ranch house, the clock in the car read 2:35.

The old couple, asleep inside the house, had less than thirty minutes to live.

The car doors flew open and two people got out, bickering nonstop all the way up the walk to the porch until one of them shoved a key into the front door lock. They stepped inside the darkness into a tidy living room made darker by paneled walls and ugly brown carpeting. Stumbling around in the blackness, one of them bowled over a lamp and the other one caught the thing before it crashed to the floor.

"Do you think you could have remembered a fucking flashlight?"

"Don't start with me. I might have if you hadn't been in such a damned hurry to leave the house. We don't need a flashlight. Just flip on the lights, they're dead to the world, remember? Could we just get this over with? I'm sick of listening to you talk it to death, sick of listening to you bitch."

"Me? It's you who complains about every little thing."

"Like hell. Why is it you never give me credit for anything? Wasn't it my idea to drug the old farts' tea with sleeping pills earlier? If we do this right, they'll never wake up; it'll be a piece of cake."

"More like taking candy from a baby."

They snickered like school children.

Completely at home in their surroundings, they showed no concern for waking the old couple as they entered the tidy but outdated kitchen. One of them reached to flip on the light switch, looking around in disgust. "Look at this dump. This place must be fifty years old. Can you believe people actually live like this?"

"Well, not for long, huh?"

That made them start giggling again. They began pulling open kitchen drawers, digging around until one of them let out an excited squeal at finding a large butcher knife. A gloved hand brought it down in a wide arch as the sharp blade carved air in a practice swing.

"Perfect. You ready?"

"I still have to load the gun."

"You should have done that already. For chrissakes..."

"Look, I've never actually fired one before, just handled a prop. I told you that. And this is one of those big ones, a .357."

"Fine. I'll be down the hall. I knew you'd flake on me."

Leaving in a huff, the one with the knife left the kitchen and walked down an unlit hallway using the wall as a guide, heading toward the master bedroom.

Once inside the room, moonlight framed the window, casting eerie silhouettes on the walls. But the intruder never noticed. Standing next to the man's side of the bed, the shadowy figure watched as the old man's chest rose and fell, watched as he slept.

After all the months of planning, it came down to this one moment in time. At the thought of actually plunging the knife into flesh and connecting with bone, the intruder's hands started to shake so much that the knife fell on the ugly, carpeted floor. In the blink of an eye the amphetamine rush faded, offering one last chance for reason. While bending down to retrieve the knife, there was still hope.

They didn't have to do this.

But movement in the doorway added one more shadowy outline to the room.

"You can't do it, can you? All that big talk; all of your big plans. You drag me all the way to Hicksville in the middle of the damn night and can't fucking go through with it."

"Shut up. I'm nervous. That's why I dropped the knife."

"Sure that's it, you're nervous because you've talked this to death until I'm sick of it. Now just when it gets dicey, you want me to do your dirty work. Figures."

As the argument grew more heated, the gun dangerously waved back and forth while the shadows on the wall mimicked their bickering movements.

Despite the sleeping pills earlier, it didn't take long for the loud voices to wake up the woman. She tried to pull herself out of slumber and sit upright. The gun went off. A brilliant flash of gunfire lit up the small bedroom as a bullet entered the woman's chest, sending her backward.

Reacting to the noise, the man attempted to crawl out of bed to try to escape. Another blast pierced the air. It went wide. But then another shot rang out. This time the bullet hit its mark, leaving a hole in the man's head.

The one holding the knife simply stood frozen in place, watching the event play out in slow motion, watched as the couple's blood splattered the headboard, sprayed the walls, and soaked the bed linens.

"Snap out of it. Don't just stand there. It's done now. You know what you have to do, right? The newspaper said the other crime scenes had words written in blood—all over the walls. Can you do that?"

Woodenly the one with the knife nodded.

"Good. Hop to it. I'll go pop open the champagne." She strolled off down the hallway, singing the tune, "We're in the Money".

Knowing what had to be done, the one holding the knife dipped the end of the blade in some of the excess blood. Using the sharp point, the letters began to take shape. Soon the words PIG, DEATH, and DIE, appeared on the wall in blood red. Checking her work, she got a little pissed when she saw that some of the letters had started to run down the wall, spoiling the perfect script. But she really lost it when she looked down and realized some of the old farts' blood had gotten on her dress.

*"Goddamn it! I just bought this outfit two days ago,"
she screamed as she viciously plunged the knife into the
already dead woman before turning to the man and doing
the same thing, hacking into the bodies with a vengeance.*

The clock next to the bed read three minutes past three.

The dream left Kit fog-brained and out of breath like
she'd been running down that dark country road. Trying to
catch her breath, she blinked around her own bedroom.

Total darkness. She fumbled toward the lamp on the
bedside table to turn on the light. Her eyes landed on the
only significant light source, the digital bedside clock,
burning in bright red numerals. A steady 3-0-3 glowed
back at her. Three minutes past three. The exact same time
the couple had died in the dream.

Trembling and sweating after watching the murder play
out, she struggled to get rid of the image of the couple's
eyes as they stared back into hers. Dead eyes.

She had seen two people die right in front of her. No, in
the dream, she corrected. It had been a dream.

Flipping the switch on the lamp, she panicked when the
light didn't come on. With her hands still shaking, she
opened the drawer of the nightstand and felt around for the
flashlight, praying the batteries worked.

Thumbing on the flashlight sent a narrow stream of
light into the dark room.

At that moment, Pepper, who'd been asleep on her bed,
went on alert, letting out a guttural growl. "What's wrong,
boy? You have a bad dream, too?"

But the dog stood up on the bed, turned his attention to
the double French doors at the end of the room. She
directed the flashlight on the doors.

"We need more light," she told the dog. But for an
instant, she was afraid to move from the security of the

covers. It seemed the death scene from the dream still gripped her in fear.

And her dog was still snarling.

She drew in a shaky breath and decided to get up. "Come on Pepper, we need to check the lights." As soon as her feet hit the hardwood floor, she threw on a robe and hurried out to the landing, trying the light switch there. No light. With her flashlight and Pepper at her side, she made her way slowly down the stairs to the second level.

When she got to the living room she flicked on the light switch. No light there either. The electricity was obviously off. With her flashlight, she peered into the open area of the kitchen, which was totally black except for the light from the flashlight. She shined the beam at the old-fashioned wall clock above the stove and saw the time had stopped at 2:30.

Pointing the light in the direction of the microwave, the clock was nothing but a black rectangle.

Rationale left her momentarily as she wondered why the digital clock in the bedroom worked. Then she remembered the clock radio came with a backup battery feature that kept it working in the event of a power failure. Relieved to know the clock worked because of practical technology, she struggled to remember the location of the breaker box. The garage; it's in the garage, she thought. Damn.

While her courage remained at a premium, she quickly took the stairs down to the first level, past the laundry room, and unlocked the door going out to the garage.

Blackness greeted her. Before stepping out into the blackened hole, however, she shined the flashlight under the Jeep and around the sides as best she could. When she determined no monster lurked there, she gingerly stepped out onto the concrete in bare feet. The cold floor had her picking up her pace.

She hurriedly approached the box hung on the sidewall and threw back the metal door casing of the breaker box. Sure enough, each breaker was in the OFF position.

Methodically, she flipped each breaker back to ON. To test her work, as she left the garage, she turned on the light by the door to the laundry room.

Light filled the space, as well as the stairwell. She left the lights on all the way as she and Pepper climbed back up to the second floor.

Once she reached the living room, she flipped on the light switch and sighed when the room lit up like Christmas.

She headed to the kitchen, but got no further than its entrance when fear had her stopping. She thought she heard voices. *I'm losing my mind.* But then the voices grew fainter, and she heard only the familiar sound of ocean surf outside.

Were there tourists walking on the beach at three in the morning? she wondered. Is that why Pepper had growled?

When Pepper gave a half-bark, she looked at him and shook her head. "No way. We are not opening that door and taking a stroll outside now. You'll just have to hold it till morning. Or not. Either way, we're not going out there in the dark."

But her unease didn't abate. Whether it was the disturbing dream or Pepper's behavior, something seemed—off.

To make sure she was alone in the house, she walked each room with Pepper by her side. It took under fifteen minutes for her to determine that no one else was in the house. Still rattled, it was apparent she could not return to sleep in her bedroom. For a moment, she thought of calling the police, but thought better of it. After all, what would she tell them? That she'd had a nightmare and the electricity had gone off and she'd heard voices outside on the beach at three in the morning?

She pictured getting a response from Max St. John. Would he put the cuffs on her right away or simply bypass jail and send her straight to the loony bin?

She considered calling Jake, just to hear his voice, but then remembered he'd had enough to deal with when he'd dropped her off. An image of what they'd almost done on the boat popped into her head and she grew suddenly hot. She desperately wanted to call him. But then realized that's exactly what a love-struck teenage girl might do.

She decided that was a bad idea.

But her mind couldn't shake the dream. She considered calling Gloria, maybe get her take. She had no doubt her aunt would find it fascinating since she'd always believed in stuff like premonitions and woo-woo psychic abilities that included dream interpretations.

Unlike Alana, Kit had never openly criticized Gloria about her weird beliefs. Alana had often called her sister crazy. In fact, over the years when Alana was particularly cruel in her comments regarding Gloria, Kit had staunchly defended her aunt. All those séances, her so-called telepathic visions, her self-proclaimed psychic abilities, might have been unorthodox, but Kit had simply taken it in stride.

But then Gloria had never embarrassed her like she had Alana. There was the time Gloria had taken out her tarot cards in the middle of a party she hadn't been invited to and enlightened the mayor's wife that her husband had been cheating. Now that had been fun to watch. Then there was the time Gloria advised Alana's potential real estate client, a Saudi prince, that it would be unwise to purchase a particular house because evil spirits dwelled there. The prince had found another real estate agent.

Each time Gloria's unconventional moments humiliated her sister, Alana would explode in a verbal attack, calling Gloria everything from a phony to a raging lunatic. Kit came to realize over the years that Gloria was just a bit different, an unconventional sort who marched to the beat of her own drum and was a kick to be around. But in reality, Kit had a harder time with Gloria's beliefs than she'd ever let on. Taking Gloria's side over Alana's was pure instinct, but in truth, Kit had never really put much store in her aunt's weird, woo-woo theories.

Until now.

Bone tired, she decided sorting out the dream at this hour was too much anyway. She decided she might as well go back to bed after all. As she climbed the stairs with Pepper, she couldn't stop thinking about those two old people in the dream. She couldn't get their faces out of her head.

And the killers—were—familiar, the way they spoke to each other, the way they bickered. The images hit a little too close to home.

Maybe she was projecting her own fears from childhood. Maybe it was the stress from the long day, the funeral, the explosion on the water. Maybe all of it had contributed to the dream of witnessing coldblooded murder.

But what exactly had brought the enemy into her head, into her bed and thus, into her sleep. She obviously hadn't put that much behind her.

When she reached her four-poster bed, she got down on her knees and hands to look underneath just in case. Of course, there was no one hiding there.

She crawled back into bed and tried to put Alana and the murder out of her mind, snuggling as far beneath the covers as possible, as if hiding under the covers would alleviate the fear she felt, the aloneness.

She lay there with Pepper by her side half of her afraid to move and the other half afraid not to, scared of returning to sleep, of closing her eyes, wondering if the dreadful nightmare might return.

As the minutes ticked on, she dozed fitfully, drifting between awareness and unconsciousness. But the faces of the murdered people in the dream wouldn't go away, especially the terror she'd seen in their eyes.

And the killers—their faces, those coldblooded eyes wouldn't go away either.

After a time, she gave up the notion of trying to go back to sleep and decided she had to get up in another hour anyway. She curled up under the covers, picked up the remote, clicked on the television, then the VCR.

Her father's image appeared on screen, this time in color, riding on the back of a beautiful black stallion. He delivered his lines, tipping back his tan cowboy hat looking as handsome as she remembered.

She finally drifted off to sleep.

CHAPTER 14

A ringing doorbell roused Kit out of a deep slumber. Before she could crawl out of bed, she had to untangle the sheets and push Pepper off her legs. Meanwhile the doorbell kept ringing. Through bleary eyes, she looked at the clock; it read 6:35. Shit, she'd overslept.

But who on earth would be ringing her doorbell at this hour of the morning? Her mind formed a mental picture of Max St. John and Dan Holloway.

As she grudgingly crawled out of bed, she pictured a contingent of police waiting on her front porch to arrest her, pictured the neighbors leaving their bowls of corn flakes long enough to come out on the street and stare as the police led her away in handcuffs.

And when the doorbell kept ringing she knew it must be the police; why else would they be so impatient? With a sickening dread in her stomach, she took her time making her way downstairs to the second level. The doorbell finally went silent, but seconds later the pounding began.

As soon as her bare feet hit the tiled entryway, an image of Collin Boyd popped into her head. So did fear. Before she ever reached the front door, she yelled at the person on the other side, "I'm armed. I have a vicious attack dog and I've just called the police."

The pounding stopped.

She went closer to the peephole and peered out. Relief washed through her knowing it wasn't the police or Collin. Jake stood there staring back at the front door, looking tired and upset as his hands rested on his hips in a warrior-like stance.

He might as well have been wearing combat fatigues instead of a dark tailored suit with a white dress shirt opened at the collar. Despite the fierce look on his face, a rush of sexual heat sent her glancing at her reflection in the mirror hanging to the right of the door.

She let out a groan. Her hair stuck up in spikes like a punk rocker. But she opened the door anyway with as much panache as she could muster.

"Why are you here so early?"

Jake noticed her rumpled mass of hair and the dark circles under her eyes. But in a matter of seconds his gaze drifted to the silky robe she wore and settled on the peaks of her breasts. She wasn't wearing anything underneath.

Not a stitch.

Kit studied his combative appearance as he charged past her into the hallway. "Early? When you didn't show up for work this morning, and you didn't answer your phone, Baylee got worried, almost closed up the shop to come and check on you. Instead, she called Gloria, Gloria called me. After what happened the other day with Collin, there were people worried about you. I drive like a bat outta hell to get here and find you just wanted to sleep late. Couldn't you have called Baylee and told her that?"

"What are you talking about? I had a rough night." Her temper shot up. "So I'm running later than usual, slept in until six-thirty. I don't understand why you're here so early—and yelling at me."

"Early? It's ten-fifteen. What makes you think it is six-thirty, Kit?"

"The clock in the bedroom said six-thirty."

"Then the clock is wrong." He held out his arm and showed her the time on his wristwatch.

The Rolex read 10:15.

She reached out and grabbed his arm, staring at the time on the watch. She glanced around the living room and then ran to the kitchen. The microwave clock flashed on and off in green digital numbers that blinked 0:00 back at her. The kitchen wall clock showed the time as 8:35. For some reason, she picked up the telephone. "There's no dial tone. The line's dead."

A cold shock went through Jake. He heard her say, "I had an electrical meltdown at three o'clock this morning. The electricity went off. Now the phone's dead. When you rang the doorbell, I thought it was...a lot earlier. The alarm didn't go off." A sob broke out of her throat. "And now you're yelling at me. Why are you yelling at me, Jake?"

"Because...damn it..." He sucked in a breath. "The whole way here I was scared shitless something had happened to you. When Gloria called and said you never showed up for work—"

She launched herself at him.

He caught her, wrapped her up. She stuck like a magnet, molding her body to his. She nuzzled his neck before he reached and covered her mouth. He moved his hand up to her neck to support her head as she ran her hands through his hair.

Kit parted her lips, returned his forceful kiss with a slick one of her own. Desire, greater than before, pulled at her belly. Holding his head with both hands, she encouraged more. Jake responded. He nibbled her ear, nuzzled the hollow of her neck before moving back to her mouth.

He nudged her robe apart.

"God you're beautiful. I want you." His fingers found the swell of a breast and stroked her nipple, popping it to peak. All the while their hungry mouths tugged, nipped.

Kit's hands sought flesh, too. She needed to feel him, all of him. She began pulling his shirt up out of his pants. Working the buttons open, she touched hot skin, ran her fingers over his upper body, felt the strength in his shoulders. He pushed her up against the kitchen wall, found her mouth again for another ravenous feed before traveling downward to her breast. Taking a nipple into his mouth, wrapping his tongue around it, he suckled.

Kit arched her back to give him a better vantage point. She could barely breathe. She captured his head at her breast, encouraging him to take his time. Jake got the message and slowed his efforts. Not only was he responsive, but he proved he could multitask. While his mouth took turns at each breast, his hands rubbed the small of her back then dropped lower to her taut rear, and began moving her hips.

Damn it, he wanted her but not against a wall. He wanted her stretched out, under him. He began moving, backing her up in the direction of the stairs. Their lips locked all the way to the stairwell. Wrapped up in each other, Kit awkwardly pulled him along with her up each step. Slowly, walking backward, she tripped once, but regained her footing, and inch-by-inch continued upward.

This was taking way too long, thought Jake. He stopped his momentum long enough to draw one of her legs up around his body. His weight shifted to take on hers. There was no doubt what he wanted her to do. Her response was quick, athletic, and in one motion she wrapped both of her legs around his body, threw both arms around his neck.

Jake carried her up the rest of the way to the bed.

They both tumbled down on the rumpled sheets. He tenderly began tracing the swell of both breasts, cupping them, before bending his head down to take a nipple in his mouth, sucking, savoring.

She held his head in place until her hands started to peel down his shirt. He pushed off her long enough to loosen his belt, toe off his shoes and socks, and strip off his trousers.

When he turned back to her, a groan as he looked at her on the bed. "My beautiful Kit."

He eased his body next to hers. His erection landed on her belly.

She gaped. *For God's sakes, don't act like you've never seen one before.* When she finally managed to meet his eyes, he was grinning down at her.

His mouth found hers. His tongue sent flitters of delight through her body while his fingers probed her slick core.

Overcome by sensations she'd either never felt or had forgotten existed, she tried to keep up as she sucked feverishly on his tongue. When her body unwittingly shattered with her first orgasm, ever, her mind locked on overload. With so much happening to her at once, so many feelings hitting her that had never happened before, she braced for what she thought was the next logical step.

Lacking a certain amount of finesse, she did everything she could to indicate to Jake that she was ready for that next step. Wanting him, ready for it to happen, she encouraged him, trying to get him to get the hint and pick up his pace. But no matter how much urging or tugging she did, the man purposely slowed his efforts, until finally he said, "There's no rush here."

"I just thought…"

"Stop thinking and feel. I want to give you…" In between deep, wet kisses, "…so much…pleasure…so much of…everything."

What did that mean?

But in less than no time Kit discovered exactly what he meant. She stopped thinking and just…let herself feel. Jake made it easy. This was no eager frat boy, college student, or novice, but a man who knew his way around a woman's body. And to prove it, his mouth moved downward to her breasts, mouthing, tasting, teasing first one nipple until it popped up firm and hard, then the other. He lingered, enjoying each flavor, the suckling of each textured, pebbled point. He took his time exploring, enjoying her moans as he tongued his way down to her taut belly, relished her belly button. He moved down her thighs, kissing, tasting before settling on a spot that had her…tensing, blocking access.

He felt her tighten up, catch her breath, give a push to his head. Warped as he was, her inexperience only aroused him more. In an attempt to get her to relax, he traveled back up to her belly button, licked and tasted there, before moving back down to her center for another try. This time, caught up in the pleasure, she didn't deny him but rather arched her back, moving her hips to the motion of his tongue. Soon her moans became little shrieks of joy.

Even with her release, he put off his own need, wanting her to come…again and again.

Delirious, out of her mind, she hadn't known this existed, had never experienced such giving, such patience. She wanted him, needed him inside her, and she persuaded him to take her by reaching for him, playing under him, bringing his head back up to hers for a devouring kiss. When he rolled to his back, she anticipated that he wanted her on top. No problem there. She straddled him. But he positioned her astride his chest just within reach of his mouth where he began, once again, using his tongue on her. Her last rational thought was that the man was a saint. And when he sent her over the edge, she could do nothing else but throw her head back and ride the wave.

Satiated, she didn't realize their positions had somehow gotten reversed. Lying under him, Jake plunged inside. His body stretched out above hers, Kit wrapped her long legs around his waist, pulling him into her. He deepened his strokes. Slow and rhythmic, Kit moved her hips. She tightened her grip on his rear. As his need became fierce, he penetrated deeper. His deliberate strokes finding their mark, he drove them both to climax.

☙ ☙ ☙ ☙ ☙

After waiting so long for this, he stayed inside her, not moving. He kissed her ear and whispered, "Amazing. You're amazing."

"Me?" She laughed. "You've got to be kidding. That was—off the map."

A slow grin formed. Easing off her, he rolled to his back. Steaming, sweating, they both lay sated. Jake asked, "Is it hot in here, or is it me?"

Still out of breath, Kit puffed out her cheeks. "No, it's hot in here."

In one quick motion, she swung her legs over the side of the bed, and wrapped up in the loose top sheet, told him, "The house doesn't have air conditioning. I'll open the doors, let in some fresh air."

He heard her feet pad across the floor as she made her way to the French doors. The breeze right off the ocean immediately made an impact, stirring the air in the room, making it somewhat cooler. He lifted his head to watch her struggle to walk back over to the bed, enveloped in the sheet.

When her long legs kept getting tangled up in the fabric, preventing her from taking a step, comfortable with him, she simply dropped the sheet to the floor, giving him a sensual view of her naked, athletic form.

She slid in next to him. In spite of the heat in the room, he didn't let her settle on the sheets too long before quickly drawing her over to nuzzle against him.

But Kit had other ideas. Her innate sexual shyness gone, she turned audacious. She'd never been the aggressor, never felt this playful or bold before, never felt the need to offer more. But after what he'd done to her body, she felt different, empowered. She took a deep breath and ran her fingers up and down his chest, ever so lightly, barely touching his skin. She pursed her lips and gently blew air over his hot, sweaty body, moving her head back and forth, hovering over his glistening damp chest to create a cooling effect. She did the same thing when she moved down to his lean belly, but this time she licked away some of the sweat that clung there and blew air onto his stomach.

"Is that better, cooler?"

His low moan told her she was on to something. Jake tried to pull her up to his mouth, but she mischievously resisted, enjoying the play.

In the driver's seat for the first time in her life, she wanted once and for all to make certain that this man no longer thought of her as that teenager he'd once known. She wanted that image completely erased from his brain, wanted him to know the full grown woman could be aggressive, assertive, and just as giving.

To prove her point, she sat astride his body, intentionally letting him hunger for her touch, taking her time, working her way up his body; finally reaching his mouth, lingering there long enough to suck on his lips, she played with his tongue before moving to his chest, licking each nipple, leaving a wet trail downward.

Barely touching his skin with light kisses, she moved down to his hard belly, where she worked to gently caress skin, then moved lower, tantalizing him, stroking him with her tongue until she took him into her mouth. Caught up in the play, running on sheer instinct, she didn't notice his moans had grown louder. It was then she took him into her. This time it was her turn to set the pace. She rode him fiercely then enticed him with slower strokes before quickening to fast and furious until they exploded into each other again.

Kit fell on top of him, breathless, sweaty, and exhausted.

Their strength depleted, they lay next to each other on their backs, trying to cool off. When Jake finally caught his breath, he reached for her. She turned and moved into his chest. He gently ran his fingers through her damp hair, playing with several wet strands before turning his attention to the curve of her body. He moved his fingers along her shape. As he held her close, he turned her face up to his. "Listen, you can hear the sound of the surf from the open doors. I could listen to that sound all day, all night. I can't think of a better sound for making love than the sound of the ocean. I love that sound."

"Mmmm, peaceful. I love living by the water, at the beach." Remembering his sailboat, what they didn't get to finish yesterday, she wanted to know, "What's it like to make love on a boat?"

"I was hoping we'd find out yesterday."

She looked at him like he was nuts. "Oh, come on, Jake, you don't expect me to believe you've had your boat all this time and haven't had a woman on board."

He grazed on her shoulder, then her neck, moved on to her lower lip. "It's true. You'd be the first. I was hoping we'd take care of that yesterday, but we got interrupted." Neither of them mentioned they'd almost been blown to bits.

"You really know what you're doing. I've never experienced anything like that before. For me, that was... no one's ever...well...I've never...had the big O before."

He lowered his gaze to those trusting green eyes. "Never? You're kidding, right?" Was she just saying that to bolster his ego?

"Nope. That was the first. And then I had..." She started counting on her fingers.

But Jake knew the count. "Four more, five total."

"You're right. Five. Wow. Could you...like...spread that out...over time?" She could do a happy dance right there between the sheets.

He ran his hands over her again, liking the feel of her. He was pretty sure this afternoon there were a lot of firsts in this bed. "And I take it no one's ever...taken the time to give you...oral before today."

She blew air into her cheeks and blushed. "Oh. Well. No. That was a first too, and ..I...was...uh....you know...sort of nervous about it." Kit thought for a moment and giggled. "I had to wait for this so long. Great sex makes up for all the times you were such a jerk to me."

He looked nonplussed for a moment, then said, "Ah. About that. I've been thinking. That isn't entirely true, that I was such a jerk to you. To some extent maybe so, but think back, you used to talk to me about the music you liked. At the time, Pearl Jam was your favorite group back then, as I recall. Do you remember?"

Perplexed at what her musical tastes back then had to do with anything, she said, "So?"

"Well, you went on and on once about wanting the Pearl Jam CD *No Code* more than life itself as I recall, and Alana wouldn't let you buy it. If I ignored you completely, how is it I bought it for you, left it in the file room on top of the filing cabinet with a note and a little pink bow on it? That's what I remember."

All at once, Kit sat up, clutched her heart, thrilled at the idea that he'd listened to her back then about the simplest thing as a music CD. "Oh my God, you bought that for me. How could I have forgotten that? Alana wouldn't let me buy it even with my own money. I remember bitching to you about that. And you bought it for me. I hid it from her in my special hiding place under the dresser in my bedroom, only played it when she wasn't at home."

Grateful, she launched herself at his chest, hugging him. "That was so sweet of you."

Jake found her reaction both amusing and touching. "I just want to make sure I understand this; because I bought you a CD, I've gone from being a rude, arrogant SOB, the scum of the earth, all the way to sweet?"

"I like knowing you listened to me, paid enough attention to what I wanted back then, that's all." As if very appreciative, she put her lips to his and gave him a deep kiss.

"If I get that kind of reaction to buying you a simple CD, what would happen if I gave you something nice now?"

She gave him a puzzled look. "You just gave me something nice, something very nice, something I've never had before." She held up her right hand in a gesture of honor, playfully, teasing him. "And I promise from this day forward never to give you a moment's grief about how much control you have. You were incredible."

And they both dived for each other again.

&&&&&

He liked Beverly Hills. What was not to like? It was the cleanest city he'd ever seen. He even got a kick out of Rodeo Drive, where he strolled down a narrow street that looked more like it belonged somewhere in Europe than it did in Los Angeles. He walked past Cartier's and window shopped at Armani before moving on to Neiman Marcus. There he actually went inside.

He had time before his next intervention, and what better place to spend time than here, among the world's richest people, the stores where they shopped, where the wealthy splurged on whatever whims caught their fancy?

It was really karma, he told himself. In life, they humored and gratified themselves with whatever whenever the mood hit them, doing it all without a backward glance to consequences. Like the Boyd, Geller, and Gatz clans and their massive greed. The philosopher in him kicked in. Well, it was payback time; time to pay the piper. The bill had come due for all of them.

And he was the collector.

He spent another hour walking around until he looked at his watch and realized it was time, time to go to work. Pulling out of the parking lot, he once again headed to Malibu.

As he had with Jessica Boyd, he was sitting in the backseat waiting for Eva Gatz when she crawled behind the wheel of her sleek late-model Jaguar and turned the key. Because the backseat of the Jag wasn't as roomy as the backseat of Jessica's Benz, the cramped space had caused the muscles in his back to tighten and his leg hurt.

He was obviously getting too old for this shit. His mood was a little dark, maybe on the bad-tempered side, so when she fought the hand over her mouth, when she screamed and tried to wriggle out of the car, it pissed him off. "I don't want to kill you right here, but I will. Now stop the fucking screaming. Got it?"

At the nod of her head, he told her, "We're going for a little ride, to the place your kind wanted so much you were willing to kill to get it."

"I'll give you anything you want; any amount of money; anything, just please, please don't hurt me."

"Now that just pisses me off even more, lady. I don't want your fucking money. Come to think of it, it isn't even your money, now is it? But I'm getting ahead of myself. We'll take a little ride, have a little talk. Then we'll take a short walk down memory lane. Rumor has it you're an even smarter legal eagle than Jess was. Is that true?" He didn't expect an answer and simply added, "You're going to need all the smarts you can manage."

It was just after two in the afternoon when Jake stepped back inside Kit's kitchen. After taking a walk around the house, it hadn't taken long to discover why her phone didn't work. Someone had cut the phone line.

His money was on Collin Boyd.

As he scoured the refrigerator for eggs and vegetables to make omelets, he wondered if it would do any good to call the police. Even now, as he began to chop shitake mushrooms and spinach and melt butter in a skillet, he wondered if the cops would do anything. He decided they might not, but at least they'd have a report on file should they need it.

He had to tell Kit.

Jake heard her big feet bounding down the stairs, and in anticipation of her walking into the kitchen got a funny feeling in his gut. He'd just had fantastic sex. He briefly turned from the stove to glance in her direction as she bounced into the room. Just looking at her made the feeling in his stomach move lower. And pure lust slammed him. He'd just shared an incredible morning with this woman but he wanted more, much more.

The aroma of coffee hit her the minute she stepped into the kitchen. She poured herself a much-needed cup and leaned against the counter closest to the stove. As she turned to take a sip of hot coffee, she noticed he was staring at her. She put down the cup and crossed to where he stood at the stove, wedged her body between his and the appliance and wrapped her arms around him, gave him a deep kiss.

Breaking apart, he patted her on the rear, telling her, "If I didn't hear your stomach growling, I'd take you back upstairs. But you need food."

She went to the table, watched as Jake beat eggs, poured the egg mixture into an omelet pan, grated some cheese, and sprinkled a generous portion on top of the sautéing vegetables. Even though he looked as if he had breakfast well in hand, she asked anyway, "Can I do something to help?"

He shook his head, "Nope, I know what I'm doing."

And did he ever, she thought, as she stared at him standing at the stove with his back to her. Watching him cook caused her juices to flow—again.

She'd just had the best sex ever. And now understood for the first time what Baylee and Quinn had tried to explain to her all those years before. Great sex made a difference. And then it hit her—was it just about the sex for him? The thought caused a sick feeling in her gut. Well, she'd wanted him to treat her just like he'd treated every other woman, hadn't she?

She suddenly took a long look at him at the stove. He was fixing her breakfast in the middle of the afternoon when he should be at work tending to his own problems, but here he was unselfishly—and then it dawned on her. The thought speared straight to her heart. She almost fell out of the chair as the idea sank in. Good God, I'm in love with him—and it's a hundred times worse than what I felt at fifteen. The shock of it inexplicably had her blurting out, "Shit. Shit."

"What's wrong?"

She hid her thoughts with aplomb, took a sip of strong coffee hoping it might ward off insanity. God, he'd run like a deer if he knew how she felt. So she lied. "Uh, I was just wondering…how…why do you suppose my phone went dead?"

"Because someone cut the line outside. Did you turn your cell phone back on?"

"Cut the line?" The warm, fuzzy feeling of love shifted into cold, hard fear. "Collin," she said with dread.

"That'd be my guess. I'd even venture to say he had something to do with that boat exploding. What exactly happened here last night, Kit?"

Should she mention the nightmare about the elderly couple? She decided to keep that to herself. She closed her eyes, let the caffeine kick in, and went into a detailed account of what happened.

When she finished, the look on Jake's face told her he was having trouble with the logic of it. "I don't think it's a coincidence that both the electricity went off and the phone went dead at the same time. That only happens during a bad storm. And those breakers didn't flip by themselves."

The idea of that gave her chills.

Jake slid a perfect omelet onto a plate and set it down on the table. "From what I saw of Collin, you have reason to fear him. He's obsessed with you."

Famished from not having eaten since yesterday, Kit attacked the eggs. Without answering Jake, she focused on the tasty omelet.

But when she didn't answer, Jake persisted, "How long have you had this problem with Collin?"

In between mouthfuls of egg, she said, "I told you we grew up together."

"That doesn't answer my question. You were kids then. The man that showed up on your doorstep is dangerous. You can see it in his eyes."

"I see it. Why do you think I didn't want to be alone with him? I've seen that look in his eyes for years and tried to avoid him. Fortunately, I stopped spending summers at The Enclave when I was twelve. My situation changed somewhat at the time and I gained a little leverage over Alana. So the summer visits stopped. But I was still near Collin in school and then around him whenever we ended up at the same kid parties, that type of thing. But every time he'd ask me out, I always said no. Much to Alana's regret. You can bet, I did my best to avoid being alone with him over the years. I knew how he felt. I knew he wanted something more. I've known it for a long time." She thought about all the times he'd bullied her, how many times he'd hit her. She remembered the time he'd cornered her in the cabana.

"You've had other encounters with him where you've had to call the police."

She took a long time before she said anything. "Yeah. Once when I was in college. But I wasn't alone then. Quinn and Baylee were there. Then there was the one I mentioned two years ago. He showed up here, unannounced, and drunk. He got physical, started pushing me around, but I slugged him and got away; ran next door to my neighbor's and called the cops. This isn't Beverly Hills. This time when they got here, they arrested him, made the man cool his jets overnight in a county holding cell until he made bail. That pissed off Sumner and Jessica. Their anger wasn't directed at their son, of course, but rather at me for getting him in trouble. Somehow, the whole thing ended up being my fault. Couple of days later, Alana called and tried to persuade me to drop the charges."

Jake fumed. "Have there been any other strange events like the dead telephone and the electricity since Alana's murder?"

"What about almost getting blown up yesterday? Don't forget that."

"I haven't forgotten. Anything else?"

She hesitated. "Just the weird dream I had last night. This omelet's good, very good, best omelet I've ever tasted. How'd you get to be such a good cook?"

"You're ravenous; you'd have eaten anything I put in front of you and said the same thing. I cook one thing well, omelets. You've just eaten the specialty of the house." He watched her enjoy the food. "What kind of a dream?"

The man was persistent. "It was kinda weird."

"Kinky weird?"

She laughed and took another bite. "I like a man who can cook. It's an extremely sexy thing for a man to cook for a woman."

"How sexy?"

"Very."

"Are you going to tell me about the dream?"

"You'll just think I'm crazy."

"I won't."

"You don't let go of an issue, do you?" Giving in to his determined look, she told him, "I dreamed about this couple, two older people, asleep in their bed—or rather, they're murdered in their bed at three minutes past three in the morning. I know because in the dream there was this old fashioned alarm clock by the bed. The time read a few minutes past three. And that's what time I woke up."

"You see the exact time on the clock? That's a pretty detailed dream, Kit."

"It is."

"And how exactly are these two people murdered?" He sat down at the table, indicated with his hand that he wanted more details. "Let's hear it all."

"Well, the couple looks like they're maybe in their late sixties. They live out in the country, like on a ranch or something, very isolated. They're asleep, sleeping in a back bedroom. These two people show up and go into their house...it's dark...one goes into the bedroom down this long hallway carrying a knife, but when she gets to the bed, for some reason she can't kill them, like she's having second thoughts or something. But then, her partner has a gun, and when she comes into the bedroom she gets angry that the one with the knife hasn't killed them yet. They have a heated argument. The noise wakes up the woman, and when she sits up, bam, the one with the gun shoots the woman, then the man. I think the dream is about a murder that's already happened because the house looks old, like maybe it's from another decade. The car, however, looks like a new model, but it's dusty from the country road. And the furnishings inside the house look old." When she noticed his stare, as if he were having a hard time grasping the concept, she stopped.

"Your dream is so detailed you see all that right down to what the house looked like and the furniture? And the car has dust on it from the road?"

"Oh yeah, the dream is very vivid, in color. I see what kind of car the killers drive: a Mercedes, a white one with tan interior. And when the car turns off the road, as they drive down the long gravel driveway, they drive past an old wooden sign painted white with orange lettering that says...hmmm, that's weird, I can't recall what the sign says, but it's the name of the ranch. The name of the ranch is on the sign in orange letters.

"And the blood...I see all the blood after the couple dies, the blood's everywhere, on the walls, the headboard, the floor, the bedding." She paused long enough to rub her arms as if she'd just gotten a chill. "But that isn't the worst part. One of the killers dips the knife into the victim's blood and uses it to write graffiti on the walls with the knife. Ewww, that part's just gross."

"What?" The hair stood up on the back of his neck.

"Yeah, I know, it's disgusting. But one of them writes the words, PIG, DEATH, and DIE on the bedroom walls in blood. I see the murder scene, the bedroom; I see all the blood and the graffiti written on the walls in detail; it's horrible, Jake. It's the worst nightmare I've ever had, and believe me, I've had some doozies. And after they kill this old couple, one of them goes into the kitchen, opens a bottle of Dom Pérignon, starts chugging it down before the other one comes back into the kitchen. I see them celebrate with a whole bottle of champagne, toasting, laughing, and singing, *We're in the Money*."

Jake had a stunned look on his face. "Kit, do you realize you've just described a crime scene that's eerily similar to the murders the Manson family committed back in 1969?"

"Wow. It is, isn't it? Wow. That might explain why the dream looks like it takes place in another era, why the furnishings look so old, like they belong in the '60s. It explains why the Mercedes looks brand new but is a dated model now."

"The killers drive a Mercedes. I think that rules out Manson."

"You know I could do some research online, find out more details about the Manson murders."

Just then the doorbell rang, causing Pepper to let out a low guttural growl. Kit frowned at her usually docile dog, looking at Jake and then back at the dog before Pepper trotted off to the front door, alternating between barking and growling. The last time Pepper acted like that...

"He's been doing that a lot lately."

"What? Growling?"

"Yeah."

Jake trailed after the dog, was the first one to reach the front door and look through the peephole. He groaned.

Curious, Kit stood behind him, and when he moved she took her turn looking—and stared at Dan Holloway and Max St. John. At the sight of both of them standing on her porch looking perturbed, Kit went white. "Is it significant they're here at the house?"

Even though Jake thought differently, he tried his best to sound convincing when he said, "Don't read anything into it. Just remember, if at any time you don't want to answer a question, just tell them you want a lawyer. Be insistent. That will end the interview and they'll have to leave or..."

Kit knew what that meant and told him emphatically, "If they arrest me, call your friend Reese. I'm not relying on a Boyd or a Geller or a Gatz for my freedom." Noticing Jake had a strange look on his face; Kit suddenly understood his anxiety and her heart went out to him. "Oh, Jake, you can't be happy to see St. John here. This is too much, I'm sorry Gloria dragged you into this mess."

"It isn't that. But I don't think my being here will help you any. It didn't the other day at the bookstore. It just made St. John more determined." He rubbed the back of his neck and reached to open the door. "Let's just get this over with."

CHAPTER 15

Boston and Griffin. Together. The idea rankled St. John as he followed Holloway into the living room and settled next to his partner on the sofa. When St. John looked up, he met the cold hard glare of the angry man sitting across from him on the opposite couch.

The two men had stared each other down at Alana's funeral, and now, Jake sat with his jaw clenched, looking like he might explode from the tension. St John did his best to ignore him, concentrated instead on the woman in question; who stood with her arms wrapped around herself in a protective lock, and noted how nervous she was.

Holloway, the good cop, started the interview with a gentle voice, wanting to know, "Ms. Griffin, we need you to tell us more about the relationship with your mother. Tell us about the abuse. When did it start? When did it stop? The neighbors tell us you rarely saw your mother these days, that they rarely saw you at the house after you moved out as a teen."

What was he saying? She'd never once gone back to that house after she'd moved out. Thinking back to her past, a cool, detached mask slid over her face. She started to feel pressure build up in her chest just as it had so many other times when she'd talked about her childhood with Dr. Strasburg. She tried to make herself relax. "That's true," she said barely above a whisper.

She looked into Dan Holloway's dove gray eyes for any friendly sign. Despite the soft voice, those eyes didn't relay an ounce of sympathy but rather cold hard steel rods searching for the truth.

She reminded herself that he was simply doing his job. This time she needed to do better, answer his questions. She wouldn't freeze up. She'd focus. If she didn't answer correctly—there was so much on the line now. Jake was in her life. She had so much to look forward to. She noticed Holloway's mouth moving.

"You want to elaborate?"

"There were the usual bruises and broken bones." Now she was wringing her hands.

She heard Holloway suck in a breath, heard an impatient voice coming from St. John, the bad cop. "You inherit your mother's sizeable fortune, an estate that amounts to millions, and you act as if you don't really care that she's dead. You didn't cry at the funeral. You didn't seem all that upset when we told you she'd been murdered, brutally." He let the words stick, before adding, "When was the last time you saw her?"

Kit drew in a deep breath, let it out. Her eyes glazed over. "The first of January, her birthday. I dressed up, wore a dress. I always wore a dress, had to; she wouldn't allow me to wear jeans. She didn't like it when I wore pants of any kind. Let's see, where did we eat? Oh. We had lunch at Luigi's; she had the shrimp scampi. I had the broiled chicken. The meal lasted an hour and a half." Ninety long minutes, she remembered now. "I gave her a five-hundred-dollar Cartier's gift certificate. Anything less would have been unacceptable. Cartier's was one of her favorite places to shop."

Jake noticed Kit had that distant, faraway look in her eyes. They'd asked her about the last time she'd seen her mother, and she was talking about lunch. He wanted to wrap his arms around her, get her away from these two cops. Couldn't they see how much it hurt her to talk about the past? Short of butting in like he'd done at the bookstore, mentioning an attorney, he wasn't sure what else he could do. And damn, if she wasn't doing it again, speaking in that detached, unemotional tone, as if she were bored with the subject at hand when the subject at hand was the death of her mother.

Jake watched both detectives. The good cop looked as if he wanted to shake some feeling into her, and Max St. John was simply so red in the face that when he spoke Kit jumped at the sound of his voice. "Look, Ms. Griffin, your mother was a wealthy woman, and yet robbery wasn't a motive; nothing was taken from the house. Not a piece of artwork, not a book, no loose change. Maybe you woke up on Mother's Day—of all days—and decided if she intended to cut you out of her will it was time you did something. So you decided to put twenty-one stab wounds in her as your way of saying, hey mom, Happy Mother's Day."

Kit visibly paled, wincing at his callous phrasing. She grabbed at that veil of cool indifference and, in a calm tone, defended herself. "I didn't kill her. I don't want her money. I never...expected it."

Jake wasn't buying that coolness she was trying so hard to exhibit. When he saw that her hands were shaking, he dragged her down to sit next to him on the sofa. The minute she made eye contact with him he noticed she acted as if she'd just realized he was in the room. Her knees were shaking so much he put his hand on her thigh to calm her down.

Holloway picked up the pace. "Okay, so there were hard feelings between the two of you about the abuse. Understandable. If you could talk to us, give us your side of the story, help us better understand how you felt."

Stony silence.

Holloway tried again. "Did the two of you ever get along?"

She shook her head.

Holloway and St. John exchanged furtive glances, but it was Holloway who continued, "Maybe there's someone we could talk to, someone who knows your side of the story."

"My side of the story?" Kit looked genuinely confused.

Jake had to hand it to Kit; no matter how the detectives pushed, she managed to stay on the offense. The only question was how long she could keep it up. If she could just show a tad more emotion...

But just then St. John erupted, losing all patience. He snapped out, "The coroner determined this morning Jessica Boyd's death was the result of homicide. You should know we consider you the link to both murders. Where were you Monday night, the night Jessica Boyd died, say between ten o'clock and two in the morning?"

Kit's answer was quick, and Jake had no time to answer for her. "Probably sleeping."

But St. John wasn't the only one who'd lost patience. Jake spoke up, stating flatly, "The night Jessica Boyd died, Kit was with me."

"Ms. Griffin says she was sleeping. Now she was with you? Which is it?"

Jake stared at St. John in disbelief. "If you think about it long enough, you'll figure it out. We were together the entire night Jessica Boyd ended up dead. As you recall, we were together at the bookstore and from that time on into the next morning. Kit couldn't have killed Jessica Boyd. I have a receipt from the restaurant here in San Madrid where we had dinner. You can talk to the waiters to verify how long we were there. The rest of the evening, you'll just have to take my word for it, we were together all night."

But St. John wasn't giving up. "It doesn't take her off the hook for her mother's murder, now does it? Unless, of course, you're willing to provide her with a much-needed alibi for Saturday night or early Sunday morning, let's say between the hours of seven o'clock Saturday night and noon Sunday."

But Jake was just as stubborn. "You just said you considered the two murders connected and that Kit was the link to both. Kit has an alibi for one. As I see it, you've just lost your link."

Holloway changed tactics, putting his hands up for peace. "Let's back up for now. What about your mother's ex-husbands? What do you remember about them?"

"I don't remember much about the men she married after my father. They weren't around long enough. For all I know, husband number two might have been Smith or Jones. Look, I just don't remember; I was three at the time. She married the other guy when I was five. As a child, I remember thinking his name sounded a lot like an Italian tuna. You'll have to get the rest of the details about her marriages from public records."

Jake watched Holloway pull two plastic evidence bags from his jacket pocket. He held them up to Kit. "Have you ever seen these two items before?"

Taking her hands for the first time out of Jake's grasp, she took both bags from Holloway. It didn't take long for her to recognize the contents. The bags held identical gold-minted cowboys, the same heavy feel and depiction of a cowboy sitting atop his horse in front of a rounded sunset in the background like the one she'd found at work by the cash register. A sick feeling came over her when she remembered that she'd thought it resembled her father.

"They're just like the one I found at the store."

St. John and Holloway exchanged looks. Holloway wanted to know, "You found one of these at the bookstore?"

Kit got up, walked over to her desk under the stairwell and retrieved the gold cowboy from her purse. She held the bags up as well as the loose cowboy. "See, it matches the ones you have in the bags."

Holloway met Kit at the desk, examining them all. "We have cowboy number three. You say you found this in the store? When?"

"Last Tuesday. It was sitting on the counter by the cash register. I thought maybe a child lost it and Baylee picked it up, put it there for safekeeping. But Baylee didn't know anything about it."

"Could these cowboys have belonged to your mother?"

She shook her head with certainty. "Oh no. They didn't belong to Alana. Even if they are pure gold, Alana would not have owned anything so...so western, for lack of a better word. She would not have allowed these in her house. Where did you get them?"

It was St. John who answered. "One came from the front seat of Jessica Boyd's car. The other one—the coroner found stuffed down your mother's throat."

Kit dropped all three cowboys to the floor with a thud. The loose one scattered under the desk. She glared at the detective. "That's disgusting. You did that on purpose."

Up to this point Jake had been fairly patient, but eyeing how upset Kit was pushed him to tell both detectives, "That little stunt was uncalled for. You obviously have no leads. If you had leads, you wouldn't have had to resort to something so base. It seems all you've got is a daughter who didn't get along with her mother. Here's a news flash, guys, lots of people didn't get along with Alana. As I see it, the killer has just handed you a connection tying the two murders together, and you're sitting here throwing accusations at Kit."

Kit swallowed hard and spoke up with a renewed interest. "Someone took great pains to have those cowboys custom minted, not to mention the intricate artwork that went into the detailed sunset in the background. That kind of detail had to cost a small fortune, considering that the pieces are made from pure gold. The fact that the pieces must be from a matching set only increases their value."

As Holloway bent down to pick up the three gold cowboys from the floor, he smiled. "Give the lady a prize, Max. That's exactly what we think both pieces came from...a matched set. And now we have a third."

Jake pointed out, "And you don't see that maybe Kit isn't your suspect here but rather a potential target? Why leave one of those trinkets for her to find unless the killer wanted her to know he was out there?"

Or, thought Holloway, it's the killer's way of telling us she's not the killer.

It was St. John who said, "But that's just it, Mr. Boston. Ms. Griffin supposedly found this at her store and she's alive, the only one that is. The other two are deader than dirt, now aren't they? How come Ms. Griffin here is so special that he doesn't kill her? How do I know for sure that she didn't just hand us one of these toy trinkets to throw us off?"

Jake was up off the couch like a shot. "So let me make sure I understand this. You're saying that because she isn't dead, because the killer hasn't gotten around to killing her yet, you think this is some kind of ploy on her part. Maybe there's some order to his killing. Did you ever think of that? Maybe he just hasn't come around to Kit—yet."

Jake threw his hands in the air. "You guys never change. What exactly passes for an actual investigation where you come from? She has an alibi for the night Jessica died. She willingly offers you the gold cowboy she found at the store. As I see it, you should be protecting Kit from whoever's out there killing women, not harassing her."

Kit was convinced that the only thing that kept the two men from going after each other right there in her living room was the ringing of St. John's cell phone.

She watched as St. John excused himself from the living room and headed off to the neutral corner of the entryway. The other three waited without talking as they caught only muffled parts of St. John's conversation.

When he hung up, he looked at Holloway and said, "There's been a development. Jessica Boyd's sister, Eva Geller Gatz, one of the partners at the law firm, is missing. Has been since around lunchtime. They found her car abandoned at some rundown strip shopping center in the Hollywood Hills. There was blood on the front seat."

"Missing since noon? If this one turns up dead too, that's another murder you won't be able to pin on Kit. She for goddamned sure wasn't in Hollywood this afternoon. Sorry to disappoint you, but she's been with me...all afternoon."

The two men glared at each other for several heated seconds before Holloway walked past Jake, grabbed his partner's arm and moved him in the direction of the front door.

Reluctantly, St. John went.

When the two cops were finally gone, Jake turned to her with such intensity she thought he might hit something.

"That man's no different than when he investigated Claire's murder. He's looking in the wrong fucking direction, focused on the wrong person...again. The Gatz woman turns up missing; if you ask me, that's another link to the law firm, and St. John is too goddamned stubborn to admit the connection. Did it ever occur to him that all three of these murders have been women, older women, somehow connected to BBG&G? Why is that?"

Of course there was a connection, but with everything happening, she'd shut that part off. But when she saw the look on Jake's face, saw his jaw lock in place, something inside her melted.

Knowing he needed to calm down, she softly said, "Jake, don't think about it anymore. If they arrest me, if it happens, I'll deal with it. I'll call that lawyer, that friend of yours, and let him handle everything. We're not going to worry about this anymore now."

"Like hell we won't. That man is not going to do to you what he did to me. That SOB made my life a living hell for a year. Since St. John doesn't seem to want to do any real police work, can't seem to focus on any suspect other than you, we need to find him another suspect, someone that takes the heat off you. Knowing Alana, the suspect list should be longer than the Bible. So we start looking into Alana's past, hand St. John some other possibilities." He walked over to Kit's desk, opened her laptop, and booted it up. "It's time to do a little searching and investigating on our own."

For the next hour, Jake put his hacker skills to work. He started his search with a public records database, specifically marriages. Something Kit had said to the detectives about Alana's marriages had him curious. Had Alana actually been married only three times? It was common knowledge she went through men like water through a sieve. He'd seen it for himself. And besides, he had a hunch. He'd learned a long time ago that when you have a hunch you simply run with it until you hit a brick wall.

Searching public records, he got five hits. Like every other aspect of her life, Alana Stevens had not been entirely truthful about her marriages. No surprise there. But the additional divorce information he wanted took less time to find than her marriages. And it was as he'd feared. The divorce information had been there all along for anyone to find if they had bothered looking. And in the end, the information was one more revelation that Kit would have to deal with. After hitting the print button, he looked up from the laptop only to realize she'd left the room.

He found her in the kitchen clearing away the dishes. And her face told him she suspected something was up.

"What did you find?"

"Listen to me, Kit. What I found is all about Alana. It has nothing to do with what kind of a person you are. I mean, it was Alana's life, her mess, her lies."

He handed her the computer printouts, one listing Alana's five marriages, the other listing her five divorces. He watched her study the names, the dates, look from one printout to the other, until finally she said, "This can't be right, Jake."

"The information came directly from public records, Kit. You yourself said that Holloway should get the info from public records. That's what made me think to do just that." He tugged on the piece of paper she held in her hands. "This is it."

"But this doesn't list a marriage to John Griffin or a divorce from him, either. That can't be right. There's no mention of my father here. And none of these dates fit the right timeframe for when I was born. According to these records, Alana wasn't married to anyone when I was born."

Jake nodded. "And if there was never a marriage, there was no contentious divorce."

"How can that be? They both told me time and time again they'd been married and divorced. Why lie about that?"

"They obviously wanted you to believe it."

"Because they weren't married when I was born, is that it? Keep the information from the child for the benefit of the child. Does that sound like Alana to you? I'm not surprised she didn't tell me the truth, but what about him? He lied to me. The father I trusted never told me the truth."

"I'm sorry, Kit."

"Okay, they kept that from me. My parents weren't married, big deal. But it does explain a lot about their private war. Maybe I was the result of a one-night stand or maybe a rape, something that happened at one of their decadent Hollywood parties and that's why Alana never liked him or me. Every time she looked at me I was a reminder of that night or that party or something horrible." When she saw the skeptical look on his face, she added, "Well, think about it. She certainly didn't like him, and I know she didn't like me. That much was genuine. Something bad had to have happened between the two of them."

Jake didn't want to speculate, so he switched to the computer printout, to the facts. "This says she was married three times before you were ever born, the first time in 1967 to a William Forrester, an environmental engineer, of all things. Can you see Alana married to any kind of an engineer? He listed his place of employment as McKetrick Construction. Talk about opposites, and they divorce after only a few months of marriage."

Reading from the list, Kit added, "Her second marriage to Robert Carlton, a real estate developer, lasts a little longer. Now that's more her style: a developer, a rich guy with money. They were divorced two years later."

"And look at lucky number three. Frank Geller. Jessica's brother. There's a surprise."

"Oh. I was almost related to the Boyds by association or something. It's a good thing that marriage took place before I came along. Again though, it didn't last long. Years go by before she marries again. I was five years old when she marries number four, Anthony Tunicelli, from Las Vegas."

"And then, there's husband number five. Four years ago, she marries one of her real estate agents, Scott Barlow, fifteen years her junior. Maybe he's our suspect. The other day when I went through some of the paperwork you dropped off, it was apparent Alana was taking an extra cut from her agents on top of her regular commission. That might not sound like much, but when you consider all the commercial real estate she handled, she took in a lot of money under the table from her agents. Maybe this guy this, Scott Barlow, got tired of paying an extra cut and killed her."

"Okay, that might explain Alana's murder. But Jake, what possible connection would her real estate agents, including this Scott Barlow, have with Jessica or Eva Gatz? And then there are those three gold cowboys, two of which were with Alana and Jessica. Why would Scott Barlow kill Jessica?"

"I wished you'd told me that you found that gold cowboy at the store. I'd say the killer's been to the Book & Bean."

That was creepy. She thought of that strange man who'd been in the store the other day, but then remembered she'd found the cowboy earlier before he'd even showed up that afternoon.

Jake looked at Kit. "There's no suspect here, is there?"

Kit shook her head. "Doesn't look like it. But I still haven't recovered from knowing they lied to me, Jake, about their marriage. Do you think Gloria knew? We need to ask Gloria about all of this." She immediately got up from the table and walked to the phone but then remembered it didn't work. She reached for her cell. Jake put his hand on hers before she could dial.

"Baby, it's late." He pushed her hair off her shoulders to give him better access and nibbled her neck while his hands encircled her breasts, his fingers found their points until she moaned.

"We'll ask Gloria whatever you want to ask, just tomorrow; let's ask tomorrow." He knew if she found out something bad from Gloria, she wouldn't sleep a wink. So he tried to distract her.

She let him graze on her neck, let his fingers work the magic before melding her body to his. She gave in with a sigh. "You're right. It's late; let's go to bed."

With L.A. traffic in typical gridlock, it took St. John and Holloway two hours to make the drive from San Madrid to the Hollywood Hills. The Gatz car had been found parked near an abandoned strip shopping center.

By the time they arrived, a patrolman had discovered the body of Eva Geller Gatz some two hundred yards from her Jaguar. She'd been shot in the left temple, just like Jessica, this time with a .38.

Sometime later, it was another detective who pointed out a shiny gold trinket left on the passenger seat of her car. The trinket depicted a cowboy riding off into the sunset.

The questions came like the opening of a floodgate. Why had the killer brought Eva Gatz to a rundown storefront in the Hollywood Hills? And once here, how had he left the area?

It was St John who had trouble defending his position. "Okay, the Boyd woman was shot, just like this one. I know what you're thinking. Kit Griffin has an alibi for

Jessica Boyd and the Gatz woman. She still could have filleted her own mother. The two didn't get along and she inherits everything. Despite the gold cowboys he's left behind, tell me, if it's the same killer, why shoot the Boyd woman and now Gatz but stab Alana Stevens twenty-one times with a knife? We have different murder weapons. It's just too early for me to merge the three together. I'm still convinced Kit Griffin killed her mother. I agree that the same killer killed the Boyd woman and now Gatz. But we don't try to link these two with the Stevens murder."

But Holloway was unconvinced. "I might buy that if I could discount the three gold cowboys. And the gold thing was stuffed down Alana's throat. Maybe the killer had cause to hate her a little more than he did Jessica and Eva. And come on, Max, you can't tell me you don't see the look in Kit Griffin's eyes every time we talk to her about her mother. That distant, unemotional tone isn't an act. It's like she goes someplace else so she can deal with anything that has to do with her mother."

When St. John made no comment he went on, "The gold trinkets show up with each murder victim. And now we find out that maybe the killer left one of these gold things at her store. Why would he do that unless he put it there specifically so we'd know she didn't do it? Did you consider that? Sounds crazy, I know, but maybe we're dealing with a psycho. What's the significance of these cowboys? The killer's leaving something of himself with each victim. You know Kit Griffin's father was a cowboy actor. I checked. Maybe he isn't dead at all. My vote is we start from scratch and find out what happened to John Griffin, the cowboy star."

Reluctantly, St. John agreed, but added, "I'm not ready to discount the fact that Kit Griffin had motive in her mother's murder. The inheritance is motive. And she's hanging out with Jake Boston. We just may have to dig a little deeper to find what we need."

CHAPTER 16

*S*he heard the loud rock music blaring from inside the car first before she watched the Mercedes make the sharp turn onto that familiar gravel driveway and drive past a sign with faded orange lettering that read, The Sundown Ranch. Even in the dark, she saw the car pull up to the weathered farmhouse—and knew what was about to happen to the old couple sleeping inside.

There was something familiar about the two people who got out of the car, something in the way they swaggered along the path, past blooming coreopsis heavy with blossoms, past fragrant lilacs, and brilliant red hyacinth that lined the foot path up to the front porch. She watched as they walked past two rocking chairs that sat empty, gently swaying in the hot night breeze.

One of them took out a key to the front door. The old couple had trusted them enough to give them a key to their house.

Inside the living room, family pictures lined the walls. She moved with the killers along the wall, looking at the old wedding photographs first, then at the baby pictures of a young boy with doting parents. As the boy grew, there were pictures of him smiling, sitting on top of a horse.

There were school photographs; more photos of the same boy, gapped-tooth, holding a bat in his baseball uniform, and then finally, one of a solemn young man in his soldier's uniform. In slow motion the scene moved into a neat, tidy, and old-fashioned kitchen. But they were *messing up the order of the place, going through drawers, pulling everything out, leaving clutter behind in their wake.*

The killers wore gloves and dark clothing. She could see that clearly now as she watched one of them pick up a knife, exchange words with her cohort before moving out of the scene while the other one stayed back, started shoving bullets into a handgun.

But then the scene shifted to the bedroom. She tried to warn the people what was about to happen. She shouted at them to wake up, to move, to get out of the house before it was too late.

But soon the shadow fell across the bed. And no matter how loud she screamed, the sleeping couple didn't wake up, didn't move.

She heard a string of obscenities, shouting, and an ugly argument. There was something familiar about that, too, as she listened, and she knew the commotion would wake up the woman.

She tried to scream they were coming, to get out but they didn't hear her.

Sure enough, when the gunman saw the woman start to sit up, the gunman took aim and fired, hitting the woman solidly in the chest. She watched as the gunman fired again, this time hitting the man in the middle of his tanned, weathered forehead, just like before.

The couple was dead. And nothing would ever change that.

⚅ ⚅ ⚅ ⚅ ⚅

Kit woke clutching her throat, trying to breathe. She had to fight for every breath, had to have air. She tried to scream.

Her squirming woke Jake, who only saw that Kit was having difficulty catching her breath. He quickly tried to calm her down by rubbing her back and shoulders, trying to get her to relax her muscles long enough to slow down her need for air. As he did so, he caught the time on the digital clock beside the bed. Three minutes after three. "I'll be damned." When he met Kit's eyes, he said simply, "You had another dream."

Jake cradled her in his arms, gently rocked her, and started rhythmically rubbing her chest, talking to her. "Relax, just relax; there you go. Calm down. Catch your breath, nice and easy. Nice and easy; breathe, calmer, calmer; come on, breathe out. Breathe in, slowly."

He started massaging her neck and shoulders. When her breathing returned to normal, he helped her sit up. But she was still shaking as if cold. The room felt warm to Jake, not chilly enough for a blanket, but Kit acted as if it were twenty degrees below and colder than a night in Alaska. He got up and grabbed a blanket from inside the box at the foot of the bed. He threw the blanket around her, wrapping her up in his arms. Her body shook with little spasms, and she made little hiccupping noises in her throat.

"How about some water?" he asked.

She shook her head and squeaked out, "Don't. Leave. Me. Alone."

He climbed back in bed, crawling over her legs and Pepper. She rested her head on his shoulder, and they both leaned back against the headboard. They stayed like that until Kit closed her eyes, and he laid her back down on her pillow.

Jake finally drifted off.

But Kit never really got back into a sound sleep. Even with Jake there, she tossed and turned. Her mind raced with a dozen questions. *That couple...who were they?* It had happened a long time ago. But now, she knew without doubt why the killers seemed so familiar.

And how did she feel about the fact that both her parents had lied to her, lied about a fake marriage, a fake divorce. Why would they do that? What had brought the two of them together in the first place? She wondered if Gloria might be able to offer up any clue as to why.

After some time, she looked at the clock on the nightstand; it was four-fifteen. She might as well get up and do the baking. But when she turned over, Jake was sleeping on his back. Her breath caught in her throat just realizing she had him in her bed.

The longing hit her.

She weighed her options. She could crawl out of bed, start her day, let him sleep in peace, or she could play. For a woman used to sleeping alone, Kit decided to take advantage of the situation.

With the tips of her fingers she followed the outline of his mouth. He didn't so much as stir. She put her lips to his and gave him a tugging kiss. Other than moving his lips in and out in a kind of sucking motion, he kept right on sleeping. She nuzzled his neck, placed tender little kisses in strategic places on his chest, and then moved down to his belly hoping he'd wake up enough to take her in his arms. But all he did was utter a half-hearted little moan. She lightly traced around his lips with her tongue, slowly working her way into his mouth little by little.

Suddenly, he reversed their positions. More awake, he covered her mouth. "You're killing me, woman. You know that, don't you?"

She wrapped her arms around his body. "Killing you is counterproductive. Let me show you what I had in mind."

☙☙☙☙☙

As it got lighter outside, Kit stayed curled up next to him with her rear end snuggled up against his stomach. They'd had one incredible night after one incredible afternoon, and he still wanted more. He wouldn't mind waking up like this for the rest of his life.

Beside him, Kit stirred. Strands of hair fell across her face. With his fingertips, he pushed them back before running a hand down the length of her body, coming full circle to rest his hand on her breast, rubbing a thumb against her nipple.

Without turning over to face him, Kit responded to his touch by nestling into his body. "Why do you suppose they call it sleeping together when that's the last thing you get to do?"

"We spent the night together."

"There you go."

"I didn't hear you complaining at four o'clock."

She shook her head. "No; as I recall, that was you."

"I came through, didn't I?"

"But I did all the work."

"It was your turn to do all the work."

"Really? We take turns?" She asked, as she burrowed her bottom into his stomach, still facing the opposite way.

"Oh yeah, we take turns. That must mean..." As he drew back her hair to nuzzle her neck, Jake noticed a small rounded scar on the upper portion of her left shoulder where the shoulder ends, just before the arm begins. He hadn't noticed it until now, but he'd been exploring more interesting aspects of her body. The moment he touched the indentation, he felt her tense. It was smaller than the size of a dime, but he could feel the mark it had left on her otherwise perfect skin. He gently rubbed the surrounding area, feeling the round groove with the tips of his fingers and wanted to know, "Where'd you get this scar on your shoulder?"

She could lie to him, make something up about falling out of a tree when she was little, or say that she'd had some kind of nasty accident. But she hated the idea of outright lying. And what if Gloria had already told him? But then if he already knew, why would he have to ask?

To Jake, the scar looked like a punched-out, exit wound from a bullet. Then to satisfy his curiosity, he turned her slightly to see if there was a matching one on the front. Sure enough, there was a much smaller indented mark on her upper arm. "I don't know much about bullet wounds,

Kit, but I'd say if I didn't know better this looks like a gunshot wound. How'd you get that?"

Without explanation, she broke from his arms, flopped over on her stomach, rolled her pillow up in a ball, and hid her hands underneath. "It's just a scar from a long time ago. It isn't important."

Rolling almost on top of her, he draped his arm over her back, rubbed it before stroking her hair. Her reaction told him there was more to it. He gently prodded, "Tell me about the scar, Kit. How'd you get it?"

She didn't answer right away. With her eyes closed, she pretended to drift back to sleep. But then barely audible, she said into her pillow in a soft voice, "It's a bullet wound."

Stunned, he felt his own body tense, felt his anger rise, so much so that he was grateful she wasn't looking at him. Why had he asked if he hadn't been prepared for the answer?

"Honey, who shot you?" But even as he asked, he felt the raw knowledge close up around him.

He moved her hair out of the way, looked at the scar again, and felt the damage. From its size, he guessed it came from a small handgun, maybe a .22 caliber.

"Alana. It happened when I was twelve. She paid a doctor to come to the house to treat me so that she wouldn't have to take me to the hospital. Hospitals ask questions about gunshot wounds, especially when you bring in your twelve-year-old daughter. I thought Gloria might have mentioned it." *Push the memory away. Don't let it ruin this perfect morning after such a great night.*

Jake swore. Gloria knew? Of course she did. Mention it? Once again anger rose within him. No, Gloria had conveniently left out the fact that Alana had shot her own twelve-year-old daughter. There had been no mention of it; even that day in his office when he had pointblank asked Gloria about Kit's abuse. Why hadn't she come clean about it then?

With his fingers, he pulled back strands of hair from her face. He got her to turn over and took her into his arms, cradling her to his chest. "Come here honey; let me hold you. Just let me hold you. I can't believe she hurt you like that." He leaned his back up against the headboard and held her in his arms, as much for himself as for her.

His mind raced with questions, but for the moment he kept them to himself. He tried to imagine what sort of circumstance might produce that kind of violent outburst even from Alana. He knew firsthand the woman had a vicious temper, had seen it in action on more than one occasion, but how could a mother shoot her own twelve-year-old child?

She'd been left in that environment too long. Knowing what she must have endured tore something apart inside him. What else had she gone through? And the sudden thought that there might've been more, broke his heart as he remembered that she'd wanted his attention as a kid, that he'd done everything he could to ignore her on every level. Suddenly, it hit him that Gloria and Morty's move from Maine had come soon after the shooting.

No wonder Kit hadn't cried at the woman's funeral; why would she? Remembering how the two detectives had used that to their advantage, and might still use it, burned him.

It felt so good to have Jake's arms wrapped around her, holding her, keeping the memory at bay. She felt at peace. But she noticed he'd grown silent. The silence was more than she could take. Finally, she said flatly, "Jake, don't pity me. It isn't necessary to feel sorry for me. That's the last thing I want. It was a long time ago and I've put it behind me." Even though it wasn't completely true, she wanted him to believe she'd done just that.

"Was it an accident?"

Kit shook her head, but stayed quiet.

"You aren't going to tell me what happened, are you?"

"I just can't talk about it, okay? I don't want to go over the morbid details. I've tried to put that night out of my mind. And this is nice. The last thing I want to talk about right now is that night. I don't want to ruin this."

He stroked her cheek with his fingertips. "Okay. I'll leave it for now. But I'm not going anywhere; when you want to talk about it, tell me what happened, I'll be right here. And just so you know, I don't pity you, honey. I care about you. I want to help. How can I make it better?"

All he could do now was hold her or listen to her when she wanted or needed to talk. He stared into her eyes and saw that distant sad look form there in the liquid pools. How would he ever get that sad look out of those beautiful green eyes?

He bent his head down, moved her hair out of the way, kissed the scar and promised, "I won't let anyone hurt you like that again...ever."

What was he saying? Didn't he want to bolt, run the opposite way, and get as far away from her as he could? What would he do when he found out all of it?

"What are you thinking?" he asked.

She pushed the memories to the back of her brain. "That it was a great night last night."

"And the morning will be even better."

To prove it, he started working his way down her body with his mouth.

CHAPTER 17

Several hours later, Ginger knocked on the door of the conference room in the middle of Jake's Friday morning staff meeting, telling him, "I've got a Baylee Scott on the phone; she says it's urgent, insists that I tell you it's about Kit." Jake was up out of the chair in a burst of movement, surprising everyone sitting around the conference table, except maybe Dylan.

Dylan watched Jake head out the door like a shot, heard him tell Ginger that he'd take the call in his office, and wondered just how deep his friend's feelings for Kit Griffin ran. After their heated exchange the other day, it was apparent he couldn't talk any sense into him.

Dylan didn't want to see his friend suffer again at the hands of another greedy viper. So he'd keep an eye out for his friend. No woman was going to get her hooks in Jake for his money again if he could help it.

In his office, Jake picked up the phone, noting Baylee didn't mince words. "Couple of minutes ago Kit headed out of here after getting a call from Connor Boyd. It seems someone broke into Alana's house, messed it up pretty badly, from what I gather, and Boyd convinced her she should go in and check the place out. Even got the all-clear from Holloway to go back inside and look around."

Baylee took a deep breath. "Before you say anything, I tried to talk her out of going. When I couldn't, I offered to go with her if she'd just wait until Sarah woke up. But she decided to go alone. I didn't speak to Connor myself, but whatever he said convinced her to head over there by herself. I know she told you about her childhood, but I don't think you know—everything about her past. I just don't... I...don't think she should go back in there alone. God, I'm not even sure she can, Jake. But she told me it was time she faced her demons. And I guess, she's trying to do that by going back. I think it's a mistake. I'm not sure she's strong enough to face that house, let alone face her demons."

Jake agreed. "How long's she been gone?"

"Five minutes, tops. I thought...maybe...you'd want to know. But frankly, if you don't go after her, I'll have to."

"I'm glad you called, Baylee. I need an address."

⚭ ⚭ ⚭ ⚭ ⚭

Kit gunned her Jeep through the yellow caution light and made a fast right onto Shannon Way, leaving behind the traffic on the busier Stone Canyon for the more peaceful, less-traveled streets of exclusive Bel-Air. Going much faster than the posted speed limit, she reminded herself what an idiot she was for coming over here by herself.

Hadn't Baylee offered to come with her? Why had she thought she could face her past now, alone? She might not even be able to unlock the front door, and if she did manage that much, could she take that step inside, step back into the house that held not just bad memories, but so much pain, so many nightmares?

As she pulled her car into the familiar circular driveway on Bel Green Drive and came to a stop, her hands began to shake in spite of the fact that Alana Stevens wasn't waiting on the other side of the front door. Even knowing Alana couldn't hurt her anymore, she still broke out in a cold sweat. Her hands even turned clammy.

She knew Alana was dead. She'd gone to the funeral, seen the casket. Alana Stevens could no longer hurt her.

Remembering that didn't seem to help. The shaking didn't stop. And she could feel the sweat pool on her face.

Why wasn't the car's air conditioner working? She absently adjusted the vents and stared at the house, shuddering at the memory of living here. She shut her eyes against the images of things that went on inside.

She sat in the security of the car, afraid to open the door. As if Pepper understood, instead of chomping at the bit to get out, he remained at her side.

Today she came here trying to overcome—what? Her fear of this house? Why should she fear a house? The house hadn't been cruel, but rather a blond bombshell of a woman who could change in and out of moods on a dime, sweet one moment, offering her little girl refuge on her lap, cruel the next, knocking her to the floor and laughing about it. All at once, Kit heard Alana's laughter as if it was coming from inside the car. Alana's laugh bellowed at her and only grew louder...

Kit's change of heart happened in an instant. She grabbed at the gear shift to put the car into Drive and jumped when Jake tapped on the driver's side window.

All the fight went out of Kit as she slumped her head on the steering wheel and without looking, she felt for the button that lowered the glass. Her hands were shaking so much it took several tries before she found the right button to work the driver's side window.

When it finally rolled down, she heard Jake say, "Sorry. Didn't mean to scare you."

In a voice so soft Jake barely heard, she said, "You followed me."

"You're upset."

Her body started shaking. "You followed me," she said again. A wave of relief washed over her as she realized she was no longer alone.

"You're angry I came."

"No. Not that. I've never been so glad to see anyone." She laughed, but it was a strained high-pitched sound that didn't sound quite genuine. "You knew I couldn't go in alone."

"Not at all. I wanted to be with you when you did."

Oh, what a sweet man.

Jake had never seen Kit so white. The woman had beautiful, flawless skin with a gold quality to it. But not now. Her skin had turned the color of paste. And her whole body was shaking, just as she'd been after waking from the dream last night.

He wasn't sure what to do, but he knew he needed to do or say something. Before he could speak, she asked, "What are you doing here? How'd you find...find me?"

He smiled at her and realized she wasn't thinking straight. "I followed you, remember?"

"I'm...I'm glad...glad...you did."

"What do you want to do, Kit?"

"I want to leave...this place."

"Okay, we will. But how about this, you stay here in the car, sit here with Pepper, give me the key to the house. I'll go in and check everything out? How about that?"

Shaking her head, in a low voice she warned, "You don't want to go in there, Jake. Bad things happen in there."

"It'll be okay, Kit. There isn't anything in there that can hurt me. I won't let it."

That sound came through her lips that was supposed to be a laugh, but wasn't. When she saw Jake reach into the driver's side window and take the key ring Connor had sent her, she heard him, as if from a distance ask, "Which is the key to the front door, Kit?"

She felt it her duty to try to reason with him. "I don't think you should go in there."

"You stay in the car, honey. It won't take long to look around. I'll be right back."

As she grudgingly watched him walk up to the front door, she put a shaky hand on top of Pepper's head. Feeling seven years old again, she told the dog, "He'll be sorry he went in there, won't he boy?"

The minute Jake stepped inside the marble entryway, a creepy feeling he couldn't explain hit him in the gut. Closed up now for almost two weeks, the house smelled musty. As he looked around at the furnishings, the whole place seemed as if it lacked any kind of warmth.

But right away he saw evidence that someone had definitely tossed the place. He examined the front door, found no sign that it had been tampered with, nothing to indicate anyone had gained entry by any other means than using a key. He made a mental note to check the other doors before he left.

Every stick of heavy furniture in the living room and dining area had been set off to the side of the rugs, as though the intruders had been looking for something in the floor—like a floor safe maybe.

The condition of the house told him they hadn't found what they'd been looking for either. After stepping around overturned furniture, he headed in the direction of the kitchen. Here every drawer, every cabinet, even the pantry had been ransacked. They'd opened cereal boxes and strewn food all over the kitchen floor.

After checking the back door and the doors leading to the terrace and finding no broken locks, no forced entry, he went back to his original assertion.

Whoever had done this must have had a key.

From the kitchen he used the back staircase leading to the second floor. Once he got to the landing, he began mechanically checking out each bedroom one room at a time. He found each one in as bad a shape as the rest of the house. They'd left no stone unturned when it came to their search.

Inside the master bedroom he noted the cleanup crew had done a half-assed job after the murder. Here, the pale Berber carpet still held that unmistakable brownish stain where blood had congealed.

Staring at the crime scene now took him back to another time, another place, when he'd walked into another bedroom, the one that had belonged to Claire when he'd found her bloodied body. And it suddenly hit him that there was no way Kit could have walked into this house and dealt with this particular scene.

Under his breath, he cursed Connor Boyd for sending Kit back here. What would have happened if she'd come upon this room by herself?

Ten minutes later, he again stood in the center of Alana's overly-decorated French living room, surrounded by what he was pretty sure used to be ugly Louis XIV antiques. It looked as if someone had taken an instant dislike to her taste in furniture and hacked each piece apart before scattering the contents throughout the room.

☧☧☧☧☧

Back in the car Kit fidgeted, checked her watch every few minutes, and decided Jake had been in there a really long time. When Pepper started to whine, she realized the dog needed a potty break. As she cut the Jeep's engine and opened the door, she watched as Pepper sprinted off to hunker down on the lawn to take care of business. Kit shook her head and muttered, "Alana sure wouldn't have liked that."

After locking the front door, for all the good it did, Jake found Kit and Pepper standing on the front lawn about forty feet from the car. At first he thought she'd overcome her panic attack and left the car. That was a good thing. But the minute he approached her, the minute she heard his footsteps and turned to look at him, he knew something was wrong. She had that distant look in her eyes that he'd seen so many times in the last couple of weeks, but this time it was as if she really were physically far away from him.

And it scared the shit out of him.

"Kit, are you okay?" He felt stupid asking. He knew she wasn't. He could see it for himself. "I don't think

Alana would be too happy if she could see the house now. They trashed the place pretty good."

She smiled, but it didn't reach her eyes. "I don't care what they did to it as long as I don't ever have to see it again or go inside again. It's a shame they didn't burn it to the ground, don't you think? It would have looked so much better in ashes or rubble. They could start over then. The new owners could build something new from the ground up, something suited to a family, a real one."

"Well, it's your house now, Kit. You can..."

But she didn't let him finish. She whirled to face him. "You just don't get it, do you? It's not my house. It was never my house. Growing up here..." She caught herself. "Yes, it appears I'm going to end up with it after probate. They'll force me to take it. But it's not my house. It was never my house. Living here was never a home, more like prison."

Jake reached for her, and placed his hands on the small of her back, gently nudging her toward the car. "We need to get out of here." He directed her in the general direction of the car. "Coming here wasn't a good idea."

But walking toward the car also meant walking toward the house and all at once Kit stopped and turned to face him. This time with more control, in a level voice, without emotion, she said, "You want to know what happened here, Jake. Where should I begin? How about when I was very small and Alana bought me a playhouse. It had wonderful toys inside: a tea set, cute little furniture. It's my first memory.

"Any little girl would have loved a playhouse like mine. And I did until she locked me up, locked me inside and wouldn't let me out, wouldn't let me out to eat or go to the bathroom. That playhouse became a prison, my personal little-girl prison when I was no more than three. And it was just the beginning of things to come. Any time Alana wanted me out of the way or wanted to punish me for some reason, she'd lock me inside my playhouse. Sometimes I was there for a really long time. It happened over and over and over again. So many times, I can't count. Do you know what it's like to be locked inside a small space, unable to get out to use the bathroom, or to get something to eat when you're hungry? I'm convinced there were times when she forgot I was there. It might be a paradise of a playhouse on the outside, but inside, it was a cell for a little girl."

Her voice caught before she continued. "But it didn't take long for me to outgrow my playhouse, and when that happened, I was locked in an upstairs closet, Alana nicknamed Kit's Closet; I was in the dark for hours; sometimes, depending on her mood, it was for more than a day without food or water, unless, of course, the housekeeper or the cook would hear my kicking and screaming, take pity on me, and sneak me something to eat.

"Come on Jake, this is what you want to know, isn't it? You want to hear all of it, don't you? Would you like to see the closet just off the alcove upstairs where Alana locked up her willful daughter to keep her in line more times than I care to count?" She moved past him toward the house, "Let's go take a look at the upstairs closet for old time's sake. How about it? Let's go back inside."

Before she took another step, Jake grabbed her arm. "Honey, look at me. Look at me, honey. It's okay to get angry. You can be goddamned angry at Alana for what she did to you."

As if not hearing him, she went on, unemotionally. "Then there were all the beatings, the broken bones, the bruises; let's skip all that boring stuff and just fast forward to when I was twelve. One night she and my father were arguing. My father had told me he was finally taking me away from here, finally getting me out of the house. So I went upstairs to pack. But I heard them arguing, and I knew I needed to intervene because he'd promised me many times that he would take me away from here but for some reason he always ended up backing down, giving in, always, always leaving me here. I remember thinking, please don't change your mind this time don't leave me with her again. So, I came into the room, and I saw that Alana had a gun. I heard her tell my father that she'd see me dead before she'd let him have me. When Alana saw me in the doorway, she turned around with the gun, faced me, aimed it directly at me, and then deliberately pulled the trigger. But as I watched her aim, I turned at the last minute and the bullet went into my shoulder, my upper arm." Absently, her right hand moved up to her left shoulder and she rubbed the spot as if it still hurt.

"A twelve-year-old girl sees her mother intentionally point a gun and fire at her because she'd rather see her dead; I can still hear the gun go off, remember the sound it made, the searing pain, all the blood. I woke up in my own bed. She'd paid a doctor to come to the house.

"Of course, my father was nowhere in sight. That was the worst part, you see, about that night, my father leaving me here with Alana…again. That hurt far more than the bullet ever could." A sob broke out of her throat. "I left this house at sixteen and I want no part of it now."

Jake brought her into him. He stood there with his arms wrapped tightly around her. She was trembling again so hard her teeth chattered. The realization hit him that it was better she got all of that out of her now with him rather than with St. John. They stood there like that until Jake said, "Kit, I'm sorry you had to go through all that. Do you feel better talking about it?"

"No. Do you want to get away from me now?"

"I don't understand?"

"Leave. Do you want to leave?"

He started closing the distance to where the Jeep was parked, walking her toward the car once again with his arms wrapped around her. As they got closer to the car, however, she stopped and said, "No, I mean hearing all that—don't you want to leave me? You can't possibly want to be with someone like me."

He stood there smiling, and tucked several strands of hair behind her ear. "Honey, I want to be with you for as long as you'll have me. Hearing all that stuff once, we never have to talk about it again unless you want to."

"Okay."

She'd thought once he found out he wouldn't want her. Her revelation had shaken him right down to his soul, but for her sake, he tried to appear outwardly unaffected.

For a long time, he simply held her, trying to get his bearings. He wanted to ask the question, but fear had him holding his tongue. He wanted to ask the question that nagged at him. Was there more? What else had she suffered in this house, at the hands of Alana or rather, at the hands of one of Alana's special friends? He wanted to ask the question, but didn't dare, couldn't.

He'd wanted her to tell him, confide in him, hadn't he? Was he really prepared to hear the answer? And what would he do, could he do, if there was more? But now he racked his brain to think of some way to get her to switch gears, get her mind off the humiliation of what she'd told him, if only briefly.

He picked the silliest and most stupid thing he'd ever done as a child and gave it life, hoping it was enough. "Now it's my turn to tell you something about my childhood, something embarrassing, something no other living soul knows.

"One summer night when I was nine, I was bored with nothing much to do. So I got on my bike, rode down to the square in this little town where we lived at the time. I ended up behind Chang's Cleaners & Laundry. There was this mass of lint behind the building. I mean a huge ball of this stuff just sitting there waiting for a dense kid like me to come along with matches. Yeah, I was carrying matches—had considered I might try cigarettes at some point, but anyway, I had matches on me. I got curious wondering if this huge ball of lint would catch on fire. So, being the inquisitive and slightly stupid kid I was, I lit a match and threw it into this enormous ball of lint. I waited around but nothing happened so I lit another one and then another. After I'd tossed in close to six matches I waited around, but still nothing. I thought, okay, lint doesn't burn. Bored, I hopped back on my bike and rode down the alley the way I'd come and the next thing I knew, I heard sirens, fire engines approaching from several different directions. The police showed up and everyone was rushing over to the dry cleaners. I rode my bike back up the street and watched as the firemen donned their equipment, pulled out their hoses to fight the fire that I'd started. It took three engines to put out that fire. Lucky for me, no one got hurt because Chang's had been closed for several hours. I set fire to a dry cleaners, almost burned the place down. It was the last time I ever set fire to a bunch of lint and the last time I ever played with matches."

Kit grinned at the stupid story. "No one found out it was you?"

"Nope. I was so ashamed I never confessed. You're the first. And now you know I was an arsonist at nine."

His story had gone a long way to take the edge off her abysmal tale. Grateful, she said simply, "Thanks Jake. I needed that."

He kissed the top of her head; let his hands wander down to her waist and up her back before bringing her mouth up to meet his. Her lips parted, and he felt her melt into him. His body reacted as it always did. "I like you better naked."

Kit pushed back long enough to catch her breath and look into his eyes. "Your car or mine?"

His eyebrows went up in mock surprise. "I liked it when I woke up this morning and you were exploring my body. Anytime you decide to ravage me in my sleep, or get carried away, which brings up…We haven't talked about birth control..."

He saw her visibly pale.

"Oh. Well. I can't be a mother."

Jake's heart skipped a beat. He wanted to make sure he'd heard her right. "You can't get pregnant?"

"No. Well. No. Not that. Well. I don't know. I mean...I just can't be a mother."

He let out a breath he hadn't known he was holding. "Why do you say that, Kit? I've seen you with Sarah. You look at her as if you want one of your own."

"Well...I...just because I want a baby...doesn't mean... Sarah goes home at night...and I...I just don't think...I just can't...be a mother."

He set her back from him to look directly into her eyes, but she dropped her head, wouldn't meet his. He lifted her chin up, forcing her to look at him. He kept his gaze locked on hers, until she finally said, "Okay. What if I...I might...I might turn out...I might be mean like Alana. Abuse usually cycles. And I'd rather die than be like that."

"Oh, honey." Pulling her back into his chest, he told her, "Stop that. You're nothing like Alana. You couldn't hurt a child. I've watched you with Sarah. I've only seen two other women, my sisters, care for a baby as well as you care for Sarah. And Kit, they've both been mothers a long time."

He thought of something and asked, "Kit, how long have you had Pepper?"

Puzzled at the change of subject, Kit tightened her brow. "What? How long? Well. Almost six years. I took him from a puppy mill when I was a sophomore in college. I don't mean I stole him or anything. The SPCA busted this puppy mill and they had all these different kinds of puppies that were in really bad shape. It was on the news. Pepper was one of the puppies that almost didn't make it. He was really sick. That's why he isn't exactly the brightest bulb on the tree. We weren't even supposed to have dogs in our apartment, but I wanted Pepper so much that Baylee helped me sneak him in, and when Pepper needed to go out, we'd wrap him up in this old blanket we had and take turns carrying him up and down the stairs so the neighbors wouldn't know we had a dog. But then the apartments got new owners and..."

Jake listened patiently letting her rattle on in typical Kit-fashion until she'd finished with her story, and then said, "See Kit, you can't even stand to see a dog mistreated. In the six years you've had Pepper, how many times has he peed on the carpet and you beat him for it."

Appalled, Kit put her hand to her mouth. "I've never hit Pepper; not once, not even when he did worse than pee on the carpet. And it was quite a challenge getting him housebroken since he isn't the smartest dog. I never...I wouldn't do that."

"See, you treat your dog better than Alana treated you. And let's not forget about Baylee. Her childhood was abusive, maybe not like yours, and yet it didn't stop her from having a child. She has Sarah now. She's a good mother from what I've seen. You'd be a great mother, Kit, and don't you believe otherwise."

"You'd trust me to care for a child."

"In a heartbeat." And then he brought her into him and crushed his mouth to hers, gave her a searing kiss. As his hands moved from her waist, down to her rear end, more solemnly, he whispered, "I love having my hands on you."

"I love feeling your body on top of mine, feeling the weight of it on me."

Getting seriously aroused now, he countered with, "I love being inside you."

"I love having you inside me, coming inside me."

Hot. It was suddenly very hot.

Just as he unbuttoned her jeans, a car pulled into the driveway, parked behind his Mercedes, putting an end to the moment.

Reluctantly, quickly, he buttoned her up, and stared down Connor Boyd, who looked like a late-thirties carbon copy of his younger brother, Collin.

Even when the man walked up to where they were standing beside Kit's Jeep, Jake never dropped his arm from around Kit's waist, and she didn't bother stepping back.

"I didn't know you two knew each other," Connor lied.

"Yeah, we get that a lot," Kit said to Connor in an amused tone, though her eyes never left Jake's.

Still staring at Connor, Jake said flatly, "You shouldn't have suggested Kit come back here, Boyd. What I can't figure out is why you wanted to meet with her, here of all places, specifically today. What did you want?"

A sheepish look crossed his face. "She needed to check the place out, protect her investment. Think ahead about what needs to be done to put the house on the market. I am, after all, the attorney of record handling Alana's probate."

"Screw this house, screw probate. You sent her to a recent crime scene by herself without so much as preparing her for what she might find inside." He finally let go of Kit long enough to open the Jeep's door, called to the dog to jump into the front seat ahead of her, and said to Kit, "Are you okay to drive?"

Feeling as though she'd been given a precious gift, she looked at Jake and said, "I'm great."

"Then go back to work. I'll take Boyd on a tour of the house. Let him see the damage for himself and meet you back there in about an hour and a half. Okay?"

Kit didn't argue, didn't hesitate, but rather gave him a quick kiss on the mouth before starting the car. As if they'd been together for years, she said simply, "Don't be long."

When she'd disappeared down the lane, Jake hung back, letting Connor Boyd take the lead to the front door. Jake watched as the man dug into his trouser pocket, pulled out yet another key ring, and used it to unlock the front door as if he'd done so before.

A thought ran through Jake's mind, and he wondered if St. John had ever bothered to check how many people had keys to Alana's house.

CHAPTER 18

Going back inside the house, this time with Boyd leading the way, Jake felt as if he'd stepped back into a time warp when Kit had lived there as a child. He looked at the house differently than he had before. Now knowing what she'd endured in this house, unlike earlier, that creepy feeling had him downright pissed off.

What had it been like for Kit to grow up here, endure here, and suffer here?

As he accompanied Boyd through the tour of the downstairs, Jake nodded politely at the right times, used a civil tone whenever he responded to the man's weak attempt at outrage about the condition of the house, but Jake's mind was elsewhere.

His thoughts wandered to the upstairs, to the alcove, to the closet where Kit had been locked up. He'd walked right past it earlier, unaware of its existence.

As he followed Boyd up the front staircase right off the foyer, he became more aware of his surroundings. Once he got to the second floor landing, raw emotion swept over him and his apprehension about the place grew stronger. He separated from Boyd and continued walking down the long hallway covered with thick, white Berber carpet that softened his every step. He walked past several bedrooms and closet doors until he got to the rear of the house.

When he reached the landing that led to the back staircase, he realized he'd gone too far and backtracked. On the left, tucked away off the beaten path of the main corridor, was the alcove, a small niche of a space with a sloped ceiling and a door at the far end. Away from the bedrooms, thought Jake.

He walked down the small passageway, his heart thudding faster with every step. He told himself it was probably nothing more than a poorly-located linen closet. But for some reason he was drawn to the space. Stopping directly in front of the door, he took several deep breaths before turning the knob. He noted that unlike the other closets along the main corridor this one had a deadbolt lock installed on the outside of the door. A deadbolt lock to keep a little girl locked inside.

This had to be it. Kit's Closet.

He swallowed hard, opened the door, and peered inside. The space was no more than three feet by three feet, and with the sloped ceiling, it was even smaller than a normal closet. For a closet in a house where the owner had lived for thirty years or more, this space was completely empty. That seemed strange to Jake.

There was no Berber carpet here, no tile either, but rather a concrete floor. There was no rod for hanging clothes, no shelves for storage. He looked around for a light switch, and realized there wasn't one. A tiny closet with no light and a deadbolt lock on the door. As he studied the inside, he thought he saw something on all three walls near the baseboard. He lowered his head and wished he had a flashlight. Stepping inside the tiny space, his large frame took up most of it.

◈ ◈ ◈ ◈ ◈

He bent down and sat on his heels to get a better look in the dim light. Just above each baseboard inches off the floor, nicks and holes and scuff marks lined each of the three walls, as if the walls had received blows, too many blows to count. The inside of the door contained quite a few more irregular nicks in the wood and more scuff marks. With his fingertips, he felt the rough edges of each of the indentations, the holes in the peeling paint and plaster, and the damage left by a child's small kicking feet and hands.

How much time had she spent locked inside this closed up space? Now, he understood why she was claustrophobic. Then he remembered her reaction at Crandall House that day when she'd opened up that tiny closet.

At that moment, he decided to tear the walls out and make the space fifty times the size. On instinct, sitting inside on his heels, he closed the door and blackness descended. As a full grown adult, who had to bend at the waist to fit in the tiny space, Jake tried to imagine what Kit must have felt like as a child locked in, unable to get out. But the only feelings he could manage were the obvious ones: the fear she must have felt at the thought of not ever getting out, and the anger for being put there in the first place.

Suddenly, he felt like throwing up.

☙ ☙ ☙ ☙ ☙

On the drive back to the store from Bel-Air to San Madrid, Kit had calmed down enough to think about what she needed to do. Jake had said her dream had uncanny similarities to the murders that had taken place back in 1969. She needed to find the connection to those murders and the old couple who lived on the property called the Sundown Ranch.

When she got back to the shop, Baylee was out front helping a customer. Kit waved and nodded as she quickly walked past them, headed straight for her office upstairs, and closed herself off with her computer.

When she Googled the murders from 1969, she got over four million hits. She couldn't believe the vast amount of information written about the grisly 1969 murders committed over a two-day period on August 9th and 10th in Benedict Canyon and Los Feliz.

Chills ran down her spine as she read the gory details. When she found several of the actual newspaper articles from that timeframe, she realized many of the details from the crime scenes had been made public. Days after both murders, it was common knowledge that the killer or killers had left behind graffiti, specifically the words PIG, DIE, and DEATH written in the blood of the victims. The articles also revealed that the killer or killers had used both a gun and a knife, that there were multiple victims at both crime scenes, and that the murders were savage and senseless, and robbery didn't appear to be the motive.

Also, at the second murder scene, the one in Los Feliz, the police initially believed it to be the work of a copycat killer, someone who had mimicked the first murders in Benedict Canyon.

What if someone read the newspaper articles got the idea to copycat the murders using the details described in the papers? If they'd been planning murder months beforehand, getting a built-in description of the other crime scenes might come in handy when they needed to cover up one of their own, like the one that night at the Sundown Ranch.

Granted, it was a far-fetched idea. But she didn't have anything else to hang her hat on at the moment. She couldn't explain it, but the more she thought about it, the more the idea stuck.

And Jake was right about the similarities between the 1969 crime spree and the murders of the old couple in her dream. But there were also major differences. Elated at her findings, Kit pulled out pen and paper from her desk drawer, and began making a list.

More than an hour later, Baylee knocked on Kit's office door. When Baylee walked inside, she saw the intense look on Kit's face. Mistaking it for distress, believing Kit was upset about going back to Alana's house, she put the blame for that on the one person she felt responsible, Connor Boyd.

"Why the hell would you listen to him anyway? Just because he phones and tells you the house has been broken into, you drop what you're doing and take off by yourself. What were you thinking? And don't give me that stuff about demons. If you felt that way, then why go alone? Why didn't you let me go with you? I knew it was a bad idea for you to go back there."

"I thought I could do it, Baylee, and go inside by myself. But I couldn't. Jake showed up. Thanks for calling him. He said he followed me, but after I calmed down, I knew you must have sent him. I was never so glad to see anyone when he walked up to the car. I couldn't go in. Obviously, I haven't put a thing behind me after all this time, all that therapy, just a waste of time and money. Sitting in the car, it was as if it had happened yesterday. And Baylee, I could hear Alana laughing."

Tears came suddenly. She got to her feet and started toward Baylee, who met her halfway. The two women hugged and Kit buried her face in Baylee's hair. Baylee let her cry it out as she had scores of other times, annoyed at seeing her so vulnerable, having to revisit memories no one should have to relive.

Jake found them like that, Kit wrapped up in Baylee, as he stood watching from the open office doorway. Her tearstained cheeks, red nose, and water-filled eyes told him she still hadn't recovered from her visit to Beverly Hills. Seeing how upset she was incensed him all over again.

But when Kit spotted Jake in the doorway, she abruptly left Baylee and sought comfort in his arms.

"I'd like to stomp Connor Boyd into dirt right about now," Baylee said to Jake.

"You'd have to get in line."

Kit snuggled up to Jake as close as she could before saying. "Thanks for coming after me, Jake. I didn't tell you that before."

"No need to thank me. I'd have been upset with Baylee if she hadn't called. Why'd you go over there alone anyway?"

"See," Baylee pointed out, "There seems to be a consensus on that. Next time…"

"There won't be a next time," Kit told them. "It's better if I just put that place out of my mind. Gloria's right. I'll get one of those estate liquidators to go in there and take care of all the furnishings, get them ready to sell."

"Well, after getting a look inside there won't be that much furniture to liquidate."

Kit wiped her face with the back of her hands and seemed not to care about the house or the furnishings at all, so it was Baylee who asked, "Connor said someone broke into the house, but they vandalized the furniture, too?"

"Didn't say they broke in, but somebody sure turned it upside down looking for something."

Kit wasn't paying a bit of attention to either one of them. She went back to her desk and picked up the list she'd been working on. "I've done some research online. You were right about the murders being similar to Manson's crime spree. There are definitely similarities to the murders of the old couple, but there are also differences, enough, I think, that my old couple was killed by a pair of copycat killers that wanted the police to think the murders were part of the killing spree. And it worked."

Jake stared at her. "That's a helluva leap, Kit."

But Baylee wanted to know, "What old couple?"

Kit ignored her. "No, I don't think so. Hear me out. I think the killers wanted to take advantage of the fact that these murders took place back to back, the ones that were so obviously plastered all over the newspapers at the time. They had to act quickly. Timing was everything. The papers published detailed accounts of the crime scenes. The killers could have read the newspaper stories about both murders, gotten all the gory details they needed, including the words found printed in blood. Now that's a detail the police might have kept to themselves, but they didn't. I mean, you've got the entire city of L.A. gripped with fear over these gruesome murders. The public thinks there's a killer out there targeting the wealthy, or celebrities, and they're just scared. So the killers in my dream jump on the bandwagon—seize the opportunity, so to speak. All I know for sure is my killers in the dream have nothing to do with the Manson family, other than maybe the fact that they're all just evil. They have that in common.

"But the killers in my dream drive a Mercedes. I see all this detail from the dream enough to know the killers are women."

She ticked off what she saw. "When they get out of the car, they walk like women. When one of them writes graffiti on the wall in blood, she gets upset when the blood stains her clothes. Then there's the champagne. They crack open a bottle of champagne afterward in the kitchen. Come on, that's such a girlie thing to do, don't you think? I can see guys having a beer, or a shot of whiskey, but champagne?"

Jake and Baylee gaped at her, then at each other. Kit quickly relayed every aspect of the dream, even the ones she'd held back until now. It was Jake who said, "You've seen a lot more detail since you first told me about it. And in your dream you're sure the one left in the bedroom with the knife stabs the old couple even after they're dead?"

As if all that wasn't bad enough, the last sounded downright gruesome.

"Yeah. If they were going to pull this off, make it look like a continuation of the crime spree, it was an essential part to make it look like the knife played a role in their deaths. But if we could find out who owns that ranch, the Sundown Ranch, maybe look for any murders of an elderly couple that occurred right after the more famous ones. We'd have names, a place to start, come up with maybe a motive."

Impressed, but still skeptical, Jake told her, "Okay, we'll check the newspaper archives for any murders that might have occurred after the crime spree hit the newsstands, search the files they keep on microfiche, try to narrow down the timeframe."

"What does this old murder have to do with Alana?" Baylee asked.

"Oh, she's connected. But guess what Baylee, get this, Alana and John Griffin were never married."

Now that had Baylee more shocked than all the talk about murder. "Say what?"

"Jake pulled the information from public records. That whole private war they had going on wasn't about a contentious divorce. So why'd they hate each other? Any clue? I mean, you were around my father. You were around Alana. It was a great ruse on their part, wasn't it?"

Fist under her chin, Baylee was attempting to remember all the times she'd spent around Kit's parents. "I'll say. I've got to think about this Kit. They were so...so...horrible to each other, always at odds, always threatening to sue each other, always arguing over custody, making outrageous claims against each other, shouting insults." She turned to Jake. "You're sure the records you pulled were accurate?"

"Yeah, I'm sure. They weren't married, Baylee."

Kit scrunched up her nose, and then point-blank said to Baylee, "Maybe I'm the result of a one-night stand that occurred at some Hollywood party, or worse, maybe rape. Maybe that's why...you know...she...hated me."

Jake didn't know what to say to her now any more than he had when she'd brought up her theory last night, and looking at the expression on Baylee's face, Baylee didn't know how to respond to her either.

Baylee shook her head, walked to the door, and stopped. "Look, let me think about this. I guess you could be right...I mean...it would make sense. But," she shook her head, "I've got to think about this."

Once Baylee left them alone, Jake shut the door. In one quick motion, he had Kit up against him, wrapped in his arms. His mouth found hers. Jake broke off the kiss long enough to say, "Now, where were we? I want you...out of those clothes. We can use your desk."

Just as teasing, Kit calmly pointed out, "In case you haven't noticed, my office door doesn't have a lock. Baylee might come back."

Not one to be deterred, he reasoned, "No problem. We'll put a chair up against the door." Bringing her with him, he took a couple of steps backward to the desk and leaned on it, positioned her between his legs.

Kit countered, "What about your desk? It's a lot nicer. And I know for certain your office door has a lock on it."

Logical to a fault, he nibbled her ear while rubbing his hand over the swell of one breast, and rationalized, "No, my office won't work, at least not until everyone's cleared out for the day. Besides, there are less people to deal with here than there, and we'd have to move from this spot. No trust me, here would be much better. And we don't have a lot of time, so start taking off..."

Kit feigned a pout. "So this is a quickie? What happened to the full service treatment to which I've become so accustomed?"

"Define quickie."

She put a little more husky tone to her voice, and pronounced each word with great care, "The opposite of slow, taking your time like before, putting all that control you're so famous for to good use."

"Depends on how comfortable this desk is, don't you think?" Letting go of her breast long enough to run one hand over the desk, he added, "Feels pretty comfortable to me."

"If it feels so comfortable then you take the bottom."

He shrugged. "Not a problem, baby; I like you on top. I thought I proved that already."

With both of his hands resting on her hips, he brought her closer, nudged her top up slightly, then set to work with his tongue exploring her belly button, licking, sampling, tasting.

"Your belly button is a real turn-on. I've got this thing for it," he teased. All the while, Kit enjoyed the motion of his tongue, kept his head in place between both hands, as if he might somehow get away from her. For the second time that day, he unbuttoned the top button on her jeans, ran the zipper down to its base, and was just moving down to enjoy the possibilities when a knock at the door interrupted their play.

"Go away," they both shouted in unison. Clearly annoyed with the intrusive knock, he made his intentions clear, "That's the second time today we've been interrupted. Tonight, we're having dinner on the boat, sleeping on the boat; no phones, no cops, no well-meaning friends or co-workers. If I have to take us five miles out of port to do it, we're going to be alone. Got it?"

Smiling at the prospect, she quickly buttoned her jeans and said, "That's a great idea. I'll leave early, go home, and pack a bag. I'll stop by the market, pick up some groceries. We can fix dinner and have the whole evening to ourselves."

When Kit took too long to open the door, it opened anyway, and Quinn stood in the doorframe, obviously just as annoyed. "What are you guys doing in here?"

"Geez, do you need me to draw you a picture? Jake and I were just…talking…we were talking…about…books. He wanted to know if we had Bruce DeSilva's latest novel."

Quinn looked around the tiny office. "Yeah. Right. And there are just so many books stored back here. This must be where you keep the sale items, right?" She cocked her head and looked at Kit. "You always were a terrible liar." Then to Jake, "It's been awhile."

"It has. How are you, Doc?"

Quinn grinned as if she just remembered. "No Dr. Quinn medicine-woman jokes, okay? I heard them already."

"What are you doing here?" Kit finally asked.

"Got an update from Baylee, came on the fly. Seems like there's something you two have completely forgotten about."

Kit's face tightened. She blinked in confusion. "What are you talking about?"

"It's a good thing I have a memory like an elephant. Do you remember spending a very weird Fourth of July weekend at your dad's house when we were fourteen? Well, you weren't, but Baylee and I were. He was leaving after the holiday for another shoot, on location, somewhere overseas. Anyway, it was the summer before he died. Your dad had been drinking. He took a phone call, a long distance call, just as we were about to go surfing. Afterwards he was so upset, he started rambling, even started crying. We were so freaked out we didn't know what to do."

A chill went through Kit. She closed her eyes briefly before asking, "What else do you remember?"

"He started talking to himself about some guy named Benny who lived all the way over in Ireland. Benny, Kit. Baylee told me Jake uncovered a son who's getting your dad's residuals, a son who lives in Ireland. I remember because, hey, born in Ireland here. But then your dad started talking about how he couldn't live with himself because of what he'd decided to do."

For a moment Kit had a stunned look on her face, but then a light went off. Slowly, she turned to Jake. "We need to find Ben Griffin. He might hold some of the answers."

CHAPTER 19

That night on board the *Sea Warrior*, they shared the cramped space in the galley preparing dinner. As she watched Jake whip up a marinade for their sea bass, squeezing fresh limes into a bowl before adding garlic into the juice, a thought occurred to her. "You're left handed."

When he just looked at her strangely, obviously puzzled over her observation and didn't say anything, she pursed her lips and said, "Well, haven't you noticed?" She stopped slicing veggies in mid-chop long enough to hold up her left hand, which held a very large, sharp knife.

"Noticed what?"

"Oh, for crying out loud, I am too."

She was getting wound up. Amused at her behavior, he teased, "Am too what? Are you left-handed, too? Huh. I hadn't noticed."

In the tiny galley, she was an arm's length away. He didn't hesitate to bring her into him, knife and all. He nibbled at her lower lip before telling her, "I've been much more interested in other areas of your body to notice which hand you use. But if you'll drop the knife, I'll be happy to show you how good I am at using both hands."

As the knife clattered to the cutting board, in between his nips and kisses, she pointed out, "Well, I think it's cool, even if you don't. No bumping into each other when we eat. And it's a known fact that left-handed people are much more creative."

At the moment, he was showing her exactly how creative he could be. His hands roamed down her body. When she giggled, sudden heat spread over him that had nothing to do with cooking. He'd been put off all day. All he could think about was having her right here, right now. But she'd wanted food and they had to eat at some point. Besides, she looked so happy in the galley, so comfortable in this domestic scene after the kind of day she'd had, that he tamped down his desire and turned back to the marinade.

She poked him in the ribs, telling him, "You said that omelets were the only thing you could cook; yet, you look like you know your way around that marinade."

"Marinade is for grilling. Beach bums grill—anything." He spread a little butter on both sides of the fish before dropping each piece into the marinade to saturate. After wiping his hands, he took a long pull on his beer, watching her finish chopping the mushrooms. She dumped them into a skillet to sauté for lobster bisque.

While the veggies cooked, she mixed together the rest of the ingredients for the cream sauce, before adding chunks of lobster meat to the thickening mixture. While the soup simmered, he watched her throw together a batch of homemade cornbread from scratch. Jake stared at the woman in wonder. She could flat-out cook. After several minutes, he said, "Not only beautiful, but you move like a five-star chef."

"Oh, I doubt that. But if you enjoy the food, next time you see Glo you should thank her. She's the one who showed me preparing a meal could be like an art form. Glo not only taught me how to cook, she made me feel good about myself. I didn't have that until Glo. She gave up owning a bed and breakfast in Maine to move here. Imagine that, and she was a pretty good cook."

While the cornbread baked, Jake slapped the fish on the grill and turned it to low heat. He sat back to watch the fish and realized Kit was talking a mile a minute about setting the table. No, she was talking about decorating the table. He'd never seen a woman get such a kick out of finding a festive blue tablecloth and matching napkins in one of the lockers than when she discovered red dishes and an assortment of red candles to go with it.

As she chattered on for five minutes about the red and blue color scheme, Jake watched, loving every minute of her enthusiasm over something so mundane. She got so much pleasure out of the smallest ordinary things most people took for granted. But then he realized that she hadn't grown up with many chances at ordinary.

After Kit ladled out lobster bisque and sliced off chunks of warm, steaming cornbread, Jake opened two more beers.

Kit watched with satisfaction as he hungrily dug into the soup and cornbread, stopping long enough to tell her, "This soup is delicious. And this cornbread's as good as my mom's."

Kit liked this homey setting. Preparing a meal for Baylee and Quinn had always given her a kick; however, cooking for Jake was more like cooking with love. She had to admit everything she did with him was unlike anything she'd ever done before. Okay, she had it bad.

Forcing her mind to think of other things, Kit asked, "Do you think we'd get anywhere if we found Alana's ex-husbands, starting with the first one? That environmental engineer, what was his name, Forrester? Start from the beginning."

"Good idea. I checked McKetrick Construction and it's no longer in business." When he saw the surprised look on Kit's face, he added, "It seems the company lost a major lawsuit in '67 to BBG&G and was bankrupt by '70. I'm still digging, searching in between everything else. I'm trying to locate Forrester." As he finished off the meal, he asked, "If you're thinking the killers of that old couple were women, are you going to tell me who you think they were?"

He thought he already knew.

"Good ol' Lana and Jess. I just can't figure out why, although my guess would be money. I've never seen two people love money more than they did. It was like a competition with them, who could get it, who could keep it, who could spend it in record time. Did you make any progress on finding out when her bank balances went south?"

"No. And I'm not sure I'm ready to hack my way there yet. But even though we don't have access I'd bet money that someone dipped into those accounts recently."

"Any progress finding Ben Griffin?"

"No. What I can't figure out is the residuals are going to an address in Galway. Slam dunk there, but I can't get a phone number. If it's a P.O. Box that would explain why. You know, we might have to hire a private investigator to go over there and check it out. We could use the guy I hired to look into Claire's murder. Jordan Donovan works with Reese."

"No offense, but he didn't exactly hit a home run there. Maybe I could go over, check it out."

"Alone? No way. We'd both go."

She sighed and picked up her wine glass. "I doubt St. John would be happy to see me board a plane and leave the country just now. Until I'm no longer that person of interest, I'm not going anywhere. You know, I've been thinking, the land that ranch sat on had to be worth a small fortune. With Alana in real estate maybe..."

"Was Alana into real estate back then, in 1969 I mean? I thought she was still acting and that came later as a sideline."

"You're right. She often said as a single mother she needed the extra income after I came along. Well, it was just a thought."

After they finished eating, they both began to clear the dishes. Kit opted to wash while Jake dried. Soon, it became a game. Whenever Kit had her hands submerged in the water, Jake took full advantage. Standing behind her, he did his best to toy with every part of her he could reach.

Alternately, she would wash a plate while he nibbled at her ear. After he'd dry whatever she'd washed, he'd go back to nibbling the back of her neck, dry a dish, then gnaw at her shoulder, dry something else, and then chew on the tender part of her arm. It was the most fun she'd ever had doing dishes.

But after nibbling her ear once too often, he finally threw the towel down on the counter and cleverly moved his hands to cup her breasts; his fingers found her nipples through the fabric of her top, rubbing back and forth until he felt the peaks go hard.

She finally leaned her back into him, dried off her hands on the towel he'd thrown down, and teased, "Show me what you got, Sailor Boy."

"My kind of woman," he said huskily as he turned her around to face him, dragged her into him, found her mouth, and devoured. They began to move toward the stateroom wrapped up in each other and worked at getting each other's clothes off.

By the time Jake got her to the bed, all she had on was a pair of black panties. He unzipped his jeans, threw them in the corner, pushed her gently to the bed and followed her down.

He covered her mouth with his, rode the kiss out before sliding her panties past her long legs. Then his fingers dug into moist heat. Kit rode each stroke out, lost in the pleasure, matching his pace until she hit the curl in one big O. As soon as she came, Jake moved to a breast, began to lick and taste there.

But Kit used her newfound confidence to take the reins. Wanting him inside her, she began to stroke him, taking him out of his rhythm. Struggling to maintain control, he slid his hands around her body and rolled her to her stomach. Running his hands up and down her back, he leaned down and whispered in her ear, "I've wanted to do this all day."

"Show me...I want you. Now, Jake."

He nuzzled her ear, brought his hands around between her silky wetness. He lifted her hips and in one smooth motion slipped inside her from behind. She was wet and tight. He tried to slow his pace, slow his thrusts, but Kit would have none of it. When she began to rock back and forth into him, they both lost the battle and rode the peak toward completion.

Moonlight drifted through the room's skylight, bathing them in shadows. As they lay on the bed uncoupled, content, and sated, Jake recovered on his back, while Kit lay on her side with her head resting in the crook of his arm. Her hand draped across his chest, she toyed with a few hairs.

"You know I'll always remember my first time making love on a boat. Without much effort, a woman remembers moments like this—I'll be eighty, sitting around the nursing home. Someone will be talking about boats. The conversation will remind me of tonight and I'll tell them I remember the first time I made love on a boat."

Entwined in each other, he took her chin, turned her face up to his and looked into her jade eyes. "We'll be in the same nursing home. I'll be the guy talking about boats. You'll turn to me and ask if I remember the first time we made love on a boat. I'll say, of course I remember that first time. I may be old, but how could I forget that? It was spring, a beautiful May evening, but as beautiful as the night was it could never compare to how beautiful you are now and how beautiful you were the first time we made love on a boat."

Tears pooled in her eyes. The usually talkative Kit went silent for a long time before telling him, "No one's ever said anything like that to me."

He kissed her brow. "I know, but it's time someone did."

"Do you really think it's possible to stay together with someone for that long?"

"If you'd have asked me that question years ago, I'd have said no way…" He chose his words carefully. "But now…I'm beginning to think if you find the right person…" He didn't tell her he hadn't felt this way about the woman he'd married. When it came to Kit, he felt a rebirth, energized, as if all he'd ever need was her.

But he didn't say that to her now.

"Maybe it's just sex."

He put his fingers to her mouth. "Hmmm, don't you feel it every time we're together?"

"I thought it was just me."

"It isn't." He yawned. She yawned. Two days of not very much sleep finally caught up with both of them. Happier than she was used to feeling, she stretched out her long legs and curled up into his pillow.

They fell asleep in each other's arms.

☙ ☙ ☙ ☙ ☙

The little four-year old girl with a tearstained face sits on the floor of the black hole closet with her arms tightly wrapped around knees drawn up to her chest, gently rocking back and forth. Surrounded by blackness, in the dark, confined to the small space, she uncurls her little legs long enough to kick at the door to no avail.

Locked inside its parameters, unable to get out, she sits, lies, crawls a short distance on the floor, which is hard and unyielding. The hardness of the floor prevents the child from getting any actual rest or finding any comfortable way to sit or sleep.

There's no pillow for her head, no blanket to wrap up in, no toys to play with, no stuffed animal to keep her company. As part of her punishment, it's always the same. She is never allowed to bring anything into the closet with her. Crying has made her eyes hurt, and her thin face shows puffy red cheeks. But she knows there isn't much she can do that will bring anyone to the door to let her out of the darkness anytime soon; even when she has to go to the bathroom, no one will come. When she gets hungry, no one will bring her food. No matter how long she cries, or how loud she screams, no one will open the door and let her out of the black hole closet.

⚭ ⚭ ⚭ ⚭ ⚭

Jake woke to an empty bed. He turned on the bedside light. Looking around the stateroom, his eyes locked on Kit, sitting on the floor hugging her knees, rocking gently back and forth next to the cabin wall.

In the sudden bright of the room, her eyes met Jake's. The look of pure panic in her huge green eyes told him this wasn't like the dream from the other night. And the time wasn't three minutes past three, but rather one-thirty in the morning.

And this was different, her face looked—terror-stricken.

Jake crawled out of bed, slipped on his boxers, and went around to the end, approaching her with care. In an even voice, he asked, "Kit, are you all right?"

She shook her head.

"Did you have a bad dream?"

She nodded and wrapped her arms around her naked body.

"Do you know where you are?"

Some of the fear left her eyes momentarily because she looked at him as if he'd asked a really stupid question. "Your boat. I woke up and wanted to go up on deck, to get outside, but it was dark...and I couldn't find my way...I got...I couldn't find my way out, couldn't find my clothes. I'm not...I'm not used to your boat. I got...confused... I just needed to get outside, but I couldn't. I just wanted to go up on deck...get out..."

"If you'll come over to me, I'll get you outside." He said this as he pulled a T-shirt over his head and put one leg then the other into a pair of shorts.

"You'll take me outside?"

"Come over to me, baby, and we'll go outside together."

She uncurled herself and threw her whole body in his direction, wrapping her arms and legs tightly around him. And in turn, he wrapped his arms around her, holding her close. Kissing the top of her head, he brought his hands up and held her head so that he could look directly into her eyes. "Do you want to stay like this for a while or do you want to go up on deck now?"

"I want to go outside, but I don't want you to let go of me."

He set her down to walk but kept his arm around her waist as he stopped at the built-in dresser long enough to dig into the bag she'd packed for the night. He found a robe and threw it around her shoulders.

On their way through the door of the stateroom, with one hand he grabbed a blanket from the bed to wrap them both up in and made his way through the salon; all the while he held Kit firmly against him.

The steps that led topside were narrow even for one person, so he set her behind him, had her wrap her arms around his waist, and guided her up and out on to the starboard side of the deck.

As soon as she hit the open space, she breathed in several deep breaths of ocean air and looked skyward at the mass of brilliant stars in the early morning sky, never letting go of Jake.

As he held her close, he asked, "Is that better, Kit?"

"Much better. Thanks for letting me out of there."

"Where?"

"The closet—I mean the bedroom. Thanks for getting me out of there."

"Did you have a dream about being locked in the closet?"

She nodded. "I couldn't get out. I haven't felt that way in a really long time. I'd gotten past all those fears, but for some reason, it's all happening in my head again. I woke up and couldn't get out."

He held her tighter. "It's okay now. You're outside."

"That's one of the reasons I like your boat. It's like camping, but on the water."

"We'll stay out here for as long as you want. You don't have to go back inside tonight. I wouldn't much like it locked in a closet, too confining for me."

Even with the darkness Jake saw Kit smile, take another deep breath. "Not only that, but you get scared even when you know you're the only one in there and the floor's cold and hard and you have no idea how long you'll be in there."

Jake took a deep breath of his own. At that moment, for the first time in his life, he contemplated murder. If Alana Stevens wasn't already dead, he might have killed her himself. How could she have treated her own child so horribly?

Underneath the stars, they got comfortable in a chaise lounge, curling up together beneath the blanket. While Jake played with a few strands of her hair, she wanted him to know, "I'm not crazy, Jake. I'm just going through a rough time right now. Since Alana died..."

He laughed. "I don't think you're crazy, Kit. If you need to talk about it, though, we'll talk. But if you don't want to, that's okay, too. I think I understand how tough it is to go back in your mind to that time. So we won't, unless you want to. But I'd never think you're crazy. Do you want to talk?"

She thought for a moment. "No." Snuggling up against his body, she kissed him. They stayed like that until Kit eventually fell back to sleep.

Jake, however, had a tougher time. He thought about his own childhood and how lucky he'd been to have parents whose worst form of discipline was banishing one or all three kids to their rooms for an evening as the dog stood guard outside in the hallway. His thoughts went back to his dad, the soft-spoken, supposedly tough-talking disciplinarian who, when it came to his kids, gave in more often than his mother. He made a mental note to call both of them just to say hello. He thought back to that afternoon, to the few minutes he'd spent in the cramped closet with the door closed, and the grown man shuddered.

He looked down at the sleeping woman in his arms, remembered exactly what she'd looked like when she was fourteen. It hit him then like a punch to the gut. And it had nothing to do with lust, pity, or sympathy. At the realization, a peace descended, and he finally drifted off to sleep.

੪ ੪ ੪ ੪ ੪

The sun peeking through the eastern sky made the water sparkle and glisten. With the first rays of morning light the marina's bird population chirped to life, welcoming daybreak. Before Jake opened his eyes, he felt weight on his legs and lower stomach. When he blinked awake, he saw that Kit had slid somewhat down his body, curled up in a ball and ended up with her head resting on the lower half of his stomach. His right leg tingled. He tried to move to stretch it out without waking her. But she was already awake and in a playful mood. "I feel something hard in my ear."

"It isn't your ear that it's interested in."

She turned her head to look up at him, rested her chin on his stomach and grinned. "What's it interested in?"

"Come here and I'll show you." He reached to pull her up for a kiss.

She responded by slinking up his body. "Morning. Sorry you had to sleep in a deck chair most of the night." She stretched like a cat. "I like sleeping on the boat. Where else can you get up in the middle of the night, take a stroll over the Pacific Ocean?" She yawned. "And we started the day off with a built-in sunrise. How great is that? I can tell you right now, I think we should chunk our boring lives and sail away some place exotic."

"I knew it. You've been bitten by the bug. From now on whenever you're back on land, you'll daydream about being on the water. You won't be able to think of anything but sailing."

She yawned again, lazily stretching out her long legs, but turned serious. "I may be going through a difficult time right now, feeling vulnerable since Alana died. But it's important to me that you know that before this, I was very self-sufficient. I've been on my own since I was sixteen. I run my own business. I may be going through this rough patch, the dreams are upsetting me, there's no denying that, but I don't need someone to take care of me. I'm not high maintenance."

Like Claire, he thought. "I know that, Kit. You're anything but." He started nibbling her ear before his emphasis shifted to the shape of her body through the short, silky robe she wore.

He pulled her up out of the chaise with him and took her hand in his.

"Let's go below deck, there's a softer surface with our name on it."

CHAPTER 20

Recognizing the familiar ring of his cell phone, Jake fumbled toward the built-in nightstand for his phone. When he didn't locate the thing, he reluctantly crawled out of bed to follow the distant ringing; eventually finding it where he'd left it plugged in to charge in the salon.

Rubbing his eyes, he looked at his watch, 8:15. They'd fallen back to sleep. Before that they'd had incredible sex at the crack of dawn. His lips turned up.

After ten rings or so, he finally got to the phone. Caller ID told him it was Dylan. "Jake, the office is a fucking mess. Someone broke in here last night and completely wrecked the place. I just walked in, found stuff everywhere, called you. I'm pissed, and more than a little rattled. It doesn't look as if they took anything, at least I don't think they did. Looks like the computers are still here and so is the other office equipment. I haven't completely checked everything. It looks more like they were looking for something. What do you want me to do?"

The words "looking for something" triggered a reminder of the mess he'd seen at Alana's house. "Did they hack the network again?"

"I can't answer that yet, but I'm on it."

"Call the police. I'll be there as soon as I can."

Back in the stateroom, he stared at a still-sleeping Kit, facing the other way, curled up in a ball, which seemed to be her favorite way to sleep.

He sat down on her side of the bed and began stroking her hair, moving a few strands off her face. Leaning down to her, he rubbed her back, hoping the motion would wake her up. But when she didn't move a muscle, he nudged her, rocking her slightly with a shaking motion. When she still didn't stir, he reached under the covers, found bare skin, and tickled her ribs. She started to wriggle under his touch, and he whispered in her ear, "Kit, you have to get up. Someone broke into my office. I have to go and you have to go with me. I don't want to leave you alone on the boat."

He didn't think it was the right time to mention that he wasn't planning on letting her out of his sight until he found out what the hell was going on. And he suspected something was definitely going on.

Half asleep, not having processed much of what he'd said, Kit turned her head to look at him and noticed he was already dressed. Confused, she stated, "Oh. Good. You're going to get food."

"Come on, sleepyhead. You have to get up and come with me."

"To get food? What time is it? Can't I just stay here?" She yawned and stretched, rolling over in bed. In one fluid motion, she threw her arms around his neck, drawing him down to her level, and gave him a wet kiss. "It's Baylee's turn to work the Saturday morning shift. We can sleep late. I say we make the most of it." She wiggled her eyebrows up and down in a purely sexual invitation.

He knew she considered herself to be somewhat inexperienced, but she was proving to be anything but. Thinking about that right now just made it tougher. When she started moving her hands up under his T-shirt, for a few moments, he didn't put up much of a protest. But then he gently set her back from him. When she looked surprised at his disinterest, he told her, "I've got to get to the office, Kit. Someone tossed the place."

That got her attention. As she rubbed the sleep out of her eyes, she replied, "Just like Alana's."

"Yeah, so until I find out what's going on, the rule is simple: where I go, you go and vice versa; no putting up a fuss."

Minutes later as Kit got dressed, she asked, more awake now, "Did they take anything?"

"Dylan didn't think so. I don't think they were there to steal the equipment, more like they were looking for something." He cocked one brow her way and didn't even have to say it.

She finished for him, "You think whoever went through Alana's place paid you a visit. But why?"

"Good question, honey." He lightly tapped her fanny. "Now hurry up, we gotta go."

Forty minutes later they walked into Billing-Pro Software. For the second time in two days, Jake walked into a mess where someone had gone through everything. He looked around at the desks, where the contents of the drawers had been dumped on the floor. Chairs were overturned, office equipment ruined. And here, just like at Alana's, it didn't look as if they'd taken a single item, but rather tossed stuff around or destroyed it altogether. But unlike Alana's house, this time it was personal.

Dylan met Jake in the hallway. "I've got good news. You just aren't going to believe this. I've got them on tape. They didn't realize we have surveillance cameras set up all over the place."

As he talked, Jake followed him into what they affectionately called, "Command Central," a computer geek's version of paradise. The room contained eight computers dedicated as servers, along with every top-of-the-line, state-of-the-art gadget and device you would expect from the computer world guaranteed to keep Billing-Pro Software on the cutting edge of technology.

Jake watched as Dylan sat down at a computer terminal, and tapped in a few keystrokes. They watched as a grainy, digital image flickered in extremely slow motion on the flat screen monitor. "But you just aren't going to believe who did this." Dylan tapped the keys to enlarge the image, and then said, "Look at who we have here, caught on tape. Recognize anybody, Jake?"

Jake stared more intently at the monitor. "Gerald Auslo and Mark Taft." Maybe this wasn't connected to the mess at Alana's house after all. But it was still a helluva coincidence. And he didn't believe in coincidences.

Kit came up behind Jake and Dylan. They were watching the security tape and alternately cursing as the intruders on tape ransacked desk drawers, scattered papers on the floor, overturned chairs, and generally wreaked havoc on their offices.

"Who are those guys?"

Jake let out a sigh, "Two not-so-bright former employees who worked in testing for about six months more than two years ago."

"So it doesn't have anything to do with Alana's place."

"I didn't say that."

"Who's Alana?" Dylan asked casually, turning his attention from the monitor to watch with interest the interaction between Kit and his friend.

Kit looked at Jake for help, until finally he said, "It's a long story."

Dylan leaned back in his chair. "I've got nothing better to do while we wait for the cops to show up. How about you?"

Kit didn't want to listen, so she excused herself with the offer to make some much-needed coffee and headed to the break room.

In the meantime, Jake told Dylan the short version of what Kit had been going through since Mother's Day, minus all the personal aspects, until Dylan finally wanted to know, "Why would Auslo and Taft ransack Kit's mother's house? Why would you think the two incidents are related?"

"Good question. But here's an even better one: why would two former employees wait two years after their termination to break into our offices? Why now?"

Dylan's eyebrows went up. "Excellent point. So you don't think it's just maybe a coincidence?"

"No way."

When Kit reappeared with the coffee, she had two uniformed officers in tow.

While Jake and Dylan dealt with the police, Kit wandered off to assess the damage to the rest of the offices. Looking around at the destruction, taking mental inventory of the damage, it started to sink in.

For the first time in days, she went through a mental checklist. First, the boat had blown up. Their trip had been a spur-of-the-moment decision made after the funeral ended, unplanned. Yet, someone had known they were on the water that day and what their precise location was.

That same day someone had put Jake's company at risk by hacking the network. The company hadn't just lost valuable data, but their security had been breached, client information compromised. The company Jake had worked so hard to make successful was in jeopardy. And now today, someone had ransacked his offices. All because of her. This was all her fault. If he hadn't gotten involved in her problems, his business wouldn't be at risk now.

For the next two hours Jake and Dylan were busy with the police, reviewing the surveillance tape. The police took the tape as evidence and pretty much assured they'd have no problem getting an arrest warrant for Auslo and Taft.

After filing the lengthy and detailed report, Jake set out to find Kit, who seemed to have disappeared while he'd been occupied with the police. He found her in his office cleaning up the mess. She'd put his desk back in order, picked up all the papers littering the floor, and straightened out most of the files.

He dropped into one of the two chairs facing his desk, and conveyed, "You didn't have to do that, Kit."

She didn't say anything, but continued alphabetizing the rest of his files. One thing he knew about her without a doubt was when the woman wasn't talking it meant she was upset about something. When she finally looked up at him, he saw her moist eyes.

"I'm so sorry, Jake."

"About what? There's nothing to be sorry about. None of this is your fault." Distracted, he joined his fingers like a steeple and leaned back in his chair, as if deep in thought.

She couldn't believe he wasn't upset. She'd seen him as a young programmer just starting out in business, a very intense man who could lose his temper when the slightest thing went wrong with the software. Now his entire company was at risk because of her.

Didn't he understand it was her fault? Finally she said, "Of course it is. If you weren't involved in my problems, your offices wouldn't have been broken into, your system wouldn't have been hacked. And your boat wouldn't have been almost blown up, and you with it." She noticed he wasn't really listening to her and wasn't surprised when his change of subject came out of the blue.

"Kit, if Alana wanted to hide something, something she didn't want anyone—not even dear old Jessica—to find, where would she hide it? Was she the safe-deposit-box kind of woman or the under-the-mattress kind?"

Tears started now and her voice broke. "Didn't you just hear what I said? If we'd gotten closer to that old boat that blew up...you might be...dead. I...I just realized...today looking at this mess...all of this is happening because of me. Someone wants to hurt you, your business, and the company you worked so hard for because of me."

Calmly, Jake got out of the chair and walked around the desk to put his arms around her. He put a hand under her chin and turned her face up to his. With a thumb he wiped away the tears running down her cheek. "Honey, none of this is your fault. It's you I'm worried about. I'm not sure why someone wanted us dead that day on the water, but I think it's you they want to hurt, not me. I'm just in the way. What we have to do is figure out why. Now, if Alana wanted to secure something valuable, hide it away so that no one would find it, what's the most likely place she'd use to stash something?"

"I have no idea. We weren't exactly close, Jake."

"I know, but did she have any weird habits?" When he saw her blink as if she hadn't heard him correctly, he laughed at himself. "Okay, the woman had weird habits out the ying-yang, not exactly Mother Teresa. Let me start over. Did she have any secret places she'd put things, hide stuff, a place she didn't like to share?"

Kit thought for a moment, bit her lip. "Well, I remember she always spent a lot of time up in the attic. She'd spend hours up there with all of her old stuff. She liked to reminiscent about the days when she was an actress, when she was younger."

"Doing what?"

She shrugged. "Who knows? Who cared? Not me. If she wasn't hassling me that was all I cared about. I lived for the times when she was out of the house or busy with whatever, as long as she left me alone." She sighed. "Look, most of the house was off-limits, including the attic. Even when I was young I knew better than to wander around the house. I never ventured up there, never wanted to. But she spent a lot of time there. Why?"

"Because someone is seriously looking for something they think Alana had. They can't find it, and now they've brought their search to my door. That makes it personal, just pisses me off. I want to go back to Beverly Hills, take a look around, and see what I can find."

"Knock yourself out; just don't expect me to go with you."

"It's okay. I'll drop you off at the store. I want you to do something for me, though. Promise me you won't be alone this afternoon. If I'm not back by the time you close up, go home with Baylee or over to Gloria's, wait there until I get back."

The idea of being treated like a child had her temper flaring.

He saw the flicker of anger in her eyes. Before she could explode at him, he added, "Just until I figure out what's going on and why. Okay?"

She wanted to argue, she really did, but when she looked at his face, looked into the depth of his blue eyes and…well shit…why did he always get to her with that look, those eyes?

"Okay," she said weakly. *So I'm not the rock of Gibraltar, for chrissakes. Sue me.*

�♰♰♰♰

A couple of hours later Jake had recruited Dylan and Reese to spend their Saturday afternoon going through Alana's musty attic, helping him look for what he didn't know exactly. All Jake knew for sure was that the three of them could cover more ground, do more digging than one person ever could. That is, if someone hadn't already beaten them to the punch. But they wouldn't know that until they'd checked the place out for themselves.

When the three of them walked up the back staircase from the kitchen to the second floor landing, Jake realized something that he'd missed yesterday, probably because he'd been so caught up in finding that damn closet. But once he got past the landing and veered to the left, this part of the second floor was like a labyrinth.

Following Kit's precise directions, Jake led the way down the narrow hallway, past the alcove, past Kit's Closet, to a remote passage leading to yet another corridor and realized that someone would have to know the attic's exact location in order to get to this spot. Based on that, there was a good chance no one had bothered searching it.

Sure enough, as soon as he got the door open and flipped on the light, it became apparent that the people who'd ransacked the house hadn't made it this far.

Larger than it looked from the second floor, the attic covered a minimum forty feet by forty feet of space. The mess here wasn't due to an intruder, but rather because Alana had been a major pack rat. It soon became clear that this room held what was important to her: possessions left from her past, stacks of boxes containing souvenirs from her days as an actress, memorabilia from a bygone Hollywood era, as well as stacks and stacks of out-of-date clothing and costumes packed away from floor to ceiling. No wonder she had spent so much time up here.

Reese groaned when he saw the condition of the place. "You can't be serious. How the hell are we supposed to find anything in this mess? Look at all this crap. There must be at least sixty cartons to go through and not all of them are marked as to what's inside."

He sneezed several times in rapid succession in response to the layers of dust and sent Jake a go-to-hell look that said "You owe me big time for this, pal."

"Look, I have no idea what's going on or what I'm dealing with. If you have any ideas, now would be a good time to let me in on it. I'm not exactly crazy about spending my Saturday afternoon up here either. If you can come up with a reasonable explanation as to why Auslo and Taft waited two years to hit our offices in retaliation for getting fired, I'll be more than happy to listen, fold my hand, buy the beer, and get the hell out of here."

Reese didn't have a reasonable explanation, but he wanted Jake to know, "I followed up with the police and there's already a warrant out for both of them. It's only a matter of time before they're sitting in a cell. Maybe then they'll feel like talking."

But if Dylan was correct, Reese had a more pressing problem to flesh out. It was time to run interference. "Let's talk about this woman, this Kit that Dylan's been telling me about, the one with the great body. What kind of a woman has a name like Kit, anyway? Sounds more like a stripper."

Jake shot Dylan a lethal glance, but Reese was on a roll. "You're entitled to a distraction now and again even if this one's a little on the young side. And Dylan says she's hot, which tells me you're finally moving on past Claire. But you need to start thinking with the head on your shoulders, not your dick…"

Out of frustration, to shut him up, Jake shoved Reese with such force he went flying into a stack of boxes. He fell back into the cartons before bouncing off and hitting the floor, busting his lip.

Calmly, Dylan walked over and helped Reese to his feet, dusting off his shirt. "Guess I should have warned you Jake's kind of touchy when you try to talk to him about Kit. Personally, I think her name's kinda cute, sort of goes with the woman. Doesn't look much like a stripper though, too classy."

Reese wiped at his already-swelling lip, saw the blood. "Jesus, Jake, I have a date tonight. What the fuck am I supposed to tell her happened to my mouth?"

"Like I give a shit. If both of you would stop needling me for five fucking seconds I might not get so pissed. Just because I fucked up once, and it was major, I'll give you that, doesn't mean I have to spend the rest of my life listening to the two of you preach at me about every goddamn relationship. I know what I'm doing with Kit. She isn't Claire, for chrissakes. Now back off."

Reese pulled his T-shirt up and used it to blot the blood from his lip, exchanged a look with Dylan, who just shrugged and said, "Jake and I already had our little run-in about her. It just didn't come to pushing and shoving."

"As your friend and attorney, I was merely trying to point out you're entitled to a little fun. But…"

"Gee, thanks."

Reese gritted his teeth. "Just don't do anything stupid like you did the last time. Just because she's Gloria's niece, just because you knew her when she was what, fourteen, doesn't mean you know that much about her now. For fuck's sake, people change."

Dylan tried to mend fences. "Jake's had a rough couple of days. Let's not forget someone tried to make toast out of him and Kit earlier in the week; somebody hacked our network, and now this morning two former employees hit our offices. I'm with Jake on this. I think everything that's happened is connected."

Disgusted now, Reese grumbled, "Let's just get this over with. I'd like to get out of here sometime today."

Dylan wanted to know, "What exactly are we looking for, Jake?"

Looking around the packed attic, trying to figure out where to start, Jake scratched at his chin. "That's the tricky part; I'm not sure. Just look for anything that might be valuable, anything that looks important enough that someone would risk the hunt. Or anything that jumps out at you and just doesn't look right. I don't know. But you saw the rest of the house. Someone tore the place up, didn't find what they were looking for, and then came looking in my direction. Until I find out why, I won't rest easy."

Anxious to get started, Jake took out his pocket knife and slit the tape on the first box that wasn't labeled. The dust flew off the carton. Tiny dust particles filled the space and filtered down through the air onto his jeans. He dug into the contents of the box as if on a mission and directed Reese and Dylan to do the same with the others. "Just pick a box and dig in."

Dylan looked around. Some of the boxes looked so old it seemed they'd been stored up here since the beginning of time.

They bypassed the ten boxes or so labeled Christmas decorations, and another half dozen or so labeled books. At least they had no interest in them for now. If they turned up nothing else, they'd save those boxes to go through last.

Dylan cut into a box, peered inside, and immediately made the determination the contents weren't worth going through since it held nothing but old clothes. However, he picked up a second carton labeled movies, organized by the year of their production. At some point in her life Alana had taken copies of her old movie reels and had them converted to VHS. Dylan started rummaging around in the box until he picked up one of the tapes. "Hey, remember this movie, *Savage Monster*? We saw it when we were twelve down at that old theater on Main with all the murals on the wall. They were having a horror film festival." Studying the picture of the actress on the box cover, he added, "Oh. I get it now. Alana Stevens is Kit's mother. This is her house. Wow. She was hot, hotter than Elvira. Both of them caused more than a couple of wet dreams back then."

He was grinning like a fool until Jake jerked the box out of his hands.

"You aren't twelve anymore. Come back from your sick fantasy world long enough to focus, okay? We aren't interested in what you used to jack off to."

While Dylan and Jake were going at each other, Reese pulled an old trunk away from the wall. Hidden behind the trunk he discovered a box of old movie reels, for whatever reason these hadn't been converted to VHS. Each canister inexplicably was marked with the letter P. Curiosity overcame Reese as he popped open one of the canisters, peeled off several inches of film, and held it up to what little light the attic provided. As soon as he saw the images, he let out a laugh and shoved his find toward Jake.

"Jesus, I think I've found blackmail material right off the bat. Looks like porn, pretty raunchy, and a bit amateurish if you ask me."

Jake took the reel and held it up to the light and swore. "Okay, our first find. Dylan, start stacking these reels into that empty box over there."

Evidently proud of her early work in the porn industry Alana had kept no less than twenty or so of her X-rated eight-millimeter films. Curiosity piqued now, Dylan waited for Jake to put down the reel he was holding. When he did, Dylan took his turn at holding the frame up to the light and whistled. "I don't care what you say; she was hot. This is pretty X-rated stuff, though." He began loading each movie reel into a box until he got them all stacked and decided to check out each reel individually.

When Jake saw what he was doing, he said, "Geez, Dylan, grow up. It'd be great if you'd do a little work here other than get off on that stuff. If you're going to check out every frame of film scene-by-scene, this'll take forever. Besides, consider how old those people on that film are now. Unless old people do it for you, really, really old people, you can't possibly think they're that hot to look at now."

Once again holding up a frame to the light, Dylan's answer was purely male. "Hey, I'm just trying to be thorough here. Old or not, and I might point out, on the film they aren't that old, and porn's porn. If I'd known we'd find porn, I might have been a little more enthusiastic about giving up my Saturday for this." As he eyed the film with closer scrutiny, he added, "These people were really into this stuff, weren't they?"

It was some time before Dylan got back to work.

The three of them rummaged through boxes containing nothing more than old real estate contracts or paperwork from some of Alana's past business dealings. And there were tons of discarded contracts and real estate documents, as if she never threw a single piece of paper away. Not knowing if any of the papers held anything of interest, they set them aside for now, but not before organizing the stacks, depending on the date, into a pile labeled Business.

Jake found a large plastic container that held old photo albums and an old scrapbook. He set them down by the attic door to take with him in the event they were of interest to Kit. Curious though, he picked up one of the photo albums, flipped through the pages thinking he'd found family snapshots and might happen upon a baby picture or two of Kit. But after several minutes he realized these were not pictures of children but rather stills of adults in various forms of undress—some in sexual positions he hadn't yet had the opportunity to try even during his college days.

When he tossed the book down in disgust, Dylan got nosy, picked it up, and thumbed through several pages, before looking over at Jake. "Have we just busted a porn ring or maybe a blackmail ring here? What was wrong with these people?"

Jake thought of Alana and replied without thinking, "The woman was just evil." Thinking about Kit growing up in that environment made him sick. Why the hell hadn't her father taken her away from Alana long before the girl had turned twelve? Why hadn't he fought harder for custody?

The porn they'd found confirmed the fact that he'd never seen a father with more ammunition on his side to get full custody of his child than John Griffin, even if the two of them had never been married. And yet time and time again he'd left his daughter with a sick, perverted woman like Alana. John Griffin had turned his back on the situation, gone on with his life, ignoring Kit's environment.

And that just pissed Jake off.

He turned his attention to another box of papers and began sorting through each piece, checking out the dates, and then further organizing them by year. He did the same with each pile until he got to the mound of business stuff.

Sifting through the papers, one piece of paper in particular caught his eye. A yellowed blank sheet of letterhead held a somewhat familiar-looking logo. Was he imagining the similarity? The logo on the stationary depicted a lone cowboy in blue sitting atop a black horse riding off into a brilliant orange sunset in the background. There was no mistaking the resemblance to the toy cowboy Kit had given Holloway. Under the logo, the letterhead read, "The Sundown Ranch, Hollywood Hills, CA." Hadn't the elderly couple from Kit's dream lived there? Folding the single sheet of paper, he stuffed it into his shirt pocket before eyeing the rest of the cartons stacked around the room.

After an exhaustive search, they had accumulated a surplus of studio contracts and real estate paperwork. For organization purposes, they separated the assortment of papers into four piles: Personal, Business, Bank Records, and Actress. When Reese found Alana's old union cards, one from the Screen Actors Guild and another from the American Guild of Variety Artists, he threw those in with the stack marked Actress. Old out-of-date cancelled checks were placed in the Bank Records pile. They found more than a dozen odd keys that weren't marked. Having no idea what any of the keys opened, or for that matter why Alana would have kept so many, Jake found a large-size manila envelope for the purpose of organization and dumped all the keys into it for safekeeping so they'd be able to keep up with them.

At one point the lawyer in Reese began to re-examine each of the items in the stack marked Personal until he came across the original deed to the house. "Look at the date, July 1969. She owned this house for more than forty years. Wonder what she paid for a house like this back then?"

"No idea. Didn't realize porn in the sixties was that lucrative."

Reese put the deed on the top of the Personal stack for later examination and decided to try to find the original purchase price of the house. But in the pile marked Bank Records, he got sidetracked when he discovered several worn-out, copies of cashier's checks, each made out for the same amount: $25,000. Each check was for a different month, dated from December 20 1967 through August 20 1969. Each was made payable to Alana Stevens, drawn on a bank in Beverly Hills that he was pretty sure was no longer in business. The color might have faded, but the printed indentations were just as legible now as they had been back then.

He counted each check…twenty checks in all, each for $25,000, totaling $500,000 over a time period of twenty months. He tapped Jake's arm to show him what he'd found. "You said to look for anything odd. You said this woman was an actress turned real estate broker, right? Well, if these checks were monthly commission checks, why was the payment made via a cashier's check when they should have been drawn on a real estate company account? And if they're for acting jobs, why are the checks not drawn on a regular business account such as a studio account? Actors aren't usually paid for a job spread out over twenty months. These cashier's checks total a half a million dollars over a two-year period. In my book, that's weird."

The cashier's checks conveniently came at about the same time Alana had purchased her house in July of the same year.

"Maybe she saved her money from these checks so she could pay cash for the house."

That's what Jake thought as well, but they needed to know how much she'd paid for the house. So Reese and Jake set out to find the original purchase contract. She hadn't thrown anything else away so it was a pretty good bet it was here somewhere; they just had to find it. It took some time, but Reese eventually uncovered the contract in the pile of real estate stuff. "She paid a hundred and twenty grand for the house. So a portion of the cashier's checks would have been more than enough to buy the house."

As Dylan burrowed further into the stack of business stuff, he discovered Alana's original real estate license dated November 5, 1969 and pointed out, "If she didn't become a realtor until four months after she bought the house, the checks couldn't have been commissions from real estate sales. If they weren't commissions or from acting jobs, then what were they payment for?"

"Let me see that." Jake checked out the date of the license. "Son of a bitch." He remembered what Kit had said last night about the Sundown Ranch and how valuable the land would have been. So Alana had had her real estate license back in 1969, years before she became a single mother in need of extra income.

But even with that, Jake wasn't sure they'd found anything important. Let down over that, he didn't expect much when Dylan popped open a box labeled Books and hit the mother lode.

Nestled under the works of D.H. Lawrence, Dylan found a small mobile safe with a key-fitting lock. Reese remembered the keys they'd found earlier and retrieved the envelope, dumping the collection on top of an old trunk. The three of them took turns trying to fit each of the keys into the lock until finally they ran out of keys.

Dylan was the first to offer a solution. "I know a locksmith. We can take this to him, get him to pop it open."

"You sure?"

"Won't be a problem. He's a...how do I say this...a former expert in his field."

"Geez Dyl, you're just full of surprises, you know that?"

"I have very diverse friends—except, of course, for you and Reese. You two are about the most conservative guys I run with."

Insulted, Reese threw Dylan a furious glare. "You think Jake and I are conservative? Is that a code word for boring?"

"Well. Yeah. Duh. Former nerd programmer, stuffy lawyer. You guys are boring."

"I hate to point this out to you, Sherlock, but you're a nerd programmer. If we're boring, that makes you one of us."

"Yeah, but I'm a lot less boring than you guys. I know how to have fun. I hate to say this, but you guys just can't help being killjoys. We never do anything fun anymore. With the two of you, it's all work, work, work."

Reese didn't care for the assessment. "We went skiing at Mammoth last year, didn't we? What about that?"

"Isolated incident."

Without waiting any longer for an apology that obviously wasn't coming, Reese threw his shoulder into Dylan, bouncing him up against the attic wall.

Before Jake could react, the two of them were pushing and shoving like two power forwards fighting for the ball. Jake stepped into the fray planning to referee, but in two seconds he was blocking blows now turned on him. They wrestled with the energy of ten-year-olds until Jake pushed between both of them and threw all of his weight into Dylan. "Knock it off. I think we're done here. Let's load up this shit. Beer's on me."

As they packed up the stuff they thought was important and loaded it into boxes to cart downstairs, Dylan wanted to know, "You planning on telling Kit that at one time her mom was the queen of porn?"

Thinking of Kit in this house as a child, Jake answered simply, "What makes you think she doesn't already know?"

CHAPTER 21

As she locked up the Book & Bean, Kit felt only a slight twinge of guilt for not following Jake's directive to the letter. But when Sarah had grown fussy with all the classic symptoms of cutting another tooth, Kit had sent Baylee home early to take care of her daughter. And since Baylee was practically living with Glo, it would have made sense if Kit had closed up the store then and gone home with Baylee. But she hadn't thought of that until Baylee was halfway to Agoura Hills.

To keep her promise to Jake, though, she'd called Gloria and invited herself over for Chinese take-out. It would be the perfect time to sit down with her aunt, get her take on the dream, and see what she had to say about the fact that Alana and her father had never been married. And while she was at it, she might as well tell her about Ben Griffin.

As Kit pulled the Jeep out of the parking lot, she didn't see the big SUV slide in behind her at the light just before the Jeep moved into traffic on the Coast Highway.

Traffic on the 1 was surprisingly light for a Saturday night. With the CD player cranked up and Pepper sitting in the back seat, Kit let her mind drift. Listening to Springsteen wonder what it was like in the back of a Pink Cadillac, she wondered if Gloria knew about Alana's marriage to Frank Geller. The thought of that union had her cringing. She remembered Frank as a rather creepy kind of guy who always appeared as if he were working on his next con, a guy with a definite used-car salesman appearance. She was grateful she hadn't been around for that marriage.

As traffic got heavier, every once in a while she glanced out over the water and mentally ticked off the list of things about the dream she needed to remember to mention to Gloria.

Deep in thought, she didn't notice the silver SUV come around the Jeep as if to pass. Instead of flying by, though, the vehicle maintained the same speed as she did. By the time she saw that the SUV intended to occupy the same lane as the Jeep, the vehicle had already crossed the dotted line, bumping the driver's side, causing her to swerve onto the shoulder.

She had to fight the wheel hard to the left to keep the SUV from completely running her off the road. The big SUV kept pace. There was no room for her to maneuver. She battled with the vehicle, trying to keep from losing control. Thinking that maybe the SUV might simply bump her and go on, she slowed down enough to give the other car the road. But when she braked to slow down so did the SUV.

Instead of moving on, the vehicle stayed glued to the side of the Jeep. Kit managed to look over and saw a familiar face smiling back at her. Meanwhile, the SUV kept coming, veering farther and farther into her until there was nothing to do but to try and maintain control of the car.

She did her best until the SUV rammed harder this time, metal-to-metal into the driver's side with such force it pushed her off the shoulder onto the rough terrain. And still the SUV kept coming. When Kit hit the brakes, the SUV did the same as if anticipating her move. Driving on the shoulder now, both vehicles were in the dirt next to the edge of the cliffs. The SUV kept pushing and pushing until finally there was no place left for the Jeep to go. It plunged off the edge and down the steep cliffs below.

⚜ ⚜ ⚜ ⚜ ⚜

At their favorite watering hole, a Mexican cantina across from Billing-Pro Software, the three men were on their second round of beers when Jake's cell phone rang. A glance at caller ID told him it was Gloria.

Jake answered the phone with all the cheer of a man relaxing in a bar enjoying a Saturday night round of drinks after a long stress-filled week. "Hey Gloria, what's up?"

The minute she started to speak, though, Jake knew something was wrong; he could sense it in the way her voice cracked. "Jake, oh Jake, I'm so glad I got you. Kit's been hurt. She…she had an accident. They've taken her to the emergency room at the Medical Center."

His world tilted. Hurt? An accident? What the hell? He stood up from the table and swayed, not so much from the beer and a half he'd consumed but from knowing that Kit had been injured and he hadn't been there to protect her. He threw money on the table about the same time he reached into his jeans pocket to pull out his car keys.

"What happened?"

"I don't have all the details. Baylee and I are on our way there now. Someone arranged for Pepper to be taken to the vet. The person who called…they said…the person that called said…they had to stabilize her before they could load her into the ambulance. Someone ran her off the road and…her Jeep plunged down an embankment. She…" Her voice trailed off and Gloria began to sob.

"I'm on my way Gloria. I'll meet you there." Jake's pace picked up as he moved toward the entrance to the restaurant with Reese and Dylan on his heels. "Kit had a car accident. I've got to go."

At the look on his friend's face, Dylan grabbed Jake's arm, only to have him pull away. Noting the glassy shock in Jake's eyes, Dylan and Reese exchanged looks. It was Reese who took Jake's keys from him and volunteered, "I'll drive."

"I thought you had a date."

"So, I'll be a little late."

⚠⚠⚠⚠⚠

Jake knew he was in the right place when he spotted an anxious Baylee pacing back and forth in front of a semicircular reception desk with a sleeping Sarah on her shoulder. When Baylee looked up and saw Jake approaching, she put out the one hand she'd been using to rub the baby's back and took Jake's hand in hers. Softly, so as not to wake the baby, but trying not to cry, she told him, "She'll be okay, Jake. She's tough."

"I want to see her. Where is she? How bad is it?"

"You will. But right now they've taken her down the hall to do an MRI. Quinn says the doctor's pretty sure she suffered a concussion, but they want to see how extensive it is, check for internal bleeding."

Jake flinched. He didn't want to think about Kit with a concussion let alone in the closed scanner. "She's claustrophobic. She won't do well in that closed up space."

Baylee gave him a sympathetic look. "She's a little out of it, Jake, groggy. I don't think she'll be aware that she's in there. Besides, Quinn's with her. She isn't alone. We lucked out having Quinn on duty tonight." Baylee made a face. "There were some lacerations...on her face, some bruising."

Jake winced.

Noticing his grimace, she explained, "From the airbag. Her head and right shoulder took the worst of the impact, as well as her right leg. Right leg isn't broken though. At least that's what Quinn said. She's been in there with her since they brought her in, says Kit will need some stitches on the side of her head." With her free hand she pointed to the side of her own head just above the ear. "When they get her shoulder back in place, she'll be good as new."

To Baylee's credit she did her best to put a positive spin on Kit's injuries, but Jake just wasn't in the mood to be appeased. He wanted answers; he wanted to see Kit, see how she was for himself. He looked around and realized the waiting area looked like any typical ER on any given Saturday night. The place offered nothing but standing room only. Since there were no available chairs, and he didn't feel like sitting anyway, he searched out Dylan and Reese, only to realize they'd been standing directly behind him the entire time. A couple of feet away he spotted Gloria for the first time; she looked upset, tears running down her cheeks.

Dylan poked Jake in the ribs with his elbow. "Aren't you going to introduce us to the ladies?"

"Dylan and Reese, you remember Gloria Gandis. And this is Baylee Scott and her daughter, Sarah." Baylee nodded in their direction, but it was Gloria who saw Dylan and Reese through misty eyes and said, "Kit will be so pleased that you came to see her."

"Has anyone spoken to the police? Can they tell us what happened and how the accident happened?"

Baylee looked uncomfortable. "Quinn talked to them earlier. There were witnesses who said an SUV deliberately ran her off the road, pushed Kit's Jeep down the side of a cliff. The SUV took off, didn't stop." She anticipated Jake's question before he had time to ask. "No one got a license plate, just a description of the car; late model SUV, silver, big."

Jake's knees went weak at the thought of Kit lying in that car, unconscious, hurt. Just then he looked past Baylee and saw Quinn heading their way. Dressed in her white coat, the woman didn't look old enough to be a doctor.

But Dr. Quinn Tyler was all business, when she nodded in greeting. "She's getting stitched up. I wanted to do the honors, but I flipped Dr. Anson for it and lost." When she realized her joke hadn't been well received, Quinn shifted back to serious. "She's still in and out of it, but you guys can see her now, one at a time. Who wants to go first?"

Jake deferred to Gloria, but obviously hoped she'd pick up on how much he wanted to see Kit. Sure enough, he saw the green light in her eyes before she nodded and heard her say, "You go on, Jake. I'll go next, and then we'll let Baylee go in and take her turn before she has to leave to put the baby to bed."

Jake didn't wait for a consensus but turned on his heels, followed Quinn down the corridor, and disappeared.

When he was gone, Dylan stared at the baby, who by now was wide awake and looking around at all the people. He also noticed how Baylee was struggling to hold her for such a long time with no place to sit down. He put his hands in his pocket and leaned closer to where Baylee stood.

He looked into her face and her huge blue—almost turquoise-colored—eyes. He'd never seen anyone with that particular shade of eyes before. In the way of most single men, he shot a glance at her left ring finger. There was no ring.

He took a step closer so he could get a better angle at the baby's eyes. But Baylee turned around abruptly. Their eyes met. Instinctively, she took a step backward, leery of the close contact. Dylan just smiled easily and commented, "That's a good-looking baby you've got there. She has your eyes. And it looks like you might need a place to sit down. Why don't I see if one of these nice folks will find their manners and let you have a seat?"

Baylee drew in a quick breath. The man looked like a surfer with sun-toned skin and blond hair pulled into a neat ponytail. He stared at her through calm blue eyes; there was an easy demeanor about him.

She immediately went on red alert. She had no business thinking about any man. She'd been fooled into trusting the wrong one once before. She knew a gentle manner could be deceiving. But when Sarah reached out to touch Dylan's nose, Baylee caved in a little and said, "Thank you, but what I really need is a place to...to feed her. Coming to the hospital is throwing her off her routine and she's getting...hungry. I'll just head outside to the car and…"

Dylan thought he understood. The woman needed a place to nurse. He looked around the room. It was overflowing with people. "Wait here," he said as he went over to the reception desk, talked with a nurse for a few minutes, and then came back to Baylee. "There's a family restroom down the hall for mothers with children. There's a place to sit and room to feed her. I'll show you where it is. Where's your bag?"

Baylee pointed over to where Gloria stood guarding an oversized, overstuffed olive green bag. He calmly walked over, took it from Gloria, and turned to Baylee. "It's just down the hall to the left, this way." He nodded his head for her to follow.

Reluctant, Baylee just stood there but then felt silly. It was a public place. He was just being helpful. When Sarah began to fuss, Baylee tagged after Dylan, who had hefted Sarah's diaper bag over his shoulder as if it were an everyday occurrence, and both of them set off down the corridor.

⚛ ⚛ ⚛ ⚛ ⚛

Quinn took the time to prepare Jake for the scene behind the curtain. "She's a little banged up." And that was putting it mildly, thought Quinn. But she didn't want the man to go nuts when he saw what she looked like. "Bruises are starting to form, turn purple, so don't be shocked by what you see. She did, after all, just go one-on-one with a 6,000 pound car and an airbag. And I don't want you passing out on me. You aren't queasy around needles, are you?"

"No," was Jake's quick reply. But as he stood, just this side of some flimsy curtain barely separating the too-small space from another patient; he thought he might not be as comfortable around needles after all. And to top it off, as if it were possible, the man stitching Kit up looked even younger than Quinn.

Kit rested on the bed with a goose egg-sized knot and a purple bruise on the right side of her forehead. Her right shoulder was wrapped in some kind of a sling and her normally golden skin had turned a pasty white. Blood loss, he knew, would account for the paleness. Her right leg was under the sheet so he couldn't assess the damage to it.

Thinking about her childhood and how many times she'd been hurt with no one to care for her, seeing her like this, so vulnerable, broke Jake's heart.

But the doctor was talking in an upbeat kind of way as he worked, and he had some sort of an accent. "Look here now, lass, it seems you have a visitor. Kit is a fine-looking lady and she'll not be the worse for wear when I'm done with her. As I was telling your girl here, I got excellent marks in school for my stitches."

He winked at Kit for effect and went on cheerfully, "We'll have her fixed up here in no time and resting in her own room. She'll be good as new; won't you, now?" He motioned at Jake with a nod of his head and said, "You can hold her hand if you like."

Jake stepped forward, wanting to touch, but half-afraid he'd hurt her more if he did. She looked so fragile. When he placed his hand in hers, found it cold, he wrapped both of his hands around her smaller one and held on like a lifeline. "I'm here, Kit. I should never have left you alone. Don't try to move. I'll just hold onto you while the doctor makes you better."

When she didn't answer, the doctor told him, "She's a little muddled right now, but she knows you're here, that she's not alone, don't you lass?"

Undeterred, Jake leaned down to her, whispering words of comfort in her ear until he heard the doctor snap off his gloves and announce he was finished.

"We'll be moving her now to her own room. You can follow her up if you like." And with that, the doctor left them alone.

Jake sat down on the bed by her side. "I was so worried, Kit." His knees were still shaking. "Are you in pain?"

Weakly, barely above a whisper, she asked, "Pepper? What about Pepper?"

He was grateful to finally hear her speak, and he had no idea how the dog was, but he reassured her anyway. "Someone saw that he was taken to the vet. I'll check on him as soon as we get you settled. Don't worry, I'll see to him, Kit; see that he's taken care of."

"Promise?"

"Promise." He kissed the palm of her hand, "Are you in pain, baby?"

"I'm okay. Throbbing, everything's throbbing a little." She wanted to just drift away, but as if from a distance she thought she heard Gloria tell Jake, "The police are out in the waiting area. If you'd like to have a word with them, I'll stay with Kit and go with her to her room. You can meet us up there when you're done. I'm told they're putting her in room 512. Baylee will want to take her turn to see that she's okay before she takes the baby home."

Jake leaned into Kit, over her, took his time trying to decide where to plant a kiss. Finally settling on her forehead first, he placed a tender kiss, lips barely touching skin, before moving on to her nose, then to her chin and finally, gingerly, kissed her lips. When she closed her eyes sleepily, he left her with Gloria, left her to sleep while he tried to get some answers out of the police.

When Jake got back to the waiting area, a uniformed police officer was explaining what he knew about the accident to Dylan and Reese. "Witnesses said the SUV crossed a lane of traffic at high speed before bumping her Jeep. Then for approximately a half a mile the SUV continued to bump the car until the Jeep finally careened out of control and went off the cliff, landing some twenty-five feet down on a drop-off point. Some of those cliffs are so steep they plunge right off into the ocean. It could have been much worse. She's lucky the car came to a stop when it did, or that the gas tank didn't take a hit and explode, or that the Jeep didn't roll over on impact.

"Unfortunately, the witnesses we've spoken to so far didn't get a license plate number and can't agree on what the driver looked like. And most of the people, the witnesses, agree the car was either gray or silver in color, but they aren't certain which. That isn't unusual with these kinds of accidents, what with dusk just setting in. The car took off, didn't hang around long enough for anyone to get any more detail than that. More than likely we're dealing with a drunk driver and that's why they didn't stop. These things take time to sort out..."

"This was no accident." Jake wasn't buying the drunk driver scenario. "You're telling us you have no fucking clue who did this to her? That you have no reliable witnesses, don't know what type of vehicle ran her down, other than it was either a gray or silver SUV? Essentially, you've got nothing?"

Reese recognized the anger building in Jake with every word. When Reese saw that Jake was about to step into the officer's face, he pushed him back a step, only to be shoved back in response. Reese hoped the physical contact with him would temper Jake's attitude toward the cop. But Jake was just warming up. Over and through Reese, he told the officer, "You need to call Homicide, talk to Max St. John or Dan Holloway, make them aware that someone tried to kill her tonight; tell them what happened here."

"Now why would I do that? Think about what you're saying. You're suggesting that someone deliberately did this. We have no proof that it was anything more than a drunk driver. We'll continue investigating. But right now, you need to calm down."

Finally, at Reese's insistence, Jake took a step backward, ran his hands through his hair, and more calmly explained to the officer, "Look, Kit's mother Alana Stevens was murdered recently. St. John and Holloway are assigned to the case. Check it out if you don't believe me. There have been two additional murders since then. I'm telling you, this was no accident and you need to at least inform them what happened here tonight."

"And you need to let us do our job."

"Then do your fucking job." A frustrated Jake spun on his heels and headed for the elevators. This was pointless, he thought. They just didn't see the connection; couldn't they see it was all related? As he punched the UP button and waited for the doors to open, he was convinced that none of the police could connect dots even if you spotted them the pattern. Right now, he needed to be with Kit.

Reese and Dylan caught up with him at the elevator. When they stepped into the car with him, he told Dylan, "Tomorrow I want you to take that safe we found and get it open. Find out if what's in there is worth Kit's life."

That stopped both men in their tracks.

"You really think someone deliberately tried to run her off the road?"

"Yeah, I do. I'm thinking after she's discharged I'm getting her out of here, taking her someplace safe."

When the elevator doors opened to the fifth floor, Jake took one look at a grim-faced Quinn standing at the nurse's station, and panic gripped his gut. "What's wrong?"

Quinn looked startled for a moment, but then took a deep breath. "They found some internal bleeding in her spleen. If it gets worse, they'll have to do surgery, remove it. Her doctor wants her to stabilize a little more first, though, give it time to stop on its own. If it does, she won't need surgery." God, she hoped that was the case.

"Surgery?" This couldn't be happening. "Can I see her?"

"Sure. I'll take you in. Gloria and Baylee are with her. I'm still on duty and will be until seven in the morning, but I'll look in on her every chance I get. If you'll leave me your phone number, I'll let you…"

"I'm not leaving."

Quinn hid her surprise. "Well, the nurses might have something to say about that." But the determined look on his face softened her so much that instead of giving him a hard time, she winked at him and offered, "I'll let the nurses know you're a member of the family." Wiggling her eyebrows back and forth, she added, "A brother, perhaps."

"If that's what it takes to let me stay in her room, I don't care who they think I am."

As soon as Jake entered the room, Baylee and Gloria stepped out into the hallway to give him some privacy. He crossed to the bed, and stared at the woman lying so still.

How in the world had she come to mean so much to him in such a short amount of time? He'd expected to care. Hell, he'd always cared about her. And he couldn't stand to see her hurt. That was all there was to it. But the urge to tell her, to say the words he'd never said to anyone else was as strong now as it had been that morning on the boat. Something stupid had held him back then. And now, to his regret, she might never hear him say those words.

What if something happened to her in surgery? He'd never considered himself weak, or scared of anything before, but he was afraid if he didn't tell her something might happen when she went into surgery. She might not wake up. At the thought of that, he leaned down next to her where only she could hear and whispered, "I love you, Kit. I love you. Do you hear me? Do you know what I'm saying to you?" He didn't really expect her to answer, but he found that saying the words had been a simple enough thing after all.

CHAPTER 22

On this Sunday morning he looked like any other typical tourist sitting on a sand dune watching the waves.

Man, he loved sunny Southern California. Since the storm had passed and brought sunshine and perfect surf, the sun had seemed to lighten the darkness that had settled over him the past two years. When he was finished with all of this, he might just extend his visit. Take some time to relax and do nothing but laze at the beach. As he sat looking out to sea, he waited once again for his prey to come to him.

Technically speaking in this case, the man would jog to him just as he'd done every day at exactly seven-thirty, come rain or shine. Hell, the man had probably been running on this same beach every day of his life at exactly the same time every morning since he'd moved here in 1970. And wasn't that just a kick in the pants. The man obviously loved this view, loved this place.

It was a good thing, too, because the man was going to die here.

At least he would die on his beloved beach. How poetic was that?

When he caught sight of the man jogging his way, he calmly stood up, brushed the sand from his ridiculous flowered print shorts. It was time to go to work.

Years younger than his prey, he jogged toward the elder man from the opposite direction, catching up with him without much effort. He had set up the scene perfectly and when he'd gotten within four feet or so of the jogging man, he said, "Wow, you're Sumner Boyd, aren't you? Wait until I tell the wife I jogged on the same beach as the great legal eagle himself. Man, she just isn't going to believe me."

Indignant that someone would not only approach him but intrude upon his private inner sanctum in such a manner, Sumner's face, already red from the physical exertion of running three miles, got redder. "How the hell did you get down here? This beach is private. Can't you goddamned tourists read a fucking sign?"

"Nice meeting you too, asshole. Oh, I can read. In fact, let me tell you a story." He calmly withdrew a .38 revolver from his pocket. The weapon got Sumner's attention. "It's not really important to know how I got down here, but rather why. I'd think you'd get down on your knees right about now and thank me for getting rid of Alana and Jessica and Eva. Of course, you aren't going to be around much longer to enjoy the solitude. But, don't tell me you didn't think about taking care of at least one of those three bitches yourself over the years."

He laughed when he noticed the shocked look on Sumner's face. "I apologize. I'm getting completely off the subject. I've been doing that a lot lately. Now, why don't we sit down on this rock here, on the beach you love so much, and let me tell you a story?"

He saw Sumner's face go from shock to fear. Good, he thought, he had the man's attention.

"Wait. I'm a wealthy man. I can give you anything you want. Just don't kill me."

"Really? Anything?"

"Yes, anything, just name it." The fear on his face turned hopeful. Thank God for his money. He could bargain his way out of this.

"Can you bring someone back from the dead?"

Sumner's face went from red to white. The hope completely drained from his face and was replaced by confusion. "Don't be absurd."

"Then you really have nothing I want, except your life. But don't worry, you'll die on your own sand on a beautiful day and if you'll sit down and listen, I'll tell you why. Have you ever heard that old saying?" He paused for effect and with his other hand twirled a finger in the air. "...what goes around comes around?"

☙ ☙ ☙ ☙ ☙

In Kit's hospital room, Jake slept covered up in a blanket, stretched out as best he could between two chairs. His head rested on the back of one while a leg and a foot dangled off another. When the door opened and Baylee walked in carrying a sack, his head popped up.

As soon as she set the bag down, she stuck her hands in her back pockets, rocked on her heels, and said in a low voice, "Sorry to wake you. I didn't realize you might still be asleep. I hate hospitals. If you ask me, you can never rest in a hospital. They're always coming up with a reason to poke and stick you."

Jake rubbed at his tired eyes and sat up erect, stretched. "It's okay. I didn't really sleep."

Little wonder, she thought, looking at the man's makeshift bed. "How's our girl?"

"She's been in and out of it most of the night. But the good news is about three this morning the bleeding in her spleen seems to have stopped on its own. They don't think she'll need surgery." Sniffing the air, he brightened. "Is that coffee?"

Baylee reached into the sack, pulled out a Styrofoam cup, and handed it off before reaching in for another. "Thought you could use a jolt right about now. Didn't used to drink this stuff. But after Sarah came along, I found out soon enough that when you wake up in the middle of the night with a fussy baby, you need that extra jolt of caffeine that you just can't get from a can of soda. After months of drinking the stuff, I'm hooked. I can't make it past six a.m.

anymore without my shot of java, even if I do drink it with a half a cup of milk."

Jake laughed before yawning and got up out of the chair to stretch his back. He started telling her about how his sisters had changed when they'd become mothers.

As he talked, Baylee noticed a wistful look come across his face. She recognized that look, an almost longing that settled in his eyes when he talked about his siblings having kids. It was possible, she thought, that he wasn't even aware of it. "Ever think about having any of your own?" Baylee asked.

Jake's eyes drifted instantly to Kit before he simply said, "Yeah."

Baylee left it at that, but wanted to know, "Were you able to find out any information about Pepper? The minute she comes around she'll want to know how he is."

"She's already asked. And yeah, I found out he suffered a compound fracture in his right hind leg as well as internal injuries, didn't get out of surgery until around two. But I left the vet my cell number and he promised to call with an update this morning. I can only hope the news is good." After taking a long drink of his coffee, Jake said softly, "I don't like seeing her hurt."

"Neither do I; she's had too much of that already." Baylee waited a beat before adding, "Has she told you all of it, then?"

The two shared eye contact for a moment. "She told me enough. I'm not making her travel down that road any more than necessary."

Baylee's opinion of the man edged up several notches as she listened to Jake go on, "You didn't see her sitting in her car the day she went to Beverly Hills. You didn't see her panic at the idea of going back inside that house. I can only imagine what it was like for her, living there with that woman. You were around Alana. You knew what Kit had to deal with."

Baylee looked away. "I did. I hated that woman. And when Holloway and St. John get around to asking, I'll tell them so."

She took a sip of coffee. "She was mean. I remember one time Kit was doing her best to ride her bike with the training wheels still on. But like most kids, she took a spill, fell off, skinned her knee, and tore her dress. It wasn't until we were older after I'd given her grief once too often about her always wearing a dress outside to play in that she told me how Alana wouldn't let her wear pants or jeans. Ever. Anyway, Kit fell off her bike, ripped her dress at the bottom. Before I could stop, help her up, Alana comes tearing out of the damned house like she'd been watching from the window ready to pounce, doesn't even take the time to check Kit's skinned knee—just yanks her up off the ground, goes to whaling the tar out of her, the whole time cursing that she's torn the freaking dress."

She drew in a deep breath, let it out. "Alana scared the crap out of me."

Baylee took another long pull of caffeine. "You might as well know Kit had it so much worse than I had it growing up. You see, my mother walked out on my father when I was about three, ran off to Europe with her tennis pro. Unfortunately, when she decided to leave William Scott, she also left me." She waited a beat until she saw the recognition flash in Jake's eyes. Her father had once been one of the most sought-after directors of action films in Hollywood. "Yeah, that William Scott. I don't remember much about my mother. I was raised primarily by the housekeeper, Tanya Lincoln. If Dad ever started that walk down memory lane, though, started reminiscing about his ex-wife, good old mom, he'd start drinking heavily. Followed by a huge mad-on, he'd start to hit on the closest and then the most vulnerable person which was usually me. Fortunately for me, my father wasn't home that often. He'd spend eighteen-hour days at the studio. Or, he'd be out of the country for weeks on location, sometimes months, directing some megabucks action flick.

"Kit wasn't that lucky. She had to put up with Alana up close and personal. Sure, she'd travel every now and again; dump Kit at the Boyd's, but not often enough if you ask me. And alcohol wasn't the reason Alana was mean. The woman was just evil without any provocation or incentive. For punishment, from anything from spilled milk to not leaving a room quick enough, she'd either knock Kit down or lock her up in a closet, might leave her there for an hour, or twenty-four, depending on her mood. And her mood swings were like storm clouds, quick to form and always violent. From an early age, I knew Kit's situation was far worse than mine, but I didn't find out exactly how bad until we went into group therapy together. Hearing her talk about it, all of it, I felt terrible for her and a little guilty. I mean, here I was talking about an occasional fist thrown my way and she was talking about agony, locked in a damned closet for God knows how long."

Baylee closed her eyes, remembering. When she opened them, she looked back down at Kit and her voice broke. "God, when we were little and I wouldn't see her outside in the yard for a day or two, playing, riding her bike, I'd panic. Even though we were just kids, I can remember not knowing how far Alana had gone, so I'd go up to the front door, gather my courage enough to ring the bell, pray Kit would answer the door and I could see for myself that she was okay. It was anguish not knowing if Alana had finally lost it and done something horrible to her."

She took a moment to rub her eyes, compose her thoughts.

Hearing the door open behind her, Baylee looked around; saw Quinn standing in the doorway.

Quinn walked up beside Baylee, wrapped her arms around the shorter woman, and rested her head on top of Baylee's. They stood there like that until Baylee looked into Quinn's tired eyes and asked, "Do you remember Alana's laugh, Quinn? She had the most evil laugh, which

I guess pretty much made her a natural for all the horror films she made."

After a brutal twenty-four hour shift that had included a busy Saturday night in the ER, Quinn let out a worn-out sigh. "I remember. That laugh was enough to send chills down my spine on more than one occasion. But then I got over it." Her voice sounded tired when she asked, "Why are you telling him this, Baylee? It won't help Kit."

"Maybe it's practice for when the police get around to interviewing me. Maybe I want to be ready. Maybe I just want to once and for all convince those two cops that she didn't go back inside that house and take a knife to Alana."

More awake now after listening to Baylee's tale, those other questions Jake had been harboring snapped into his brain, and he knew it was time to ask. "What kind of a man was John Griffin? Why didn't he ever follow through on his promises and get her out of there?"

Quinn stepped back from Baylee, crossed her arms over her body. "See what you've started? You've opened up old wounds that are best left in the past."

"Don't blame Baylee. I'm the one who asked, the one who wants to know. Kit's wondered, too. It bothers her. You know it does. There's no use pretending."

Quinn looked long and hard over at Kit, still sleeping. "I don't know how Baylee feels, but I always thought Kit's dad was a good guy. He'd take her places, do stuff, spend time with her; he'd let us girls spend the night over at his house whenever Kit spent the weekend, you know, like a girl's sleepover. Alana never allowed that. I thought he was a cool dad. But he should have taken her out of that situation, no argument there. I don't know why he didn't. Neither does Kit."

Baylee chimed in, "Ditto the nice stuff. I've got nothing bad to say about the man, other than him leaving Kit 'in that situation time and time again. But after…after…Alana…" She faltered and looked over at Jake again, but when she saw Jake's slight nod, as if he knew, she went on, "When Alana shot her, that was it for me. I thought, okay, Kit will be moving away any day now. I'll lose my best friend. She'll go live with her dad now."

She shook her head. "But it didn't happen. And Kit changed. She wouldn't take anything off Alana. After what happen, well, she just wasn't as close to her dad either. But then he left one day to make a movie and she never saw him again."

Quinn started to pace the small room. "Well, why would she be close to the man after that? Alana could have killed her that night and he knew it. He was there, witnessed the entire thing happen right in front of him, and what does he do? Instead of calling the cops or Protective Services, he helps Alana cover it up. I'm in agreement with Baylee though. After the shooting, I no longer trusted her dad. I don't think Kit did either."

The room grew silent as Baylee asked. "What will they do when they find out how bad the abuse was?"

Jake looked at the floor a few seconds before answering. "Knowing St. John, he'll use it to get her to agree to an exhaustive interview where he takes her through the past bit by bit, wears her down; then he'll use whatever he finds out in the process of interrogating her to further the investigation. Maybe use it to get a warrant."

Horrified at the idea, Quinn fumed, "You can't be serious. You mean if Baylee's father ends up murdered or my stepfather pisses off the wrong person one day and gets himself killed, Baylee and I would be suspects because the bastards beat on us when we were kids. That's ridiculous."

Taken aback at Quinn's revelation, Jake stared at the two women. Here they were, three beautiful women who'd grown up in one of the wealthiest neighborhoods in the world, and yet, they'd had monsters for parents. His heart went out to all three of them. He was considering their abusive childhoods when Baylee pointed out, "I guess it isn't practical to bring up all those times the three of us wished Alana dead, now is it? If you don't mind, that's something I'll leave out of my statement when the time comes."

Quinn nods in agreement. "Okay. I'll concede that we did wish that—a lot, but we were kids, Baylee. Surely, this St. John can differentiate between murderous adult and a kid's childish thinking."

"Don't bet on it," Jake said flatly. As if he were reluctant to bring it up, the question kept nagging at him and wouldn't go away. He had to get it out. "Did either one of you know Alana was in to…" he'd almost said porn, but decided to take a more tempered approach. "…adult parties? How exposed was Kit to that type of environment? Did any of Alana's friends ever get…did they ever take notice of a little girl kept in a closet or back bedroom?"

Baylee went white, before her demeanor changed to hot, red fury. "What are you really asking? You're asking if Alana's friends took pity on the little girl and offered to help her out. They didn't. Or you're asking if she was molested by one of them? She wasn't, thank God." And then as if something had just occurred to her, she turned her temper toward Quinn. "She wasn't, was she? Did she ever say anything like that to you? That wasn't something she discussed in group. Did she talk to you about it? She would have said something to me, wouldn't she? She'd have told me about it, right?"

Quinn reached out for Baylee's hand. "She never said anything like that to me. There was that one time in group when she mentioned venturing out of her room to see what the noises were coming from Alana's bedroom were. She was about eleven, I think, and she followed the music, saw the adults doing the down and dirty, and went back to her room, shut the door, stayed there, and as far as I know never made that mistake again. Being in that type of environment was one of the reasons she waited so long to…" She shot Jake a scornful look. When Baylee tried to stop her from going any further, she shook off Baylee's arm and said, "No, he should know. The way she grew up was only one reason Kit waited so long to lose her virginity; the other reason was that she was crazy about a guy who never gave her the time of day."

"I can't change the past, Quinn. But I'm here now. And I'm damned sure not going anywhere."

But Quinn's temper spiked again. With little sleep, that long shift caught up with her. She turned on Jake. "Is that what you're after here, the dirt of it all, the dirty little things that the press, if they find out, will have a field day? Well, if that's what you're looking for, you can go straight to hell."

He stepped closer to Quinn, kept his voice level. "Calm down. I'm after the truth and whatever helps Kit get through this. My goal isn't to hurt her, but rather to be prepared. I don't want the police springing things on her, finding out some dirty little secret they'll just use against her. It's St. John's way. I'm worried about Kit and what St. John can do to her, not the goddamned media."

Kit stirred and Jake closed the distance to the bed. Gingerly, he picked up her hand, touched her bruised face, and softened his voice. "Hey sleepyhead, you decide to finally come back to us? Baylee's here to see you and so is Quinn. We're all waiting for you to wake up and talk to us."

She opened her eyes, tried a weak smile, and then winced in obvious pain when she tried to turn her head. "Everything hurts. I feel like I've been hit by a truck."

"No honey, just a big-assed SUV," Quinn pointed out as she went into doctor mode, taking her pulse, adjusting the drip going in to her vein. "You've got an IV drip here for the pain. Just push this button and out comes the good stuff."

"No. No. It makes me sleepy."

"That's the point, Einstein. You need the sleep to help your body recover."

She tried to sit up. "I need to check on Pepper." When she didn't quite make it upright, she weakly slid back down.

"They're keeping you until they're sure that head of yours isn't going to fall off."

"A car bumped into me, fast. I tried to get out of the way as best I could, but it hit the side of the car again and again. I saw…Collin sitting in the passenger seat."

Jake's jaw tightened. "That son of a bitch."

Quinn's fury exploded. "I knew that bastard would cross the line one day. They're all rotten, every last one of them."

A little groggy from the IV drip that Quinn had increased, Kit fought the feeling, but reminded her through a fog, "There was a time you thought Cade was different."

"I made a mistake, okay. But didn't I pay for it? I'll never let Cade get the chance to hurt me again. And I'm not scared of those bastards just because they have money."

Jake wanted to get both women back on track, but curiosity had him leaning into Baylee, asking, "What are they talking about?"

In a low voice, Baylee explained, "Over our objections, several years back Quinn and Cade went out." She waited a beat, "They dated. During which time, Cade showed his true colors. I think it's a Boyd family trait. Quinn wanted to end it. Cade had other ideas. Seems to me, the Boyd men have a little trouble understanding what the word no means." And she could attest to that firsthand, couldn't she?

It sounded to Jake as if all three sons had a major problem with women. But he wanted to get them all back on topic, so in mid-chatter, he bent down to Kit, interrupting the flow of conversation, and asked, "What do you remember, Kit? What kind of car hit you?"

Her words slurred, she spoke slowly, drawing each word out, "Silver. And big…like one of those Cadillac…things."

"An Escalade, you think it looked like that? Did you get a good look at the driver? Could you identify him if you saw him again?"

The pounding in her head increased. She wanted to drift away, sleep. "He had blondish hair, sort of sandy brown, kind of spiky on top." She made a weak attempt to sit up again. "If I had some paper I could sketch him."

Jake reached down and planted another kiss on one of her bruises that had her going down for the count. "Later. You'll draw him later. That's my good girl. Now go back to sleep."

Just then, the door opened and Gloria stepped inside the room carrying a small suitcase, which she set down by the door without coming completely into the room. Instead of saying anything to Kit, as if she hadn't even noticed her, Gloria motioned for Jake to follow her outside. "I need to talk to you out in the hallway." Only then did she ask, "Did Kit have a good night?"

Upbeat now, Quinn replied, "She did. The bleeding's stopped. But she needs to sleep, get as much rest as possible, and let her body recover." Quinn noticed Gloria seemed upset, distracted even, and hadn't yet spoken to Kit herself. Believing that Gloria's behavior meant she'd brought bad news about Pepper, Quinn attempted to divert Kit's attention with a steady stream of chatter about something inane, until she realized Kit had drifted back to sleep.

Jake and Baylee followed Gloria out into the corridor. As soon as the door closed behind them, Gloria blurted out, "I stopped by Kit's house this morning to pick up a few things I thought she might need, but when I went inside, the house had been turned upside down. Someone vandalized Kit's house, tore through it like a cyclone. It's a mess. It'll need to be put back in order before she comes home from the hospital. She can't walk into her house in that shape."

Baylee exchanged looks with Jake. "Just like at Alana's."

"They moved to my office, and now Kit's. Baylee, they're looking for something they think Alana hid. Got any ideas?"

"Not a clue."

"What about you, Gloria, got any ideas what they might be looking for?" As soon as he got the words out, Jake noted she'd gotten that befuddled look on her face she so often used when she was either nervous or was reluctant to own up to something. It was the same look she'd used when he'd quizzed her about Kit's abuse that day in his office.

Without looking at him directly, without answering, Gloria simply changed the subject. "They wouldn't let me bring Morty in, so I had to leave him in the car." She turned to go back into the room. "I need to check on Pepper. Kit will want to know how he is, don't you think?" Without further comment, she calmly walked back into Kit's room, leaving him and Baylee standing in the corridor wondering whether Gloria's confusion could be attributed to the early stages of Alzheimer's or had been rehearsed.

They were all correct about Kit. When she woke up a couple of hours later, the first question out of her mouth was about Pepper. The vet had called to let Jake know the dog's vital signs were holding steady. He'd suffered no ill effects from the anesthesia and was being fed intravenously. If the bleeding didn't reoccur over the next twenty-four hours, he'd recover. He wasn't completely out of the woods yet, but his condition was far better than anyone expected.

Knowing her dog was on the mend made Kit feel better, even though her head hurt like she had her own personal jackhammer pounding away inside. And with her right shoulder in a sling every little movement was a struggle. But if Collin had been in the car that ran her and Pepper off the road, she wanted him to pay, which meant she had to do something about it even in her weakened state. She'd volunteered to sketch what the driver of the car had looked like. So with Gloria holding the paper and Baylee guiding her every motion, Kit began to sketch with her good left hand.

While Kit drew, Jake headed downstairs to meet Dylan for breakfast in the hospital cafeteria. Quinn walked out with him, got on the elevator with him. "I'm sorry I blew up, but it wasn't really at you. I don't like to think that Kit's in this mess because Alana knocked her around when she was a kid. Kit's like family, my sister. I don't expect you to understand, but I never knew my real father; I'm not close to my mother, and certainly not close to my stepfather. I won't go into the details, but I do agree with Baylee that Kit had it far worse than either one of us. Alana was just…she was crazy, Jake. I think she might have been a sociopath, not right in the head. After listening to Kit in group, I gave Alana's particulars to a psychiatrist friend of mine, got him to do a behavioral profile. He agreed with my amateur diagnosis. She was abusive, both verbally and physically. She locked Kit up, often. Treated her badly, and never seemed to show any remorse or guilt about any of it. Throw in the fact that she was often erratic, unpredictable, and narcissistic, and you have a bona fide sociopath. Whatever it takes to get this St. John off Kit's back, I'll say and do. Just tell me what you want to know, how I can help, and I'll not only cooperate every step of the way, but I promise not to fight your efforts."

When the elevator doors dinged at the first floor, Quinn looked straight into Jake's eyes and said, "And if you can get that son of a bitch Collin Boyd to hang for hurting her, I'll be indebted to you for life."

☙☙☙☙☙

Over runny eggs and stale coffee, Jake brought Dylan up to speed about what Kit had told them earlier.

After listening, Dylan had one question. "So this Collin isn't a former boyfriend?"

"Remember when we sold our first major law firm here locally? Boyd Boyd Geller & Gatz? We worked on them for months before we finally got them to sign on the dotted line. When the deal was done, they asked us out to their compound in Malibu called The Enclave to that decadent party known as the Boyd Bash, over Memorial weekend. We went, we drank, we made nice. Remember how impressed Claire was, surrounded by dozens of Hollywood celebrities?"

"Well, I'm glad you brought that up right about now, Jake. I can see how relevant that is to the topic at hand."

Ignoring the sarcasm, he told Dylan everything he knew about Collin, including the fixation he had for Kit, his hot temper, and how volatile he could be when he drank. Jake went over the ugly scene at Kit's house. "Now you've got Alana dead, Jessica, and Eva Geller Gatz dead. You want to tell me there isn't something that connects all of it? Half the founding partners of that law firm are gone, out of the picture for whatever reason."

Dylan suddenly understood. "Holy shit, the family has money, power, and more political influence in this state than you or I could possibly imagine. We have to be careful how we tread here, Jake. Are you sure you know this woman well enough to put everything on the line for her like this? And don't go biting my head off. I'm just asking a simple question, trying to look out for you."

"I love her, Dylan." Why did he have no reservations about telling Dylan but had such a hard time saying those three words to Kit?

But hearing Jake use those three words, words he hadn't even used about Claire, stopped Dylan flat. How was he supposed to argue with love? "Well, hell. When did this happen? You don't think you could slow this thing down a little, take a step or two back just long enough to think it through?"

He took another long look at Jake. A million questions formed in his head but looking at Jake's face, he had his answer. "Of course you can't. But there's more at stake here. If you go after him for what he did to Kit, you better be prepared. You don't take on a family like the Boyds without a serious battle plan. You can't fight these people conventionally; they're too powerful. You have to hit them where they hurt. I just hope you know what you're doing."

"What would you have me do, sit back and wait until he kills Kit the next time?"

"Of course not, but there's something else going on here other than Collin getting pissed off at Kit, isn't there? Like who's killing the partners off one by one and why? And what does all of it have to do with Kit's mother? And what the hell are they looking for?"

"Can we trust this guy where you dropped off the safe we found?"

"He's working on it now, and yeah, we can trust him. When he pops it open he'll call. And don't look at me like that."

He glanced at his watch. "The man's only had it for about thirty minutes. I know you're in a hurry, but stuff like this just takes time."

"How would you know?"

"I read thrillers, mystery novels, watch my fair share of those forensic shows. It always works itself out with a little patience."

At that moment, his cell went off. Grinning, he moved his eyebrows up and down. "Burke here. Okay. What'd you find? That's it? You're kidding. Okay. I'll be there in thirty to pick it up."

When he hung up, Jake waited. Patience was not a virtue at the moment. "Well?"

"He got the safe open. There was $200,000 in hundred dollar bills, a .357 Magnum, a passport in the name of Alana Chambers, and Kit's birth certificate."

"That's it?"

"That's it."

Jake thought for a moment. "Why would these guys be interested in Kit's birth certificate or a lousy two hundred grand? It has to be the gun they want."

"If, and I emphasize if, the safe is what they're looking for at all. Looking for a gun doesn't make much sense, unless maybe it was used in a crime of some sort. What do we do now?"

"We call the cops and let them know Collin's mixed up in this whole thing. When you pick up the safe, don't let it out of your sight. And Dylan, call Reese, tell him I need Jordan Donovan to drop whatever he's working on."

厥厥厥厥厥

With only one good hand, it took Kit twice as long to do the sketch as it normally would have. But when she'd finished and Baylee held it up so that Jake and Dylan could take a look, they both did a double take and blurted out in unison, "Gerald Auslo."

"You know this guy?" Baylee asked.

"One of the guys who ransacked my offices yesterday morning caught on the surveillance video. There's already a warrant out for him, but it looks like we might have to bump up the charges to attempted murder."

"Now wait a minute, why in the world would this guy be driving the car that hit Kit and be hanging out with Collin Boyd in the same car?"

"Good questions, and ones I intend to ask the cops." He took out his cell phone. "But right now, I don't think it's a good idea to leave Kit alone. Even with a half dozen nurses around, I don't want her left by herself for any reason."

When he noticed Kit had drifted off to sleep again, he turned to Baylee and offered, "If you need to take off, go home to be with Sarah, I'll be here."

"If it'll help, I can take a shift," Dylan offered.

Baylee smiled. "It makes more sense to take shifts. Go home, Jake, try to get some sleep, grab a hot shower, a change of clothes. I'll stay here till you get back. That way, she won't be left alone."

She turned to Dylan. "And we may take you up on that offer later, thanks."

As Jake stroked Kit's hand, he hesitated. "I don't like the idea of leaving her."

"You aren't. She'll sleep while you're gone; she won't even know you aren't here." Watching him hesitate, Baylee added, "I'm not going anywhere, Jake. Tanya has Sarah."

"Okay. But call me the minute she wakes up. I want to be here when the cops come."

CHAPTER 23

A half a mile or so down the same stretch of beach where earlier that morning Connor had stumbled upon his father's body, the three Boyd brothers sat on the deck of a luxuriously furnished beach house, once again knocking back Johnny Walker Blue.

Shaken by the events of the morning, the brothers drank shot after shot. They'd buried their mother only days earlier. Now their father was dead—dead from a bullet wound to the head just like their mother, just like their aunt. But at the realization that someone was exterminating their family one by one, all three adult men were scared shitless, feeling like cornered prey, ready to lash out at the first thing that moved.

"What the fuck is going on here?" Cade raged.

"Someone has to know," Connor suggested. "It's the only thing that makes sense."

"I'm telling you it has to be Kit. She's at the bottom of it."

Patience running thin, Connor shook his head. "And how exactly does that work, Collin? These murders were carried out by a professional, had to be, too neat, too clean. Kit might have offed Alana, but I'd venture the rest of it has nothing to do with her. But by God, whoever's targeting this family is in for a fight. I'll be damned if I just sit back and wait until some sleazebag comes after us one by one and destroys everything we've worked hard for."

Entrenched in his theory, Collin refused to give up. "Kit's the most likely, the one with a longtime grudge. There's been a war going on with us since she was twelve."

Cade scoffed at that. "Bullshit. Her war is with you, little brother, not with us. Everything was fine with our little surrogate sister until the day you cornered her in the cabana house and tried to rip off her clothes. She ran screaming from you then and hasn't wanted to have anything to do with your charming self ever since."

"Yeah well, she had me arrested didn't she? Just like Quinn had you arrested four years ago for assault. Women. If you ask, me they're good for one thing only."

"Oh really? So when did you close the deal with Kit, little brother? When did this happen and I missed it?"

Collin rose up from his chair with clenched fists, as always, ready to fight, and shouted, "You son of a bitch, come on; I can whip your ass any day of the week."

Cade stood up too, as if ready to do battle. "Anytime you say the word, baby brother. And that thing with Quinn, that was simply to let her know who was in charge of the relationship. The little tease needed someone to set her straight. From the start Quinn was too damned independent, too unstable; look at her background, look what she came from: half-Indian scum, half music dirt. Nothing came of it anyway. And I'm not still hung up on Quinn like you are Kit. Once dad persuaded her to drop the charges, I at least moved on."

Connor had heard enough. "Both of you sit down and shut the fuck up. Fighting among ourselves isn't going to get us anywhere."

Collin sat back down, but began to fidget, shaking his leg up and down, nervously tapping his fingers on his thighs. He had to tell them what he'd done. "There's something you guys need to know. I took Auslo and Taft out last night and things might have gotten a little out of hand."

A warning bell went off inside Connor's head. Used to Collin's immature antics, his brain went on alert. "What things?"

Collin began to squirm, and looked away not making eye contact with either one of them. "I only meant to scare her, but Auslo had other ideas. He got a little carried away, stepped on the gas and before I knew what was happening, the car went out of control and…"

"And what? What are you saying, Collin?"

"The car Auslo was driving might have clipped Kit's car out on the PCH, knocked her Jeep off the road. She might be a little banged up."

Connor exploded. "Goddamn it. What were you thinking? Oh that's an even more absurd question on my part. You weren't. You never do. You're such a fuckup." He slapped the side of Collin's head with his open hand. "Dad was right about you; you've got the brains of a piss ant. You've got nothing upstairs. No wonder you haven't been able to pass the goddamn Bar. At this point, thinking with your dick would be a step up, wouldn't it? Goddamn it, Collin we don't need this right now."

Ready to fight a few minutes earlier, now Cade was his brother's loyal defender. "Stop railing on him. He just told you it was Auslo's fault. You know how dense that Auslo guy is and weird to boot. What are we going to do about this whole fucking mess, Connor? Someone's after us. And no one's taking me down without a fight."

Connor rubbed at his forehead, feeling the beginnings of a migraine coming on, and tried to assess the damage. "Can they connect you to the car, to Auslo and Taft?"

"I think Kit might have seen me."

"Shit. You're fucked," Cade decided. "Count on Quinn and Baylee to come after you, make trouble anyway they can. Those three are tight…always have been."

Connor pointed out, "Not Baylee. She's left town. Gone."

Collin laughed. "To hell you say. I saw her the other day at Kit's little bookstore in bumfuck township. She's dyed her hair some shitty brown color."

Something feral glazed in Connor's eyes. But even as his head pounded, he was quickly reeling in the fury coursing through his head. Forcing himself to pull in those familiar feelings, he got himself under control so he could think more clearly. One problem at a time, he told himself, before turning his attention to what Cade was saying.

"What about that guy we used last year, the guy who took care of that little political problem we had with the judge? We could use him to take care of Auslo and Taft, get them out of the way."

More composed now, in control of his emotions again, Connor suggested, "We take care of this mess ourselves. First up, we make sure no one finds out about Collin's little scare tactic. We take care of Auslo and Taft, then Kit, even if we have to go through Baylee and Quinn to do it. Despite what Dad thought before he died, I think somebody out there knows. And if it gets out, everything goes down the tubes."

"Dad should have taken care of Alana a long time ago," Collin chimed in.

"Guys, there might be someone else besides the women we have to go through." Cade added.

"Jake Boston," Connor said in agreement. "That just puts another flavor in the punch, doesn't it?"

Cade walked over to the railing, looked out into the water. "We're in this together and that means we take care of Auslo and Taft together and whoever else gets in our way. Agreed?"

"Maybe we should increase security around this place, utilize the round-the-clock, twenty-four-hour protection."

With a bitch of a headache starting to form behind his eyes, Connor was growing more tired of Collin's mouth by the minute. "Yeah, like that did Dad any good. For once, Collin, stand on your own two feet." Pacing the length of the deck with his hands jammed in the pockets of his khaki shorts, Connor looked at his brother in disgust. "Thanks to genius here, we need to get to Auslo and Taft before the police do. If they get picked up and spill their guts, we're all screwed. They know too much.

"And if they haven't turned up the damned gun by now, what good are they? I told Dad that was a mistake." Connor added.

"I vote for taking care of those two dickheads. Getting them out of the way is priority one. Then..." Cade hesitated. "We think about how to get rid of Kit. If we get Auslo and Taft out of the picture, she's the only other witness, right?" He looked at Collin for confirmation.

Collin merely nodded, glad to be off the hook. But he'd been working on an idea of his own. "What if Auslo and Taft were good for one last job? We make sure they carry it out, maybe plant some evidence around, you know, pull back, make it look like Auslo and Taft did the whole thing, then let the police try to figure it out. We make sure our hands are nowhere near the scene. That would lead the cops straight to them, not us."

Cade raised his eyebrows. "Not bad, little brother. What's the plan?"

At the praise, Collin sat up straighter and shared his idea.

When all three men were in agreement, Connor raised his glass in the air. "To a successful mission." He downed the whiskey. "We need women."

"Good idea. My treat," Cade offered, as he pulled out his cell phone and punched in a number to call the escort service they frequented.

☙ ☙ ☙ ☙ ☙

He didn't like it. They were up to something. Looking through the telescopic lens of the high-powered rifle, he decided the three brothers were in panic-mode.

He'd seen Collin in action with Auslo and Taft. He'd followed the SUV, witnessed the hit-and-run on Kit Griffin. And he'd observed Collin's pathetic attempt at using explosives in the hope of blowing up Boston's sailboat.

They were getting desperate. And desperate people were dangerous.

If he needed any more proof of that, there was no better example than their parents. They'd all been desperate once, a long time ago, and look what they'd done for the almighty dollar. They hadn't been content with the money they'd received just winning the lawsuit. No, they'd taken it one step further and taken the lives of an old couple who'd never harmed anyone.

As he began to take the rifle apart and pack it away, he considered his mission essentially finished. Four out of five wasn't bad. If Frank Geller happened to be lucky enough to be half a world away, so be it. Was it fair to let Geller live? Probably not. But then he'd essentially met his goal and gotten rid of the source, the core.

He considered the scene he'd just witnessed between the brothers. There was evil still there. All three men were replicas of their parents. And that he couldn't tolerate. He couldn't walk away knowing it was only a matter of time before they spread their evil, like a disease, infecting their plague on everyone around them.

With the sons still breathing, walking away wasn't an option.

Without knowing it, the three Boyd stooges had just upped the ante, and he was more than willing to play.

Strangely, that burned out and useless feeling he'd carried around with him for so long had miraculously been replaced by an invigorated rejuvenation of sorts. He knew the moment he'd started to feel it, too. As he carried his bag to the car, he weighed his options. He liked this new feeling. Hell, the fact that he was feeling anything again was a refreshing change of pace, one he'd forgotten existed. And if he stayed, he'd have to get his hands on that painting.

As he loaded the car, that idea had his lips curving.

𑀸 𑀸 𑀸 𑀸 𑀸

Sitting up in bed, Kit had so many pillows propped up behind her head she felt like she might tip over. Since she'd awaken from a foggy sleep, the man sitting on her bed spoon-feeding her bites of a hot fudge sundae, one slow spoonful at a time, had seen to her every whim. Thanks to the generous IV drip, she was feeling no pain at the moment. She'd just slurped down a big spoonful of ice cream when she looked up and saw Dan Holloway standing in the open doorway. At the sight of him, she choked.

Jake dabbed at her chin with a napkin and rubbed at her back until she stopped coughing. Then he noticed the reason. He swore.

Holloway stepped into the room and spoke to Kit. "Sorry to interrupt, but if you're feeling up to it, I need to talk to you."

Realizing he'd just been ignored, Jake calmly set down the bowl of ice cream. "The police just left, took her statement about the hit-and-run. If you're here to hassle her about Alana, you won't. She's been through too much over the last twenty-four hours. I'll go get her doctor before I let you upset her."

"That's the last thing I want." Holloway came further into the room to stand by the bed. "The media hasn't gotten wind of this yet, but it's only a matter of time before they do. About seven o'clock this morning Sumner Boyd apparently went for his usual run on the beach. When he didn't come back, his oldest son, Connor, went looking for him. He found him on the beach…dead. He'd been shot in the head." He pointed to the left side of his own head and then held out his other hand, turning it palm up. It held a miniature gold cowboy inside a plastic evidence bag. It matched the others. "This was found in his mouth. In light of what happened to her last night, I'm here to tell Ms. Griffin that she's no longer a suspect in the deaths of Jessica and Jessica's sister, Eva Geller Gatz."

Patience, thought Jake. Holloway wasn't saying what he wanted to hear. After several long seconds of staring each other down, impatience won out and Jake finally said, "Okay, that's big of you to stop by and tell her. We appreciate it. But it seems to me a car had to run her off the road before you guys came around. What I don't hear is that you've cleared her as a suspect in Alana's murder. And you haven't done that. Even though you found one of those gold things…" A quick glance at Kit had him saying, "At Alana's."

Even though he understood the man's thinking, Holloway was in a difficult position. For the first time in three years, he was in disagreement with his partner. "It's true all four murders had one of those things left on or near the body. But Alana's murder is different. She died from multiple stab wounds, not a gunshot. That's the big thing Max can't get past. Until we find the link, Kit's still the person of interest there."

Jake missed the fact that the detective's voice lacked total conviction. He sucked in an irritated breath before telling Holloway, "Let's step out into the hallway for a minute."

Reluctantly, Holloway followed him through the doorway and watched as Jake pulled the door closed behind him.

"Patience was never my strong suit, so I'll just get this off my chest. I've about had it with this ridiculous notion that Kit has anything inside her that remotely resembles the kind of rage needed to kill her mother the way Alana Stevens died. It's not just that she couldn't do it, but she wouldn't go back inside that house if you paid her. She didn't know she'd inherited a dime from Alana, and didn't care. And just so you know, I'm in the process of skimming over some of the papers Connor Boyd sent her to sign. So far, I don't like what I'm seeing. Alana's will is a little too tidy and predictable for a woman who didn't give a shit about her daughter. And the money isn't adding up, either.

"Now, having said all that, the killer is obviously trying to tell you something and you guys are too stupid to figure it out. Those gold cowboys he's leaving behind with each of the victims mean something to him. And you may not like it, but you can't ignore one of those things was found with Alana."

On a roll with no intentions of slowing down, Jake kept going. "As you're already aware, Detective, Alana's house was ransacked. My office was broken into and now this morning Gloria found Kit's house in the same condition. Someone's looking for something they haven't been able to find. Don't you see how it all fits? And then there's the fact that Alana wasn't a very nice person. She'd made a lot of enemies through the years."

He took a step closer. "Widen your circle. If you want to get to the bottom of this whole fucking mess, you need to find what dirty little secrets Alana had."

He thought of the stuff still sitting in the trunk of his car, considered handing it over, but decided he'd hold the stuff as close to the vest for as long as he could. "I shouldn't have to do your job for you, but I did a simple search of public records. I found out Alana was married for a short time to Jessica's brother, Frank Geller, long before Kit ever came along. Is it relevant? I don't know, but that's one more connection to the law firm and to the Boyd family. I'm not sure what else you need at this point to clear Kit, but coming here to question her today was a bad idea on your part."

He reached into his wallet and pulled out a business card. "From now on, Kit has an attorney, Reese Brennan. In the future any interviews you want with Kit should be scheduled through his office with him present."

A visibly agitated Holloway stood his ground. "Look, when we find the solid connection that links Alana's murder to the others, I can assure you Kit will be officially cleared. These things take time. I heard what happened to her last night and I wanted to stop by, see how she was doing. Someone handed me a copy of the report minutes ago and I wanted to check it out for myself, ask her some questions about what happened."

When he saw he had no chance at getting past this guy, Holloway changed tactics. "Look, I've found out some things about her mother that might move the investigation in another direction. Namely, Alana and Jessica girls' night out was a little more than we were initially led to believe. I'm working on another angle. Just give me some time to make my case. I'm telling you this as a courtesy and as a direct result of what happened to Kit last night. In the meantime, I'll let Max know he needs to go through Reese Brennan for another interview." He paused, changing the subject back to why he'd really stopped by. "Did she really see Collin Boyd in the car with Auslo?"

"Yeah. And there's history there." He went into a brief explanation about Collin's behavior in the past. When he saw the skeptical look on Holloway's face, he said, "Check it out, if you don't believe me. She's called the police on him twice."

"I'm sure you're aware the Boyd, Geller, and Gatz families are very powerful, not just in this city but the entire state. I need to make certain that this accusation isn't motivated by some vendetta you two have cooked up to get back at the Boyd family for whatever reason."

Red fury ran through Jake like a swift current. He inched further into Holloway's space. "Do your job, Detective, that's all I'm asking. For once, stop thinking about the political power the family wields and go after the bad guys." With that, he turned on his heels and went back inside Kit's room.

When Kit looked up and saw he was alone, a smile brightened her bruised face, and she asked, "Where's Holloway?"

"Gone."

"You got rid of him?"

He wiggled his eyebrows up and down and then grinned at her. "Sure, was there ever any doubt?"

Oh God, but she loved this man. The drugs made her blurt out, "My hero. I dreamed last night you told me you loved me."

Gently, he sat back down on the bed, putting both of his hands down on opposite sides of her pillows. Leaning over her, inches from her mouth, he whispered, "It was no dream."

Kit swallowed hard. Dry mouth took over. The drugs were coursing through her veins. This really was a fantasy. She was dreaming again. That had to be it. She'd play along. "Okay. So if you really feel that way, I'm awake now. Say it again."

"I love you, Kit."

How long had she waited to hear him say that? It seemed like forever. As if absorbing the shock of it, all she could say was, "No one's ever told me that before."

"You know, I may be relatively new at this, but when I tell you I love you, I'm pretty sure there's something you're supposed to say back to me."

"Well. Geez." She threw her one good left arm around his neck, drew his mouth down to hers, and planted a sloppy kiss on his mouth. When she pulled back, she told him, "I thought you knew already. I love you. I'm pretty sure I've loved you since I was fourteen."

He kissed her mouth, lingered there, and then rested his forehead on hers. "That thing at fourteen was a crush. I hope you aren't going to tell me you still feel like that."

"It's the real thing, all right. You don't think I could have fallen in love with you at fourteen?"

"Not a chance." He had so much love stored up for her that it scared him. His head was telling him to take a step back, but his heart was saying go for it. And since he'd never felt this way before, he decided to follow his heart straight over the falls. His mind had wandered and he realized she was talking.

"Why? Because I was too immature to know my own mind or because you were such an arrogant ass back then?" Seeing the surprised look on his face, she laughed. "Well, you were an ass; don't even try to argue the point."

"Arrogant? Maybe. An ass? Never." He grinned. "That was a long time ago though. I've never felt this way about anyone before. This…it's…scary."

"Scary? Now that's what every woman wants to hear when she's come out of a mini-coma. Scary isn't very romantic." She giggled. "Next, you'll be telling me that maybe there's an antidote out there somewhere and you're leaving on a crusade to find it."

She'd no sooner spoken when she saw the hurt look in his eyes. She tried to lighten the mood. "It's the drugs. They're making me say things I normally wouldn't say, think crazy thoughts."

"I admit your being in the hospital isn't exactly the ideal time to tell you for the first time I'm in love with you. I should have said it sooner."

"You're sure what you're feeling is love then and not pity?"

"Are you sure what you're feeling isn't the drugs talking?"

"Okay, fair question. I'm a little loopy, but I'm in love with you right back. We're in love with each other. I like the sound of that."

Just then, the door to Kit's room opened and a man walked in that Kit had never seen before. Great. Just what they needed was another cop to drag this special moment down into a deep abyss. But Jake calmly looked over at the man who was dressed in an Oxford shirt and dress pants on a Sunday afternoon and said, "Took you long enough."

Reese wasn't comfortable watching his friend hover over the blonde. In spite of the purple bruises and the bandaged look, it didn't take a blind man to see how attractive she was, and how, according to Dylan, Jake had taken the fall—again.

What was it about a beautiful woman with a great looking-body that turned a smart, successful man into a blithering idiot who couldn't or wouldn't protect his own interests? Reese didn't trust the woman. And now it seemed she was days away from being arrested for murdering her own mother. In Reese's estimation, Jake had taken a giant step down from the gold-digging Claire. Reese wanted nothing more than to keep his distance while at the same time inject Jake with a little common sense serum, make him see what she was really after…his money. But at some point today things had changed. Reese found himself getting pulled into the middle of the fray by an old nemesis. He was less than pleased with the turn of events.

Kit noticed the man looked slightly annoyed and seemed tense, but what came out of his mouth alarmed her.

"Apparently, I came by to meet my new client. Maybe I should tell you about my very interesting morning. First, Dylan called, said I might want to stop by, talk about you putting Jordan Donovan to work. Then I was just pulling into the hospital parking lot when I got a call from a very pissed off Max St. John not five minutes ago wanting to set up an interview the moment Kit's well enough to leave the hospital. He figures if she's well enough to go home, she's well enough to talk to the police. Officially. I had to wing my response, which of course was not only clever but brilliant. I didn't have a clue what he was talking about. But since I'm the best damn criminal lawyer in southern California, I told him I had everything under control."

As Reese watched Jake plant a kiss on Kit's bruised lips, he added, "When you're done with her mouth there, Jake, I need to confer with my client."

"Meet Reese Brennan, your lawyer," Jake said.

At that, Kit's face lost all color...again. "I need a lawyer? Oh my God, they do plan to arrest me."

"Not if I have anything to do with it," Reese said emphatically. And he meant it. Reese might not trust Kit Griffin, but he disliked the bulldog detective Max St. John ten times more. After spending two years sparring with St. John over Jake's troubles, Reese had no intention of walking away from a fight.

"That's why I'm here. That's why... when St. John threw down a challenge..." But Reese stopped in mid-sentence when Quinn entered the room. Completely distracted, his preplanned speech derailed as he gaped at the exotic resident doctor he'd seen only briefly last night. The woman had an athletic body, long black hair, and the biggest brown eyes he'd ever seen. Reese stared at her as if he'd been on a desert island for a year and she was his first meal. He had trouble finishing his thought and actually stammered, "...uh...uh..."

"Just wanted to check on you before I start my shift," Quinn said, as she came all the way into the room. The moment she realized Kit was upset, her gaze landed on the man who couldn't form a complete sentence. Giving him a sharp, accusing look, she asked, "What did you do to upset her?"

He found he could speak after all. "Me? Not a thing. I'm here to save the day. We haven't met. I'm Reese Brennan, Kit's attorney." Impeccable manners had him holding out his hand to the resident in polite introductory fashion.

All Quinn heard was that he was Kit's attorney. At the news, her eyes went wide. Ignoring the outstretched hand of the attorney, Quinn automatically grabbed hold of Kit's.

Confused about what was happening, she turned to Jake. "Why does she need a lawyer? Collin tries to kill her with a car and she's the one who needs a lawyer. That's bullshit."

"Holloway was here. They still won't come off the idea that she killed Alana."

"When I inherit her money, I'm their best bet, Quinn. I'm the most likely suspect." Kit said.

Quinn turned icy eyes on the lawyer. "What are you going to do about this? You can't just let them arrest an innocent person. She had nothing to do with Alana's death. If you can't make them understand that, then you aren't much good to us, are you?"

She let go of Kit's hand long enough to poke Reese's chest. "She didn't murder Alana. If you're any good, you need to hire an investigator, dig into Alana's past, and keep Kit the fuck out of jail."

For an instant, the passion he saw in those chocolate brown eyes had him wanting to make promises he might have trouble keeping if St. John had his way. One thing a criminal lawyer learns early on is not to make promises he might not be able to keep. Instead of promising her anything, Reese simply said, "I'll do everything within my power to keep her out of jail. But St. John wants an interview the minute she's released."

But Quinn demanded more. "Are you any good?"

Reese wasn't insulted, but took the question as an opportunity to tout his own abilities. "They never arrested Jake, now did they?"

Puzzled, Quinn looked down at Kit. "Why would they want to arrest Jake?"

Kit's head wanted to explode. She suddenly felt tired and looked into Jake's eyes, found the go-ahead to tell Quinn about Claire. If Quinn needed to hear about Jake's troubled past, Kit thought it might sound better coming from her. So she went into a brief account, telling Jake's story for him.

When she'd finished, it sounded to Quinn as if the two were mirrored bookends. Having watched Kit over the past two weeks struggle with being a murder suspect, Quinn looked at Jake now with newfound respect.

And an idea blossomed.

Turning to Reese, Quinn suggested, "So if St. John wants an interview whenever she leaves the hospital, what say we arrange to keep her a few extra days until we can prep her, get her ready for the best damned interview of her life?"

Jake stood up a little straighter. "You mean keep her in the hospital until she's stronger, more confident, and ready to face St. John on our terms. That's not half bad, Quinn."

"In the meantime, we start with a strategy session here and now, today. We've got the lawyer here and who knows when that will happen again." Quinn gave Reese a disgusted look that said she didn't care much for his profession, glanced at her watch, and said, "I have to go on the clock in thirty. You've got me for half an hour before I have to be in the ER. After that, you can page me and I'll come up on a need-to basis. If we don't finish today then we set up another round for tomorrow and the next day."

She smiled at Kit. "It'll be just like cramming for an exam. I'll call Baylee; get her on board with the plan."

To Jake, she reminded him, "We've been there with her through most of it. We'll get Kit in top form so she'll be ready to go one-on-one with this St. John guy."

Quinn turned to Kit and softened. "I know you're reluctant to tell the police everything, but girl, it's time to kick a little ass here. You have to set this St. John straight about all of it. If you can't do it alone, then Baylee and I will insist on being with you during the interview, verify everything just the way we did with Dr. Strasburg."

Upbeat now for the first time since walking through the door, Quinn added, "Dr. Strasburg would be another good source, a go-to guy for the defense if it comes to that. He'll be more than willing to testify on Kit's behalf."

Kit laughed, feeling somewhat better about her situation. "Guys, meet Super Quinn. Hard to believe she gets her degree in three years, goes to med school, graduates with honors, and now, she's the newest resident at the ripe old age of twenty-five."

"Twenty-five?" Reese looked stupefied.

Ignoring the interest she saw in his eyes, Quinn gave the lawyer a go-to-hell look she'd honed over the years to ward off all comers.

Jake, on the other hand, wasn't so forgiving after Reese's comments yesterday. He'd watched Reese become a blithering idiot the minute Quinn had walked into the room, so he went around the bed, slapped Reese on the back, whispered in his ear, "Don't even think about it old man, she's clearly way too young for you, don't you think?"

Reese's response was an elbow shot to Jake's ribs, which he managed to dodge like a boxer. The minor scuffle caused raised eyebrows from the women, a purely female reaction that said there was too much testosterone floating around the room.

Reese continued. "Well, I'd hoped this initial meeting would be a bit more private, but I can see that isn't going to happen. The truth is we'll make more progress when everything's out in the open anyway. And the more I know, the better I can serve my client. I have a ton of questions, though, so let's get started."

Over the next three hours, Reese wasn't sure what he'd expected Kit to say, but he certainly hadn't expected to hear the story she told about her childhood. All the jokes they'd cracked in the attic the day before about the porn queen didn't come close to portraying Alana Stevens as a mother. At times Reese had trouble keeping up, but with Quinn backing up Kit's story whenever necessary from the third grade on, Reese sat there appalled by what he heard.

And when Quinn had to leave to start her shift, whenever Kit needed help remembering some essential detail there was Baylee Scott, the petite brunette with the baby from last night, picking up the narrative and was able to go even further back than Quinn to when Kit was age five, providing more confirmation.

By the end of the third hour, the mistrust Reese had felt earlier for Kit had dissipated into sheer respect. She'd not only answered his questions in straightforward fashion, but she'd alleviated any remaining doubt he might have had that she had murdered her mother. It was apparent there'd been no typical Beverly Hills upbringing for Kit Griffin but rather a chilling real-life horror she'd finally escaped at the age of sixteen.

When it was done, Jake planted a kiss on a tired and drowsy Kit. "You did great, honey. Now get some sleep."

"Will you be back in the morning?"

"I'll be back in ten minutes. I'm not going anywhere."

"Jake, you can't spend another night sleeping in a chair. You have to get some rest."

"How about if we argue about this when I get back? I'll walk Reese and Baylee to the elevator and be right back. We can fight about it then."

"We don't fight."

"I know. Now go to sleep." He kissed her again and walked out of the room with Reese and Baylee.

When they got outside in the hallway, it was Baylee who cross-examined Reese. "What are her chances? I mean, how do you think she came across? It's the first time in about four years that she's actually talked about it and certainly never like that in one sitting from beginning to end. How do you think she did?"

"She did fine. She might need a little work on relaxing. But given the subject material, I know it must be difficult for her to talk about it."

Baylee looked mortified. "The woman's on drugs, Reese. If you don't think she's relaxed enough now, what are her chances when she talks to St. John minus the IV drip? You know, when St. John finds out about Kit's childhood, it'll only help build his case."

Baylee shook her head. "Every instinct I have tells me we're going about this all wrong. We have to search Alana's past. As mean as she was, she had to have pissed off any number of people over the years. We should be concentrating on Alana."

Reese assured her, "And we will. For starters, that stuff we found yesterday in the attic—like the porn—can be used in our favor. If it comes to that, I won't think twice about putting this particular woman's past on trial."

"Porn?" Baylee eyed Jake, suspiciously. "You asked about adult parties; you didn't say anything about porn. You found honest-to-God porn in Alana's attic? What else did you find we might be able to use?"

Jake ran his fingers through his hair and ticked off the list of things in the safe.

"You found Kit's birth certificate?" Baylee asked.

Just then, Quinn walked up on her break. Not even a third of the way into her long shift, she had more energy than all of them combined and proved it by shooting them rapid fire questions. "How'd it go after I left? Did she tell you all of it? How's she feeling? I better go check on her. How'd she do anyway?"

"Okay," was all a deflated Baylee had to say and the look on her face told Quinn something was wrong.

"What happened?" Quinn shot Reese a dubious glare. "Don't tell me she couldn't talk about it?"

"Oh, she talked about it. I don't know about these guys, but I'm sick to my stomach from having to listen to it all over again. I thought after all these years, it wouldn't still have this effect on me, but I was wrong. Right now, I'd like to put my fist through the wall because Reese says that if she's honest about all of it, we're likely handing St. John a reason to charge her. And get this, they found porn in Alana's attic. Now that doesn't surprise me in the least. But why would Kit's birth certificate be locked away in a safe?"

"What?" All at once Quinn grabbed Baylee's arm. "Oh my God, Baylee, you said her parents were never married, right? You don't suppose that one day Alana felt a tiny maternal quiver and actually went out and adopted a child, do you? You know, like the real Mommie Dearest? Weren't Joan Crawford's kids adopted?"

Baylee went white. "Come to think of it, that would explain a lot. Now that you bring it up, I remember when Kit applied to college there was some issue with her birth certificate. Alana said she couldn't locate the real deal and Kit thought it was just a stall tactic to make it more difficult for her to get into school. The birth certificate issue held up Kit's paperwork and she almost had to sit out the first semester. But at the eleventh hour, Alana sent it over by special messenger. Remember? Kit must still have a copy somewhere at home; if not, the registrar's office would."

In two seconds Jake had his cell phone out and was talking to Dylan. "Could you bring over Kit's birth certificate from the mobile safe? Good. See you in twenty."

A half hour later, stunned into silence, a shocked Jake, Baylee, and Quinn sat around a table in the hospital cafeteria with Dylan and Reese taking turns examining Kit's birth certificate, as if they might somehow be able to change what they'd found.

As Kit's friends, Baylee and Quinn felt obligated to say something, anything. But as they stared in disbelief at the name on the line next to Mother, speech eluded both of them. When Quinn's pager went off and broke the silence, she stood up and tried to speak, but her voice quivered as if on the verge of tears. "I guess it's too much to hope that there's another Gloria Chambers. What in God's name is this going to do to Kit when she finds out?"

Reese summed up what everyone was thinking. "So the aunt isn't really the aunt but the mother?"

With tears forming in her eyes, Quinn turned on Reese. "Oh, you're brilliant, aren't you, ace? Nothing gets past you. Where'd you get that law degree from anyway, The Internet School of Law?"

Dylan cracked up.

"Shut up, Dylan." Reese muttered.

"Hey, I didn't say it. But Quinn's pretty funny."

When she realized how rude she'd been, Quinn quickly apologized. "I'm sorry. You didn't deserve that. I'm not usually so insulting, but…I'm upset. How could Gloria do it, just give away her baby to a monster like Alana?"

Jake shook his head. "All these years you think you know someone. Gloria doesn't seem the type that would relinquish her child to a psycho like Alana, move three thousand miles away, and just abandon her to that kind of environment. But Gloria had to know what Alana was like. They were sisters. And she told me the other day that every time she'd talked to Kit over the phone she sounded sad. Well, in that kind of situation, yeah, I'd say the kid was sad. And what did Gloria ever do about it? Nothing. Just like John Griffin did nothing." John Griffin's name had been listed in the space under Father. At least Kit hadn't been lied to about that, thought Jake. But at the moment, he was livid. Like Quinn, he wondered what the knowledge would do to Kit. How much more could she take?

Even though Quinn knew she had to get back to work, she was reluctant to go. She swore when her pager went off for the second time. But before she left, she had to know, "Who's going to tell her?"

Hoping it wouldn't be her job, she wasn't about to volunteer, but Baylee had a point to make. "You know, she trusted Gloria. There was a time when she was small that she thought her Aunt Gloria was her fairy godmother. I suspect when she finds this out, this is going to break her heart."

Jake looked around the table. Every eye turned on him. "Now wait a minute, why me? If it's all the same to you, I think Gloria should be the one to step up to the plate and tell her. What about you, Baylee?"

"Good idea, but who confronts Gloria?"

"Oh, I don't have a problem confronting Gloria. In fact, I'll relish the moment. Who wants to go with me?"

While everyone else looked away, Baylee was the only one to maintain eye contact.

As the only mother here, she knew firsthand about holding her own child for the first time.

"I can't wait to see her face when we confront her."

CHAPTER 24

Baylee stood on the path connecting Gloria's house and the guest cottage, waiting for Jake to get out of his car. She'd made arrangements for Tanya to stay with Sarah long enough for her and Jake to meet with Gloria.

For fifteen minutes, over the phone, they'd discussed strategy, only to decide the situation required a simple and direct approach. Surprise was on their side since they'd decided not to call Gloria and tip their hand. There was no small talk between Jake and Baylee, only steely eyed determination as they made their way up to the front door.

Jake rang the doorbell and the moment the door opened Gloria acted as if she knew something was up. As she led them into her living room, Jake noticed the condition of the place and understood that Auslo and Taft had finally gotten around to searching Gloria's house. From the looks of the damage it had been recent.

"When did this happen, Gloria?"

"When I got back from the hospital last night the house was like this. Someone turned every plant in the house over, broke things, sentimental things that belonged to Morty. It's taken me all morning just to put the kitchen right again. Would either of you like a cup of tea?"

"We didn't come for tea, Gloria. But thanks."

Gloria started toward the kitchen anyway, until Jake commanded, "Sit down, Gloria. Please. No one wants tea or coffee; we came here to talk to you. It's important we have your full attention."

She recognized the tone to his voice, his body language, his demeanor. He was angry with her.

Trembling now, almost in tears, she nervously sat down. "What's this about? Has something happened to Kit?"

Gloria watched Jake pull out a piece of paper from his pocket, unfold it, and hand it off to her. When she saw that he wanted her to read what was on the paper, she grabbed her glasses from the end table, adjusted them on her nose, and turned white after only a few seconds.

"God. No. No. No. Where did you get this? Has Kit seen this? Oh no, Kit."

Mortified, she started sobbing uncontrollably.

Unmoved by her tears, Jake scoffed, "Obviously, you didn't think anyone would ever see this. You want to tell us about it, Gloria?"

In between sobs, she tried to explain. "You must think I'm such a terrible person, but I'm not. It isn't what you think. I never gave Kit up. It was Alana. Alana took her away from me when she was born. After I gave birth, she had me admitted to a psychiatric ward three thousand miles away in Maine. She and Jessica saw to it that I was locked up in a mental hospital for almost eighteen months after Kit was born."

She waved the birth certificate toward Jake and Baylee and hurriedly went on, "I kept the hospital release form with the date on it so that she'll know. She'll know I'm telling the truth. She'll have to believe me. The day she was born, Jessica filed papers in court for Alana to adopt her, said I was an unfit mother, that I was crazy. Jessica made certain it was all legal. They took her away from me in the hospital. I never got to hold her…my baby daughter. I never got to name my own child.

"That first day, I waited for the nurses to bring her to me. I asked every nurse that came through the door about my baby. But nobody would tell me anything. I began to suspect that maybe something was wrong with her and they didn't want me to see her. At some point, they must have drugged me because days later I woke up three thousand miles away in Bar Harbor, Maine, at a private psychiatric hospital called Sierra Manor, where I stayed until they let me out eighteen months later.

"You have to believe me. I have the paper to prove I was there." Wild sobs poured out of Gloria making her a little incoherent.

Jake and Baylee watched as she suddenly started talking as if Kit were in the room, rocking back and forth, trying to explain everything all over again. "I never got to be your mother. Alana and Jessica stole you from me. I wanted so much to be your mother but they took you away. It's haunted me. It's haunted me for years. I was locked up, don't you see, three thousand miles away."

Baylee and Jake exchanged exasperated looks. It was Baylee who said, "I suppose it's possible. We all know what a cruel streak Alana had. But why? Why did she take your baby from you, Gloria? She had the maternal instincts of a viper. No, scratch that, she had zero maternal instincts. Why would she want a baby?"

Through tears, Gloria sobbed. "She wanted to get back at me. She and John dated off and on for years. It was never serious between them. They'd always end up at each other's throats. John liked me though. We started seeing each other. One thing led to another, and we had an affair that lasted about a year. When Alana found out she went nuts. The idea that John preferred me over her was unthinkable. Alana and I argued over John. And when I got pregnant, from the moment she found out about it, she was horrible to me. Then a couple of months later, out of the blue she came to see me, offered me a place to stay, said I could move in with her until the birth. She and Jessica must have plotted it all out for months, planned every detail. I was so stupid to believe she'd had a change of heart.

"That night I went into labor, she and Jessica drove me to the hospital. I had no idea what they planned to do. I swear I didn't know. If I'd known I would have gone somewhere, anywhere, left L.A., but I didn't know they intended to steal my baby. You believe me don't you, Baylee?"

Because she'd known the woman for years, Baylee tried to give Gloria the benefit of the doubt. "It sounds like something Alana would do. But Gloria the adoption had to be illegal unless you signed something relinquishing the baby."

The look that crossed Gloria's face had Baylee's stomach dropping.

"They said I did, the people at the psychiatric hospital told me every time I brought up the subject of my baby. I'd tell them what happened and they'd look at me sympathetically and calmly explain that I'd given up my baby for adoption and that I was simply having regrets. The doctors and nurses would tell me that I'd signed adoption papers giving my baby away. But I wouldn't, I wouldn't have done that."

Baylee looked skeptical. "What about confronting Alana and Jessica after you got out of the hospital, Gloria, coming back to L.A., just showing up on their doorstep, getting in their faces?" It's what she would have done, she noted. If anyone had taken Sarah away from her like that, but then, she thought, she hadn't been locked up in a mental ward for eighteen months.

"Don't you think I wanted to? When they finally let me out of the hospital, I was broke, didn't even have money for a bus ticket back to L.A. So, I found a job, went to work as a maid at a bed and breakfast about five miles from the hospital. I saved every dime I made to get her back, but it never seemed to be enough. I knew I couldn't compete with Alana's money or Jessica's legal expertise. One afternoon I was so depressed I walked into a law office downtown to get legal advice. That's how I met Morty. He was so nice to me. He listened to my story and decided to contact Jessica, one attorney to another. But after he talked to her, he told me it was too late. Jessica and Alana swore it was a legal adoption, that I'd signed papers. Morty told me there was nothing I could do. I cried for a week."

It suddenly occurred to Jake after listening to Gloria talk, how much she and Kit looked alike, the same skin tone, the same hair coloring, and the same mannerisms, the same chatty way they talked. How had he missed their similarities over the years? Watching her now, the resemblance between the two women was uncanny.

But there was something Jake needed to know. "What about Kit's father, Gloria? What about John Griffin? Where was he while all of this was happening?"

"He was of no help to me either. When Kit was born, he was out of the country on location. He wasn't around during my pregnancy. By the time he got back to L.A., Alana had Kit. Jessica made sure of that. And I was out of the picture. They convinced John that I had abandoned the baby, disappeared shortly after Kit was born, that I'd signed the papers for Alana to adopt her. He said he tried to find me. Even if he had tried, he wouldn't have been able to find a trace of me. They convinced him that I had willingly given her up for adoption, willingly given her away to Alana and just disappeared. From what he told me years later, Alana played her part very well, acted as if she had done such a noble thing by giving her a home so she wouldn't end up in foster care. John believed all of it without question.

"But he wanted to be around Kit. That's something Lana and Jess never counted on. And legally, he was her father. So they couldn't very well keep him completely out of the picture. Every now and then, they let him visit whenever he was in the mood to play daddy. It wasn't until after Morty and I married, when I had some money, that I paid Alana a surprise visit. By that time Kit was about three."

At the memory, she let out a gasp. "I found Kit...she had...her arm was in a cast...her arm had been broken. She didn't know who I was of course, but when I asked her how she had hurt her arm, she told me, Alana had a temper tantrum and threw her down the stairs. I was horrified. I went to Morty, I begged him to do something. So he got back in touch with Jessica, sat down with her, and reviewed all the adoption papers. He found everything in order, nothing he could do he said. I'd just have to learn to be my daughter's aunt. But because Kit had said how mean Alana was to her, I tracked down John in Europe and asked him to do something, to take Alana to court, get Kit away from her.

"Finally, after several more broken bones, he petitioned the court. But the next thing I knew he'd withdrawn his petition. It seems Alana financed one of his films."

She sobbed again before going on, "Alana bought him off. There's no other way to say it I suspect over the years, it happened quite often."

Sickened at the newfound knowledge, Baylee told Jake, "Even as a kid, I suspected it was something like that."

"Me too. It's the only reason that made any sense. She kept buying him off, dangling the money to produce and finance his films as the incentive not to fight for custody. It worked once when Kit was five, so why not keep financing his damned movie career while at the same time keeping him under her thumb. Either way it was a win-win situation for both of them. The only one who lost was Kit."

"And knowing Alana, she had to get off on the control factor, knowing she could control him with the money anytime she wanted. The night she shot Kit, he must have upped his demands and she went ballistic, wanted to prove a major point."

"At Kit's expense," Jake finished for her. She'd been twelve years old that night, he reminded himself. That caused a tidal wave of anger to build up in him.

"And when exactly where you planning on telling Kit the truth, Gloria?"

❧ ❧ ❧ ❧ ❧

Kit had just finished taking her first walk around the fifth floor still attached to her IV drip, when she practically collapsed back on her bed from exhaustion. She was still trying to catch her breath and let the dizziness pass when she looked up and saw Dylan stationed in her doorway. After telling her he needed to take care of something, Jake had been gone all of five minutes and now, here was Dylan, dutifully taking his turn as guard dog.

Smiling, in spite of the fatigue, she muttered, "Your turn to watch me, huh?"

Dylan grinned. "We can't have you getting in trouble again, now can we?" He'd volunteered to take a shift, but now he noted how pale Kit looked. He approached the bed and asked, "Are you okay? Can I get you something?"

"Some water would be nice," she said, as she fell back into the mountain of pillows.

He poured water from a plastic carafe and handed her a cup, only to realize that when she took it, her hands were shaking. It was then he noticed the pain on her face. Glancing at the IV, he reminded her, "Don't hurt. That's what it's there for. Go for it."

When she laughed, Dylan saw past the bruises and knew what Jake had found in her, a gentle soul who seemed genuinely in love with him.

"Are you going to tell me where Jake went?"

He stuck his hands in his pocket and grinned again. He was there to look out for her while Baylee and Jake confronted Gloria. He wasn't about to give anything away. So, he wiggled his eyebrows back and forth, and opened up a new avenue for discussion. "What can you tell me about Baylee? Is she seeing anyone?"

Kit choked on the water, but motioned for him to take a chair. "Oh Dylan, we so need to talk."

☖ ☖ ☖ ☖ ☖

When Jake walked into the room, he found Dylan, sitting cozily beside Kit's bed, chatting like the two were old friends. She looked up, spotted Jake, and gave him a come hither grin, cocked her head to one side, and said, "Give us a kiss."

Jake noticed it was a fair attempt at an Irish accent. It was then he noticed how sauced Kit acted. In protective mode now, Jake turned accusingly to Dylan. "What did you do to her?"

But it was Kit, with a slur to her speech, who tried to explain, "We've been getting to know each other. He's been telling me about his visit to Ireland several years back. Donegal, wasn't it? Up there it's different, right Dylan? I told him about the brother I've never met in Galway. He's been telling me how we should all go to Ireland, see the countryside. Quinn was born there you know." She actually giggled.

But Jake glanced over at Dylan, saw him get to his feet. Dylan simply smiled at the hint of jealousy on Jake's face and pointed to the IV drip. "Wish I could say it was the Burke charm, but the drug's making her loopy. She was up walking when I got here. It seemed to take everything out of her. When she fell back to bed she started pushing the pain button."

Jake couldn't help himself, he laughed. He needed something to laugh about after having to drag Gloria here kicking and screaming.

When Quinn walked through the door, quickly followed by Baylee, followed by a bleary-eyed Gloria, Dylan tried to excuse himself, but to his surprise Kit pointed a finger at him, and warned, "Oh, no you don't. Something's up. Look at this bunch. Can't you tell?"

Finally, Quinn stepped to the side of the bed, checked the IV drip, and wanted to know, "How much Demerol have you had, Kit?"

"You told me to push the button, so I pushed it and pushed it and pushed it, but nothing came out." She found that hilarious and started giggling again.

"Oh God," Jake groaned. Alarmed, he started to say something else, but then Quinn shook her head. "She can't get more out of the drip than she needs. It doesn't work like that. It's a micro drip with a very low dose."

Worried, Baylee pointed out, "But she acts like she's high."

"Oh, she's feeling no pain that's for sure. Since she's never taken anything stronger than ibuprofen she's a little more susceptible than most."

Jake said flatly, "I guess this isn't the best time to do this."

But to his surprise, Quinn suggested, "On the contrary, I think it's the perfect time to drop the bombshell. She's drugged enough it'll take some of the sting out of it." She shot Gloria a look of contempt.

Jake took Kit's hand and cautioned, "Honey, Gloria's got something she wants to tell you."

Everyone made room for Gloria to stand next to Kit's bed. "Glo, you don't look so good. What's wrong? Tell Kit what's wrong." She'd lost the Irish accent.

But when Gloria opened her mouth to speak, nothing came out. Kit leaned in to her, telling her, "You'll have to speak up Glo, I can't hear you." She giggled like it was the funniest thing she'd said all day.

All of a sudden tears formed in Gloria's eyes and water ran down her cheeks. Kit reached over with her good hand, took Gloria's hand in hers, and then clumsily tried to wipe some of the tears from Gloria's cheek. But the tears kept coming.

"I've done something bad, Kit, and I can never, ever undo it or take it back, but you have to know what I've done and why. It's time you knew." Gloria breathed deeply, looked around the room at everyone staring at her and then looked back into Kit's face. As if her courage came from Kit, she reached to touch her cheek and took in another deep breath before saying, "It's time you knew the truth."

From her pocket, with hands shaking, she took out two pieces of paper and unfolded them, smoothed out the creases, the lines on the paper. "This is your birth certificate, your real one. Alana took you away from me when you were born. She had me admitted to a psychiatric ward. She and Jessica saw to it that I was locked up in a mental hospital for almost eighteen months after you were born."

She waved the other piece of paper toward Kit. "And this is my discharge paper from the psychiatric hospital I was in, dated with the date of my release so that you'll know I'm telling you the truth. The day you were born, Jessica filed papers in court for Alana to adopt you, told the court I was an unfit mother, that I was crazy. Jessica made certain it was all legal. They took you away from me in the hospital, Kit. I never got to hold you...my baby daughter. They locked me up, you see."

The sobs poured from Gloria again and made her a little incoherent. "I never got to be your mother. Alana and Jessica stole you away from me. I wanted so much to be your mother, but they took you away from me, Kit, and sent me three thousand miles away from you."

Kit felt a little sick at her stomach. Even sitting up in bed, she swayed back and forth looking at everyone in the room. "This is a joke, right? You guys are just messing with me, right?"

When Gloria started crying again, more uncontrollable sobs formed in her throat and she started shaking her head. But it was Jake who stepped up to the bed, took Kit's hand in his and said, "No honey, this isn't a joke. Do you understand what Gloria's telling you?"

"Yeah, I think so. She's telling me that fucking bitch wasn't my real mother. Isn't that what you're telling me, Glo? That I'm not Alana's real daughter." Kit started laughing. "How about that guys? How about that? Gloria's not my aunt, she's my mother. What do you think about that, Baylee?"

Gloria's hands were still shaking, her face was still wet, but the sobs had ceased when she looked at Kit and asked, "Aren't you angry, Kit?"

With a heavy slur to her speech, Kit said, "Hell no. As long as I know that bitch wasn't my real mother, everythin's fine, jus' fine."

$$\maltese \maltese \maltese \maltese \maltese$$

It was hours later before dawn that Kit came awake in her hospital room to streaky bits of light peeking from underneath the hospital drapes covering the window. Trying to focus in the dim light, she thought she could make out someone sitting in the darkened corner by the bed and asked, "Jake, is that you?"

But it was Gloria who popped up from her chair and reached out to touch Kit's face. "No sweetie it's me. How'd you sleep?"

"Like the dead. The last thing I remember was…" She blinked further awake. "Everyone was in my room and you were telling me…"

"That I'm your mother. Yes, sweetie it's true. It wasn't a dream. You can still call me Gloria if you want. I don't expect anything…expect you to feel…I don't expect you to be…to call me…"

Tears pooled in Kit's eyes. "I love you Gloria. Gloria is a name I trust. The word mom on the other hand is as foreign to me as another language. Maybe someday I'll be able to wrap that word around my tongue, and it'll just roll right off when I see you without thinking, but for now, you're still just Gloria. The woman I've loved and trusted like no other for so long."

Sobbing, Gloria put her arms around Kit in spite of the bandages and drip. "Oh Kit. I'm so sorry, so very sorry. I wanted to make it right, travel across the country to come back to L.A. get my baby back, but I was locked up. Locked up all that time, knowing what they'd done, what I'd lost almost made me crazy for real. For eighteen months, they gave me shock treatments once a week. When they released me, I was flat broke, didn't even have a car, couldn't afford a bus ticket to five miles down the road much less to get back to L.A. to come back for you. I thought about ending it then."

"Oh, Gloria."

"But I wasn't on any medication so I didn't have any pills I could take. I didn't own a gun so I couldn't shoot myself. One afternoon, I walked out to the harbor and sat down on the pier there, watching the boats for a while. It's different from L.A. there, quieter, a little more serene than here. But right there in the harbor, I thought maybe I could just walk off into the ocean and drown, just sink down into the depths of the water, and leave my problems, my messed up life behind.

"But I didn't do that, Kit, because I thought of you. The one person in the world that was mine, the one person I loved above all else. I walked back to town then, got a job as a maid at the bed and breakfast on the outskirts of town and started saving every penny, every dime I could scrape together to get a lawyer to get you back.

"That's how I met Morty. I went into his office about six months later and told him the whole story. And the day he told me that the adoption was legal because Jessica had some piece of paper that said I gave you up, I cried for a week. I didn't sign anything, or at least I don't remember signing anything. But Alana had you just the same and I didn't. And by that time you were almost two, I had never even laid eyes on you so in my mind I told myself that Alana would be good to you. That since she did something so despicable she must have really wanted a child. I told myself that Kit every day, I told myself that to keep from going insane for real. I had to keep telling myself everything would be okay if you were with Alana. Lord knows the woman had the money to take care of you better than I could. That's what I told myself.

"But then when Morty and I got married, he asked me where I'd like to go on a honeymoon. I chose L.A. He brought me back here and I got to see you for the first time. You were three years old by then. You were such a beautiful little girl, all blond with big green eyes just like mine. But your right arm was in a cast. I'll never forget it. I asked you how you'd hurt yourself and you said..." She stopped long enough to blow her nose into a Kleenex. "You said that 'the mean lady hurt you' and I knew then, I knew Kit, I knew from that point on. I wanted to kidnap you, just grab you up and run, but Morty, of course, ever the lawyer, talked me out of it, convinced me to let the courts handle it. To get your father involved.

"I tracked down John in Ireland, told him what was happening. He promised me he'd do something. But he didn't. Oh, he'd petition the court every now and then, go through the motions for a while, but then when it came right down to it, Alana would promise the incidents were isolated or that he was exaggerating the extent of your injuries, and she'd keep financing his next picture. She bought him off, Kit."

By this time the tears were trailing down Kit's face. She sniffed. "Oh Gloria I always suspected it was something like that, because he'd make promises to me, too and then back down, give in to her every single time, and he'd always take me back to her."

"Oh baby, I'm so sorry, sorrier than you will ever know."

"We can't change the past Gloria, you said so yourself. Jake said something to me the other day about going forward from this moment on. That's what we'll do Gloria, from this day forward, we'll start over as mother and daughter.

"You know, when I was little I used to wish that you were my mother. Of course, for a time there, I also did that with Maya, the Boyd housekeeper."

She smiled with a twinkle in her eye before going on, "But I wished more often and harder that you would fill that role. And now, you're my mother. It's like I've been granted a wish after years of wishing on a star. You were always like my fairy godmother, you know, showing up at the worst possible times to help me out, make things better."

"I missed everything though, those years I'll never be able to get back, your first steps…" Her voice trailed off in a broken whisper.

"Hush now. Don't think about it. We'll make up for it Glo, somehow, someway, we'll make up for it. Maybe with grandchildren, how would that be?"

"Oh Kit, I could only dream and hope for this kind of reaction from you. You're the sweetest angel. I thought you'd hate me."

"I couldn't. Will you do me a favor?"

"What's that?"

"Go check on Pepper today. Stop by the vet's. Let me know how he is. I mean Jake hasn't left my side long enough to do it. I'm worried about Pepper."

"I stopped at the vet's this morning, but I'll stop by and check on him on my way home. You do realize, honey, that Pepper may need to stay at the vet's for some time, don't you?"

She sighed. "I know. I just hope he'll make a full recovery. What are you doing here so early, anyway?"

"I woke up at three o'clock—couldn't get back to sleep. So I drove here to sit with you for a while."

Kit caught the time and sat up straighter. Was it possible? Casually, she asked, "Bad dream?"

"Oh, it's just this recurring dream I've been having off and on over the years. It hasn't surfaced for quite some time. But since Alana died I've been having it every night, waking up at exactly…"

"Three minutes past three." The hairs on the back of Kit's neck stood up and chills shuddered down her arms to her fingertips.

Gloria looked shocked. "How do you know that?"

"Because since the night we got back from sailing, the day the boat blew up I've been having a nightmare that wakes me up at three minutes past three about an old couple who lived in the Hollywood Hills on a place called the Sundown Ranch. How much detail do you see, Glo?"

"When I first started having the dream I'd just turned fifteen, there wasn't much detail to it, just like two people stumbling around in the fog, a misty scene hard to make out sometimes. But for the past week, the details have gotten clearer, more vivid."

"Vivid as in color or black and white?"

"Like an old black and white movie. I see their car drive up to the house. I see how they get inside. The killers use their own key, so it was someone that knew the old couple, someone they trusted. I see them stumble around in the dark, turn on the lamp, go to the kitchen, take out the knife from a drawer. Then one of them creeps along the hallway to the bedroom where the couple's sleeping, while the other one stays in the kitchen loading some kind of a gun. Then the one with the gun comes into the room and just starts shooting."

Kit picked up the rest. "After the couple's dead, the one with the knife stabs them, uses their blood to write the words PIG, DEATH, and DIE on the walls of the bedroom. Afterwards, they go back into the kitchen to celebrate with a bottle of champagne."

"What? They do what? I don't see that. That's just horrible."

"I told Jake about it. Because of the graffiti on the walls, he thought the whole thing sounded similar to the Manson murders."

"Oh my God, I remember that. I've been having this dream for so long I didn't see the similarity. Of course, it's like that. How could I not have seen that? But why would I be dreaming about the Manson murders, why this particular old couple?"

Kit told her about her theory that the murders were a copycat of the more famous murders and that she believed the killers were Alana and Jessica.

Gloria was so stunned she had to sit back down. "Some psychic I am. What does it all mean?"

"I don't know. Without proof, who on earth is going to believe us?"

CHAPTER 25

Two days later, Kit left the confinement of the hospital after claustrophobia descended. She wouldn't stay cooped up in that hospital room a minute longer. She had to break outside, lap up some sun and breathe fresh air again no matter how much Quinn wanted her to stay until she was ready to face St. John. And Kit was equally resistant to Jake's plan to whisk her out of town for security reasons. She simply turned a deaf ear to his fears and suggested she recoup on the boat.

If Collin hadn't tried to kill her, taking her to the boat to recover might have been a great idea. But taking her to such an exposed place, out in the open where Collin might reach the boat from the water, was risky. Jake tried reason, logic, and common sense. But Kit refused to budge. She wanted to recover on the boat.

Granted, he'd wanted to cave the minute he'd taken one look at her sorry state. She still had stitches in her head. And the purple and yellowish bruises still covered most of her body. But what really had him giving in was when he'd looked into her pleading green eyes and fell into their depths. Against his better judgment, he'd thrown in the towel right then and let her have her way.

He promised himself he wouldn't keep her locked up like Alana had done. If Kit couldn't have the freedom to come and go, to enjoy life outside, she'd feel as if she might already be in a jail cell. And since that was exactly where St. John intended to put her, Jake refused to treat her like a prisoner.

But just because he'd given in, didn't mean he was happy about it.

Looking over at Kit wearing a bright red bikini, stretched out in a deck chair enjoying the sights and sounds of the marina, his mouth watered. But he had no intentions of acting so carelessly. Taking the chair across from her, he rigidly watched her like a hawk for any signs she might be in pain.

After so many days pent up, and with so many people around them at the hospital, Kit was aware that for the first time in days they were truly alone. On the trip to San Madrid, she'd felt that pull in the belly at the idea of getting him naked. Despite the bruises and soreness, her body revved with a sexual energy as she recalled what terrific things he could do with his mouth, things she yearned for. Her juices went slick in anticipation.

As hungry gulls bomb-dived for their supper, as the water gently slapped the sides of the boat, one glance at Jake told her he had no intentions of making a move toward her that way. Still dressed in his Dockers and Polo shirt, he sat stiffly watching her as if she might explode any second.

So it was up to her.

She patted the chair next to her and suggested, "Why don't you come over here and sit beside me?"

He stared at her through the sunglasses he wore, but said nothing as he stood up, moved to oblige and sit down next to her.

"Aren't you hot in all those clothes?" She all but purred the question, as she watched a single brow arch over his dark glasses in response. When she awkwardly leaned toward him, he continued to stare without uttering a word. Determined, Kit fanned her face. "Why don't you take off some of those clothes so you'll be...cooler and I'll get to see ...all of you." Reaching up with her good left hand, she took hold of the back of his neck, brought his mouth down to hers. She tugged on his bottom lip before opening her mouth, drawing in his tongue. Feverishly, she gave him a wet kiss then tried to lift her injured right arm to put her other hand around his neck—and shrieked in pain.

Patiently, he gently lifted her right arm and put it back down on the chair, placed both hands down on either side of her. "You're in no shape to be fooling around. And I tried to tell you not to remove that sling from your shoulder, but you wouldn't listen. It's there for a reason. You need rest and sleep to get your body to recoup. Now behave yourself."

"You just think you're so smart don't you, Mr. I Know Everything. I've been sleeping for five days until I'm loopy. I've been cooped up inside. It's such a beautiful day. I don't want to behave. I want to feel alive, make love. Make love with me, Jake. I want to feel you inside me."

"You're getting bitchy, honey."

"I'm not bitchy. I'm just…can I help it if my juices are revved. Don't you want me?"

He sighed. "Kit, if I touch just one of those bruises, I'm liable to hurt you. The last thing I want to do is to put you in any more pain."

"It hurts no matter what activity I do, so why not do something I really enjoy, one we both enjoy. How about if I show you where it doesn't hurt, how would that be?" She cocked her head, took one of his hands in hers, and placed it on her breast. With her fingers on top of his she started kneading her breasts using his fingers. Soon he was rubbing her breasts for real through the fabric. "Kiss me, touch me, Jake. When you touch me, I feel so alive."

"Woman, you are killing me here. I'd like nothing better than to get you out of that bikini, but I might hurt you." Then he saw the wounded look in her eyes and gave in, again. As his mouth covered hers, his arms moved under her to carry her below deck. "We're doing this in a bed. I'm not giving the damned nosy neighbors an eyeful they'll be talking about at the Book & Bean."

"Let them talk. It'll increase business."

"You say that now, but when I rip off this bikini, they'll whisper about it with awe in their voice."

"You like my bikini." It wasn't a question.

"What's not to like," he said, as he gently laid her on the bed. "In about two seconds, you aren't going to be wearing it."

"Show me."

Twenty minutes later she was still lying on top of him, with his arms rubbing up and down her back, when he said, "I didn't hurt you, did I?"

"No." Her shoulder was killing her. But she played along with the teasing tone when she asked, "Did I hurt you?"

"I think I might have a couple of bruises myself."

"Poor baby."

"I'm not complaining."

She kissed his mouth, whispered softly, "You have a gentle touch, Mr. Boston. I feel safe when I'm in your arms, safer than I've ever felt before." In one motion she swung off of him, rolled over to reach her bag on the floor, dug around until she found a prescription bottle, and poured out a blue pill into her palm. She downed it with a couple of sips of bottled water from the nightstand.

He sat up. "I did hurt you."

"It's nothing. Just so I don't embarrass myself though I'm taking a nap. I'm not sure Baylee and Quinn will ever let me live down the day Gloria 'fessed up and I was blitzed. And poor Dylan, after our drama, Quinn said he practically ran from the room like a man possessed trying to get as far away from the hysterical females as he could."

"We were all worried that you'd be so upset you'd have a setback. But then we got there and you were…giddy as hell. I bet you're a fun drunk."

"I'm a blast."

"I plan to put that in the data bank, use it for later, when maybe you're pissed at me."

"Oh, stop it. I still can't understand why you guys thought I'd be upset. Let's think about this for a minute, what is the downside here? I had Alana for a mother. Hello. Then I find out the woman I've loved for years, the woman I'm closest to is really my mother. I just don't see why I should be the least bit upset about that.

"I believe Gloria when she says she didn't willingly give me up. It sounds exactly like a scheme those two women would cook up in retaliation for some slight Alana thought she'd received. Think about it, Alana manipulates Gloria into thinking she's befriending her, all the while planning to take away her baby. That idea took time to plan. After all, Jessica had to prepare for immediate adoption proceedings the minute Gloria gave birth, even if it was with phony, forged documentation. Then before Gloria knows what's happening, maybe she starts to ask too many questions, kicks up too much of a fuss while she's still in the hospital, and boom before she knows what's happening she's on the other side of the country locked up in some mental ward. You know Jake, Gloria's lucky they let her out of that hospital at all. What a punishment though, taking me away from her. No wonder, Alana treated me like a dog. To her, I probably was no more than that.

"If I'm upset with anyone, I guess it would have to be my father. He just lets Alana have me. I mean, he knew the truth. He knew I wasn't Alana's and yet, when he found out about the adoption, he didn't go to the judge, petition the court, and say 'hey, this is my daughter, my kid, I'm the father Alana's just the adoptive mother. I want custody.' No, I have to face facts, he didn't want me. For a man traveling around the world doing exactly what he wanted to do, he couldn't have a kid tagging along. I'd be too much trouble. I'd have been in the way. You know, it makes me realize Baylee's father did a decent job all those years, except of course when he drank. But I mean at least he kept her, tried to be a father to her."

"You're a helluva woman, Kit. I thought for sure, you'd be pissed. But here you are logically going through it in your head, sorting it all out. That's why I love you."

She rolled back over the bed into his arms, nuzzled his chest, and said. "Mmmm, I love you, Jake Boston. How could I possibly be in anything but a blissful state right now? I'm not pissed, just hurt, disappointed. Life's too short to be mad at Gloria for something she had no control over. How can I blame her when at least she came back into my life at the age of twelve? And frankly, Jake, as long as I know Gloria's my mother, I never have to think about Alana in that role, ever again. Right now, here today with you, I'm a happy camper."

Later, waking from a nap, she found Jake's body pressed up against her back with his arms locked around her. It felt like heaven. Still basking from the afterglow of their lovemaking, she could easily stay wrapped up in him like this and just bake in the knowledge he was hers. Her mind drifted lazily into dreams of marriage and kids. With the knowledge that Gloria was her mother and not Alana, she could actually look forward to the future, the dreams she'd had about having a family, having children of her own, might now become a reality. It seemed to her that the future somehow held brighter possibilities.

The phone ringing somewhere in the cabin put a slight ding in her bliss. But even as Jake moved to answer it, even as she heard him say something about Reese's office, she knew the phone call was about her. She rolled over in bed to study Jake's body language for any sign of what the call was about. She saw him tense up, saw him run a hand through his hair, then after several more minutes, heard him end the call by saying, "We'll be there."

After hanging up, he crawled back in bed, and put his arms around her. "That was Reese. He wanted us to know two things. St. John wants his interview. Reese set it up in his office in the morning at ten." As soon as he looked at her face, he wanted to take away the fear he saw there. As his hands moved up to stroke her hair, he reassured her, "Baby, just go back to sleep, don't worry about it now."

But how could she not worry. Just when she began to think about the future, had a reason to plan ahead, the past reared its ugly head again, sending her back to a time she so wanted to forget. When she came out of her funk, she asked, "What was the other thing?"

"The private investigator found Will Forrester."

⚭ ⚭ ⚭ ⚭ ⚭

After spending an uneasy night and morning fearing the worst, the interview with St. John lasted under thirty minutes and brought with it her first ray of hope the police might go in another direction. During St. John's attempt to get her to say something incriminating, Reese dropped a bombshell of sorts when he presented St. John with a copy of the coroner's findings. The M.E. was convinced the stab wounds on Alana's body came from an angle suggesting the killer had been right-handed.

"Read the report," Reese had demanded when St. John protested. "My client's left-handed. This should be a no-brainer for you. Kit did not kill Alana."

But St. John had taken the report and huffed, "It's a theory, nothing more."

"He's the same guy who theorized the time of death. You need to pursue other suspects on this one, Max, and stop harassing my client."

St. John had stormed out of the office.

Later, Reese had explained the interview had been little more than a scare tactic, a power trip that made sure Kit knew she was still a suspect.

Even though the meeting had taken everything out of her, she insisted on stopping at the vet hospital to sit with

Pepper for a while. The dog was coming along well enough, but would still need to stay under the watchful eye of the vet in the ICU.

As she laid her head near Pepper and began to talk to him softly, it broke her heart to see her dog so banged up. "Will he make a full recovery?" Kit asked Dr. Phillips, the veterinarian who had operated on Pepper.

"He should, although he might have a slight limp in his hind leg, the one that snapped at the joint. But the good news is there's no post-surgery bleeding, or signs of infection."

"When can I take him home?"

"Give it another few days."

"I have a lot of stairs in my house. I'm thinking perhaps he should go stay at Gloria's until he's able to maneuver around."

Dr. Phillips agreed, "Stairs won't do. We don't want him tearing the stitches. But when he's better he'll need to have some kind of rehabilitation. I understand you've been in the hospital yourself."

"Yes, but I'm getting along okay."

Jake rolled his eyes. "She's out and about way too early. But she's determined to push the envelope."

The vet smiled. "It'll take both of you some time to recover. Neither of you should try to do too much too soon."

"See, even the vet agrees with me," Jake said smugly as they reluctantly left Pepper in the capable hands of the staff in ICU.

But Kit was ready for a fight when Jake offered to drop her off at Gloria's on the way to the public library while he went through the newspaper archives without her. "Do you intend to have someone baby sit me for the rest of my life?"

"If that's what it takes to keep you safe."

"That's ridiculous. I'll be going back to work in a few days. Do you intend to bring your laptop to the Book & Bean and run your company from the coffee shop?"

"Who's being ridiculous now?" But as the idea sunk in, he thought it had merit. "And going back to work in a few days is out of the question."

"Says who? I have to earn a living, Jake. I won't live life with a babysitter. You can't be with me every second of every day. And I won't let Collin or any other Boyd dictate how I live my life. I've no intentions of letting them have that kind of power over me. They've bullied me my whole life. I'm done with letting them."

"Hard-headed woman," he muttered, before offering a suggestion. "At least ask Gloria for some help. She could take some of the baking off your hands."

"Now that is a good idea. I'll call her."

He clasped her hand. "I just don't want you hurt again."

How could she fight that kind of heartfelt sentiment? She let out a frustrated breath. "Just so you know, if you're headed to the library, you aren't going without me."

CHAPTER 26

They had been at it for hours, looking through slides of newspaper articles, archives on microfiche, until both of them suffered from blurry vision, and so far they hadn't found a single mention of any unsolved murders that fit the timeframe after August 10, 1969. There had been murders back then all over L.A. county, lots of them, but none that matched what they were looking for. Now that she'd had some time to think about it, Kit wondered if the whole idea was just a little too far-fetched.

"Maybe we should turn this over to a professional who knows what they're doing, drop it in their lap, like one of those investigators who specialize in cold case files. Isn't that what they're called?"

"Jordan Donovan is damn good, but he's concentrating his efforts right now on Alana's murder. His plate's too full to go chasing a half-baked idea like this."

"Gee, thanks."

"You know what I mean. This is a reach even for us." Then he saw the forlorn look on her face, and added, "But it won't hurt to eliminate the possibility. Then we can go on to other ideas, other theories."

"Such as?"

"For one, it occurs to me that maybe county tax records from back then might yield a name. We look up the Sundown Ranch on the tax rolls see if we can come up with an owner's name that way."

Kit gaped at him. "God, I love you. You're brilliant. How do we do that?"

"We can look up the county tax records online. I just don't know how far back they go. It might take a trip into the office where we search the old-fashioned way through stacks of old records one at a time." He saw the incredulous look on her face and concluded, "Well, it beats nothing."

"No, I'm impressed. It tells me you're putting a lot of thought into this. If I haven't said so, I just want to say thanks. You've been in my corner from the beginning on this, willing to believe in what I saw in the dream, and I just want to say...oh wait, go back one frame. Look at this, Jake." She pointed to the screen where the headline read:

Elderly Couple Found Slain In Hollywood Hills
Dated August 17, 1969

The L.A. County Sheriff's Department confirmed the identities of the elderly, Hollywood Hills couple who were found brutally slain in their Sundown Ranch house on Friday morning August 15. Authorities believe Pete Parker, 69, and his wife, Mary, 67, died from gunshot wounds or multiple stab wounds. Sheriff's deputies are investigating the murders of the couple as a double homicide. Local attorney, Jessica Boyd, discovered the bodies of the couple in their bedroom when she went to check on them after they failed to show up at her law office for a morning appointment.

When interviewed for this article Jessica Boyd wanted everyone to know, "They were always so reliable. It was out of character for them to run late or to not keep their appointment. With all these recent murders in the news, when they didn't show, I immediately became concerned. Their deaths are such a shame, too. They were such a sweet old couple."

Upon arrival, sheriff's deputies found a gruesome murder scene that included graffiti written on the walls in the victim's blood. There were no signs of forced entry.

Autopsies of the couple have been scheduled for Monday by the Los Angeles County Coroner's Office.

Pete Parker gained notoriety in the '30's and '40's as a former cowboy film star, starring in such westerns as Hills of Wyoming and Mountain Siege. After their only son, Noah Parker, an Army Ranger, was reported missing in action in Vietnam in May of this year, it was determined the couple had no other living relatives. The Parkers made history two years ago when they were awarded a fifteen million dollar settlement against McKetrick Construction, the largest settlement of its kind at the time. Funeral arrangements are pending.

&&&&&

"Wow, Pete and Mary Parker," a dejected Kit said as she rubbed the back of her neck, and slumped in a defeated posture in the uncomfortable metal chair she'd been sitting in for the last several hours. "I thought I'd feel better knowing who they were, but I don't." Instead of feeling elated at the discovery, all of a sudden, she felt sick to her stomach. "Pete Parker was a former actor, a cowboy star. I bet that explains the gold cowboys, Jake. I wonder if my father knew him."

"What if the son, this Noah Parker wasn't dead at all, but was alive and eventually found out who killed his parents, decided it was time for payback?"

"But why would it take him so long. It's been over forty years."

Jake frowned. "Good point. But if he thought Alana and Jessica killed his parents for the money that would explain a lot. And if we found this article, maybe he did too. Isn't it convenient that Jessica not only found the bodies that morning, but she even managed to work into the interview about the other murders. Looks like your dream was right on the money, Kit."

And that was an understatement, he thought. He didn't know quite how he felt about what they'd just unearthed on their own because of Kit's dream. As he hit the PRINT button to make a copy of the article to take with them, he rested his hand on Kit's shoulder, and considered the woman.

He had to admit he hadn't really expected to find anything about a murdered couple on a ranch, yet here they were sitting in the library reading about their deaths, and the deaths were just as Kit and Gloria had described from their dreams. The whole thing was more than a little spooky. He looked into the green eyes of the woman he loved, and wondered silently if she might have some sort of psychic ability. He'd known Gloria had always claimed to be intuitive. She'd been right on target about Claire. Despite his affection for her, he'd always thought Gloria was a tad odd, but now it seemed he owed her an apology.

And Gloria was Kit's mother. Had Kit inherited some of the same intuitive tendencies from her mother, her real mother?

☘ ☘ ☘ ☘ ☘

Back on the boat, he was still thinking about Kit's uncanny dream and how it had led them to identify the Parkers when he logged onto the Internet to try and find more information about them.

He hit pay dirt in a database containing L.A. County court records. It seems in 1966 Sumner and Jessica Boyd filed only one lawsuit that year on behalf of the Parkers, who owned a six-thousand-acre cattle spread in the Hollywood Hills, known as the Sundown Ranch.

Parker believed McKetrick Construction was responsible for dumping toxic waste on his ranch, killing his cattle and polluting his land. It had taken a year for the case to go to court, then in the middle of the trial, before the case had gone to the jury, the construction company had abruptly settled for $15 million dollars to be paid out to the couple over a three year time period, starting in 1967 and ending in 1969. The final payment had been delivered in August 1969.

Just in time for their murder. The same timeframe agreed with those copies of checks he'd found in Alana's attic, the ones totaling half a million dollars paid out over the same amount of time. Could those checks be payment of some kind, maybe Alana's share of the winnings?

When Kit hobbled up behind him and wrapped her arms around his shoulders, he brought her around to sit on his lap, nuzzled her neck. Cuddling was new to him. Funny, how it seemed so natural now. Without letting her go, he deftly tapped keys on his laptop, switched to another web browser, brought up a secure site designated for Vietnam veterans and typed in the name Noah Parker.

"Found anything?" Kit asked as she nibbled his ear, not really interested in what he was searching for, but doing her best to get his attention.

While he waited for a result to pop up, he told her what he'd found out about the Parkers and what he hoped to find out about their son using the only bit of information the newspaper article had provided.

After several seconds, the web site rendered the date Noah Parker entered the Army, his pay grade, rank, serial number, date of birth, and marital status. To make sure he had the right man, he added a caveat. He asked for the city where he'd been inducted into the Army. When he got Los Angeles, he asked for the date this particular soldier went MIA. The date came up May 1969, matching the date mentioned in the article.

Jake sat up straighter when he caught sight of the line with the date Noah Parker had been found alive. He shifted Kit on his lap, typed in a command looking for a discharge date. When he came up empty, he planted a wet kiss on Kit's mouth and declared, "Looks like Noah Parker may have survived Vietnam. And he was attached to a sniper unit during the war."

"And that's significant because…"

"Who else would have the training and the greatest reason to avenge the murder of his parents?"

"Oh. We should let the others know what we found out."

& & & & &

That evening, everyone gathered around Gloria's dining room table for lasagna. They were a noisy bunch even with their mouths full. And no one enjoyed it more than Gloria. She listened as Jake and Kit good-naturedly bickered over when she should head back to work. She got a kick out of watching Dylan interact with Baylee and Sarah, curious to know when the baby could start eating solid food. She noticed Reese seemed to be a little lost without Quinn who hadn't been able to get out of her shift at the hospital.

Gloria knew they were here to talk about murder. But it didn't much matter to her why only that they were here like a family, her family. After so many years, she not only had Kit, but the family she'd always wanted. Somewhere Morty had to be smiling at all of them.

Over a fresh pot of coffee and Baylee's chocolate cake, Jake told them about the newspaper article they'd found and how the Parker murders happened right on the heels of the Manson crime spree splashed all over the news at the time.

"And the son, this Noah Parker, would now have every reason to go after Alana and Jessica, like a revenge factor," Dylan surmised, as he scarfed down every crumb of the chocolate cake on his plate.

"But why wait almost forty years to make his move?" Baylee asked. As she scooped up Sarah out of her infant carrier, she noticed Dylan get seconds of the cake she'd baked and grinned before making her point. "He'd have to be in his sixties by now, wouldn't he?"

"Good point, but that doesn't mean he's any less pissed off his parents were murdered for their money," Dylan said, as he licked fudge frosting from his fingers.

"And I thought it was for the land," Kit said.

"Probably both. Like you said before, they were sitting on prime real estate worth millions." Jake turned to Reese. "What exactly happened to the ranch after they died?"

"After you called this afternoon I did some checking. That land used to be horse and cattle country. The ranch was sold to a developer named, Robert Carlton, four months after they died."

"Wait a minute," Kit said to Jake. "Alana was married to a Robert Carlton?"

Jake shuffled some papers around. "Husband number two. Son of a bitch."

"Guess who handled the sale?" Reese looked around the table.

But it was Gloria who answered a little sheepishly. "Alana. It was her first sale as a realtor. And before you ask, I don't know everything Alana and Jessica were up to in those days other than they were almost inseparable back then. I was ten years younger and had my own circle of friends. I didn't start hanging around Alana until much later, a couple of years before Kit was born."

"But you knew she was married to Frank Geller and this Carlton?"

Gloria nodded. "But her marriages never lasted for long."

"But Carlton turned the property into a strip shopping center. It's abandoned now, like a ghost town."

"Didn't they find Eva Gatz's body somewhere in the Hollywood Hills at an abandoned strip mall?" Kit asked.

"They did. So wouldn't it stand to reason, someone's figured out who killed the Parkers and wants justice forty years after the fact. If we go by Kit's dream that leads right to Alana and Jessica."

"We've got smart people in this room. We need to come up with facts and fast."

"Before St. John gets an itchy trigger finger and arrests me," Kit added with a grin.

"Here's the newspaper article," Jake offered as he passed around copies to everyone.

When Dylan read the article, he turned to Kit. "I can't believe your dream was so on target. I have to admit when I heard about it, I thought you were nuts."

"Me too," Kit agreed. "Jake's the one who made the connection to the Manson murders. If it hadn't been for that I'd have never come up with the right time frame."

"And just so I'm clear," Reese asked, wondering if he was stirring up the masses even more. "You think Alana and Jessica killed the Parkers for the money they got in the lawsuit. Jessica plans to find the body, gives the interview to the paper, and then steps into a goldmine when she's conveniently named executor of the Parker estate. I checked the probate records, it's true. No pesky son in the picture to show up and want his share of the inheritance. That's a nice tight scenario and might explain a few things."

Jake frowned, picking up on Reese's undertone. "You want to share?"

"Over the years there've been rumors that BBG&G isn't exactly on the up and up. I didn't put much stock in the rumors until now… But after reading this article, after learning Jessica found the bodies…after going through old probate files this afternoon and finding out there was a change to the Parker will after the son reportedly went MIA. With no other relatives, Jessica saw an opportunity, a big one."

Up to now, Jake had been busy organizing the box of stuff from the trunk of his car so they could go through everything. But now, he stopped, stared at Reese with furious eyes. "What are you talking about? What rumors?"

Reese sighed. "There's been talk among lawyers, common knowledge really. Some people believe that if

BBG&G doesn't have the documentation to prove a case in court, they somehow manage to get it."

When Jake didn't seem to understand the implication, and no one else in the room did either, Reese said flatly, "Manufacture the evidence, guys. They have a history of surprising the other side in court with nice tidy little packages of evidence that wasn't listed during the discovery phase, in other words, they're more than a little lax about complying with discovery. After searching details about the Parker case this afternoon, it sounds like there may be something to the rumors."

Listening from the doorway, an outraged Quinn pointed out, "But that's disgraceful. People knew this and let them get away with it all these years. That's against the law. They get fined for not complying, right?"

Reese looked up, surprised at the little jolt of lust he got in his gut just looking at her. "Sanctions are at the discretion of the court, more accurately the judge. It's common knowledge BBG&G has a lot of political influence in this state. And all of the partners wield a considerable hold over some of the state's most influential judges, or at least they did."

Jake hissed out a breath. "You know I'm getting tired of hearing that as an excuse to let these guys get away with crap like that, like they did with Kit's adoption."

Reese agreed. "Exactly. But a long ago adoption is the least of our worries. If we can prove this, if the murders happened like we think, if all this comes to light, how they won the court case, it would ruin the firm's reputation. We're talking about ruining a legal empire here, guys. We can't go off half-cocked."

Jake fumed. "You knew about these rumors and never said a word these last few weeks knowing how much we didn't trust these people? And knowing what kind of spot that left Kit in?"

"Look, rumors are one thing. Proof is something else. At the time I had no idea about the Parkers, okay?"

"Still you could have said something," Jake said.

But Kit spoke up. "If I get your drift, you're saying that the firm has this history of doing shady stuff with evidence they don't have."

"The rumors go back to the beginning, ever since they pulled a last minute victory over McKetrick Construction," Reese clarified.

"If Jessica changed the Parker will to benefit her, suppose she changed Alana's will, not for the money this time but to implicate me. Maybe Alana really did leave it all to Jessica, just as we all suspected. Maybe when Jessica found out Alana had been murdered, she panics. She conveniently alters the will where everything is left to me to solidify a motive for the police. That would certainly take the heat off her or the law firm. But then she gets herself killed, too."

"Well, when you put it like that it sounds ridiculous."

Kit moved closer to Jake, but kept her eyes on Reese. "But that's what you're saying, isn't it? They've done stuff like this before, produced forged documents in court that the people didn't sign, or didn't know anything about. Now that whole scenario would make a lot more sense than believing Alana named me the beneficiary."

Now, Kit did turn to Jake. "If Jessica was used to getting away with it, why not do it now when everything, so to speak, was on the line. Jessica couldn't have the police looking into Alana's murder, and learning she was the beneficiary all along. If that happened, the cops might possibly have connected her to a forty-year-old double murder where Jessica was also named the Parker trustee. Jessica couldn't take the chance."

Jake lifted her chin. "Is this intuition or speculation, Kit?"

"A little of both. Something just doesn't feel right about that will."

Reese sensed he needed to be the voice of reason here before the crowd got carried away. "Not provable, guys. If the documents are there to back up the will, there's no proof Alana left her estate to Jessica." Looking directly at

Jake, he continued, "That's why I hesitated mentioning any of this. Without proof it's just bull—it's conjecture. Maybe just angry litigants who feel they were ambushed in court without proper discovery, nothing more."

But Baylee spoke up, "According to Gloria, that's what they did to get Kit, isn't it? They wanted custody and produced whatever documentation they needed in court." And if Jessica did it once and got away with it, she would have taught her sons well and they could do it again. That had Baylee, once again, considering going on the run, getting as far away from L.A. as she could. But first, she needed to know, "So you're saying if all the paperwork is in order, the court just goes along with whatever the piece of paper says that makes it all legal? Even though it isn't, right?"

"This entire conversation is getting out of hand."

During the back and forth, Kit had moved to the box of stuff on the table. Now she was bent over the open mobile safe examining the gun. Out of the blue, she said, "It's rather large, isn't it? The gun." She turned to face everyone. "You need proof, right? Something concrete that might link Alana to the murders. This gun, it's the one in my dream. The one used to kill the Parkers, I'm sure of it. Couldn't we have it tested?"

Jake got up and went to Kit. "That's why it was locked up, hidden away. Alana could have thrown it away, gotten rid of it, but she kept it around all this time hidden in the attic. This has to be what they've been looking for."

"I knew it. I just knew it was the gun," Dylan stated, as he leaned over the box, inspecting the weapon and got into the spirit of the game. "Could be she locked the gun away and forgot about it, forgot where she hid the safe. We did find it in a box labeled books. Then again, she could have kept it around for a little additional insurance, blackmail maybe in case Jessica ever got the urge to make a point."

Grabbing a tablet and pen off the buffet, Quinn sat down at the table. "We need to make a timeline, something to connect the dots. We need to go through all this stuff you found, piece by piece, get it organized. If it's solid enough, we could take it to Holloway."

"Now we're talking," Jake said. But when he noticed the dubious look on Reese's face, he asked, "What's wrong?"

"Jake, this is nuts. None of this constitutes proof of anything. It's speculation, nothing more."

"That's why we need to connect the dots. Look, I know it's far-fetched, but it's a start. Let me ask you something, can you guarantee me that St. John won't prematurely arrest Kit tomorrow?"

"Well, no."

"Then sit down, grab a handful of those papers out of the box, and shut the fuck up."

☙ ☙ ☙ ☙ ☙

A couple of hours later, they'd gone through the entire box. With Quinn keeping track of each document, acting as gatekeeper, they'd made an inventory list of Alana's activities and dates that covered two years prior to the Parker murders and five years after.

They knew, for example, that Alana had married Will Forrester in 1967, an engineer employed by McKetrick Construction, a company involved in a major lawsuit brought by the Parkers, and that Jessica Boyd, Alana's best friend had represented the Parkers from day one.

The copies of the cashier's checks showed Alana had received $500,000 over a period of twenty months starting six months after their court victory on December 20, 1967, and ending August 20, 1969, five days after the Parkers had been found dead. And Reese found documents confirming that Alana had brokered the Parker real estate deal with her future husband Robert Carlton as the buyer.

Looking around the room, an invigorated Kit announced, "I'd say we're on to something."

But it was Jake who opened his cell phone, dialed Jordan Donovan. As soon as the private investigator picked up, Jake told him, "When you interview Will Forrester, I want to be there."

CHAPTER 27

Jake wasn't about to leave Kit alone no matter how many protests she made about having a babysitter. But when it came time to talk to Will Forrester, the former McKetrick engineer, he'd made up his mind. At nine o'clock Sunday morning, he dumped Kit at Gloria's guest cottage into Baylee's waiting arms under the guise that Baylee needed help with a fussy Sarah. It had been a weak excuse, one he might have to pay for later, but she'd gone along without complaint. In the meantime, he headed to Van Nuys where Forrester had agreed to meet him and Jordan Donovan at a coffee shop on Sepulveda.

When he got there Jordan, a big man at least six-four and a former cop in his late thirties, was already deep in conversation with a slightly built, balding man in his early sixties, sitting at a booth in the back.

At the mention of Alana it didn't take much prompting for the man to start talking.

"She was a secretary in another division of McKetrick. New at her job, and not very good at it from what people said. But Christ, she was a looker. I mean gorgeous from head to toe. When she approached me, I thought it was some kind of a joke. The first night we went out, we ended up in bed. She was...incredible." He looked a little embarrassed. "Four weeks later we were married. I know I was stupid. Even after all these years, it pisses me off that she played me like a drum. I mean, it doesn't take a genius to figure it out. Immediately after the Parker trial ended, she quits her job, runs off to Reno. I get divorce papers within the week from Jessica Boyd."

"What exactly was your role in the trial?" Jake asked.

"I was subpoenaed to be a witness for the Parkers. I figured Alana had something to do with that, too. She knew I dealt with the toxin reports that I knew which carcinogens were in the waste. I had nothing to do with the actual dumping, mind you, but I knew we were getting rid of some very toxic chemicals like pentaerythritol found in surface coatings, and hexamethylene tetramine found in phenol-formaldehyde resins. After Parker filed suit, management told me to shred all the toxin reports related to the dump sites. I did what I was told."

Jake exchanged looks with Jordan, before he asked, "Did Alana know the documents were gone?"

Forrester nodded.

But it was Jake who asked, "Then there were no documents lying around proving McKetrick dumped anything toxic on Parker's land."

"Exactly. But then one afternoon a copy of a report showed up on my desk I knew for certain I'd destroyed. That's when the phone calls started coming in the middle of the night, telling me I'd better come clean. I knew those chemicals were highly toxic to animals and humans. I knew McKetrick had a habit of dumping the stuff in rural areas. I felt guilty about that. So when they subpoenaed me, I testified for the other side. Imagine my surprise when more documents showed up at trial, documents that looked real enough but ones I knew I'd shredded. When I testified under oath, I'd shredded certain reports myself at the direction of management, the next thing I knew, McKetrick's lawyers asked for a recess and settled out of court.

"But I didn't put it all together, didn't suspect a thing until after Alana left the company, and disappeared. By then of course, the trial was over, the Parkers had won their lawsuit, the lawyers got their cut, and I was divorced and out of a job. The lawsuit bankrupted McKetrick. What was I going to do about it then, admit to the world that I'd been maneuvered by a gorgeous blonde who didn't give a shit about me?"

"So you never told anyone, no one ever asked you about this until now?"

"I never talked about it with a living soul until today."

"Did you know the Parkers personally?"

"No. But after the trial Jessica ended up as the trustee of their estate. I read it in the paper. After the Parkers died I wondered what happened to all that money."

&&&&&

Later when Jake relayed the story to Kit while she rolled out pastry dough, in preparation of going back to work come Monday, in typical Kit-fashion, her sympathy was with Will Forrester. "Poor man. I bet he was in love with her."

"Well, he got over it pretty quick after she dumped him without a backward glance. I got the impression that until the day he dies, he won't be thinking kind thoughts about Alana."

"So this proves the half a million was payout for her role in the whole charade?"

"Not according to Reese. Just because Will's story is a sad tale it isn't proof Alana and Jessica killed the Parkers. But layer by layer we're working on building all the evidence we need to make a case before going to the cops. And we've got the gun. Jordan is contacting the sheriff's office to see if he can rattle someone's cage over there."

"To someone like Alana and Jessica, millions of dollars would be a tempting motive for murder. Think about it, they see the Parkers as old, and bless their hearts they'd just gotten word their only son was missing in Vietnam. Alana and Jessica view them as vulnerable, heartbroken, pathetic. My God, to Alana and Jessica they must have seemed like sitting ducks." As Kit opened the oven door, she added matter-of-factly, "But what we need is something solid, something irrefutable."

❧ ❧ ❧ ❧ ❧

At six o'clock the next morning, Jake packaged up the dozens of individual spinach and asparagus quiche tarts Kit had baked the night before while she worked on getting the chocolate chip muffins bagged to transport to the car.

When they opened the front door of the house to carry out the first load of food, they saw the hordes of people loitering at the end of the driveway. And they all seemed to have either a camera or a microphone clutched in their hands. Word had finally reached the media that Kit might soon be arrested for the murder of Alana.

The minute the reporters spotted Jake and Kit trying to make their way to the car, they came alive, hurling questions and accusations at them both in rapid-fire succession. Not all of the questions were about Alana's murder. A few of them had done their homework and uncovered all the gory details about Claire Boston's murder as well, which made Jake and Kit an odd and interesting couple on the morning news. All the way to the Book & Bean, the press hounded them. The siege from the media made the ten minute trip take twice as long.

Even though they parked behind the store, the minute they started unloading the car, an on-air personality with a camera crew in tow, surrounded them and began firing questions. But Jake and Kit refused to take the bait, refusing comment.

Once they were inside the store though, Jake told her, "We use this to our advantage. I need to get Reese out here to make a statement on your behalf, standing in front of the coffee shop. From this point on, every time these guys ask, you just keep telling them you did nothing wrong, you have nothing to hide, and that you're being harassed by the police."

With all the media descending on the Book & Bean, business tripled. Kit and Baylee were so busy they alternated between handling the lines behind the counter in the coffee shop to digging for titles and ringing up sales in the bookstore. When the quiche and chocolate chip muffins disappeared by eight-thirty, Kit wished she'd had the foresight to have baked more.

With so many news people and strangers milling around the place, Jake stuck to Kit like glue. At one point, he even stepped behind the counter and did his best to fill simple orders for coffee since he had no idea how to work any of the equipment.

By the time Gloria got there, Kit welcomed the influx of items she brought to the already dwindling inventory. The customers pounced on the mint brownies, the oatmeal raisin cookies, and cherry tarts before Kit had a chance to unpack the goodies.

"You're a lifesaver, Glo," Kit commented, as Gloria stepped behind the counter to help fill orders.

"Well, if I'd known I'd be on the news, I would have worn my black dress, the one that makes me look like I'm fifteen pounds thinner. And I called Quinn told her if she got the chance to DVR the news at noon."

As the morning wore on, the atmosphere became more like a party. The coffee flowed, sales picked up inside the bookstore, and the locals turned out in defense of their girl.

Kit had never been more proud of the whole town.

Reese showed up in time to give a live interview in front of the shop for the mid-day newscast. He answered questions for half an hour from every media source from as far away as Tijuana. When they asked about what evidence linked Kit to Alana's murder, Reese pointed out there was none, then volleyed insults back at the police, questioning their dogged pursuit, if not downright hounding of his client. When they brought up Kit's abuse, Reese managed to turn the tables, reminding them that Kit was the victim here. The question though, cemented his belief that St. John had leaked the information to the press. How else would they have known about Kit's abusive childhood?

By mid-afternoon, the hubbub had died down somewhat when most of the reporters took their film and lead-off story and headed back to L.A. to make their evening deadline.

As Kit propped her feet up on one of the chairs, exhausted, she had to admit it had been one of the most successful days in sales in the four year history of the Book & Bean. "I'll just put a sign on the door that says we're sold out of food and books and coffee. I'll have to re-order coffee. They drank every flavor I had in stock. I even managed to get rid of that raspberry flavored crap I mistakenly ordered weeks ago. Do you think they'll be back tomorrow? How much food should I bake?"

Jake couldn't believe her demeanor. "You're worried about how much to bake? You're taking this a lot better than I am."

"Difference in personalities. Difference in histories. And besides you're a guy. Hey, I'm just practicing that old adage, when life gives you lemons, make lemonade."

"What's that supposed to mean?"

"You've never heard that expression?"

"No, not that."

"What? You mean the fact that you're a guy. Well, it's all about ego..."

"Not that, the history thing, what do you mean by that?"

"Oh that. Our histories are different that's all. You're successful, come from a calm, stable home environment. So you don't react very well to chaos. My history is reaped in chaos. It's the only atmosphere I had going for me for years. So I'm used to it, while you're not. Understand?"

"Yeah, I do." And the sad thing was he really did.

At five-thirty Kit and Jake pulled into the garage at Kit's house and began to unload the bakery trays from the car. She gathered everything from the back seat, while Jake emptied the stuff from the trunk. Their arms laden down with empty pastry trays and metal food carriers, Jake took the house key out of Kit's hand and made his way around the car to unlock the door going into the first floor laundry room. The minute he stepped inside, Kit heard a thud, and then the sound of metal hit the tile floor. As she got to the doorway, she looked in and saw Jake sprawled on his stomach, face down.

She dropped the stack of trays and rushed inside.

Collin stepped into her path.

Standing over Jake was a man she recognized as Gerald Auslo. She turned around and bolted for the door. But Collin caught her by the hair from behind and pulled her backward. She began punching and kicking and screaming.

Collin yelled for Auslo. "Leave that son of a bitch and get out here. Help me with Kit. And tell Taft to bring the van around."

As if on cue Auslo stepped out into the garage behind Collin and began talking into a two-way radio. Collin tightened the hold on her hair and started backing her out of the garage toward a van, now parked at the end of her driveway.

"You can't run from me this time, Kit-Kat. God knows you've tried all these years, but this is the end of the line. You can't get away from me this time. Boston can't protect you. And this time I mean to have you, understand? I mean to have what you've been giving that piece of shit Boston."

"Why are you doing this, Collin? We grew up together."

"You told the cops about me. Some detective came to see me, wanted to know where I was the night you lost control of your car, I gave him a very convincing story, told him I had an alibi. Cade and Connor backed me up. Surely you didn't think the cops would believe you over me, did you? He can't touch me now, Kit-Kat, but that doesn't mean he won't come after me later. I won't spend time in jail. You hear me. And without you they'll be no witness for later."

Kit didn't intend to make it easy. With her long legs, she kicked out at Collin, and sent him sprawling onto the concrete floor. She took off running. But Auslo soon caught up with her.

"Goddamn it, Gerald, get the fucking needle. I wasn't going to do this, Kit-Kat, but you're pissing me off."

As soon as he got to his feet, Collin backhanded Kit across the mouth. The blow sent her reeling. She fell back against the wall of the garage, knocking over a stack of paint cans.

Collin ordered Auslo, "She isn't going without a fight. Give her the damn drug."

In one quick motion Auslo pulled the syringe from his jacket pocket and plunged it into her arm. "She's a fighter. I like that in a woman. I wouldn't mind a go at her when you're done with her, Boyd."

"Shut up, Gerald. Kit belongs to me and don't you forget it. She's mine, she's always been mine, got it?"

Kit looked at the man she'd known all of her life and saw nothing but cold, stony eyes, not a shred of compassion. But she tried to reason with him anyway. "Collin, you won't get away with this. This is kidnapping. This is crossing the line. When Jake finds out, he'll come after you. We can…" But as the drug started to work, blackness descended.

Her last conscious thought was of Jake, as she fell into the arms of Collin and Auslo, who carried her to the waiting van.

⚜⚜⚜⚜⚜

Jake sat on the sofa in the living room holding his throbbing head in his hands as what constituted as the law in San Madrid, a sheriff's deputy from Ventura County, took his statement.

When he looked up, he saw Reese and Dylan rush into the room. They took one look at Jake and saw the miserable look on his face—and the guilt.

"Collin took her. He was inside the house waiting for us. And I bring her right in, hand her to him on a silver platter."

Dylan reached out, rested his hand on Jake's shoulder. "We'll find her, Jake."

"How? How the hell will we do that, Dylan? Where do we start looking?" He looked at the deputy. "Or where do they look? She's gone. And it's my fucking fault. I couldn't protect her."

CHAPTER 28

He'd followed the van from a safe distance back. Through night vision goggles, he watched as they unloaded the girl, carried her inside what looked like an abandoned warehouse, surrounded by an eight foot chain link fence.

He got out of his car, surveyed the terrain, gauged the best location for his kill zone. Deciding in an instant, he opened the trunk of his car, took out a black case and began to assemble the Remington rifle. With a rhythmic motion that comes from having done this more than a thousand times, he snapped the scope into place, slid a bullet into the chamber, gathered up another magazine, and took off up the hill. As he crouched behind whatever cover he could find, adrenalin pumped through his veins.

"I've killed others far less deserving than these three," he muttered to himself, as he took up his position on the hill overlooking the warehouse. The only question in his mind was which one of them he would take down first. Before he had time to think, that question answered itself as the man known as Taft moved from behind the wheel of the van into his line of vision on the way to the open doorway. He locked on the target through his telescopic lens, sucked in a breath, steadied his gun, and slowly squeezed the trigger.

On target, a bullet through the head, Taft lay dead.

When Auslo came into his line of sight to check on his buddy, he squeezed off another round before the man had time to react. The bullet hit Auslo in the chest. He watched Auslo grab his shirt, stagger two steps backward before falling inside the doorway of the warehouse.

Two down.

I'm coming for you, Boyd.

He charged around the side of the warehouse, scanning from left to right, watching for any movement out of the corner of his eye. He could hear Collin screaming at the two dead men, ridiculously trying to find out what was going on. He recognized the voice for what it was. Collin's voice trembled with panic—and fear. He'd seen Collin's type many times, the man was a weakling, and would either run at some point or would try to bargain for his life. Either way, Collin would be dead before the night was done.

As he reached the corner of the building, he peered through a broken window. He had no clear shot. The son of a bitch had taken up position in a crumpled mass trying to use the girl as a shield as she lay on the floor. He moved to try from another vantage point. As he made his way around the side of the warehouse, he heard Collin shout, "Who's out there? You come any closer, I'll kill her. I swear I will."

He knew as long as he didn't answer Collin, the silence would unnerve the man, so he kept holding to the side of the building, kept moving, and kept checking each window for his clear kill zone. He knew if he wasn't careful a bullet at this range might exit Collin and keep going, so he had to make sure the girl was not in the line of fire.

As he came to an outside stairway going up to the second level, he realized he could get a clear shot from above. Swiftly and silently, he ascended the stairs. As he went through the doorway at the top of the landing, he spotted a narrow catwalk midway up. With Collin below and to the right, he'd found his clear shot.

Silently, he dashed onto the wooden catwalk. Even from this distance, he could smell Collin's fear. He lowered the rifle, sighted him in, held his breath, and put his finger on the trigger. As he fired, the rotted wood beneath his feet gave way, and he fell to the first floor below. He knew before he hit the floor, the shot had been off target.

Jarred by the fall, it took him almost a full sixty seconds to scramble to his feet. Outside, he heard the van's engine roar to life, tires squealed, gravel spitted, and he knew at that moment he'd missed.

And he had never missed.

As he dusted himself off, he approached the girl with caution. But as he got closer, he realized she was still unconscious, drugged. He searched for a pulse, found it slow, but steady. Untying her hands, he laid her back on the concrete floor. He looked around for something to put under her head and noticed the sizeable amount of blood on the floor. Well, well, well, he hadn't completely missed after all, he thought. The bastard would need a doctor for that, and he'd be easy enough to track.

He saw nothing he could use for a pillow and shrugged out of his jacket, making sure the pockets were empty. As he gently lifted her head, he slid the jacket underneath and placed the gold cowboy in her hand, closed her fist around it.

Looking down at her, his thoughts inexplicably turned to the daughter he'd once had from a lifetime ago, a little tow-head blonde who had once been the light of his life, who'd followed him around wherever he went. She'd looked exactly like her mother. Had his wife and daughter lived, his life would have been far different from the one he had now. All at once, snapshots of the people he'd once loved went off like a collage inside his head. He pictured his wife, his daughter as they'd been in life. Realization hit him. Kit Griffin reminded him of his daughter. She was causing emotions to surface that had long since died, emotions he'd put on hold for so long, it was as if someone else was standing there…feeling.

He came out of his reverie long enough to push a lock of her hair from her forehead. "Looks like it's time to call that man of yours and have him get his ass over here to pick you up. Maybe next time he won't be so careless."

He stripped off his leather gloves, replaced them with a fresh pair from his pants pocket.

"You should know Collin and his brothers aren't likely to just let this go. They're bound to regroup. But don't worry. I'll be watching out for you and the people you care about."

Noah Parker would have expected nothing less.

♲ ♲ ♲ ♲ ♲

Kit woke up swinging, both hands bunched in tight fists as she punched at the air.

"Whoa there, honey. It's me," Jake announced as he blocked the jab she'd thrown at him. He'd been sitting beside her hospital bed for the last couple of hours waiting for the drug to wear off.

Kit heard a familiar voice through the haze in her brain and collapsed back down on the bed, her body spent. Trying hard to get rid of the cobwebs clouding her head, get her eyes to focus, she propped herself up momentarily, only to slide back down again. She tried to open her eyes but the room spun. She realized she was back in a hospital room.

She focused on Jake standing over her and whispered, "How'd you find me, Jake? Take me home, I want to go home."

"I'll get you out of here just as soon as we know you're okay. What do you remember?"

"I remember fighting, kicking at Collin and his two thugs. Then that Auslo guy took out a needle and gave me some kind of shot." She reached to rub the site of the injection on her arm. Then as if she'd just remembered he'd been hurt too, she touched his cheek. "What about you, how's your head?"

"I'll live. The doctor thinks they might have given you something called a hotshot, a very fast-acting drug, a cocktail mixture that's gonna leave you with a helluva headache."

She scrubbed at her face and laid a hand on her belly. "My head's pounding and I'm sick to my stomach." Clearly a bit disoriented, she asked again, "What happened, Jake? How'd you find me?"

"I was in the process of giving my statement to a sheriff's deputy, when I got this weird phone call. The man on the other end told me where to find you, said you were okay, not to worry, gave me the location of a warehouse, and the directions on how to get there."

He paused, rested his forehead on hers to clear his head. He'd been out of his mind with worry, afraid he'd never see her again. He touched his lips to hers for a chaste kiss. "I jumped in the car with Reese and Dylan. We followed the police car to this abandoned warehouse near Thousand Oaks. When we got there we found Auslo and Taft lying dead, each from a single gunshot.

"When we walked inside the warehouse there you were lying on the concrete floor with a jacket underneath your head and this in your hand." He held out his palm, and showed her the gold cowboy. "Do you remember anything, honey, about the man who helped you?"

She picked up the gold cowboy with a confused look on her face. "I don't remember anything, except the fight with Collin." She paused and then added, "And the fear, I remember the fear knowing Collin planned to kill me." Her voice began to shake, and the tears came. "I vaguely remember hearing another man's voice, a voice that oddly tried to reassure me that everything was going to be all right." She rubbed her throbbing head. "The voice sounded familiar, you know, like I'd heard it before. The voice wasn't Collin's or those other guys, that's for sure. I thought it sounded like my father."

Jake shook his head. "I promise you Collin will never get another chance to hurt you again. When I woke up and found you gone I've never been so scared in my life. I'm so sorry, honey. I won't let him near you again. That's a promise." He wrapped her up, placing kisses on both cheeks, her nose, her lips.

Her brain might have been foggy, but she knew one thing for certain. "You can't make that kind of a promise, Jake. No one can. What happened wasn't your fault. It's ridiculous to think we can spend every waking minute of every day with each other. We can't live our lives afraid to go about our daily routines. We can't live like that, and I won't have you blaming yourself."

When she looked up, she sucked in a breath. Jake felt her body tense and followed her gaze to the doorway.

Dan Holloway stood just inside the room.

"Sorry folks, but I need to talk to both of you for a minute."

"Now's not a good time. Can't you see she's wiped? Her head's pounding. She's been awake for less than ten minutes. She's in no shape for an interview."

Holloway shook his head. "No, we need to talk. Collin Boyd showed up at the police station a couple of hours ago, turned himself in on the advice of his attorney, Jacob Gatz, who happens to be his cousin. I thought you might want the short version of what Collin said on the record."

Hearing that, Jake spun around to face him and noticed the expression in his eyes, a weary look that said he'd come as a courtesy and didn't have to be here. "We'd appreciate that."

Holloway stuck his hands in his pockets and started talking. "No surprise, but Collin's story differs quite a bit from the one I got from the deputy sheriff who took you out to Thousand Oaks. Collin claims Auslo and Taft forced him at gunpoint to help them kidnap Kit. Seems Auslo and Taft learned she'd inherited a lot of money and figured even if she didn't actually have the money in the bank yet, there was always you, their former employer who was more than a little loaded and good for a pricey ransom. They figured you'd pay anything to get Kit back.

The way Collin tells it, Auslo and Taft needed a big score before they left town after the hit and run on Kit, while at the same time they'd get back at you for firing them. So they approach Collin, coerced him into participating."

When Jake started to protest, Holloway gave him a stern look. "Let me finish. The story gets better. Collin's version is that once they got Kit to the warehouse, Collin managed to wrestle the gun away from Auslo, shot him, and then Taft in self-defense. He was wounded in the ensuing gun battle trying to save Kit. And get this, he says he disposed of the weapon by throwing it in the ocean on his way back to Malibu because he panicked and was disoriented from the loss of blood.

"But that isn't the best part. And you're just going to love this. He claims he's the one that made the phone call from a pay phone to you, telling you where you could find Kit."

The story rattled Jake so much he had to sit down on the bed. "I've never heard such bullshit in my life. That voice on the phone did not belong to Collin. The voice on the phone had a slight accent, like a brogue. Please don't tell me you guys believe that fabrication of his and you're letting him off the hook on the kidnapping charge?"

"Well now, his story is so full of holes it's like a sieve, and had it been up to me, I'd have kept him locked up in a cell, but…"

Jake swore. "He's out?"

Holloway checked his watch. "About thirty minutes ago he got a sympathetic judge who set bail at a paltry five grand. He's probably back at the Enclave now nursing an ugly wound to his shoulder."

"Damn it, he should be locked up."

Clutching the gold cowboy in her fist, even with a pounding headache, Kit explained, "Collin definitely was not coerced. He was the one in charge, telling Auslo and Taft what to do. It was Collin who told Auslo to give me the shot. And he planned to kill me. He told me so. He told me I was a witness and wouldn't testify against him, that he wouldn't spend jail time…"

She ran out of steam. She held her hand out, palm up, showed Holloway the gold cowboy. "Jake found this in my hand." She watched as Holloway reached to pick it up, saw the look of disbelief on his face.

"Don't look at me like that. I don't know how it got there. I'm telling you the truth."

"I know." It was said simply and took some of the venom out of Kit's temper.

Jake didn't trust what he was hearing. "You know? Then you believe me about the phone call from the guy with the brogue?"

"Yeah. But it doesn't matter a damn what I believe only what I can prove. First of all, I'm starting with those holes in Auslo and Taft and working from there. To me it looks like they came from a high-powered rifle from some distance away, not from a gun battle at close range. But I'll have to wait for something definitive from the autopsies. Even though I didn't get to inspect Collin's bullet wound since he drove himself to the hospital before turning himself in, if what I suspect turns out to be true, I intend to find out what kind of bullet made that hole in his shoulder and to do that I'll have to interview the doctor who treated him and soon. Right now, I've got my work cut out for me. I just wanted to stop by and tell you, Ms. Griffin, there will be a hearing. And I take it you'll testify against Collin Boyd?"

"We both will," Jake said before Kit could answer.

Holloway nodded. "Good. And don't worry. We'll be keeping an eye on Boyd. He may be out on bail, but he's on our radar now. I don't intend to lose him."

"Does this mean I'm no longer a suspect?"

Holloway grinned. "That's the other news. The coroner convinced Max the angle of your mother's stab wounds had to come from a right-handed person. Just do me a favor, don't ever pick up anything with your right hand around Max." He winked and left the room.

Thirty minutes later, Jake checked Kit out of the hospital. On the drive back to San Madrid, Kit made sure she kept the window rolled down giving her a chance to breathe in the moist night air along the coast. When they got to the city limits, Jake unexpectedly took a detour down a gravel covered driveway, pulling up in front of the Crandall House. He looked over and noticed Kit's head rested on the back of the seat. Her eyes were closed. It probably wasn't the best time to do this, but after what happened earlier when he believed he'd lost her, he wasn't letting another minute slip away.

As soon as he cut the engine, Kit's head popped up. It took a minute for her to get her bearings. When she saw where they were, she asked, "What are we doing here?"

"How do you feel?"

"Better."

"Let's take a walk then."

"I could use the fresh air. With everything that's happened, I haven't asked you about the progress you've made on the house."

They got out of the car. Jake appreciated her graceful stride, her long elegant body, which he planned to take advantage of as soon as he got her home. But in a sense they were already there. They walked up to the wraparound porch, which was no longer dilapidated but rather sported brand new wooden planks.

The stars glittered overhead, and in the stillness they could hear the waves crashing against the rocks in the distance. Despite the spur-of-the-moment stop, this felt right after all.

"One of the first things I did when I got back to town was buy this house, knowing it needed a lot of work, but hoping one day, you and I could live here together. Hoping you'd give me a second chance, or a third chance or even a fourth."

He took her chin in his hand. "I want to live here with you, Kit. Make a home here, have kids, the whole package."

Her throat went dry. She turned to face him, afraid she'd misunderstood. "What are you saying?"

"I thought I'd lost you tonight. It ripped me in two. I've been waiting for you to grow up. I love you, Kit. It took leaving you and missing you for me to realize how much I need you in my life. Marry me. I'm tired of waiting for us to be together. Our time is now."

"And all these years I've waited for you to come to your senses. I'd say it's about time."

With that, she launched her body into his.

Dear Reader:

If you enjoyed *Just Evil*, please take the time to leave a review. A review shows others how you feel about my work. By recommending it to your friends and family it helps spread the word. If you have the time, please Tweet/Share that you've finished *Just Evil*.

If you *do* write a review, by all means let me know via Facebook or my website. I'd love to hear from you!

For a complete list of the author's other books please visit her at. www.vickiemckeehan.com

Want to connect with the author to leave a comment? www.vickiemckeehan.wordpress.com/ blog www.facebook.com/VickieMcKeehan

Go to the next page for a preview of
Deeper Evil
Book Two of the Evil Secrets Trilogy

DEEPER EVIL

Sunny Southern California was turning out to be better than he'd originally thought, much better. It was warmer for one, late May with spring still blossoming and coming to life around him.

Even though the locals kept mentioning something they called May Gray and grumbling about the upcoming June Gloom, he hadn't really noticed. The days seemed no more overcast than the ones he'd grown up with in his native Ireland.

But Los Angeles definitely had its advantages. From his little hotel patio he could sit and enjoy the beach as it slowly filled each morning with female bodies slicked with oil, baking in the bright warm sun. Like this morning. He had started his day watching six gorgeously toned women play a game of beach volleyball wearing, God bless them, tiny little strips of fabric that barely covered tits and ass. Who needed Aruba when he had only to kick back and enjoy those hot bodies mere steps away from his own door?

He was living in paradise, enjoying the fruits of his labor.

And he hadn't felt this invigorated in twenty years.

Weeks earlier, he'd been burned out, ready for Prozac. But now for the first time in years, thanks to this last mission, he was actually enjoying life. In a way, helping Kit Griffin last night made him feel as if he were making up for all of his mistakes.

And there were plenty of those. But he wasn't going to waste time dwelling on them.

At his age, this might be his last chance to do something positive, make a change, and maybe take that first step towards cutting back on his nicotine and alcohol intake. God knew he loved the ten cigs he allowed himself daily, as well as his late-night measure of Jameson.

Had the media not labeled him an overnight hero, he might not be thinking about taking better care of himself.

Amused at his own thoughts as well as the swell to his ego, he did his best to imagine himself as one of the good guys.

And just couldn't bring the image into focus. He'd crossed over into the dark too many years ago for that picture to fully take shape.

Last night, as part of that first step, he'd promised Kit Griffin he'd keep her and her friends safe, a different direction for him to be sure. It wasn't like him to promise anyone anything. The less involved you got the better. That had been his motto for decades, something he lived by. He made very few promises.

But those made were always kept.

In his line of work that might be unheard of. Hit men rarely lived by a code of honor. But then, the few, the proud, hadn't been trained by Noah Parker.

As he glanced across the cobbled Main Street towards the Book & Bean, he realized the role of protector might be new. A hero he wasn't.

But even now, he knew Baylee Scott was inside the store alone with her baby daughter, working in place of Kit this morning because Kit Griffin was still trying to recover from her kidnapping ordeal from last night.

From the moment he'd opened his eyes that morning, his instincts had kicked in. He'd learned long ago never to ignore a gut feeling. Something was up. Years of tracking the quarry had him feeling antsy. It was the reason he'd driven up to San Madrid at the crack of dawn, the reason he'd left those hot bodies playing on the sand.

And even if he happened to be wrong this morning, because he'd seen no signs of the Boyd brothers, there was no way he could walk away now. No, the last couple of weeks had already set the wheels in motion. There was no going back. He'd been prepared to accept the consequences then, whatever they were.

And he still was. Today was no different. Looking back would get him nowhere.

He could not have predicted the chain of events the past few weeks would set in motion, nor the rippling effects. Who knew the three Boyd sons would throw down an entirely different kind of challenge, one he wouldn't be able to walk away from now.

Add in the fact that he still had a score to settle with Collin Boyd for kidnapping Kit last night and he had all matters of unfinished business with the Boyd clan.

Collin had a nasty wound to his shoulder. He ought to know, he'd put it there. He intended to finish the job first chance he got just as soon as the bastard came out of hiding. And if he didn't crawl out from under his rock, he'd go in and dig him out. It was just that simple.

It was true he still had a few things left on his to do list before he could call it quits in L.A. The remaining law partner for one. At some point, Frank Geller would have to be taken down. It wasn't fair to let him off the hook, to escape payback when he'd been in on the ground floor of the plan from day one like his sister, Jessica, and her husband Sumner.

Those two had already paid the ultimate price for their greed. He'd seen to that. In time, so would Frank Geller. But now was not the time to get impatient or careless or tip his hand too early. He might be unaccustomed to this role of guardian, but he intended to do whatever it took to see this thing through to the end.

The way he saw it, quite a few lives depended on it.

✿✿✿✿✿

Standing behind the scarred oak counter inside the Book & Bean, the only coffee shop in San Madrid, the tiny fishing village north of L.A., Baylee Scott put the finishing touches on a latte.

At just after seven in the morning, she glanced at the line snaking out the door and wondered how many of the customers were there for the coffee and pastries or how many were reporters or curiosity seekers who had watched last night's newscast and wanted to catch a glimpse of the kidnap victim.

Baylee shook her head at the idea of people coming to gawk at Kit Griffin, her lifelong friend and owner of the Book & Bean.

What kind of people did that? she wondered. Because she didn't recognize most of the people as regulars that alone told her the people in line were more than likely reporters of one sort or another, who had made the trip hoping to get a quote or pick up some glimmer of gossip they could pass on, and sate whatever audience they attracted.

The whole media circus didn't sit well with Baylee. Not only did she feel incensed at the intrusion on Kit's behalf to her friend's personal life, but she very much feared this entire ordeal would bring to her door a person she'd been trying to evade for more than a year.

As she steamed milk for another latte, she did her best to calm her nerves and think like practical Kit did. She tried to concentrate on how much extra business these prying parasites might bring in today.

But it was difficult to tamp down her fear in lieu of how good this would all be for the bottom line.

Baylee recalled yesterday's mad house when the media had invaded the little town with their crews and cameras in tow, hoping to edge out the competition to get an exclusive interview with the prime suspect in the Alana Stevens murder. She was sure the police had purposely leaked the fact that Kit had suffered years of physical abuse at the hands of her mother or rather the woman who had merely raised her. That had brought the reporters swarming like vultures over a dead carcass in the road. And once they'd discovered that Kit was involved with Jake Boston, the software mogul who was still the prime suspect in his wife's slaying two years earlier, the media had played that relationship angle to the hilt.

Two separate murder cases, two murder suspects linked together as a couple, the press had gone wild, Baylee mused now, as she poured coffee into an oversized mug and plated a couple of cinnamon rolls for the next customer.

The way the media had portrayed Jake and Kit, one would have thought the two presented the biggest single threat to the greater Los Angeles area since The Hillside Stranglers.

But as ludicrous as it had seemed yesterday, the store had experienced its most successful day money-wise since opening four years earlier.

Even though Kit and Jake's connection to each other had created a firestorm of interest—at least it had for about forty-five minutes, the news of Kit's kidnapping last night had changed everything.

Baylee shook her head just thinking how fickle the media could be. She glanced at the wild-eyed, sleep-deprived reporters waiting in line. Some of them looked as though they had been up all night.

Funny what a difference 24 hours could make, she thought.

It had taken a kidnapping to put another twist in the story and brought them back full circle to the Book & Bean for Round Two. Today, they seemed to be working the sympathetic angle, convinced Jake and Kit had been wrongly accused. She could laugh now because they certainly hadn't been convinced yesterday of the couple's innocence.

But once they discovered the wealthy Collin Boyd, son of slain murder victims Jessica and Sumner Boyd, had taken Kit hostage, the story had dominated the six o'clock newscast. Then at ten o'clock, those same news reporters had announced her rescue. And that was before anyone had known about the faceless, unknown stranger who had come charging in to an abandoned warehouse in Thousand Oaks where Collin had been holding Kit, and saved the day.

He'd shot Kit's captors, including Collin, and then called Jake to come pick her up.

By the time Jake had arrived, the stranger had already disappeared. Jake had found Kit still unconscious. Luckily by the time she woke up in the hospital, she hadn't remembered a thing about the kidnapping other than the role Collin had played in the whole thing.

The fact that Jake had found one of those mysterious gold cowboys that had been left with each of the other victims clutched in the palm of Kit's hand suggested that the man who had come to her rescue was the same one who had murdered Alana as well as all the others—and now for whatever reason had decided to play hero.

No one close to Kit felt like complaining.

Kit was alive, thanks to the stranger and tucked away in her little bungalow along the water's edge.

As Baylee waited on yet another customer, she thought the whole thing sounded like the plot from one of her father's action movies.

No wonder the media had shown up again, she thought moodily, as she wiped down the counter once more before taking another order.

Looking out over the strange faces in the crowded shop, Baylee thought she recognized some of the same on-air television reporters from yesterday. As more news vans pulled up in front of the store, it was clear they were staking the place out, hoping to find out more about Kit's mystery savior.

Even now, they were clamoring to get another story for the noon newscast. It made her stomach burn to think the sharks were circling. They were obviously waiting for Jake and Kit to make an appearance, so they could jockey for a quote on camera no less.

Well, they'll be sorely disappointed on that score, thought Baylee, as she expertly worked the espresso machine, mixing together java with steaming milk, working on making the perfect blend. She doubted Jake intended to let Kit out of his sight for days yet.

Baylee sighed. She hoped they weren't staking out Kit's house at this very moment. Her friend desperately needed some downtime.

That was the reason why she'd offered to open up for the next couple of mornings even if it meant she and Sarah had to get up extra early to make the drive in from Agoura Hills, from the sweet little guest cottage she'd rented from Gloria.

Baylee didn't mind. Kit was more like family, more like a sister than her best friend. They would do anything for each other. The least she could do was mind the store to keep Kit away from the prying eyes and the inane questions of the pesky media. Even though it might mean she and Sarah risked wandering into the spotlight right along with Kit and Jake.

She shook off the alarm that wanted to creep in. Chancing a quick look at her almost six-month old daughter, who sat in her swing behind the counter, content for the moment to chew on a red plastic teething bracelet, Baylee sucked in a breath. Knowing Collin had been desperate enough to kidnap Kit last night was bad enough and sent chills down her arms in spite of the heat from the espresso machine.

But as she methodically passed the finished product, the latte, to the waiting hands of her customer, she fought off images of what Collin's brother, Connor, might do if he found out she was here in San Madrid, and had been for months.

She needed to think about leaving L.A. for good. The problem with taking off again though, meant she'd be leaving behind her dying father, not to mention the fact that she'd have to go on the run with Sarah.

How could she keep doing that to her baby daughter? Sarah deserved better. To Baylee it seemed she'd been on the move ever since the baby's birth, unsettled, moving from place to place.

She had to get her life back on track. But how could she do that when she was so terrified Connor would find out about the baby. The idea put the reality of her situation front and center.

As she wiped down the counter again for the twentieth time that morning, Baylee thought about what she wanted. She wanted for her and Sarah to be left alone, to feel secure again, she wanted her life back the way it had been before Connor Boyd had crossed her path and shown her the dark side of his life. She wanted to be left alone to raise Sarah on her own. And she'd do anything, absolutely anything, if he never ever learned Sarah existed.

Was that asking too much? If she hadn't had to come back to L.A. because of her father's cancer, she would still be living in Denver, where she'd given birth. Living back with her friend, Blair Rafferty, the person she'd turned to during her pregnancy, and who had given her a job.

She knew she'd hurt her friends, Kit and Quinn, by doing that. By shutting them out, they had been excluded from participating in Sarah's birth. But how could she explain what had happened? She couldn't take the chance that Connor wouldn't have followed through on his threats.

No, she thought, she would continue to keep her secret. Kit had too much going on in her life right now, too much to deal with to get bogged down with her problems. And Quinn, Quinn was a brand new resident doctor, just a month into her first year of residency. Others might not recognize her as "doctor" Tyler just yet, but as far as Baylee was concerned, Quinn had earned the right to focus on her future, her career, without the added problems she brought to the table.

Baylee sucked in a nervous breath and made a promise. She'd been handling the stress and pressure of it all for the past fifteen months—by herself.

She would handle this on her own as well. She had to.

Don't miss these other exciting titles by bestselling author

Vickie McKeehan

The Evil Secrets Trilogy
JUST EVIL Book One
DEEPER EVIL Book Two
ENDING EVIL Book Three

The Pelican Pointe Series
PROMISE COVE
HIDDEN MOON BAY
DANCING TIDES
LIGHTHOUSE REEF
STARLIGHT DUNES
LAST CHANCE HARBOR
SEA GLASS COTTAGE
LAVENDER BEACH
SANDCASTLES UNDER THE CHRISTMAS MOON
BENEATH WINTER SAND

The Skye Cree Novels
THE BONES OF OTHERS
THE BONES WILL TELL
THE BOX OF BONES
HIS GARDEN OF BONES
TRUTH IN THE BONES

The Indigo Brothers Trilogy
INDIGO FIRE
INDIGO HEAT
INDIGO JUSTICE
THE INDIGO BROTHERS TRILOGY BOXED SET

ABOUT THE AUTHOR

Vickie's novels have consistently appeared on Amazon's Top 100 lists in Contemporary Romance, Romantic Suspense and Mystery / Thriller. She writes what she loves to read—heartwarming romance laced with suspense, heart-pounding thrillers, and riveting mysteries. Vickie loves to write about compelling and down-to-earth characters in settings that stay with her readers long after they've finished her books. She makes her home in Southern California.

Find Vickie online at
https://www.facebook.com/VickieMcKeehan
http://www.vickiemckeehan.com/
https://vickiemckeehan.wordpress.com